FULL NAVAL
HONORS

THE HONOR SERIES BY ROBERT N. MACOMBER

At the Edge of Honor

Point of Honor

Honorable Mention

A Dishonorable Few

An Affair of Honor

A Different Kind of Honor

The Honored Dead

The Darkest Shade of Honor

Honor Bound

Honorable Lies

Honors Rendered

The Assassin's Honor

An Honorable War

Honoring the Enemy

Word of Honor

Code of Honor

*This novel is dedicated with deep love and respect
to my wife and co-adventurer
Nancy Ann Glickman*

*Gifted teacher of the wonders of the universe,
the creatures of the sky, and mysteries of the earth,
and fearless guardian of the Honor Series
and its somewhat antiquated creator.*

No CO has ever had a better XO.

Thank you, my beloved, for it all . . .

An Introductory Word with the Reader

Over the years, readers around the world have asked me how long our fictional hero Peter Wake lived and served, whether his descendants continued the Wake tradition of naval service, and what—and where—is the mysterious Wake Shelf of naval intelligence secrets. Here, in the seventeenth and final novel in the Honor Series, you will learn the answers to these and many other long-held questions. For a bit of background, I offer the following timeline of Wake's life until this point. It has been far from dull.

Timeline of Peter Wake's Life from 1839 to 1907

1839—June 26. Peter Wake is born into a seafaring family on the coast of Massachusetts.

1852—Wake goes to sea at age thirteen to learn the coastal cargo trade in his father's schooner.

1855—Wake is promoted to schooner mate at age sixteen.

1857—Wake is promoted to command of a schooner at age eighteen.

1861—The Civil War begins. By 1862, Peter's three older brothers—Luke, John, and Matthew—are already in the Navy and fighting the war. Two will not survive the war. The third will die of yellow fever shortly after. At his father's desperate plea, Wake remains a draft-exempt merchant marine schooner captain on the New England coast.

1863—As the war drags on, many merchant marine officers lose their draft exemption. Wake is about to be called up, so he volunteers for the U.S. Navy. Sent to Key West, he is commissioned an acting master and given command of the small sailing gunboat *Rosalie*. Successfully operating against blockade-runners in Florida and the Bahamas, he is promoted to acting lieutenant. In Key West he falls in love with Linda Donahue, daughter of a virulently pro-Confederate merchant. Irish-born boatswain's mate Sean Aloysius Rork joins *Rosalie*'s crew, and the two men become lifelong best friends (as depicted in *At the Edge of Honor*, first novel of the Honor Series).

1864—Wake chases Union deserters from the Dry Tortugas to French-occupied Mexico, where he confronts Rebel gun runners, creating an international incident. He marries Linda at Key West, with Rork as best man. Wake conducts coastal raids against Confederates in Florida, and his quick thinking attracts the notice of the squadron commander (as depicted in *Point of Honor*).

1865—Wake's daughter Useppa is born at the pro-Union refugee camp at Useppa Island in southwest Florida. After the tumultuous end of the Civil War, Wake is sent to assess ex-Confederates who have fled to Puerto Rico, where he confronts his nemesis from the war (as depicted in *Honorable Mention*).

1867—Wake decides to stay in the Navy after the war and is given a regular commission as lieutenant. He is now a rarity among naval officers—one of the few who did not graduate from the Naval Academy. His only son, Sean, is born at Pensacola Naval Station.

1869—As executive officer of a warship off the coast of Panama, Wake relieves his drug-addicted captain of command and is charged with mutiny. He is subsequently acquitted of the charge, but his reputation is permanently tarnished (as depicted in *A Dishonorable Few*).

1874—Wake is involved in questionable activities in Spain and Italy when a beautiful married Frenchwoman enters his life, but he is serendipitously saved from further disrepute by Jesuits. He later rescues the woman and other French civilians in Africa, is awarded the Légion of Honor by France, and is promoted to lieutenant commander (as depicted in *An Affair of Honor*).

1880—Wake embarks on his first espionage mission during the South American War of the Pacific and further cements his relationship with the Jesuits in the Catacombs of the Dead in Peru. He is awarded his second foreign medal, the Peruvian Order of the Sun. While he is away, his beloved Linda dies of cancer. After a period of deep depression, he plunges into his work and in 1882 helps form the Office of Naval Intelligence (ONI) (as depicted in *A Different Kind of Honor*).

1883—On an espionage mission into French Indochina, Wake befriends King Norodom of Cambodia, is awarded the Royal Order of Cambodia, and warns Emperor Hoa of Vietnam about a coming battle with the French. Rork loses his left hand in the battle. Wake returns home and is promoted to commander, but sick of Washington politics, he and Rork buy Patricio Island in southwest Florida (where they served in the Civil War) and build bungalows there for their annual leave (as depicted in *The Honored Dead*).

1886—Wake meets young Theodore Roosevelt and Cuban patriot José Martí in New York City as he is beginning an espionage mission against the Spanish in Havana, Tampa, and Key West. He forms close friendships with Martí and Roosevelt and begins a twelve-year struggle against the Spanish secret police (as depicted in *The Darkest Shade of Honor*).

1888—The search for a lady friend's missing son in the Florida Keys, Bahamas, and Haiti becomes a love affair and an espionage mission against European anarchists. During his perilous escape, Wake's shadowy relationship with the Russian secret service, the Okhrana, begins. He proposes marriage to his lover and is rejected (as depicted in *Honor Bound*).

1888—During a mission to rescue ONI's Cuban operatives from Spanish custody in Havana, Wake is designated a "Friend of Freemasonry" by Master Mason Martí, which forges a lifelong relationship with Freemasons around the world (as depicted in *Honorable Lies*).

1889—Wake is sent to the South Pacific on an espionage mission to either prevent a war or immediately win it during the armed confrontation between Germany and America at Samoa. He is awarded the Royal Order of Kalakaua by the Kingdom of Hawaii and earns the gratitude of President Grover Cleveland, but is ashamed of the sordid methods he felt forced to use in Samoa (as depicted in *Honors Rendered*).

1890—Wake learns that his 1888 love affair produced a daughter, Patricia. His lover died in childbirth, and Patricia is being raised by her maternal aunt in Illinois. He sends a stipend for Patricia's care and education but is refused visitation by the aunt. Wake leaves ONI espionage work and returns to sea in command of a small cruiser. Sean graduates from the U.S. Naval Academy.

1892—Wake has a love affair in Washington with María Abad Maura, widow of a Spanish diplomat. Brought back into espionage work on a counter-assassination mission in Mexico and Florida, Wake saves Martí's life and returns to sea in command of another warship (as depicted in *The Assassin's Honor*).

1893—In April, Wake is promoted to captain and Rork to the newly established rank of chief boatswain's mate. In May, Wake marries María, and his daughter Useppa marries her Cuban fiancé, Mario Cano, in a double wedding ceremony in Key West with Martí attending (as depicted in *The Assassin's Honor*).

1895—Wake's dear friend José Martí is killed in action while fighting the Spanish at Dos Rios in eastern Cuba on May 19.

1897—Wake ends seven years of sea duty with orders to be the special assistant to the new assistant secretary of the Navy, his young friend Theodore Roosevelt. Together they ready the U.S. Navy for the looming war against Spain (as depicted in *An Honorable War*, the first book of the Spanish-American War Trilogy within the Honor Series).

1898—January to June. As calls for war with Spain mount in America, Roosevelt sends Wake inside Cuba on an espionage mission against the Spanish. Wake is in Havana harbor when *Maine* explodes, and later that night finally kills his longtime nemesis, Colonel Isidro Marrón, head of the Spanish secret police. Several months later, Wake commands a coastal raid against Spanish forces in Cuba, poorly planned by ignorant politicians in Washington. Afterward, he is shunned by the naval and governmental leadership for employing shockingly brutal tactics to accomplish the impossible mission, save the lives of his men, and get them all home. Wounded during the action, he convalesces in Tampa, nursed by María (as depicted in *An Honorable War*, first book of the Spanish-American War Trilogy within the Honor Series).

1898—June and July. Recovered from the worst of his wounds, Wake is ordered back inside Cuba as a liaison officer with the Cuban and then the American armies ashore. He is captured during a reconnaissance mission and imprisoned on a Spanish warship, where he observes and narrowly survives the climactic naval battle at Santiago. María, a volunteer American Red Cross war nurse in the war zone, falls ill and is sent home, and Wake begins a new sea command (as depicted in *Honoring the Enemy*, the second book of the Spanish-American War Trilogy within the Honor Series).

July–August 1898 and October 1901—In October 1901, while in Washington on the final assignment of his naval career, Wake is grilled about decisions he made while commanding the cruiser *Dixon* in the Caribbean during the Spanish-American War. The interrogation is a trap set by his professional and political enemies to ruin his reputation and thwart his retirement and pension. Expecting a demand for his resignation, Wake is shocked when President Theodore Roosevelt instead asks him to stay on active duty, accept a promotion to rear admiral, and work as a special presidential aide conducting high-level missions around the world. Wake's career evolves into a new and exciting phase (as depicted in *Word of Honor*, third book in the Spanish-American War Trilogy within the Honor Series).

1904—In Europe ostensibly on a goodwill visit, Rear Admiral Wake is really on a false-flag espionage mission to procure Germany's plans to invade America. The mission is successful, but Wake is embroiled in the turmoil in Russia and ends up as naval observer with the Russian fleet that is steaming around the world to face the Japanese at the cataclysmic naval Battle of Tsushima. En route, Wake befriends a remarkable young Russian naval officer. His perilous escape from Tsushima leads him across revolutionary Russia from Vladivostok to the *Potemkin* mutiny in the Black Sea, with lasting consequences for himself and his descendants (as depicted in *Code of Honor*).

In This Book

Readers of *The Honored Dead* will recall that in 2007 Wake's sword and memoirs were found inside a Vietnamese trunk stored in Agnes Whitehead's attic in Key West. At last, we have the story from the man himself. Part 1 of this book ("Honor's Call") is the final memoir in that collection.

Peter Wake remained active to the very end of his life. In this book you will accompany him on the epic 1907–9 voyage of the Great White Fleet around the globe, a 1914 espionage mission for newly installed Assistant Secretary of the Navy Franklin D. Roosevelt against German spies in Central America, and the 1917 visit of Theodore Roosevelt to Wake's home islands in Florida.

Part 2 of this book ("Honor's Legacy") narrates Wake's final year and then follows the considerable naval exploits of the next generations of his family to this very day. In World War I, World War II, Vietnam, the Cold War, and the War on Terror—Wake's descendants are there when the nation needs them, helping to make the history that shaped the nation.

A Note about Wake's Writing Style

Peter Wake wrote with unusual candor and personal details so that family and friends would know the truth of what really happened in his career. His descriptions of people may not be considered sensitive and tolerant today, but Wake was remarkably liberal for his time. His various grammatical mistakes, in both English and other languages, have been kept to enable the reader to better appreciate the man and his limitations. His assessments of personalities, policies, and events were frequently at odds with the norm back then, but one-hundred-year hindsight has proven them uncannily prescient.

Chapter Notes, Research Bibliography, and Appendix

At the back of the book are notes to most of the chapters explaining the people, places, and events described in the book. The bibliography of my research materials that follows the notes offers reading suggestions for those whose curiosity demands further knowledge. And for those who are fascinated by details about the man himself, I have included something new—and I hope helpful—in this final book: an appendix summarizing Peter Wake's family tree.

———

Onward and upward—
for Wake, for us all, on this final voyage . . .

———

Robert N. Macomber
Distant Horizons Farm
Pineland Village, Pine Island
Florida

Rear Admiral Peter Wake's
Preface to This Volume of His Memoirs

Back on an October evening in 1901, my energetic friend Theodore Roosevelt declared to me that for men of action like us, retirement means giving up in life and vegetating while waiting to die. He disdained the very thought of that sort of tortured existence and predicted I would soon be miserable if I ever succumbed to such a preposterous notion.

Of course, at the time Theodore was loving every minute of a vigorous and productive life. Twenty years my junior, he was the father of an active young family and had become, against all political prophecies, president of the United States of America at the beginning of an exciting new century.

My situation was completely different. The children were grown, successful, and living far away. María was exhausted by the trials and tragedies of life, by her worry for me in my work, and by the morale-sapping duplicitousness of Washington's denizens. I was old and tired, and old wounds were a painful reminder of my age. I also had a very jaded attitude about the Navy, the government, and certain political winds starting to be felt in the country.

Retirement sounded damned enticing. Wonderful images beckoned me: cuddling with María well past sunrise, playing with our grandchildren, tending our gardens, having time to deepen my Episcopal-Methodist faith, and maybe even allowing the luxury of peace and hope. Perhaps scowls could be replaced by smiles after all.

And yet, the moment Theodore made that comment in October 1901, something deep inside me realized he was right. Even as my heart damned him for it, my mind agreed with him. He understood that I needed a mission to feel truly alive. After only a moment of reflection, I said yes to his offer, which meant continuing my national service, with the attendant stress, the strain on my beloved wife, and another delay of her dreams. Somehow, I managed to convince her not only to go along with it but to join me in the new assignment in ways she had never done before.

The next six years were a succession of presidential envoy missions, posh diplomatic soirées, luxury hotels and ocean liners, and intriguing tinges of espionage, usually with María and Sean Rork by my side. I was busy on important matters, solving problems and sometimes in peril (especially during that German mission and the subsequent Russian disaster in 1904–5). I was useful and appreciated. I felt alive.

And then, on a hot June afternoon in 1907, Theodore came up with my final mission, a grandiose scheme that both thrilled and concerned me with its audacity. It was to be the grand finale of his remarkable presidency and of my long career; a seemingly impossible, but possibly history-making, naval endeavor of global scale.

The mission was also an opportunity to gain deeper insight into the insidious efforts and plans of our burgeoning adversaries—Germany and Japan—whom I had long feared my son's generation would have to fight somewhere, or everywhere. After this final mission, Roosevelt and I agreed, we could both retire knowing we had done all we could for the future of our country and her Navy.

Little did we know then what each of us would face in the future. I sometimes think it is a profound blessing that God severely limits our foresight, lest we be too frightened of what is yet to come. This is that story. . . .

Rear Adm. Peter Wake, USN (Ret.)
Casita Porfina, Grunt Bone Lane
Key West, Florida
29 June 1919

Part 1

Honor's Call

1

The "Wonderful
Second Honeymoon"

SS *Siberia*
1,173 miles south of Honolulu
bound for Auckland, New Zealand

Monday, 20 July 1908

The Gentlemen's Bar on the Promenade Deck was crowded and smoky. Rork glanced about and lowered his empty glass, fixing me with that warning look, his words emerging in a low rumble. "I'm thinkin' this voyage's gone far too easy, sir. An' all this posh livin' makes me nervous. Somethin' bloody nefarious is afoot." He nodded. "Trouble an' treachery."

"You're a Gaelic clairvoyant, Rork. I was thinking the very same thing. South America was easy compared to what we'll face here in the South Pacific—old enemies with long memories. But this Bundaberg rum *is* damned good, so let's have another glass while we think it over."

Rork was right. The voyage *had* gone too smoothly, and I was increasingly nervous about that. After eight long months, four passenger liners, and nine ports in six countries on two continents, we were now bound for our third continent. We'd gone 18,000 miles so far, and there were still many more to go before journey's end. By design, we had remained three weeks ahead of America's "Great White Fleet," sixteen battleships that proclaimed America's might. The world was watching that fleet. And certain people in the world were watching *us*.

By this point the shine had worn off our first-class accommodations, the pampering servants, the haut cuisine, the tea parties, and the magnificent balls and soirées on board and ashore. The events all blurred into one, as did the ports, as did most of the "cultured" people we encountered.

We'd slogged south down the stormy Atlantic to the bottom of the Western Hemisphere, pushed through the Strait of Magellan, and steamed up the equally stormy Pacific coast to California, then followed the setting sun west to fabled Hawaii. From there we headed south through the sweltering equatorial doldrums, spying from afar the remote islands of the central Pacific on our way toward British New Zealand and Australia, where the fleet steaming behind us would be welcomed in grand style. But for us, there would be a slight course deviation to German Samoa, where several passengers would disembark. It was a place I remembered vividly from twenty-five years earlier. Lest I forget, I still had the scars to remind me.

After this extensive geographical preamble, the reader is probably wondering—as we did ourselves at the time—exactly why María and I and an elderly Sean Rork were in the middle of the Pacific Ocean.

María insinuated it was because of my ego. At the beginning, with his signature sly grin and a rum fizzle in his good hand, Rork had declared it a marvelous lark. I consistently stuck to a more elevated view: we were there to help ensure the safety and efficiency of the fleet steaming along weeks behind us, thus maintaining the untarnished image of the United States of America.

I formed that opinion on good authority: the president of the United States had told me. The previous summer, as we were planning the Great White Fleet's international training and goodwill cruise, Theodore Roosevelt informed me that my eyes and ears were needed out in front, smoothing the course ahead. But he knew full well that for me to go, María would have to be with me. And, of course, "that lovable old rascal" Rork as well.

The president knew his old combat comrade Rork would jump at the chance. Fully aware that María would be the real obstacle, Theodore got first lady Edith Roosevelt to invite her dear friend and confidante María, and me, to a private dinner at the White House.

It was just the four of us that evening. María, who is no fool, suspected it wasn't just a social visit. Undeterred by her wariness, Theodore put on his most charming manner as he presented his case. He started with describing the voyage as a "bully adventure!" Next came "a wonderful second honeymoon," followed by "a posh tourist cruise which few but the richest of European royalty are fortunate enough to experience." All reasonable expenses would be covered, naturally, for we would be representing our country to the world.

Roosevelt himself was "positively *envious!*" because he would be stuck in his "dreary office" in Washington while María, Rork, and I "gallivanted around the world in pampered luxury, seeing exotic lands, spreading the fame of America, and reaping the *adoration* of foreign cultures" ahead of the Great White Fleet's arrival bringing goodwill to their ports.

And, of course, María's linguistic abilities in Spanish and Portuguese would be a "*beautiful* touch to show our genuine friendship for the fellow republics" of the Americas. Slowing down to a more spiritual tone, Theodore suggested that María's and my style of genuinely heartfelt diplomacy could ensure peace for a generation, just as it had helped end the war between Russia and Japan two years earlier.

I thought he was laying it on a bit too thick, and I could tell María was about to dampen his ardor.

But the president wasn't done, preempting María's expected question with a smile and nonchalant wave of his hand. "And not to worry, Peter will not command the fleet, with all the stress *that* entails. No, quite the contrary, my dear. As my personal envoy, Peter's only real responsibilities will be to stay ahead of the fleet on board a luxury passenger liner, keeping a weather eye out for diplomatic, logistical, or espionage problems that might possibly come up. If any do, they'll be simple to handle—no doubt over a nice dinner with some friendly dignitary. María, everyone will be happy to host you and Peter, and later, our Navy boys!"

Theodore ended the performance with his patented toothy grin. At that point I wouldn't have been surprised if he'd curtseyed as well.

María turned and evaluated me—Theodore's co-conspirator—for a moment. I could see her shrewd mind cogitating the potential for good or bad outcomes of this endeavor. I smiled and reached for her hand. The president took the cue and reached for Edith's. There we were, two loving, mature couples having a nice discussion about a remarkable opportunity. But there was palpable tension in the air. I waited for the explosion. María looked at her friend Edith, who gazed back with just a hint of pleasant resignation. A feminine signal to surrender on this one?

María leveled a doubting eye at the president. "Your *word*, Theodore—this is our last assignment? With no dangers? Peter still has to walk with a *cane* since his last assignment, which got you the Nobel Peace Prize and got him nearly killed."

He never flinched at her social insubordination, but leaned toward her, removing his spectacles in a gesture of sincerity. "Yes, my dear. No danger. You will be diplomats, not warriors. And yes, this is my final request of Peter, and of you. The fleet returns just before I leave office and Peter retires, a last hurrah for both of us and a great service for America. For peace."

She glanced again at Edith, then at me, and sighed. "Then I suppose. . . ."

The tension evaporated. Theodore proposed a toast "to the upcoming second honeymoon of the gallant sailor and his lovely lady!"

The next morning in his office, a far grimmer president discussed the realities of the cruise with me. "As you well know, the Germans, British, and Japanese are watching our every move on this. They expect—and want—us to fail. Your proper attention to diplomacy, logistics, and espionage in advance of the fleet can *prevent* our national image from being tarnished. Your crucial responsibility is to handle problems *before* the fleet arrives in a port."

He paused, looking expectantly at me. I dutifully gave the expected reply, "Aye, aye, sir."

Then Roosevelt appended an ominous clause to my orders. "If, and more probably when, you encounter espionage—and especially its darker side, sabotage—you will use your unique expertise to deal with it quickly and effectively. But most of all, *quietly, out of sight*. Can you still accomplish that, Admiral Wake? American sailors' lives depend on it. I must have no doubts on this whatsoever."

The president and I regarded each other closely for a moment. I understood exactly what he meant, and what the consequences might be for me, María, and Rork. It was also not lost on me that none of these orders were in writing.

Without using my cane, I stood up and faced Roosevelt. "Aye, aye, Mr. President."

2

The Captain's Table

SS *Siberia*
At sea

Monday, 20 July 1908

It was one of those sultry, windless nights so common in the tropics. The ocean was glass. Fortunately, *Siberia*'s forward motion provided a refreshing breeze over the first-class promenade deck. On the eastern horizon to port, an incandescent half moon rose out of the sea, its light tracing a silvery pink path to my feet. I stood transfixed by the most romantic moonrise I'd ever seen in more than fifty years at sea.

Better yet, I was with the beautiful woman who loved me. She'd been visibly admired by the men and women at the captain's dinner table just minutes before, and now I had her alone in front of that stunning backdrop. It was the stuff of sailors' dreams and writers' novels. But my wife didn't even look at the moonrise.

María's tone was no longer the lighthearted banter of the previous three hours. Such repartee was merely a practiced façade, and very effective at extracting information from arrogant swells who loved to hear themselves talk. Tonight, the swell in question had been her German dinner partner.

María kept her voice low. "Gaston von Eberhardt knows a lot—far too much—about you. He knows you were at Samoa in '83, in the Caribbean in

'92 and '98, met the Kaiser in Hamburg and the Tsar in St. Petersburg in '04. Nothing accusatory, just that you are *famous*."

She let me digest that. *Infamous* in German intelligence circles was what von Eberhardt really meant. Those were all places I'd confronted German espionage or military operations.

I could tell she had more to say. "What else did you learn, my dear?"

"He asked me your opinion about current German activities in the Pacific. When I asked why he wanted to know, he said he was just curious because you are so experienced, and he would value your views. I feigned feminine ignorance of such weighty matters and told him we are on an extended second honeymoon."

"I doubt he bought that, but go on. What happened then?"

"I switched the subject to the famous lovely ladies of Samoa. He said they are too dark-skinned, and he prefers lovely ladies of Spain."

"He was buttering you up."

"Yes, the conceited bastard thinks I am utterly fascinated by his Teutonic manliness, charm, and brilliance. By the way, I am sure he is with the Nachrichten-Abteilung."

I couldn't help smiling at María's astute ability to spot adversaries. "Yes, I agree. We'll have to be careful around him as we find out what he's really up to out here."

Ever since von Eberhardt had boarded the ship four days earlier in Honolulu I'd seen signs that he was with German naval intelligence, probably the N-I counterespionage branch of Nachrichten-Abteilung that handled intelligence operations in the Pacific.

He portrayed himself as a bon vivant, a senior executive in the Telefunken Company's Pacific cable and wireless telegraphy operations. With his amiable manner and fluent English, von Eberhardt had quickly become a friend to all nationalities on the first-class deck. With a disarming smile, he explained his work as helping remote colonies—especially the British, German, and French islands out beyond Australia—communicate via wireless with their home countries.

Von Eberhardt was accordingly fluent, or seemingly so, in the new scientific jargon about wireless transmitters and receivers, wattage, voltage, distance attrition, band wave size, and electromagnetic induction. Such stuff was way beyond me—and everyone else listening to him. Oh yes, Gaston von Eberhardt was the perfect image of a smart, modern, hardworking, trustworthy, thirty-seven-year-old son of the Fatherland serving German commerce and world humanity overseas.

But not quite perfect enough. He stood parade-ground erect at all times, his steady gaze was a bit too calculating, the camaraderie too stilted at times. He never shared personal information, and most notably never showed any sign of inebriation—rare for a German in the Pacific, or anywhere, actually. Yes indeed, Gaston von Eberhardt was suspiciously self-disciplined—especially for a man who had lived in the energy-sapping indolence of the Pacific islands for many years. Even German discipline didn't last long there.

I was almost certain the Telefunken connection was a ruse. Back in Washington I'd heard a vague report of a German South Seas Wireless Telegraphy Company being quietly formed, possibly run by German intelligence. The operation's potential for mischief was clear. In the event of war, the company would be able to access—and interfere with—the British, French, and American cable and wireless networks in the Pacific. I wondered further: *and during "peacetime" as well?*

"So, what did you learn tonight at your end of the table?" María asked, now belatedly appreciating the moon rising over the glittering water.

"My table neighbor tonight was a Mr. Tanaka, a rather unimaginative alias, don't you think? Speaks English effortlessly. He very shyly explained he is a moderately successful, middle-aged, widowed owner of several barbershops in Honolulu and Sydney. He dreams of expanding his barbershops to Pago Pago, Guam, and Fiji so he can increase the money he sends home to his dear elderly parents in Yokohama; that's why he's disembarking at Samoa. He was very impressed by the dignity of the late Queen Victoria and admires the energy of our President Roosevelt. Thinks the U.S. Navy is the finest in the world and the Statue of Liberty is a wonderful symbol of freedom. Quiet, pleasant, polite, boring fellow—totally forgettable in every way."

María turned away from the moon. "So, he is in the Black Dragon Society," she said dryly, "and therefore Japanese intelligence and tied to Major Yoshida in Singapore, the *Kasato Maru* that has been following us, Kyoichi Aki in Chile, and that strange fellow in Honolulu."

"Yes, it appears so, my dear. And from his age and bearing I get the impression Tanaka is a senior officer. Probably has a better idea of American and British naval assets in the Pacific than I do. I just get official reports. He gets the real story from drunken sailors and officers stopping in for a haircut—and other things."

She nodded. "And what about that obnoxious Australian seated near you?"

"Ah, yes, the one and, thankfully the only, Parker Newton. Claims to be a businessman, self-made. Grew up in Western Australia. Now lives in Sydney. No wife. Despises the 'damned Orientals.' Said they're lazy and up to no good—then said, 'No offense' to Tanaka, who just stared back at him. Disdains the Brits because they've gone soft. Americans are naïve."

"What kind of business is he in?"

"Middleman broker. Exports cattle to French Polynesia, grain to Britain, rum to the Dutch islands. Imports manufactured goods from Britain. He went on about an impending war between Britain and Germany. Says Australia needs its own navy because the British will concentrate theirs against the Germans in the Med and North Sea and leave Australia defenseless."

War talk between Germany and Britain *was* escalating, both in the newspapers that came on board at every port and among the men in the first-class lounge. María sighed. "Well, he does have a point there. Germany has a first-rate raider squadron in the Pacific. Did he mention German influence in Australian cable and wireless communications?"

"No. I was about to ask, but the old lady next to me got him talking about kangaroos. Turns out he eats them, and some sort of creatures called wombats too. Says they're delicious. By the way, while Newton was bragging about his diet, Tanaka suggested to me that we have lunch tomorrow at the promenade café. I agreed. And now, darling, really, shouldn't we concentrate on this vista?"

She snuggled up to me, and we gazed out over the sparkling night sea. Words weren't needed. There in the fabled South Seas moonlight, I once again realized how very fortunate I was to have María's love and wisdom in my life. We were an extremely unlikely pair. When we first met, neither of us imagined that fifteen years later we would be happily married and working together to ensure the safe passage of an American fleet around the world.

I pulled her close and lifted her chin for a kiss. And with his usual abysmal timing, Rork showed up, a bit unsteady and slurring his words. "By God, you two should find yourselves a cabin. But first, we've a bit 'uv important business to attend to, Admiral—if ye can find the time, that is . . . sir."

María glared at Rork, then at me, and without a comment she walked away.

"Sorry to spoil yer romancin', sir," muttered Rork. "But there's somethin' truly important you should know."

3

The Lady of Spain
and the Gaelic Rogue

B efore I divulge what Rork thought so vital, I should shed some light on
these two remarkable people who were the pillars of my life.

When I first noticed Doña María Ana Abad Maura at the French
embassy's Bastille Day soirée back in 1892, my first impression was of statu-
esque beauty. A tall, slim, graceful lady with smooth, light olive skin, María
has the darkest blue eyes I've ever seen. That evening her shining black hair
was done up in the French fashion and adorned with a classic Spanish mantilla.
Her high-necked crimson silk gown could not conceal the perfection of her
figure. As I got closer, I was particularly taken by her smile at me. It was a
genuinely kind smile, a rarity at diplomatic affairs.

Because it was a stifling hot evening and the lady had no glass, I offered
to obtain refreshment for her. During the ensuing conversation over flutes
of chilled champagne, she asked about the medals that adorned my chest,
a standard polite question at such functions. I provided bland explanations
(the details of some of them are rather controversial and still confidential),
then steered her to a quiet corner near the garden to learn her personal story.

María was born and raised on the Spanish island of Majorca in the Mediterranean. She was Roman Catholic although of ancient Jewish roots (her family

converted on pain of death in 1492), had been married for thirty-two years to a Spanish diplomat in Washington who had died of a heart attack four years earlier, and had two grown sons.

She stayed in Washington after her husband's death to avoid the right-wing politics and royal foolishness current at the time in Madrid and the depressing social restrictions placed on widows in Majorca. She preferred the individual liberty and opportunity America offered her and was thinking of becoming a naturalized citizen.

I found all that intriguing enough, but there was much more to learn. The lady turned out to be multilingual, well educated, financially independent, scientifically curious, and liberal-minded about culture, race, religion, and politics. At a time when so many in Cuba, America, and Spain were stridently clamoring for open war in Cuba, María fervently wished for a peaceful solution to the Cuban people's quest for independence.

Her two sons, she said, were split on the issue. The oldest, Francisco, was a Franciscan priest in Havana who was trying to bring Spaniards and Cubans together in endeavors of mutual interest. Juanito, her younger son, was a government functionary in Havana, a strict monarchist, and an officer in the army reserve. He served Spain and wanted to crush the dangerous ideas of liberty popular in Cuba.

I found this complex woman utterly fascinating. She found me far less so, I'm afraid, assessing the naval officer sitting beside her as just another American warmonger who wanted to annex Cuba for the profits to be had there. That wasn't true, of course, but it would take awhile for her to realize it.

Ultimately, we fell in love and formed a strong partnership based on respect and humor (hers is very dry). My family and friends, even Rork, were worried for my happiness. It had been more than twenty years since my wife Linda died, and several ladies had broken my heart since then. Not to mention the fact (which Rork did) that María was my complete opposite in many respects: Catholic (like Rork), wealthy, educated, cultured, linguistically gifted, and a citizen of the country we were probably going to war against soon.

María faced the same kind of opposition from her family and friends when they learned of our relationship—I was an ignorant Yanqui barbarian, a Protestant heretic, a vagabond sailor, and too crude for a lady of her status and intellect.

We ignored them, were married in 1893, and never regretted it. María has never converted, but she enjoys the Methodist church we both attend. She did convert her allegiance from the Spanish king (a ten-year-old boy at the time) to America and became a proud naturalized citizen.

Then, in 1898, the war ignited. Francisco was killed by the Spanish secret police. Juanito fought against the Americans and was wounded and captured (by me, no less). María served in the American Red Cross in the Cuban war zone, and I was nearly killed in battles ashore and afloat. But our love has endured everything, even the last eight months afloat in tight quarters.

Rork is another immigrant story. Born in Wexford, Ireland, he fled British oppression and the lack of opportunity and ran off to sea at age thirteen. In his late twenties he ended up in Boston, and in 1861 joined the U.S. Navy. I do not know his real age, which seems to change according to whatever is required at the time by naval regulations or what a pretty lady thinks it might be. I believe he is about eight years older than me.

Tall, lanky, with a gray pigtail twisted in an old-fashioned sailor's queue, an infectious laugh, and a wicked wit, he has the arthritis common to longtime sailors, walks with a limp courtesy of several wounds (the most recent from Tsushima in 1905), and—despite what he maintains—is not as strong as he once was.

But whatever his age and ailments, Chief Boatswain's Mate Sean Aloysius Rork still has one unique attribute that is the wonder of the U.S. Navy.

His left hand.

Though it appears real, Rork's left hand is actually a finely crafted India rubber appliance. It is configured in a permanent grip that allows him to hold an oar, a belaying pin, or a bottle. Every year the hand is accurately repainted, complete with fake hairs and freckles, by a lady friend of Rork's who works the street outside the Washington Navy Yard. You have to be very close to the hand to realize it is a replica. If you are a foe, by that time you are far too close and it is far too late, for there is a silent and very deadly weapon inside that hand.

Underneath the rubber exterior is a five-inch-long bosun's marlinspike protruding from a wooden base. It is mounted at the end of a soft leather sleeve that is strapped over the stump of Rork's amputated left forearm. A sniper at the 1883 Battle of Hue in the empire of Vietnam was responsible for that. Rork's life was saved—and his appliance constructed—by surgeons and metalsmiths on board a nearby French warship. Rork misses his left hand, but he relishes his appliance, which can be removed in seconds to expose the spike.

Rork is not some ignorant brute, however. He is a self-educated gentleman, the Navy's third most senior chief petty officer, and the valued friend of admirals and presidents. He is extremely well read, particularly in poetry; can converse in Gaelic, French, and Spanish in addition to English; is the funniest man I know; and has the innate ability to charm any woman in any culture before she even knows he is doing it.

He does have a weakness: decent rum and, from our time in Russia, fine vodka.

In many spots around the world, I have had to extricate him from some calamity brought on by his fondness for drink and pretty women. Some of these situations have been quite dicey, with fathers, husbands, or very angry women seeking deadly revenge. Fortunately, Rork's high naval and political friends don't know about most of those situations.

But they do know that Rork and I have a friendship that is strictly against naval regulations, for commissioned officers do not fraternize with enlisted men, no matter how senior they may be. Our naval colleagues, both officer and enlisted, know our friendship is based on mutual respect gained from forty-four years of shared experience in combat, storms, and espionage missions around the world. Neither Rork nor I regret our friendship. But it is never displayed in front of others while we are on duty, when naval norms of courtesy and rank are scrupulously followed.

Rork has lived an adventurous life, but he does have one huge regret. While I was married to dear Linda, who gave me two wonderful children, and in my later years to my lovely María, who gives me gentle love and companionship, poor Rork has never been able to get a woman to marry him. He never has known the comfort and calm and joy of a home and family. His pride does not allow him to acknowledge this great void in his life, but I know it's there and painful, particularly now that he is in his seventies.

So now let us return to that moonlit night on *Siberia*'s promenade deck and the matter that concerned Rork so much that he interrupted a tender embrace. The moment I heard what he had to say, I knew my old friend was, as usual, absolutely correct.

4

The Okhran Man

SS *Siberia*,
South of Honolulu
Bound for Auckland, New Zealand

Monday, 20 July 1908

Duly chastened by María's disapproval, Rork straightened up and began reporting as if we were back on the bridge of a warship. Well, perhaps not *exactly* like that. Lately, he'd been adding considerable editorial comment to his reports.

"Admiral, 'bout five minutes ago some fancy-arsed toff came up to me, passed me an envelope, and told me to get it to you right away. Not asked, mind you; he *told* me. Said it was from an old friend of yours. No pleasantries, name, or discussion. Rude as hell, he was, an' me rigged out in me finest duds like a proper gentleman an' standin' right there next to me lady friend from dinner. Then the arrogant bastard walked off without so much as fare-thee-well. Damned embarrassin' it was."

The man was lucky Rork didn't shove him overboard. Probably saved from that because the lady was there. "You're getting a bit touchy in your old age, Rork. What's his description?"

"Just shy o' fifty years old, medium height an' thin build, spectacles, pomaded hair, an' one o' those sculpted goatees. Struts like a staff poser who's never heard a hostile round. Rooskie accent, an' the bloody imperial attitude to go with it. Worse than the damned Limeys, that bunch is. When I heard that Rooskie accent I had an idea who the bastard might be an' came 'round to find you straight away."

Rork could go on ad nauseum once he got started on the British and the Russians, so I brought him back to the topic at hand. "Anything else about him?"

"I asked a steward friend o' mine who the Rooskie bugger was, an' he said a Mr. Smirnikoff, what come on board at Honolulu. Cabin 143, aft end o' first class, port side. Said the bastard treats the stewards like dogs. 'Tis no wonder the Rooskie fleet mutinied." Rork wagged his head and then admitted, "But ye've got a point, Admiral. I *am* a wee bit more sensitive in me old age—just don't have the patience for arrogant snobs I used to have when we were younger."

That got a chuckle out of me—Rork had never had patience for arrogant snobs. "Thank you for your restraint, Rork. Now let's see what we have here from this arrogant Russian snob."

I opened the envelope (it was ship's stationery, found in every cabin), which contained one sheet with a note in large, rolling cursive script, the sign of uncertain writing in a second language. As I read the note, I shared the contents with Rork in a whisper so the couple perambulating by in the shadows would not overhear.

Admiral Wake,
A mutual friend you've known since Cap Haitien told me to share this information with you. Recent very good authority has it that the friends of Tamasese are planning to work with the enemies who sank you three years ago. Their goal is to add more surprises to your bunkers. That is the end of the information I have from our mutual friend. I will have no more for you. Do not try to contact me.
Kukov

Rork took in a breath, then hissed, "Oh, bloody hell, the Okhrana's on board. As if we didn't have enough trouble already with the Nips an' Krauts."

He was right, the passenger in Cabin 143—"Snobov," as we came to call him—clearly worked for the Okhrana, Imperial Russia's dreaded secret service, with which I was, unfortunately, quite familiar. No doubt "Smirnikoff" was an alias, likewise "Kukov." The snobbish demeanor was part of his cover story. He was probably a part of the same spy network as Commander Alexis Diatchkoff of the Imperial Russian Navy, who had been observing our fleet quite openly from the decks of various ships (including one we were on) in South America. We hadn't seen Diatchkoff since Peru.

I analyzed the clues in the note. "Recent very good authority" meant a primary witness or participant to an event. The "friends of Tamasese" were the Germans I'd worked against in Samoa in '89. The "mutual friend" was Pyotr Ivanovich Rachkovsky, an Okhrana agent Rork and I met in a dicey operation against a European anarchist lair at Cap Haitien back in '88. We had occasional contact over the years, but he could hardly be called a friend. Now the head of Okhrana, Rachkovsky was the man who figured out my false-flag operation against the Germans in St. Petersburg in '04. He had a female assassin try to kill me because of it, although it was she who ended up dead. The "enemies who sank you" were the Japanese at the Battle of Tsushima in '05. "More surprises to your bunkers" meant placing more bombs in the White Fleet's coal bunkers—like those already found when the fleet refueled at Trinidad and Mexico.

Very few Americans knew about those bombs, and even fewer foreigners did. *How did Rachkovsky in far-off St. Petersburg know? And what else does he know?*

"You think Rachkovsky's still feelin' bad about tryin' to kill you, an' that's why he reached out to warn you?" asked Rork. "He exposed his agent to do it, an' that oily bastard never does *that* kinda thing."

I snorted. "I don't think he ever did feel bad about that. It wasn't personal for him, it was business, to get points with the Tsar's entourage, who were angry about our operation on their soil. But you're right. Why expose an agent to warn us? Why not just send a telegram? This is about something bigger than the bombs. Rachkovsky wants us to react to this message, to do something."

"Kill that Kraut fellow, von Eberhardt, I'm thinkin'—the Rooskies hate Kaiser Willy," opined Rork. "Course, we can't really blame 'em fer that, can we?"

"Could be, Rork. The Russians *are* worried about the Germans. Or maybe Rachkovsky wants me to kill Tanaka as revenge for Russia's defeat in the war with Japan? Maybe Tanaka worked for Colonel Akashi's network in Europe back then. They killed several Okhrana agents."

"But why you, sir? His own Okhrana man on board can kill either o' those buggers. He looks like the sneaking sort who'd use poison rather than a knife or pistol."

"False-flag operation, Rork. For deniability. Same as we did to the Germans in '04. Rachkovsky would enjoy the irony of that."

"Aye, sir," Rork said. "Ye've a good point there. He's an evil bastard, an' a damned smart one."

I tried without success to fight back a yawn. "It's too much for my tired old mind to figure out right now, Rork. I'm off to bed. I'll see you at breakfast."

The Russian dominated my thoughts as I made my way to my cabin. I'd long respected the intricate convolutions of how Rachkovsky—one of the best spymasters I've ever known—planned and executed his multifaceted false-flag operations. Each one had layer upon layer of very plausible—and completely false—façades, making it almost impossible to trace the actual origins back to the Okhrana. He usually got others to betray their comrades and do the killing for him by convincing them that they were doing it for their own side's benefit. I'd seen him use that tactic against foreign and domestic Russian anarchists, the Germans, and the Japanese.

My thoughts distilled down to several questions. *Is Rachkovsky setting me up now to be his pawn? To do what to whom? Why? And what happens if I just ignore the warning?*

The answers didn't come to me. This new development wasn't one of the factors I'd considered when the president and I began planning this audacious naval operation.

María was sound asleep when I slipped into our bunk. I lay there in the dark for a long time, staring at the piping dimly outlined overhead, wondering what the hell to do. Or, perhaps far more important, what *not* to do. . . .

5
The Invitation

Apia
Upolu Island, German Samoa

Thursday, 24 July 1908

The luncheon with Tanaka confirmed my suspicions. His probing questions, artfully concealed among innocuous comments about the beauty of Japan, centered on the fleet's upcoming visit to Japan, which had been publicly announced—without details of itinerary and agenda—once the battleships arrived at California. Tanaka smilingly asked if the esteemed American sailors would get to see legendary Mount Fujiyama or visit the beautiful gardens of Yokohama; or would they perhaps go to another part of Japan and see the famous park at Kyoto? Would all the sailors of the fleet make the visit, or only a few? Would they have time to see much? He hoped so, for the Japanese loved Americans.

Underneath the lies about Japanese love for Americans was the "barbershop" owner's real question: Would the entire American fleet enter Tokyo Bay—the heart of Japan—with all that meant culturally, politically, and militarily?

I deflected his query with an amiable shrug. "I'm sure all our sailors would love to visit your fabled land, Mr. Tanaka, but I suspect they will have little time for tourism. Much depends on ships' machinery and fuel, and future port commitments in other countries. Say, this sandwich is delicious. The food on board is first class, isn't it?"

I didn't see Tanaka again for several days. He stayed in his cabin until we reached Samoa, as did the arrogant "Snobov." The German, however, continued to make friends with one and all, and the brash Australian, the one passenger I heartily wished *would* stay in his cabin, showed up for every meal and continued offending his dinner companions.

Three days later, after a raucous crew celebration of crossing the Equator (which featured a slightly tipsy Rork, as oldest man in the ship, relishing his role as King Neptune), *Siberia* anchored off the village of Apia, capital of the Imperial German colony of Samoa.

It was a bittersweet moment for me, because memories flooded my mind.

I was last there in March 1889 on an espionage mission from President Grover Cleveland, my job to either prevent an impending war between Germany and America or win it overwhelmingly and quickly. During that impossible endeavor, I managed to get shot in the hip by the German navy, bombarded by German marines, hounded by native Samoan forces, and nearly killed in a catastrophic cyclone. When all was said and done, 226 German and American sailors were dead, but war was averted. Not by me, but by an act of God.

Much had changed in the intervening years. Modern buildings had sprung up along the streets, a seawall high and long enough to serve as a defensive fortification lined the shore, and the tall steeple of a Lutheran church glistened in the sun. European men in pith helmets and ladies under parasols strolled the waterfront conversing about the unusually large passenger ship in their bay. The Imperial German flag flew everywhere, and an Imperial German Navy launch chugged busily about.

This wasn't a previously advertised port call, just a quick stop. *Siberia* was there only overnight to disembark a few passengers and offload some cargo. Many of the passengers wanted to go ashore to see Vailima, home of the late Robert Louis Stevenson. But that famous house was now the residence of the German governor, and entrance was by invitation only.

I'd met Stevenson—dear friend of the Samoan people and adversary of their German oppressors—when we were both in Honolulu with King David

Kalākaua. I had no intention of going ashore in Apia to see what the Germans had done to my friend's home. I expected the Germans had equally bad memories of my last visit. Perhaps vengeful ones.

An hour after *Siberia*'s hook went in the mud, María and I were on the broiling hot deck watching Samoan police constables in lavalavas goose-stepping with Teutonic vigor down the waterfront. I found the sight profoundly sad. We were about to head inside for lunch to buoy our spirits when the ship's captain walked up and handed me an envelope bearing the official coat of arms of German Samoa—the imperial black eagle over a row of palms set atop the blue sea. It was the governor's personal stationery. María cast a worried look at me.

"A very special invitation, Admiral!" said the captain.

"Looks that way," I groaned, giving the thing to my wife as the captain headed off with several other envelopes in hand, one of which I noticed bore Rork's name.

"Oh, joy," murmured María sarcastically when she opened it. Then she read aloud with a marked absence of enthusiasm:

To Rear Admiral Peter Wake,
Navy of the United States of North America

His Excellency Wilhelm Heinrich Solf, Governor of Samoa
and Personal Representative of His Imperial Majesty
Kaiser Wilhelm the Second, Master of the Imperial German Empire,
invites Rear Admiral and Mrs. Peter Wake to a special reception and
dinner in their honor at the Governor's Residence at Vailima
at seven p.m., Thursday, 24 July 1908. Attire: Formal.

She frowned, then went on. "Starts at seven. Well, that means it will drag on to midnight. Oh, you will love this next part, Peter. It seems the military that tried to kill you here twenty-nine years ago will be our official escort."

I countered her sarcasm with humor. "Really, my dear? And to think it was the heavy German food I was dreading."

She lifted an expressive eyebrow, then continued the narration. "Transport: A launch of the Imperial German Navy alongside SS *Siberia* at 6:40 p.m. Land transport: The Governor's personal carriage at the harbor boat landing at 6:45 p.m., with carriage escort to Vailima by the Imperial German Navy Marine Guard."

"How extremely courteous of them," I laughed.

María didn't laugh with me. She sighed. "Formal dress in this dreadful heat and humidity. I am sweating just to think about it. Is there no way for us to decline this? Sickness, perhaps? I believe I'm feeling faint. Might be malaria."

I sympathized completely but couldn't go along. "No, darling. You can stay here and deal with your 'malaria' if you wish, but I'm a personal envoy of President Roosevelt and a representative of America to the world. This is not just a personal invitation to dinner from the governor of Samoa, my dear. By political extension it's from Kaiser Wilhelm and the Imperial German Empire. I must go and show the flag. And yes, sweat. . . ."

"Very well. If you go, I will go, and we will sweat together." Her frown returned. "Seriously though, Peter, having to wear formal dress is not the only reason I don't want us to go. They hate you and might do you harm as revenge for the past."

"No, they won't, my dear. They are much smarter than that," I said in my most convincing manner, which to her ears sounded patronizing.

I regretted it instantly, but now she was angry. "Why not? Because you are a presidential envoy? That didn't stop them from trying to kill you in Europe and in Africa only three years ago. Not to mention right at this very place three decades ago!"

Tired of the argument, I held up a placatory hand. "María, those scenarios were different. This is just a dinner. And there will be many other people around, including Rork. We will dine, then we will leave. End of story."

Our luncheon was silent.

6

Samoa mo Samoa

Vailima, residence of the governor
Upolu Island, German Samoa

Thursday, 24 July 1908

As we expected, von Eberhardt made the introductions, with a theatrical (bordering on comical) flourish and true Germanic passion that was somewhat exhausting to endure. Rork, unlike me, was in civilian attire, and was therefore introduced as "Mister Rork."

Expecting a typical colonial autocrat like those I'd encountered in other German colonies around the world, I was surprised to find stout Governor Wilhelm Heinrich Solf and his lovely young wife, Johanna (twenty-five years his junior), warmly hospitable. There was no posturing, no condescension, no dictatorial ranting. At first I thought it was a clever façade, but their manner remained unchanged throughout the evening. They were genuinely nice people.

Solf was no fool, however. He knew about my past in Samoa and faced it with impressive diplomacy. "I regret you cannot stay longer than one night, Admiral, for much has changed here since 1889. I think you, and even the late Mr. Stevenson, would like our progress. The internal Samoan factions still have differences, naturally, but they solve them peacefully now. His Imperial

Majesty, our beloved Kaiser, has graciously allowed us to help the Samoans by building proper schools, roads, a water and sanitary system, a hospital, and many other improvements. And we have no tensions with our neighbors—you Americans at Pago Pago, the British at Fiji, or the French at Papeete. Samoa under Germany is peaceful and prosperous."

"I congratulate you on your progress, Your Excellency. Peace is always better than war."

"Tell that to Berlin and London!" interrupted a drunken Parker Newton, who shouldered up next to us. "And all's *not* well out here in paradise, either. You've got some bloody unhappy kanakas over on your island of Savai'i, don't you, Governor? *Samoa mo Samoa*—Samoa for the Samoans!—that's *their* cheer. Chief Lauaki and his big brown buggers're planning on ousting you Krauts out on your lily-white arses. They just might start with you, your high and mightiness. Hell, that's why you've got so many guards here tonight! Admit it."

Solf's face was a cold mask as he turned to the Australian. "Mr. Newton, your impression is completely wrong. There is only a nonviolent disagreement over copra production. There will be *no* rebellion against the authority of the Kaiser, whose representative I am. And there is only a ceremonial guard tonight, here in honor of our American guest, Admiral Wake."

Eberhardt stepped up beside Newton and took his arm. His face pleasant but his tone uncompromising, he said quietly, "Ach, Parker Newton, my dear friend, you must try some of our German chocolate cake. Look there, over on that table. Come, let me offer you a piece. I insist."

Newton refused to take the hint. "We've not had our bloody dinner yet, you daft squarehead! And take your hand off me—I'm not some Frenchman you can lead around!"

As a worried María came over to stand protectively beside me, Eberhardt's arm locked tightly around Newton's, his hand bending the Australian's right hand back to a painfully unnatural angle while walking him briskly toward the other end of the room. To cover his use of force, the German laughed at some nonexistent joke. It fooled no one. The buzz of conversation faded as the guests watched the cursing Newton marched past the cake table and out the side door.

"Aye, now that was very neatly done," said Rork, who had materialized just behind us. "Couldn't've done it smoother meself," he said admiringly.

"Personally, I thought it was a bit too obvious. Should've taken the wind out of him with a slight poke at the solar plexus. That would have eliminated the unseemly vulgarities as well."

Rork grinned. "Quite right, sir. The Kraut's technique could use some improvement. By the by, I've been havin' a look 'round. Seems to me there's more than just a ceremonial guard here tonight, sir. And the lads're lookin' a wee bit nervous. Fingerin' their Mausers, they are. An' I saw an interestin' sight in the governor's office. . . ."

Before I could digest that observation and ask for details, the string quartet on the verandah erupted into a gay, fast-paced rendition of a popular German song. The conversational buzz rose again, this time with many disparaging comments in German and English about drunken Australians. Herr Eberhardt was a hero.

The party was back on track by the time the governor's aide rang a bell and loudly declared—first in German and then in good English—that dinner was ready, and to please follow him. The crowd, still chattering away, formed a line behind the Solfs and the Wakes and headed for the dining room. María dabbed a dainty handkerchief at the perspiration beaded in her décolletage, then gave me an I-told-you-so look. The choker collar on my dress whites began to make my neck itch. We still had a long evening ahead of us. I tried to look happy.

Bang!

The first shot was followed by two more. In the commotion that followed, I saw a form dart toward a side doorway. With guttural commands in German the guards surrounded the governor and hustled him out of the room. I couldn't tell if he'd been hit. The panicked crowd surged toward the doors with shrieks and bellows.

The three Americans reacted a bit differently. Rork drew his Navy Colt .44, crouched into a firing stance, and scanned for targets. I drew the .44 Merwin Hulbert revolver from inside my tunic and scrutinized the remaining German officials, who seemed stunned. María's Remington .41 derringer appeared in her hand from a hidden pocket in her waist sash.

More shouting, this time in German and Samoan, sounded outside on the far end of the front verandah. I headed there, flanked by María and Rork. When we reached the verandah, we saw a body sprawled on the lawn by the steps—a young man in a black suit. His skull was crushed. A large Samoan constable stood nearby being questioned by two German officers. On the ground was a bloody club, of the type carried by the native constables. Parker Newton was in custody next to the driveway, with a Samoan constable at either side, being shoved into a carriage.

Solf, who appeared uninjured, emerged and walked up to the senior officer present, gesturing toward the body. I caught the words "ein Passagier auf dem Schiff." The man was a passenger from the ship, then. A subordinate showed the governor a pistol, evidently the one used in the shooting. I recognized the type: an old .41-caliber Eibar revolver, Spanish army issue. Rork shot me a grim glance. My gut began to churn. Then the senior officer held out a Spanish passport to the governor and told him, "Julio Boreau, Barcelona."

I suddenly knew who the target really was—and why.

7

Venganza

Vailima
Upolu Island, German Samoa

Thursday, 24 July 1908

I led Rork and María out of the crowd toward a quiet place on the far side of the house where we could talk. There was no time to waste.

"Rork, get to Boreau's cabin before the police do. Take anything of value to us. Find out everything you can about him, including if he has sons. When María and I return to the ship, the three of us will meet in your cabin. Go!"

Rork nodded curtly and headed off toward the line of carriages.

María stood there tensely, waiting for me to explain. She knew the basics of my past before she had entered my life, but not all the details. That's why she didn't recognize the name or the weapon from the German officer's report. I knew now that she needed to know everything.

"Obviously, the assassin was not a rebel Samoan; nor do I think the governor was the target," she declared while watching me closely. "Though Solf thinks he was, which is probably useful for us. So, who *was* the target, Peter?"

"I was," I admitted. "*Venganza*—vengeance for something that happened long ago in Cuba. Back in 1886, a lieutenant named Boreau in the Orden

Público—the Spanish secret police—was my first adversary in Havana. I've told you the gist of what happened but not the details."

She nodded. "I remember. Boreau—he worked for that evil bastard Colonel Marrón, didn't he?"

Marrón had killed her son Francisco in early 1898. A month later I killed Marrón—long an enemy of mine.

"Yes, Boreau worked for Marrón, who ridiculed and embarrassed him when I was successful on some espionage operations. So Boreau and some of his men came to Florida and tried to kill me, Useppa, and Rork. I never told you because I didn't want to scare you unnecessarily. Besides, it was long ago and no longer a problem."

"This attack on your home, on American soil, it was authorized by Marrón?"

"No. I thought so at the time, but I later learned that Marrón wasn't involved. It was personal on Boreau's part, and he damn near succeeded before Rork and I killed his men and wounded him. I would have killed him, too, but Useppa begged me not to in the name of Christian mercy. I let Boreau live, but I made him promise never to come to the United States again. He slunk back to Cuba, and I hoped that was the end of it."

She nodded, understanding the connections now. "The Statue of Liberty incident you told me about. . . ."

I nodded. "Exactly. Six months later, at the dedication of the Statue of Liberty in New York in October 1886, I caught Boreau following me. I thought he was going to kill me, so I drowned in him the harbor. Made it look accidental."

She didn't flinch at that. Instead, she calmly asked, "And that saber incident at Havana two years later?"

"*Venganza.* Boreau's naval officer son was a fencing master, and he arranged a supposedly goodwill fencing match with me at the governor's palace in Havana. I didn't know who he was until after the match started. He tried to kill me—'accidentally,' of course—but I managed to defeat him without killing him. He retired in 1902. A year later I heard from a reliable source that he had died of consumption in Spain. At that point, I was sure the whole thing was over. Until now. This Boreau is about the right age to be that man's son—the grandson of the Boreau I killed in New York twenty years ago."

"And now this one is dead." María sighed. "But there are still important questions we need the answers to, aren't there?"

"Yes, two very important questions," I said. "How did he know I was on this ship? And did he act alone, or is someone else on the ship working with him?"

We heard the governor's aide calling everyone back inside with a pleasant announcement that the "little disturbance" had ended, and dinner was about to be served. Tired of dealing with it all, I started for the carriage, trying to conjure up an excuse for leaving.

María, however, started back toward the front door. "Come on, Peter. You know we have to go through with this. We are the guests of honor. But make no mistake," she added in a steely voice, "our dear Theodore will answer to me for this. No danger, he said."

We sat stoically through a long, dull dinner of heavy German food, swatting away insects in between bites. Our hosts tried to enliven the evening, but nobody seemed to be having a good time. The German officers kept eyeing me, the governor was morose, María was tense, the native servants were jumpy, and even the usually vivacious German ladies opened their mouths only to take in food.

I imagined the ghost of my friend Robert Louis Stevenson surveying the scene, cocking an eyebrow, and letting out a satisfied chuckle over the social disaster in Kaiser Willy's peaceful little colony of Samoa.

8

Connections

SS *Siberia*

Apia, Upolu Island, German Samoa

Thursday, 24 July 1908

The three of us met in Rork's cabin as soon as María and I got back on board. Boreau's belongings were laid out on the bed. Rork immediately launched into a description of each item.

"Talked with me pal the steward, an' he let me in Boreau's cabin on the sly for five minutes or so. Bastard didn't have much, especially for a man in a first-class cabin—number 120, to be precise. Four sets o' undershirts an' shorts, two trousers, an' four shirts. As for money, he had 142 Spanish pesetas and 200 in old Mexican silver dollars—all tucked up nice an' tidy in the safe. By the by, the ship really should get better safes. I opened that little tin box with a pair o' toothpicks in a wee minute."

Rork gestured at some papers lying next to the money. "In the desk was this torn piece o' notepaper with two names written on it—Eberhardt's and Newton's. An' also a bill for the Victoria Hotel in Honolulu for the three nights before he got on *Siberia* and we left Hawaii. That's the whole sum o' his possessions. But I've discovered a wee bit more about Mister Boreau."

"He wasn't traveling alone," I ventured.

"Aye, sir. Steward told me Boreau was the nervous sort an' always ate in his cabin. Never saw the bugger outside o' it. But he did see somebody else comin' out on that first evening we left Honolulu."

"Newton or Eberhardt?" asked María. "One of them must have set all this up. To judge by his belongings, Boreau didn't have the money to travel first class on an assassination mission. I can see the Germans' motive, but why the British or Australians? And the Russians warned us, so it wasn't them."

Rork shook his head. "Wrong on both counts, m'lady. 'Twas Tanaka. An' guess where Tanaka's cabin is?"

"Next door," I muttered.

"Right you are, sir. An' would ye also care to guess where Tanaka had been staying in Honolulu? 'Tis all in the record of his luggage transfer, arranged by the ship."

"The Hotel Victoria," said María. "Same as Boreau."

"Right again. Aye, 'tis not the Spaniardos, the Krauts, the Limeys, *or* the Aussies who put this together. 'Twas those Black Dragon buggers in the bloody Japanese intelligence service. Oh, an' guess who's runnin' the laundry on board this fine vessel?"

"Some Japanese fellows," I sighed. "So, were you able to get into Tanaka's cabin?"

"Nay, sir. Sorry. He's been in there all evenin', silent as a dead man."

"But how did the Japanese know about the Boreau feud in the first place?" wondered María.

Rork looked at me. "They must've been watching you since Singapore in '05, lookin' for a weak spot. Gotta admire the devils; 'twas a good false-flag operation right up 'til Boreau buggered it up by missin' his shots with grandpa's old pistol. An' the Krauts thought Solf was the target 'til they saw 'twas a Spaniardo. Now they'll figure it must o' been *you*."

I nodded my concurrence. "Eberhardt and Newton were convenient scape-goats. I heard the Germans released Newton once they were sure Boreau fired the shots. Did Newton get back to the ship?"

"Aye, he came back on board an hour ago, roarin' like a stiffed hooker. Went to the Gentlemen's Bar straight away. Been throwin' down shots ever since, rantin' on about squareheads an' Samoan kanaka boys."

That put an idea in my head. I turned to María. "I think I could use a drink, my dear. I'll see you at our cabin in a little bit."

Her reaction was predictable. "Don't do anything *I'll* regret, Peter."

Rork's was also predictable. He raised a worried eyebrow. "Want me to go too, sir? A touch o' rum would go down nicely right about now."

"No, I'll be all right, Rork. This is just a *conversation*, and best done discreetly."

9

The War Will Come

SS *Siberia*
Apia, Upolu Island, German Samoa

Thursday, 24 July 1908

The Gentlemen's Bar, a bastion of upper-class male sophistication with its dark oak paneling and red leather chairs and banquettes, was almost empty. Except for the corner of the bar itself, where Parker Newton was boring the barman with his opinion about something. I intentionally walked close by, knowing what would happen.

A big paw reached out for me. "Wake, old chap! Come and have a drink with an accused felon! Gotta love the Krauts. They don't waste time on evidence and such. Just throw a bloke in the dungeon for attempted *murder*—of the *governor*, no less—and figure it out later. Hell'uva thing. Bastards." Newton had clearly been drinking heavily since he returned to the ship. His eyes didn't quite focus, and his thick lips were slack.

Obviously relieved to see me sit down next to Mr. Obnoxious, the barman fled to serve a table of three conversing in the back of the room. Newton had apparently been roughed up by the guards who seized him at the governor's house. His lower lip was puffy and oozing blood. He regarded me humorously. "You're a strange Yank, Wake."

34

"Am I, Mr. Newton?" I replied calmly. "How's that?"

He passed an unsteady hand across his mouth. "You're not one bit like other Yanks I've known. Too bloody damned quiet."

I hid my smile at the irony and assessed the man next to me. It was time to get candid, I decided. Very candid.

"I get more done that way, Newton. So, tell me, did you find what you were looking for in the governor's office? My friend Rork saw you searching—for his daybook, perhaps? Or was it the latest cables from Berlin? And the item in your right jacket pocket? Was that merely an innocent consolation souvenir or something more incriminating if you'd been caught with it? By the way, nice job of ditching it as they seized you, Parker. If that's your name, which I very much doubt."

His loose, vacant smile vanished, and the slurred and heavy Australian accent was replaced by a more refined British English. Kent, perhaps.

"Of course it's one of my names, Wake. A rather nice one, too. I think I'll use it awhile longer."

"On your assessment report to Osmond Brock?" I inquired, watching his reaction closely.

I must admit "Parker Newton" was quite a cool fellow. He barely showed his recognition of the name of the head of the war plans division of the Royal Navy's Intelligence Department. I could almost see the wheels turning in his mind as he decided how to answer.

It took only seconds. "No. Dear old Ossie knows me by a different name altogether. All the better to foil the evil foe, as you well know. And yes, it was only a consolation prize—a fancy letter opener. No time to grab anything of real value because Eberhardt walked by and saw me. The Germans were a bit slow, however, and didn't find it on me." He paused for a moment, a sneer edging across his face. "So now you know my little secret, Wake. I've heard that you have a great many secrets, too, including some from right here. I've met one of them. She's never forgotten *you*, old boy. And a number of aliases, if it comes to that. So, I believe we understand each other now, don't we?"

He was lying about what he took, but I didn't press it. And he had done some background on me—not many knew of the lady ruined by her connection with me in Samoa decades earlier. I wanted to know about other things, though. "Yes, completely. And since we're in the same line of work and have the same foes, why not cooperate? You can start by telling me what you know about Tanaka."

He canted his head in mock surprise, a delaying tactic while he considered how much to reveal. Finally, he said, "Fake name, of course, but you know that. Black Dragon muckity-muck and Nip intelligence colonel; but you know that, too."

I said, "Yes, of course. Tanaka's one of your *officially* esteemed Japanese allies, but you Brits already regret that decision, don't you? Much has changed in the last six years. The Japanese learned well from your example—too well. Now they act just like Europeans, probing for weaknesses, looking for territory to add to their empire. But some of those weak spots speak English, and that's a bit worrying, especially since you've diminished your fleet out here to counter Kaiser Willy's warships back home. What's Tanaka's current mission on this ship?"

His look of surprise this time appeared genuine. "You really don't know, do you? He's here to kill *you*, Wake. His bosses in Tokyo have deemed you a problem—for figuring out their plans and turning their long-admiring friend Roosevelt against them. They consider you pro-Russian and anti-Japanese because you were with the Russian fleet at Tsushima and got that Russian medal. They think *you* are behind this whole American Great White Fleet effort to steam around the Pacific and humiliate their country."

I played it nonchalant. "Really? Well, I never knew I had *that* much influence. How long have you known about Tanaka's intentions?"

"Got a cable in Honolulu. It was just a rumor, and I didn't take it seriously until the drama tonight at the governor's house. I give Tanaka full marks for audacity on that one! But then his Spanish boy botched the job and got himself bludgeoned to hell. The devil's always in the details, isn't it? Rusty old Spanish pistol failed him. I'm surprised Tanaka overlooked that possibility. He'll be in trouble when his bosses back home find out. I think he'll try again—try to redeem himself. I expect it'll be more difficult on the ship, though."

"Yes," I agreed. "Well, they *are* known for being persistent." I could see that Newton, or whoever he was, was enjoying this. Tired of talking about Tanaka, I switched to the German. "And Eberhardt?"

"Ah, the suave Commander Manfred Schiefer of German intelligence. Normally stationed up at their colony at Tsingtao to keep an eye on us at Shanghai and Weihaiwei but sent down here to keep watch over the Kaiser's empire in the South Seas. Seems Willy's getting nervous about the Nips and you Yanks."

I recalled Eberhardt muscling Newton away from Solf. "And you, too, it seems."

"Yes, he's seen through me, so that part of my game is over. Time for me to head back to Singapore. Far more civilized there, anyway. No decent gin out here. And now that I've bared my soul, or at least part of my brain, you get to fulfill your end of our quid pro quo, my new friend. What do *you* know about Japan's and Germany's plans in this part of the world?"

I had no intention of telling him everything. Just enough to satisfy him. "Nothing you don't know already, really. The Japanese fleet will equal ours soon, then they'll hit us. The first strike will be at Guam and the Philippines. This fleet cruise is meant to deter them until the Panama Canal opens in four years and cuts our response time to the western Pacific in half."

He nodded his understanding, and I continued. "I suppose you know the Germans are building a wireless network out here to assist their raiding squadron in a war with Britain. It'll be ready by 1912. They're already inside the empire's Pacific cable and wireless network. Their ocean raiders from Tsingtao and East Africa will interdict food, supplies, and manpower reinforcements from your Pacific colonies."

He made a wry face. "Yes, we know that much already, but it's good to hear your information coincides with ours. All eyes in Britain are on Germany and the North Sea right now, but a prolonged war would spread worldwide. Fighting in the Pacific, Africa, Middle East, maybe even India. The Japanese will be our allies—valuable allies—against the Germans in the Pacific *if* we stay their friends. Unless, of course, we can count on you Yanks."

I shook my head. "I doubt that. There's no political or cultural will in America for that sort of messiness. I hear that Jacky says your war will happen in 1914. Gives you enough time to thwart it." Admiral Jacky Fisher, First Sea Lord and head of the Royal Navy, was an old acquaintance of mine.

"Well, your old friend Jacky—yes, I know you two correspond—may be correct on the timing. But things are already reaching the point of no return.

The Kaiser is surrounded by sycophants and is completely unmanageable. It's about his ego now. The war will come. The only question is when."

And on that depressing point we parted. Having established a modus vivendi with the British spy, I looked forward to mining his knowledge of the countries on the U.S. fleet's confidential projected itinerary around the world. But we were both tired and a little drunk, it was past midnight, and I assumed such valuable cooperation could wait until the morning.

Seven hours later I realized my mistake.

10
Death for Breakfast

SS *Siberia*
Apia, Upolu Island, German Samoa

Friday, 25 July 1908

I briefed Rork and María about Parker Newton and Tanaka the next morning before we went to breakfast. Rork took the new information in stride. He asked if he should "pre-empt the Nip fellow." I told him no, not yet. María wasn't scared as much as angry—at Theodore Roosevelt and at me.

"This has become a nightmare, Peter. Damn Theodore for lying about the danger, and damn you for believing him! Or knowing the truth and then going along with him."

"It was only a vague possibility at the time, my dear. The Germans, maybe. But nobody knew about Boreau's grandson. How could we? And Tanaka—I never dreamed the Japanese would come after me."

Breakfast was rather a subdued affair as each of us contemplated the present situation. Then it dawned on me that we weren't moving. *Siberia* was scheduled to get under way for Auckland at dawn, yet the sun was well up and we were still at anchor. I mentioned it to Rork, who went out onto the promenade deck and soon returned with a report.

"Lads're ready on the foredeck an' capstan, sir, but there's a police launch comin' alongside. An' the ship's officers're lookin' serious." He scratched his nose. "Somethin's amiss."

Before Rork could say more, the waiter delivered a note to him. His brow furrowed as he read it. "'Tis from me steward pal. Parker Newton's body washed up at the Mulinu'u seawall this morning. No sign o' wounds. Captain thinks he fell overboard an' the flood tide took his body there. The ship's doctor'll do a postmortem."

"Drunk?" said María.

I thought about that, then shook my head. "I don't think so. He'd been drinking, but most of the drunk bit was an act. He dropped that completely once we came to terms. Of course, he might have had more whiskey later. But still, for a man his size to go over the rail. . . ."

Rork growled his opinion. "Unless there was something else in his drink. He could'a been drugged and then dumped o'er the rail. Not to bring up an ugly memory, but we all remember what happened at the Maryinsky . . ."

The attempt to kill me by poison at the Maryinsky Theater in St. Petersburg (while I was just down the hallway from my host, the Tsar of Russia) four years ago was still a very raw memory—for María, especially.

María let that pass and agreed with Rork. "Poison or some drug in his drink does seem the most likely way to incapacitate him. The barman, do you think?"

"The bar was shutting down, and Newman told me he was heading for his cabin. I saw him walk out right after I did, so it didn't happen there in the bar. He was fine when I last saw him."

"Depends on the poison," declared Rork. "He's a big man, so it might take awhile, even if the barman had slipped it in his drink much earlier."

"No," I countered. "If it was enough to kill him, he'd have started showing *some* signs. I don't think it happened at the bar."

"That means poison put in his nightcap in his cabin," María postulated. "The perpetrator must have known Newton was heading to his cabin and put it in his scotch bottle."

I stood. "That means evidence of it will still be in the bottle. We'd better get to that cabin before the police do. Maybe we can find Parker's intelligence information there as well. Let's go."

Cabin 112 was locked, but Rork, of course, had a steward's passkey. The neat and orderly room was not at all in keeping with Newton's loud and sloppy public demeanor. The bed was made up, and no depression or wrinkles disturbed its smooth surface. On the bedside table was a bottle of scotch, nothing fancy or expensive. The cork was off, the level was down a bit, and the color appeared normal. A glass containing whiskey residue was beside it. I sniffed both glass and bottle and detected no unusual odor.

In the center of the bed was a stack of cleaned and pressed underwear, neatly folded, each piece separated from its neighbor by a sheet of tissue. That raised a question in my mind. *Was the laundry delivered before or after Newton left his cabin the final time? If before, why didn't he put it away?* The tissue sheet on top of the stack was artistically folded to resemble an angry lion with a long, thick tail. The stewards enjoyed doing that sort of artistic thing—and, of course, it enhanced their tips at the end of the voyage. But something about the figure struck a chord. I took a closer look and realized it wasn't a lion at all.

It was a dragon.

Rork, who had been in Singapore with me three years earlier, recognized it at the same time. He offered an additional insight. "Remember, the laundry lads're Japanese, sir. An' they mainly work at night."

"The Black Dragon Society," observed María. "But why would they leave such an obvious clue?"

"It was meant for us," I said. "Who else? Most Americans, probably even most merchant ships' officers in the Pacific, have never heard about the Black Dragons. In their arrogance, white passengers look at a Japanese laundryman and see a dimwitted Oriental doing a menial job. It's a perfect cover for an intelligence-gathering network."

I looked at Rork. "Can you find out which laundryman delivered this last night?"

"Aye, sir, me informant'll know. But what was the poison, d'ye think? Must've been some powerful stuff. An' did Tanaka give it to the laundryman?"

Men's voices sounded in the passageway, getting louder. One of them I recognized as the doctor. I made for the door with María and Rork close astern. We dashed down the passageway in the opposite direction and took the first exit to the weather deck just as the doctor and another officer entered Newton's cabin.

An hour later the three of us met again. María had spent the time hobnobbing with the society matrons in the Ladies' Parlor, but none of them knew anything. I went to the Gentlemen's Bar and circuitously asked the barman what he knew of the situation—which was nothing except that Newton had no more drinks in the bar after we left.

It was Rork who came up with an intriguing, and terrifying, bit of news.

11

The Least around Us

SS *Siberia*
Apia, Upolu Island, German Samoa

Friday, 25 July 1908

Rork reported what he'd learned in a rapid-fire staccato. "Me informant heard somethin' a bit odd down in the stewards' mess last evening. The Nip laundry lads got liberty in Apia. Most went to a seamen's grog shop on the east side o' town. But two went fishin' on the reef just offshore. Came back to the liberty boat later with nary a single fish, but they did have a jar o' sea water with a strange-lookin' slimy creature in it with bright blue circles on its skin. Wouldn't let the other lads have a close look."

He took a breath and slowed down. "Once on board, they disappeared with the damned thing. An' one o' the two lads, goes by the name 'uv Akito, was the one who delivered the underwear to Newton's cabin near about midnight. 'Tain't usual to deliver that late, an' the night steward wasn't gonna let him in. Akito said that Newton had insisted on havin' his clean drawers delivered that night, an' he was in the bar drinkin', so he wouldn't disturb him. An' so the steward let 'im in the cabin. That's all me information, sir."

Rork looked at me expectantly. He'd done his part, and now I had to do mine. María made a noncommittal *humpf*. I concentrated on the description

43

of the creature and where they'd found it. Slimy, with bright blue circles on the skin, from the reef, fit in a small jar. No fish, just that creature brought back on board, then hidden. Thus, it was valuable, not as a curiosity to show off but for something else. I could think of only one explanation. An ugly one.

I shuddered. "Damn, it's brilliant, but truly evil. The blue-ringed octopus is one of the most venomous creatures in the world. When I was here in '89—before you arrived, Rork—I was living down on the south shore. I went spearfishing with some Samoans one day, and they showed me a blue-ringed octopus on the reef. Motioned me not to touch it. Back on the surface they warned me not even to get near one. If that vicious little animal bit you, they said, you'd be paralyzed in minutes and then start to suffocate as your diaphragm and lungs failed, and finally die of heart failure. Newton had a cut on his lip. All the laundryman had to do to poison him was coat the rim of the glass with the venom."

"Oh Lord," murmured María. "Then Mr. Newton might have been alive but paralyzed when he was carried out on deck and dumped in the water. . . ."

Rork thought through the scenario aloud. "It would've taken two o' them to carry that big bastard out on deck after he drank the scotch. They must've used a ruse to distract the night steward so they could get him out." He gave me a stern look. "An' they've probably got more of the stuff. I'm thinkin' we're next. Tanaka has to go, sir."

María didn't like that idea. "Do we really need to start a war? There must be another way."

"They've already started it," Rork declared. "Tried to *kill* the admiral with that Boreau fool. Then killed Parker Newton. We need to end this. Now."

She didn't back down. "No, this is all conjecture, Sean. We have no proof about the cause of Newton's death. Tanaka needs to know that we know about Boreau and the octopus venom. That will deter him from doing anything else."

María was in a state of denial—something I'd never seen before—which showed me she was at the end of her rope. I knew I'd best tread lightly.

"Very well, everyone's had their say. María is right. There's no reason to start killing people *yet*."

When both acknowledged that point—Rork grudgingly—I continued. "So, here's what we *are* going to do. First, the doctor will find heart failure and water in the lungs, indicating that a drunken Newton had a heart attack, fell overboard, and drowned. We'll just let that be. I don't want any extra attention to his death that might reflect on us.

"Second, today at lunch I will make it clear to Tanaka that he, Akito, and the other laundryman will be killed if anything happens to any of us three, or if we even think something *might be about* to happen. And that our fleet better have a very peaceful voyage through the Pacific and visit to Japan—because now we have proof of Japanese intent. And that President Roosevelt will have knowledge of that proof."

Rork nodded curtly. María gave me the flicker of an approving smile.

I went on. "Third, after my conversation with Tanaka—hopefully I can gain some further information or insight from it—I will warn Snobov about him. The Russians and Japanese still hate each other, and Tanaka might try something against him. Telling Snobov won't cost us anything and might build some goodwill with Rachkovsky and the Okhrana back in St. Petersburg. You never know when that might be needed.

"Fourth, we watch everyone, and everything, very closely until we're off this damned ship in Melbourne. The very *least* around us just may be the most dangerous to us. Understood?"

As they duly acknowledged my orders, the ship's engines rumbled to life. Seconds later the capstan clanked into action as it hauled in the anchor cable.

I wrote a brief note to Tanaka inviting him to lunch in the main dining room and indicating that I had important information for him. Rork delivered it to Tanaka's cabin, playing the role of dull-witted minion.

On my way to lunch, a very concerned looking Rork intercepted me in the main lobby. "Don't have to warn Snobov, sir. Steward found that arrogant Rooskie bugger dead on his bed half an hour ago. Bottle an' glass o' vodka on the table next to him. Doctor said it looked like a heart attack caused by alcohol, then joked there's been far too much drinkin' on the ship."

"I don't suppose any laundry was recently delivered to Snobov's quarters?"

"Don't rightly know, sir. An' me informant's gettin' a wee bit queasy about tellin' me stuff. So, are ye still thinkin' o' havin' your luncheon with Tanaka?"

"Definitely, Rork, especially now. But I think Tanaka won't be very hungry."

12

The Dragon, the Zealot, and the Marmalade

SS *Siberia*
Southbound from German Samoa to Auckland, New Zealand

Friday, 25 July 1908

Tanaka was waiting for me in front of the maître d's desk, which was vacant at the moment. In his plain attire and subdued manner the Japanese agent was once again the shy, humble merchant, seemingly unaware of the reason for my invitation.

He bowed. "This is indeed an honor, Admiral Wake. I thank you for your kind invitation."

"A pleasure for me, Mr. Tanaka. I'm simply reciprocating the wonderful luncheon you hosted for me earlier." Then I added anxiously, "But first, I've urgent information to give you—"

I stopped abruptly as the head waiter arrived, then shifted into a whisper. "I've heard that someone on board wants to hurt you. Let's go somewhere we can talk in private."

To the head waiter I said, "We'll be back in a moment for a table." Then I headed out the double doors onto the promenade deck, gesturing Tanaka to follow. I heard his steps behind me, trying to catch up as I ascended a ladderway to the boat deck and made my way forward among the davits and exhausts and shrouded funnels. As I expected, the boat deck was broiling hot in the tropical noon sun, and empty of crewmen or passengers.

I beckoned Tanaka into the shade of a funnel. The roar of an exhaust blower ventilating the engine room five decks below precluded anyone hearing our words. The grating covering the exhaust vent, normally latched shut, was slightly ajar, but Tanaka didn't seem to notice.

I leaned toward Tanaka with an expression of concern and spoke loudly into his ear. "We can speak confidentially here, my friend."

He regarded me intently. "Yes, Admiral. Please do."

"I am very *worried* about your safety, Mr. Tanaka."

He showed surprise, or was it wariness? "Why is that, sir?"

I glanced furtively around as if looking for eavesdroppers. "Please don't tell anyone you heard this from me, but that Russian man Smirnikoff was drunk two nights ago in the bar, and I heard him talking about killing you. He said. . . ." I stepped back and turned my gaze forward along the deck as if looking for eavesdroppers. Tanaka moved closer to me and turned his head to follow my gaze. That was a fatal mistake. He didn't see my left hand opening the grating cover—or my right hand holding my revolver with the skull-crusher frame.

Ten crowded seconds later I walked away from the funnel and back down to the promenade deck. When I strolled into the dining room, the head waiter smiled. "Table for two now, Admiral?"

"No, just one. Poor Mr. Tanaka has a headache. Seems he had a bit to drink last night. Evidently, he's not used to our strong spirits. Anyway, he decided against having lunch. Wanted to take a turn around the deck and get some fresh air and sunshine before taking a nap to sleep it off. Truly fascinating little fellow; so glad to have him as a new friend. So, it seems I will be lunching alone," I said regretfully. "Oh, but look," I motioned toward a window table. "There's Mr. Singletary, all alone. Would you be so kind as to ask if he'd like a fellow American for company?"

Singletary, a taciturn widower from Honolulu who had previously bored me with his fundamentalist religious zeal, would be a miserable meal companion but an ironclad alibi. He nodded reluctantly and allowed me to join him. He was silent until I mentioned Mr. Tanaka and praised Japanese culture.

That was too much for Singletary. He launched into a tirade on the inferiority of the darker races, quoting verses from the Bible about the curse of Ham. I did my best to appear impressed by his pontifications, which had the effect of prolonging them. I felt not an iota of shame over his unspoken but obvious disapproval of the double bourbon I had with lunch (after all, I *am* a sailor). I just smiled at his sour face, for at that moment this sailor needed the bourbon far more than that fool's racist sermon.

As I was taking the last sip from my glass, the doctor and captain, looking very earnest, strode past our window accompanied by a squad of sailors carrying a folded stretcher. Singletary disgustedly declared that some fool was probably drunk—looking meaningfully at my glass—and began a new sermon on the evils of the Devil's tool—alcohol. I raised my glass in agreement.

A few hours later, María and Rork joined me for afternoon tea in the lounge, impatient for news of my lunch encounter with Tanaka. Since there were other passengers around us, I sanitized my report.

"Turns out that Mr. Tanaka and I never had lunch," I told my companions. "He wasn't feeling well—said something about drinking too much last night—so he took a stroll up on the boat deck while I had lunch with Mr. Singletary. Remember him, my dear? That staunch defender of Christian purity we dined with several days ago?"

María rolled her eyes, and Rork snorted with amusement. I continued, "But I fear that's not the important news. I was speaking with the captain on the bridge a short while ago, and he told me that Mr. Tanaka fell down a ventilator shaft into the engine room exhaust fans while he was on the boat deck! The captain said the poor man must have opened the cover grate to peer inside, and fell in and was chopped to pieces. Shocking, isn't it?" With raised eyebrow I added, "Obviously, Mr. Tanaka was still a bit tipsy."

I paused a suitable moment, then added sadly, "What a terrible end for such a nice little man. We shall have to pray for his family. I'm certain Mr. Singletary will do likewise."

Rork and María sat there poker-faced. After several seconds, Rork wagged his head and murmured dolefully, "Aye on that, sir. A terrible thing. Seems curiosity killed the dragon, don't it?" Then he brightened. "Say, I'll have some of that orange marmalade on these delightful lookin' scones. Nothin' like afternoon tea to tide a man over till dinner, is there."

María reached out for my hand and squeezed it, her eyes never leaving mine. "It's over, then? I won't ask how. Just tell me we will be able to reach Melbourne with no more trouble."

I returned her gaze steadily. "Yes, the trouble is over, María. And we're going home early. We'll leave from Auckland instead of Melbourne. We all did as we were asked, and we're tired and need to go home. I'll cable Theodore from New Zealand. He needs to know as soon as possible about what we've learned."

María's face softened into a gentle smile, the first I'd seen from her for some time. "Thank you, Peter. I have been so longing for home."

13

You Have Done the Trick!

USS *Connecticut* (BB 18),
Hampton Roads, Virginia

Seven months later—Monday, 22 February 1909

I n spite of the cold rain and wind Theodore was exuberant. The fleet's
magnificent homecoming was the culmination of years of foreign policy.
The world—enemies and friends alike—had seen and been impressed by
America's "big stick": the U.S. Navy's battleships. All twenty of them were
home now, stretched out in two long lines under the gray winter sky, a bit the
worse for wear, their decks crowded with happy bluejackets.

The president was late arriving at the Old Point Comfort pier. The presidential yacht *Mayflower* obediently waited for her master to board, then charged
at full speed out into the chilly mist to the fleet's flagship, *Connecticut*, where
Rear Adm. Charles Sperry awaited the president and his entourage. That
assembly of self-important personages included Senator Lodge and other
congressional swells; a rather confused-looking President-elect Taft (only a
week away from assuming presidential office); Navy Secretary Newberry in
his glory, bustling about and barking orders; the presidential military staff
aide, Captain Butt; the naval aide, Commander Sims; various functionaries,
admirals, and staff officers—and in the midst of them all, me and Sean Rork.

I was in full dress blues complete with giant epaulets, all my brass and gold trim, bangles and baubles hanging from my chest, wearing the ridiculous-looking Napoleonic-era fore-and-aft cocked hat and useless sword that regulations mandated. Rork was in his best rig also, gold chevrons and hashmarks gleaming, medal-bedecked, and looking quite the most sober and dignified I'd ever seen him. *Ever the senior petty officer,* I said to myself as I watched him mentally counting the twenty-one precise intervals of the saluting cannon; surveying the smartness of the side-boys, Marines, petty officers, and officers of the quarterdeck honor guard; and listening intently as the boatswain's pipes trilled the president's arrival up to the main deck.

Rork, sitting forward in *Mayflower*'s launch, exchanged a knowing smile with me in the stern sheets. It was a bittersweet moment for the two of us. After my forty-six years in the Navy (forty-eight for him), we both knew this was the last time we would wear the uniform of our country, tread the deck of an American warship, or be in close proximity to a commander-in-chief in a naval ceremony. We'd known many other presidents over the years—Hayes, Garfield, Arthur, Cleveland, Harrison, and McKinley—and all were gone now. Roosevelt was young and strong enough to last for decades more in his post-presidency as a respected "elder" statesman. But I knew Theodore had other plans, and they didn't include a sedentary life.

Once the president acknowledged the age-old arrival ceremony, he headed straight for the foredeck where hundreds of sailors stood. His entourage scrambled to follow. Climbing up on the forward main gun turret, evoking a gasp from the spectators when he momentarily slipped, Roosevelt told everyone to gather around closer. Bluejackets beamed as they gazed up at their commander-in-chief from the main deck or down at him from the upper decks and even the rigging. Enlisted and senior officers packed in shoulder to shoulder, normally an unheard-of breech of naval etiquette. Rork stood next to me as even more sailors jammed in. The president waited, waving to the men around him, the other warships, and the hundreds of spectator vessels.

When at last he began, my young friend Theodore was at his very best. "Not until some American fleet returns victorious from a great sea battle will there be another such homecoming!" he shouted. "Do you remember those prophecies of disaster?"

With a sweeping gesture that encompassed the two lines of battleships, he declared, "Well, here they all are, returning after fourteen months—without a *scratch*!—the first battle fleet ever to *circumnavigate the globe*." The president looked around at his beloved sailors. "*You have done the trick! Other nations may follow, but they will follow behind you!*"

As he knew it would, that raised a cheer among the sailors that grew louder as it spread across *Connecticut*. Officers, politicians, and the spectators on civilian boats joined in. Rork and I were yelling like the rest. Theodore spotted Rork and me in the throng below him and nodded ever so slightly in a signal of thanks for all that we, and María, had done. He knew all of it.

I thought back to the verbal report I delivered to him at the White House the second week of September. His eyes had flared as I described in candid detail all that happened. When I finished, he was pensive, and I could tell he was assessing the consequences of my decisions.

In the end, the "incidents" in Samoa and on *Siberia* were not shared with the press and the public. The Germans didn't want the embarrassment of an assassination attempt at the governor's house. The ship's captain and doctor followed my counsel not to speculate or make a fuss, and thus harm future commerce for the shipping company. The Japanese laundrymen were dismissed at Auckland and left without protest. There were no repercussions from the Germans, Russians, British, or Japanese. None admitted anything, of course, but every one of them got the message not to cross us, overtly or covertly.

The Germans grew quieter in the Pacific. The British actually warmed up to the circumnavigation cruise and opened their ports in India and Egypt to the fleet. Though the fleet was ready for combat as it entered Tokyo Bay, the Japanese were the very epitome of hospitality. Roosevelt and I were both relieved. It could have gone very differently.

My attention was jerked back to the present as a gun on another battleship boomed its salute, followed by a thunderous roar as every ship in the fleet joined in a two-thousand-gun presidential salute—something Rork and I had never seen before and will never see again. It went on and on, a cacophony of explosions echoing in the foggy haze, ironically reminding us of the din we'd endured at the naval battle at Santiago de Cuba ten years earlier.

The president got down off the turret and headed for the quarterdeck to leave the ship, for he was going to give a speech on board each of the four division flagships within the fleet. Rork and I went ashore to the Hotel Chamberlin at Old Point Comfort. The next morning, we would take the train to Washington, but that evening at sunset we had a quiet dinner and drinks on the verandah. The vast Chesapeake Bay spread out below us, dotted with the fleet that was America's pride.

I raised my glass toward my friend. "A hell'uva last hurrah, eh, Sean?"

"Aye, that it was, sir. An' done in fine naval fashion," he said proudly, his eyes looking lovingly at the fleet.

After returning to Washington the next day, 23 February 1909, we said our goodbyes to the White House staff, walked over to the Navy Department next door, and officially retired from the United States Navy.

It felt like a funeral.

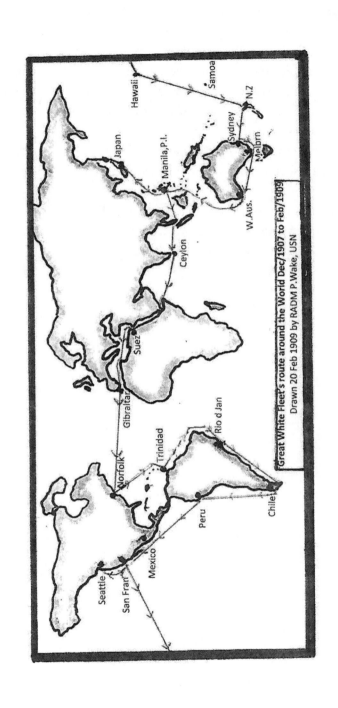

Great White Fleet's route around the World Dec/1907 to Feb/1909
Drawn 20 Feb 1909 by RADM P.Wake, USN

14

Simple, Gentle, and Predictable

Alexandria, Virginia

1909–1914

Rork moved his gear (including a panoply of trinkets gathered all over the world) into a comfortable apartment, complete with indoor plumbing, only a block away from his beloved old naval quarters in the attic of the Latrobe Gate at the Washington Navy Yard. His favorite pub, the Goat Locker, the haunt of fellow old salts, was just down the street, and his most recent amour, a lovely Irish American lady named Clotilda O'Conner, lived conveniently close by. María and I thought the two of them made a good couple. Rork even spoke of marriage.

I went home to my María at our cottage in Alexandria, but only briefly. My old bones couldn't tolerate the damp cold as well as they once had, so we left the next day for the warmth of southern Florida. That proved to be a good decision. A horrific blizzard hit Washington several days later on Inauguration Day, 4 March. Theodore later told me that Taft—who really wanted to be a Supreme Court justice, not president—had quipped at the ceremony, "I told you it would be a cold day in hell when I became president."

My nineteen-year-old daughter Patricia stayed in Virginia, engrossed in her studies at the new Fredericksburg Teachers College and planning to pursue a career in teaching. Patricia was grown up and living her own life, and we were very proud of her.

And so, for the first time since we were married in 1893, María and I were deliciously on our own, our itinerary strangely free. On the way south we visited friends in St. Augustine, Tampa, Punta Gorda, and Fort Myers.

Having sold Patricio Island to land developers, we bought a fifty-foot-long houseboat, named her *Libertad*, and lived on her. *Libertad*'s full-time caretaker was a bright twenty-year-old named Conner Gerard, nephew of my number two on the cruiser *Dixon* in '98. Conner kept the vessel and her steam engine in shipshape condition and served as crew when we were on board.

This became our routine for the next five years—Florida winters on *Libertad*, springs and autumns in Virginia, and summers in coastal Maine. It was a simple, gentle, predictable life, and the difference it made in María was profound. She looked healthier and happier than I'd ever seen her. Her greatest joy was the family. My greatest joy was watching her smile and laugh. The fear and grief and anger were gone now. Her dreams had come true.

Our grown children and growing grandchildren provided us with endless amusement and satisfaction, and some worry as well, of course. Sean Peter rose steadily through the ranks and ship commands and in early 1914 was assigned as gunnery officer on the staff of the Asiatic Fleet. His wife, Filipa, and their sons, Robert and Ted, lived in Manila. Useppa and Mario still lived in Tampa with their children, Peter and Linda.

As everyone expected, my friend Theodore continued steaming through life at full speed. No longer called Mr. President, by custom he chose a new moniker: Colonel Roosevelt, in honor of his beloved Rough Riders. The Colonel headed off to Africa to lead an expedition of fellow naturalists for the Smithsonian Institution. He trekked through east and central Africa in 1909, then continued his travels with a triumphant grand tour of Europe in 1910. A summons to return to public office and the subsequent presidential campaign followed in 1912, during which he managed to get shot in the chest *and* lose the election. In 1913 he led an expedition through the jungle rivers of Brazil. I was invited to go along on all of these endeavors, and I must admit

I was tempted, but I declined and stayed home with María—with absolutely no regrets.

Gradually I got used to the leisurely life, my monthly dinner with Rork being the only link with my naval past. We swapped sea and spy stories enlivened by considerable hyperbole and a not inconsiderable amount of Matusalem rum. Fortunately, María understood, leaving us seamen to our memories while she read quietly in our bedroom.

Rork's arthritis grew worse over the years, but the old rogue was still energetic and strong. As I did, he remained *au courant* with national and international affairs. Our concerns increased over the mounting war tension in Europe. Neither of us had any doubt it would become a worldwide war like the Napoleonic Wars a century earlier, which lasted more than twenty years and ultimately dragged in the United States. American entanglement in the upcoming one was a certainty, for the Germans were all over the Caribbean and Latin America, and Kaiser Willy had long lusted for land in our American hemisphere. Rork and I carefully kept our worries from María, though. She'd had more than enough of war and was adamantly pacifist and isolationist on that subject.

Then in mid-May 1914, two months before my seventy-fifth birthday, the telephone in the parlor of our Alexandria cottage rang. It was a warm spring afternoon, and I was on the back porch relaxing over iced tea and Theodore Roosevelt's recently published *Autobiography*. I vaguely heard María answer the telephone, speak for a moment, then stomp out to the porch. That alone told me something was wrong. One of the children? Grandchildren?

She stopped in front of my rocker, glowered down at me, and pointed to the parlor.

"Assistant Navy Secretary *Roosevelt*—the newest one—wishes to speak to you."

15

Kaiser Willy's Dream

State, War, and Navy Building
Washington, D.C.

Saturday, 16 May 1914

The Navy Department was bustling with activity. Self-important staff officers and petty officers with pensive faces and arms full of files dashed through the passageways. This was unusual for a Saturday morning, but it was completely understandable given the current situation.

The U.S. Navy was facing a difficult set of tasks as a result of President Wilson's decision to get involved in Mexico's bloody civil war, using a minor hubbub in Veracruz and Tampico as an excuse. An entire squadron was cruising the Gulf coast off Mexico, and for the last month 2,300 American sailors and Marines had been trying to occupy Veracruz. Our presence had proved somewhat stabilizing at first, but there were ominous signs that worse was to come. Hence the telephone call that had interrupted my reading the day before. The number-two civilian leader of the Navy, Franklin Roosevelt, had amiably but ambiguously requested that I "please stop by" his office the next day "for a little talk." I understood his "request" to be a command.

María was not amused by my explanation that duty—and some curiosity—compelled me to go and hear what the young man had to say. I told her I planned to take Rork along and suggested Mr. Roosevelt probably just wanted my advice about naval operations in Mexico. She uttered a very negative comment in Spanish.

It was not by coincidence that Franklin had followed in the footsteps of his larger-than-life cousin. Former New York state legislator, now assistant secretary of the Navy, and no doubt someday governor of New York, the handsome thirty-two-year-old Democrat was bright and charming. I knew the man and liked him; Rork, on the other hand, thought him openly opportunistic.

Theodore Roosevelt, who was more of an adored uncle to Franklin than a distant fifth cousin, delighted in the young man's accomplishments and frequently gave him guidance, even though they were in opposing political parties. When Franklin married Theodore's niece Eleanor, Theodore stood in for her father, his deceased brother Elliott, and had the honor of presenting the bride to the groom. I was mired in the Russo-Japanese War at the time, but María attended the wedding. She later described to me it as "quite formal, almost dutiful, without warmth." She added that the bond between the young couple seemed nothing like Theodore and Edith's openly affectionate marriage.

Now, however, Theodore was five thousand miles away in the Brazilian jungle and unable to give his cousin advice. *But why me?* I wondered. *Franklin has plenty of people working for him who could give wise counsel.*

Walking into that office felt eerily like walking into the past. Nothing had changed since Theodore, Rork, and I worked there back in '97 and early '98: the desk, the giant globe, the electric lamps, the fireplace, the government-gray wall color. I peeked in at my old adjoining office. It looked the same, too.

Franklin leaped up. "Admiral Wake! Chief Rork! Thank you so much for coming by."

After a brief exchange of pleasantries, I got to the point. "I presume this is about the Mexican problem, Franklin. Is there something I can do for you and the Navy?"

Roosevelt's face tightened. "No, it's not Mexico. The Mexican operations are going better now, Admiral, though there are still problems to overcome. No, I asked you here to talk about the war that is coming in Europe. European colonies around the world will be involved, including those in our hemisphere. As you well know, and have warned for years, the Germans have considerable influence in Latin America and are striving for more. They will use that against the British and French colonies—and us too, most likely."

I tried not to scowl when I thought back to those days. *Most of the leadership called me an alarmist when I brought up the Germans. So now they agree?*

Franklin continued. "That German influence now involves weaponry. Last month we seized a German Hamburg-America Line freighter, the *Ypiranga*, that was running guns into Mexico under an arrangement brokered by the Russian vice consul to Mexico, Leon Rasst; the Germans in Mexico; and a New Yorker named Ratner. Rasst, by the way, is an arms dealer on the side whom we suspect may have ties with your old friends the Okhrana. The ship was loaded to the gills with modern weaponry—thirty train car loads of it—mostly American made. To get around our arms embargo against shipping weapons directly into Mexico from the United States, the vessel was routed to Hamburg, then Odessa in Russia, then to Mexico."

"Unfortunately," he said, his anger clear, "legal constraints have forced us to release the ship and her cargo."

"Legal constraints and the possibility of war with Germany over the illegal capture of one of her merchant ships," I suggested sardonically. "Kaiser Willy would love to look like the stalwart supporter of liberty and free enterprise in Latin America protecting his friends against the evil and arrogant United States of *North* America."

Franklin sighed and said, "Well, yes, that too. And there is a time element. The canal across Panama is due to open this August. We think war will break out in Europe at about the same time, and our canal will be a crucial transportation link—or bottleneck. There are rumors that the Germans are sending more than farmers and shopkeepers to Central America."

I finished his line of thought. "And possibly setting up clandestine supply depots in remote areas for German raiders and for the new longer-range submarines. That way they could seize our new canal, rupture British and French colonial supply routes, and make the canal a German colony. The Colombians would welcome that. I can think of others who would as well."

"Exactly, Admiral. To that point, I've heard through friends at the United Fruit Company that some of the German lumber companies on rivers in

Nicaragua, Honduras, and Guatemala are also gathering supplies that would be useful in war. Some are loud supporters of the Kaiser."

I was beginning to feel uneasy. "Hmm, I see. So, you need what from me?"

"Nay, that would be *us*. . . ." interjected Rork with a reproving look at me. "You're too damned old to go galivantin' off on your own."

"That's ridiculous, Rork," I shot back. "You're older than I am."

With a straight face he countered, "Only chronologically, sir." Then, ignoring me, he turned his attention back to Roosevelt. "An' you were sayin,' sir?"

Franklin chuckled. "I'd like you *both* to help. The United Fruit Company charters a supply ship that services their farms on the Caribbean coast of Central America and also carries a few passengers. I want you to be passengers, just to observe and listen, for about three weeks along the coast, especially at a remote place called Wanks River at Cabo Gracias a Dios. Do you know that area?"

"Yes, I do," I said. "It's on the Mosquito Coast between Honduras and Nicaragua. Wanks River is the theoretical boundary. Some Germans and Brits live in the area."

"Precisely. Now, this is very informal. No one on the ship will know about your naval service or your mission from me. You will be United Fruit Company employees assessing the Wanks River area for a new banana plantation. When you return, I'd like a report with your observations and recommendations. That's it. This won't be fancy like your trip on the Great White Fleet cruise. This is a small steamer, and you're the only two passengers."

"Why us and not ONI?" I asked.

"Because nobody in ONI has your experience in the area, ability to see anomalies in apparently benign patterns, and understanding of the Germans' abilities. In short, I need your *brains*."

Roosevelt pulled a file from a desk drawer and handed it to me. It contained rail and ship tickets, hotel reservations, and travel expense vouchers—already prepared in our names. Roosevelt had been certain we'd accept. On June fifteenth we were to board a train for Port Tampa, where we would embark.

The plan *sounded* simple and doable. Go there, look around, come back. Rork was nodding and looking at me eagerly. *Well, it would be an interesting break from gardening and babysitting. And it's only three weeks.*

Even as I warmed to the idea, however, I knew the esteemed assistant secretary of the Navy had forgotten a critical factor. "I'll have to speak with María about this before I say yes."

"Oh, of course," he replied, a little too confidently. He knew María had insisted I retire in 1909—and stay retired—and yet he was smiling confidently.

That uneasy feeling returned.

16

Eleanor and María

Alexandria, Virginia

Saturday, 16 May 1914

I found out the reason for Franklin's confidence that afternoon when I returned home to find a pregnant Eleanor visiting María. I smiled to myself. Her uncle, President Theodore Roosevelt, had employed the same tactic several times with María: using *his* wife to influence *my* wife to say yes. It usually worked for Theodore, and it worked for Franklin too.

After Eleanor departed, and before I could even broach the subject, María said to me matter-of-factly, "Peter, you have been all I could wish for these last years, truly you have. But I know you miss the excitement of your old job. Eleanor told me about Franklin's offer, and I think this cruise with Sean on the coast of Central America will be good for you both. So I want you to know you have my full support. I love you."

Astonished but relieved, I embraced her. "Thank you, María. Really, it's only a simple voyage. Just to use my eyes and ears."

She held me tightly. "I hope so. I will not lecture you about your age, Peter. Or Sean's. Just be careful—very careful—and come home to me. I *need* you. . . ."

What exactly did Eleanor, a lady wise beyond her years, say to María to convince her to let me go? Though I've asked several times, María has never told me. It is a mystery to this day.

On the appointed day in June, Rork and I ascended the gangway to *Tocororo*, which had just finished loading 2,100 tons of supplies belowdecks and 530 tons in steam engines and generators on the main deck. The rusting relic was named after the beautiful national bird of Cuba, but one glance at her condition and her motley officers and crew precluded any further comparison.

An hour later, *Tocororo* took in her lines from the Mallory Line wharf in downtown Tampa, steamed down Seddon Channel to Tampa Bay, and headed out to the Gulf of Mexico. Rork and I stood on the main deck as the sun set ahead of us, forty years of memories of transiting that very bay, during peace and war, flooding our minds with images and emotions.

After surveying the filthy ship, an anathema to a naval seaman, Rork growled at the coppery sun, "Aye, I'm thinkin' this wee venture shan't be dull."

17

The Mosquito Coast

Off the mouth of the Wanks River
Cabo Gracias a Dios, in the disputed border region
of Honduras and Nicaragua

Monday, 22 June 1914

At dinner the night before the plodding *Tocororo* finally arrived at the Wanks River, Captain Theodosius Stadlin, a rheumy-eyed ancient as disheveled as his ship, finished his second glass of rum, slammed it on the table, and turned to me. Rubbing his stubbled face, he described Ilaya, six miles up the Wanks River on the Honduran side, where Rork and I would end our journey. He summed up the place and people with one word: *rubbish*. *That*, I thought but did not say, *is the pot calling the kettle black*.

Calling the place Honduran meant nothing, he grumbled, because political boundaries on the Moskito (the native spelling) Coast meant nothing. Both Nicaragua and Honduras claimed the area but seldom patrolled it. Neither country made any effort to provide basic services for the people there—or even bothered to fly a flag.

Ilaya was nothing more than a collection of badly thatched huts and a few shanties built from discarded cargo boxes. The sixty or so inhabitants were of every shade from sunburned white men (there were no white women) in dirty linen to mahogany Indians in loincloths, black Negroes in tattered rags, and olive-skinned mestizos in somewhat cleaner rags. Most were fishermen or loggers, plus a few farmers, and all were notorious for drunken Friday night brawls. The most substantial structures were a Protestant mission church ("Shack is more like it," he sneered) and a crude trading post. Eight or so whites—British, American, and German "renegades" who worked for the lumber companies—lived there permanently or occasionally. Many of them were fleeing the law in their native country, particularly the Americans.

His final warning of the evening (at the end of his fourth rum) was to trust no one anywhere on the Mosquito Coast: "Every damned one of the bastards, and their whorish native women too, is a stonehearted brigand who'll cut your throat for the shoe on your foot."

The next morning, the twenty-third of June, *Tocororo* threaded her way through the reefs off Cabo Gracias a Dios, slowly approached the mouth of the Wanks River, and stopped in eight fathoms. Rork was already stowing our gear in the ship's steam launch, hanging from davits on the main deck, that was to provide our transport.

I was on the bridge with the captain. Stadlin turned a worried face toward me. "You *sure* you don't want one of my men to go with you?"

"Thank you, but no, Captain. The company just wants Mr. Rork and me to determine whether the area has potential for large-scale banana cultivation. It's not a complicated task and won't take long at all. Three full days up and down the river. And then we'll see you again right here at noon on Friday."

He shook his head doubtfully. "Yeah, well, I don't want no trouble from the company if you two damned fools get yourselves killed."

"You won't get in trouble, Captain, and we won't get ourselves killed. We've done this kind of assessment all along the coast of Central America. Most places we don't recommend for commercial banana growing—but you never know until you have a look."

Heretofore on the voyage I had played the good-natured banana company functionary for Stadlin. Now my admiral's voice emerged. "Remember, Captain Stadlin, this coming Friday at noon—*do not* be late. Is that understood?"

He recoiled at my change in tone, and his own improved. "Yes, sir, Mr. Wake. Friday at noon we'll be right here."

Five minutes later, the steam launch was lowered into the muddy brown ebb tide water. The launch was relatively new and in good condition (Rork had inspected it carefully before we left Tampa), and we chugged along at four knots to the river mouth. The outflowing tidal and river currents met the usual incoming Caribbean easterly wind there, setting up a nasty chop. Every few minutes Rork would swing the lead line and call out the depth, and I would mentally record it to incorporate in a sketch chart later. The average depth at the mouth was a fathom, far too shallow for a German submarine to enter the river; they needed at least ten feet. Astern of us, *Tocororo* got under way on the 225-mile run south through the coastal reefs to the port of Bluefields, where she would offload her cargo and the machinery on her deck. And then, we hoped, return for us.

An hour later we took the first side creek to the right and followed it a quarter mile to the outskirts of a village situated on the eastern shore of a small lagoon. Locals in a dugout canoe stared at us. We were strangers, and that clearly wasn't good. None of the half-dozen men on the shore said a word as I steered the launch onto the muddy beach. I waved and called out to them, "I want to visit the pastor of the church." No response, just sullen looks. I said it in Spanish. Still no response.

Rork stayed in the launch, which was now turned bow outward for a quick escape, the boiler fully stoked, stack puffing away, and a shotgun ready but out of sight. I got out and walked toward the church. Captain Stadlin had been right. It was just another shack, distinguishable only by the whitewashed cross canting to starboard on the roof. With every step I noticed people watching me from the shadows. None smiled.

A white man in his forties, sunburned brownish red and attired in muddy dungarees, ragged red shirt with sleeves rolled up over his biceps, and a floppy panama hat, appeared from behind a shack. The anchor tattoo on his right forearm was barely discernible, but the holstered revolver on his right hip was quite obvious. He seemed like the sort used to ordering people around and made no pretense at politeness when he barked, "Why are you here?"

His question didn't bother me. His thick German accent did.

18

Brown Gold

Ilaya
Six miles up the Wanks River on the Honduras-Nicaragua border

---

Monday, 22 June 1914

I once again commenced my role as harmless fool. "Hello, sir," I said heartily. "I'm Peter Jakes from the United Fruit Company. This gentleman is Mr. Bork. We're here to see if this area's worth growing bananas commercially." I winked at him. "Might be good money in it for everybody here. We just want a little look-see at the soil, available supplies and transport, that sort of thing."

I waited for him to give his name and status, as common courtesy required. Instead, he snarled, "The answer is no. This place is no good for bananas."

Good—he's bought my ruse and dismissed me as no threat. I held my hands out wide to show I was harmless and ambled toward him, still grinning like a fool. "We won't get in anyone's way, sir. But since we're here I'd like to talk to the pastor and the shopkeeper. Get their thoughts on the subject of bananas. Are they around, Mister . . . ?"

Still no name. He only grunted, "Clarke is up the river in his boat. Belmont is with him."

I deduced Clarke was the pastor and Belmont the shopkeeper, but who in hell was this German? The people observing us from the shadows were looking at him warily. "Sorry, I didn't hear *your* name, sir."

Now that I was closer, I revised my opinion of him. He had a solid physique and moved with muscular confidence. His narrowed eyes were piercing, and he spoke American-style English, not the proper British English taught in German schools. And his skin wasn't sunburned, it was sun-leathered, and there was a long, badly stitched scar on his left hand. *This is a man who knows violence. He'll be a dangerous foe if it comes to a fight.*

His tone morphed from rude to menacing. "I did not give it. You look too old and too clean to be working for the banana company, and I have never seen you on this coast. There is nothing here for you. Go away, Peter Jakes. You will get sick or be hurt if you stay here."

Ignoring his thinly veiled threat, I continued approaching and asked amiably, "You in the mahogany trade? Tropical Lumber Company, right? Tropenholzfirma, out of Hamburg, I believe. So, how is business these days? Is 'brown gold' still valuable on the market? Say, maybe our companies could work together."

That got his attention. "How can *you* help Tropenholzfirma?"

I stopped seven feet from him and said, "Well, that should be obvious. Our boats bringing bananas downriver to freighters on the coast could also carry your logs. Our seagoing freighters could carry some of your logs too. We're not in competition against you. Everybody can win."

He seemed to be considering the possibilities when a sharp, high-pitched steam whistle on the river interrupted our conversation. One of the darker-skinned locals shouted in a Spanish-English-Miskito patois, "Bota *Deutschland* es here!"

The locals ran excitedly toward what I presumed was a German riverboat, apparently making an unexpected arrival. The whistle also had an immediate effect upon the big German, who marched off after the locals. As he passed close by me, he muttered, "We will talk later on this business."

I wandered after him. A furious exchange in guttural German ensued between my new acquaintance and a German on the boat. My German is rudimentary, and I caught only a little of what was being said, but it was enough to get the gist: "Ein problem mit den teilen für einen Körting-motor." A chill ran down my spine. The man on the boat was saying that there was a problem with the parts for a Körting motor—the same paraffin/kerosene-fueled engine used in the new German submarines.

The rumors were true.

19

The Miskito Zambo Wanki

Ilaya
Six miles up the Wanks River on the border of Honduras and Nicaragua

Monday, 22 June 1914

Deutschland was a wide-beamed riverboat, fifty or more feet long with a flush deck aft of her pilothouse that could hold tons of piled logs. I estimated her draft at no more than four or five feet, so she was capable of meeting a ship beyond the river's mouth. As she swung around to put her bow on the beach, I saw she had two engines and props. The crew seemed to be all native Indians and mestizos; only the captain was German.

The captain continued shouting until he saw Rork sitting in our launch and me standing on shore. Then he abruptly stopped. I waved a jolly hello to him, but he did not deign to reply. The big German at my side jerked his head at me and said to the captain, "Idiot der amerikanischen Bananenfirma." That got a laugh and dismissive gesture in reply.

I walked over to Rork, still seated on the thwart, right hand inside the seabag where his shotgun lay ready for use. "Pleasant jaunt ashore, Mr. Jakes?" he asked with a quick wink.

"Quite informative, Mr. Bork," I said, then stepped closer and whispered, "Unfriendly folks, especially my new German friend. But I heard enough of what they were saying to each other to learn that they've got parts for a Körting motor someplace upriver. At their mahogany depot, probably. Obviously, we need to go there and find out more."

Rork frowned. "Ah . . . not to be a naysayer, sir, but that's a wee bit beyond the limit o' Roosevelt's orders. Stay along the coast, he said, an' we're already six miles inland. An' if we ain't back at the river mouth right on time, I expect Captain Stadlin won't wait for us."

"Ha. Since when have you worried about going 'a wee bit beyond the limit' of orders?"

He replied in an infuriatingly paternal tone, "One 'uv us has to be mature an' responsible here."

"Fine, you can be mature and responsible here in Ilaya. I'm going up the river."

He held up his hands. "Jes' remindin' you o' the orders, sir. If ye think it's important, we'll go together and find what we find." He looked behind me. "Uh, oh, what's this? We've got company. . . ."

A dark-skinned, very serious-faced little boy with Indian-straight hair was standing right behind us. He pointed at a distant shack and recited in careful English, "Sir, Chief Henry the Eighth of the Miskito Zambo Wanki desires you come to him now. I will show you."

I bowed and replied with proper gravitas, "I am honored to visit the chief of the Miskito Zambo Wanki. Lead the way." This earned a big smile from the boy.

To Rork I said quietly, "This won't take long and just might be productive. Stay here with our boat and gear. We'll get under way when I return."

By this time the nasty German had boarded the *Deutschland*, which suddenly belched smoke and backed away from the shore. She headed upriver and disappeared around a bend.

"Don't be takin' too long with the local grand poobah, sir. We've no time to lose."

I followed my guide to the shack, where I entered the august presence of Chief Henry the Eighth, king of the Miskito Zambo Wanki—the Afro-Indian inhabitants of the lower Wanks River. Chief Henry, who appeared to be in his mid-thirties, was clearly in his best regalia: a top hat and dark suit with vest and bright red tie. He sat in a rattan chair-throne on a hard-packed dirt floor in the inner room of his cargo-box palace, an elegant walking stick by his side. Magazine advertisements for ladies' garments were plastered on the walls, probably as much for décor as for insulation, I figured. I found myself wondering if this Henry's morals were like those of his chosen namesake.

All this sounds comical to read, but let me assure the reader that the actual scenario was not. Chief Henry was a deadly serious man in peak physical condition, with striking grayish blue eyes set in a teak-colored face. Two men in gray trousers and red cotton shirts stood silently nearby. I saw no weapons, but they watched my every move intently.

The chief greeted me in very good British English—learned, I surmised, from a missionary teacher. "Thank you for coming, Mr. Jakes. I fear Herr Grausame was less than gracious to you. Let me assure you that he is not representative of *my* people. I understand *Tocororo* left you and Mr. Bork here with a fine little steam launch to see if commercial banana farming would be feasible. Perhaps I can assist you with information."

Impressed with his knowledge about me, I bowed and said, "Thank you, sir. I would very much like your opinion on whether large-scale banana cultivation could work in the Ilaya area. Do you think it feasible?"

He laughed. "No, not here in the mangroves, but perhaps on higher ground a bit up the river. However, the Germans control the commerce in that region through their lumber companies, so you would have to deal with them. Not all are boors like Herr Grausame and Captain Hopf of the *Deutschland*. Herr Hans Becker, their boss, is a reasonable man and I believe a Moravian Christian. I suggest you speak to him."

"What does Grausame do, sir? I saw a sailor's tattoo on his arm and a pistol on his hip."

"Wilhelm Grausame is the foreman of the German mahogany-harvesting company. He was once in the German navy, I believe, but has been in this area for the last twenty years. Quite a loud supporter of the Kaiser when he is in his cups, which is frequently."

"And this Captain Hopf fellow?"

"Gerhard Hopf has worked on the river for many years. He also sells guns to the upriver people, something I do not allow here among my people. When he is not drunk, he too is a reasonable man. Hans Becker is a decent man who tries to do the right thing, but he is young and has a difficult job, particularly with those two."

"You said upriver—how far?"

"The mahogany company's compound is about a day up the river by steamer, near a village called Plankia, where the land along the river begins to rise. There are no roads from here to there; the jungle covers them as soon as they are made. If you wish to go there, it must be by boat."

"Do they have a sawmill there?"

"They do—the only one on the lower river, which they use to cut the logs into lengths for shipping."

"Hmm. I find that quite interesting, sir. Would you happen to know what sort of engine powers the saw?"

One of the men leaned over and whispered in Henry's ear. The chief quickly stood. "I must go now, for I am expected elsewhere. Goodbye and may God go with you, Mr. Jakes. Please be careful—very careful—if you choose to go up the river."

His tone and expression seemed to indicate that he did not expect to see me again. I decided to test that theory. "Thank you very much for the information, sir. I will indeed be careful and hope to have the pleasure of seeing you again on my return here."

No response was forthcoming. Chief Henry the Eighth of the Miskito Zambo Wanki had disappeared out the back door. The interview was over.

I stood there alone for a moment, thinking about all I had just heard.

20

"Heil dir im Siegerkranz"

Approximately thirty miles up the Wanks River

Tuesday, 23 June 1914

We spent seven long hours steaming against the narrow river's current negotiating a constant succession of loops and sandbars. Finally, the sun lowered and shadows began to obscure the thick green walls of trees and bushes around us.

The Wanks' endless twists and turns had spun the compass to the point where I could no longer deduce how far we'd come or where the hell we were. The suffocatingly hot, dank air added to our mental and physical exhaustion. Fortunately, a bank of low, bluish gray clouds approaching from the northwest promised a breath of wind to dispel the insidious miasma of decaying flora and fauna. I sensed the temperature finally slacking a bit and smelled rain in the offing.

In all this time we'd seen no one else afloat or ashore, but I could feel eyes out there watching us. *They know we are here. Are they afraid of us? Angry? A disturbing thought entered my mind: Did Chief Henry the Eighth intentionally send us into a deadly trap to rid himself, and the Germans, of us?*

My coastal chart's depiction of the river ended at Ilaya, so I tried to keep track of our looping course on a page of my notebook; my sketch was hopelessly inaccurate. We got the first indication that we were nearing our destination when a distant scratchy sound, clearly man-made, wafted downriver toward us. We strained to make it out. At last Rork, whose hearing is better than mine, announced it was a gramophone. Not a very good gramophone at that, for it constantly wound down. As we got closer, we could tell the recording was a woman's voice singing plaintively in German. In the growing dusk, it was an eerie and menacing sound.

I was about to suggest we head for the shore when several large-caliber shots rang out somewhere close ahead of us. Rork, who was steering, slipped out his shotgun and surveyed the nearest bank to starboard for their source. I reached for my shotgun as well and searched the opposite side. We saw no splashes, so they weren't shooting at us. *A warning, perhaps?* Not likely; ammunition was expensive this far from civilization and not to be wasted on mere warnings.

A native dugout *cayuca* careened around the bend and rushed past us on the current. Two Indians were in the boat, one holding his shoulder and trying to steer with a paddle and the other clutching his belly in agony.

"Head for those bushes and camouflage the launch!" I ordered, pointing toward a thicket protruding from the bank. Rork rammed the launch into the center of it while I bled off the steam valve and closed the firebox flue to stop any smoke from giving us away. Then we bent branches down around the launch to hide it as best we could and readied our weapons.

As the pistons slowed and the engine grew quiet, Rork watched the land side, peering into the tangled dark mass surrounding us. I took the river side, watching that next bend intently, trying to listen for the approach of an engine-driven vessel or the splash of paddles. We waited for an enemy—German or Miskito Indian—to appear.

We heard no more shots, and I belatedly noticed the gramophone wasn't playing anymore. The jungle had gone completely quiet, a bad sign. The only sounds were the wind in the treetops and the whining buzz of insects down at our level. Soon they were crawling over us. We continued waiting. The jungle stayed quiet.

After thirty minutes had passed, Rork hissed, "I hate damned jungles."

"Me too. Blame this one on Roosevelt," I quietly countered.

"Aye, but which one 'uv 'em? The crazy one or the bloody naïve one?"

"The crazy one probably told the naïve one to use us if he ever needed help—so both."

His retort was interrupted as the gramophone sprang back to life, this time belting out stridently martial music. Though I am hopelessly deficient in musical ability, I recognized the melody as the British imperial anthem.

So did my Irish friend Rork, whose lifelong resentment of the Brits' dominion over his native isle hasn't diminished with age. "Damned if that ain't 'God Save the King.' So there's Limeys here? What the hell're they doin' makin' all that racket with Germans around? They're about to go to war with 'em."

The explanation came seconds later when several drunken male voices rose from the jungle ahead of us singing along with the music—in German. That was when I remembered that Kaiser Wilhelm, infatuated with all things to do with his grandmother Queen Victoria, and especially her Royal Navy, had adopted the British anthem, put German words to it, and titled it "Heil dir im Siegerkranz." I'd heard it played in Hamburg not long ago.

Pointing up the river, I whispered, "They're not English; they're Germans. They sound less than a hundred yards in that direction, right around the bend. We're really close."

Rork glared at me. "An' you want us to go take a gander at 'em?" He didn't sound enthusiastic.

"Of course, Rork. That's why we came upriver—to see what's in their depot. We'll have a look-see, then come back to the launch and drift down quietly with the current, then start the engine a little ways downriver and be back in Ilaya by morning."

He sighed. "Admiral Peter no-bloody-middle-name Wake, you'll be the friggin' death o' me yet." Then he wagged his head and said, "Ah, hell, after more'n forty years, might as well have it done here by the damned Krauts—if these friggin' skeeters don't suck all me blood first."

I clapped him on the shoulder. "That's the spirit, Rork. No guts, no glory. Can't live forever."

He ignored that. "So, what's your plan for when we get there?"

"I'll go have a look. You'll stay halfway between me and the launch and keep an eye on us both. Be ready to leave in a hurry. Got it?"

"Aye, sir, an' we best get goin' while they're roarin' drunk an' singin' loud. That caterwaulin'll cover the sound 'uv us movin' through this friggin' jungle."

Day turns into night fast in the tropics, and minutes later it was dark. I crawled onto the bank, crouching as I carefully moved forward through the thick bushes and vines to where I estimated the river would loop back at the Germans' depot. With Rork right astern, we headed one pace at a time through the darkness, wiggling between the thick vegetation or struggling to quietly move it out of the way. Above us, a strengthening wind foretold a storm. The treetops moved in great swishing arcs, and scudding clouds blotted out the stars.

21

Chaos in the Lair

Approximately thirty miles up the Wanks River

Tuesday, 23 June 1914

At what I guessed was the halfway mark I motioned Rork to stay in place while I got closer to the Germans' compound, a faint yellow-ish glow through the trees ahead. There was no need for stealth. The Germans were still at it, their ruckus reverberating across the jungle. Finally finding a suitable bush where I could still see Rork through the branches but could also easily see the compound, I sat down and peered at the scene.

I saw a wood-frame bungalow with a verandah, set about a hundred feet back from the river. A small barn and large paddock were on the far side. A thatch-walled building that appeared to be a warehouse and an adjoining open-sided sawmill were to my left, nearer to the dock, which ran alongside the riverbank for sixty feet. *Deutschland* was moored there, and I gratefully noted she was darkened, with no steam up. That would make our escape simpler. Thick logs in thirty-foot sections were piled five-high along the shore, apparently ready for loading.

Glass windows in one corner of the warehouse indicated an office. Three lanterns—one at the dock, one on the verandah, and one by the river side of the warehouse—shed a modicum of light across the compound.

A wagon path to my right led inland. The long, narrow building next to it was probably a barracks for the sawmill's laborers. It was dark and appeared empty. I presumed they had fled into the jungle when their boss had shot the men in the *cayuca*. I scanned around for the bane of a close surveillance, a guard dog, but saw none and allowed myself a brief sigh of relief before studying my adversaries.

Grausame, Hopf, and a younger fellow who I deduced must be Becker were sitting in rocking chairs on the verandah, drunk as coots and waving empty bottles as they belted out that damned anthem. Becker abruptly stood, swayed to starboard, and staggered inside, soon returning with another bottle of schnapps. So much for Chief Henry's belief that Becker was a Moravian Christian—and my hope that he might be a reasonable man. Grausame had his revolver out and was aiming it at various things, interspersing his singing with obscene curses. No one else was in sight.

The sawmill and office, if such it was, intrigued me. The engine that powered the mill could provide an alibi for the presence of excess engine parts ready for use in submarines. The office might have information that could help me determine whom these Germans were in contact with, and why. But I couldn't inspect the sawmill or get into the office without crossing the lantern-lit area in front of the verandah. Clearly, a diversion was needed. I decided the barn would do nicely. I felt around in my pocket and smiled when I found what I hoped was still there: two safety matches.

Circling to the right around the jungle side of the compound, I crossed the wagon path and made my way to the thatched barn. Fortunately, the animals—two riding horses, several draft horses, a surly-eyed mule, and some goats—were out in the paddock. I opened the gate and silently shooed them out. Then I lit a match and held it to the windward corner of the barn farthest out of sight from the verandah. It caught immediately, and within thirty seconds the ten-knot northerly breeze was blowing embers all over the barn. I hastened back to my previous perch in front of the verandah.

In the time it took me to return, the Germans smelled the smoke, saw the flames, and stumbled out of their rockers toward the barn. Diversion implemented, I got back to Rork, explained my scheme, and told him to wait right there—I would be coming back in a few minutes at top speed.

Minutes later, while the rapidly sobering Germans stood gaping at the burning barn, I examined the engine of the sawmill. It wasn't a Körting motor that used paraffin/kerosene fuel. It was a good old-fashioned American-made Corliss steam engine with a wood-fired boiler.

As the Germans argued over what to do, I slipped around the corner and through the open warehouse doors. Half a dozen crates of machinery parts—stamped "Körting" with other details in German—were stacked on one side. I counted fifty-two iron barrels labeled "Paraffin/Kerosene." The iron barrels, made in America by Nellie Bly's Iron-Clad Manufacturing Company, were stacked two-high along the other side. I estimated the total at about 2,800 gallons of the stuff. That much fuel could get a Type-16-class German submarine the 430 miles from Cape Gracias a Dios to the Caribbean entrance of our new canal at Panama.

The unlocked office was barely large enough to hold a makeshift desk, a rickety chair, and a filing cabinet. A few papers were scattered on the desktop, which also held an envelope addressed to Herr Mark Blumenthal, Direktor, Tropenholzmakler Company, 492 West 15th Street, New York, New York, USA. The return address was Plankia, Wanks River, Honduras.

I'd seen the name Blumenthal in the ONI files I'd studied before embarking on this mission. It was one of the aliases used by Paul von Hintze, Imperial German Navy spymaster in Mexico and Central America. The file had given his last known activity as running guns to the Huerta side in the Mexican civil war in April. *So why write to him in New York?*

Then I answered my own question. Karl Boy-Ed, head of German naval intelligence for all espionage operations in the Western Hemisphere, was in New York. From there, the letter would go in a different envelope to the German embassy in Washington, then in untouchable diplomatic mail pouches to the German embassy in Mexico City and on to von Hintze. That route was four times longer—five weeks—but far more secure than regular mail. It was a technique all espionage networks used—including our own. I estimated Grausame's message would get to von Hintze in early August.

Checking the situation outside, I found the compound suitably chaotic. Hopf was running a hose from *Deutschland* toward the bungalow, but the riverboat's engine was cold and the hose was limp. Grausame was frantically throwing buckets of water on the bungalow's roof, now afire too. Becker was inside the bungalow throwing personal gear out through the door. Satisfied they would be busy for a while, I considered how to get that letter out of the envelope in such a way it could be read and then replaced inside and sent on its way with no one the wiser to my intrusion.

One of my old techniques would work nicely.

22

Steganography

Approximately thirty miles up the Wanks River

Tuesday, 23 June 1914

The technique was ancient and very simple. That was good, because I had no modern espionage accoutrements with me. But I did have a pencil.

With my pocketknife I cut a deep slit at the pointed end, in the shaved wood near the lead tip. Inserting the pencil into the slightly unsealed corner of the envelope, I snagged the edge of the paper inside and slid it into the slit in the pencil. Then I gently twirled the pencil to wind the paper up around it. When the letter was fully wrapped around the pencil, I pulled the pencil out and unrolled the paper. It was dated that very day. The salutation was to the same fellow as on the envelope, Herr Blumenthal, and it was signed "Herr Hinkle." An alias for Grausame? Or maybe Becker?

By now the barn fire was creating enough light through the window for me to see clearly inside the office and read the brief letter, which regrettably was typed in German. Though I couldn't understand every word, I did get the impression it was written in unsophisticated basic German, the type a grizzled lower-deck man would use, because it looked nothing like the florid messages I'd seen in official German communiqués.

22 Juni 1914

Herr Blumenthal

Ihr Preis ist zu niedrig für unser typisch gutes Mahagoni. Ihr Preis muss auf 1,000 dollars, oder Sie können den Transport der verschiedenen Waren bezahlen.

Dein bayerischer Freund,
Herr Hinkle

I could only understand that the price of mahogany was U.S. $1,000, and something about transport. Nothing about engines or fuel. Obviously, it must be in code. Usually, the Germans used a five-digit numerical code, which was then translated into alphabet code, and thence into words or phrases. I held the letter up to the window to search for signs of hidden ink between the lines but saw none. That would be too easy.

Just then, the fire outside flared up and I noticed a minuscule pinprick of light shining through the paper. I saw one hole at first, then looked more closely and found other tiny pinpricks of light, eight of them in all, the holes about the caliber of a small sewing needle. Each hole was positioned directly above one letter in the word. Only one pinprick per letter. I never would have seen them if not for that bright flare of firelight from the barn.

On a piece of scrap paper from the desk, I wrote down the letters that had pinpricks above them. The "m" in Blumenthal. The "y" in typisch. The "g" and "o" in Mahagoni. The first "t" and the "o" in Transport. The "v" in verschiedenen. And the "y" in bayerischer.

M Y G O T O V Y

That combination of letters rang a bell. Not a visual bell, like Blumenthal's name had, but an aural bell. I said it aloud. *Muygotovee.* Yes, I was certain I'd heard it, but I couldn't think of where or when. It didn't look German. I went through the languages I knew or had been exposed to in my career. Spanish seemed a possibility at first, but *muy* (very) was the only Spanish word I could derive from the jumble of letters. Not Haitian Creole, Portuguese, Italian, or French. Not Japanese, Samoan, Vietnamese, Cambodian, Pidgin, or one of the Melanesian dialects. Not Arabic or Hebrew. My mind was blank. I said it aloud again. *Why do I recognize that sound? It must have some connection with von Hintze, but what?* Then it hit me, and I was embarrassed at my forgetfulness. I'd heard the word nine years earlier, almost to the day.

It was Russian.

Captain (now Rear Admiral) von Hintze had been Kaiser Wilhelm's naval attaché to the court of Tsar Nicholas II in St. Petersburg from 1903 to 1908. When I was there in 1904, we'd met at a social affair at the Russian base at Kronstadt. Von Hintze had gone out of his way to make my acquaintance. I remembered him as multilingual, intelligent, disarmingly pleasant, and quite interested in my work in Hamburg and St. Petersburg—in other words, nosy and dangerous. The events that followed that evening had driven him from my mind. Rork and I had embarked with the Russian fleet the next day on its doomed voyage around the world to battle the Japanese at Tsushima in the Sea of Japan.

As the Japanese fleet approached us on that morning in May 1905 I stood on the bridge of the Russian flagship and heard the captain say that word—or to be precise, two words—to the fleet admiral: *My gotovy.*

"We are ready."

So, a German spy in Honduras was using a Russian phrase to let his master know the clandestine submarine supply depot was ready for war. I doubted Grausame knew the language or meaning of the message he was transmitting. He was just employing a simple form of steganography—a secret message hidden inside an innocuous message—utilizing the phrase he'd been given in advance by the intended receiver. A phrase very few in Central America, or North America, would understand. I had to admit it was brilliant, a simple and effective additional layer of protection.

But as smart as he was, von Hintze could not possibly have anticipated that the one American naval officer who'd heard those words on a Russian warship in battle would be in the Honduran jungle reading German espionage correspondence nine years later. How ironic. Poetic justice indeed. For a fleeting moment I allowed a grin at my little cryptological victory.

But now I had to decide what to do next. Reinsert the letter, let the evil plot develop, and try to ferret out more of the Germans' spy network while alerting ONI in Washington and the Royal Navy's intelligence division in England? Or steal the letter and destroy as many supplies as I could by burning down the warehouse. The machine parts would probably survive, but the fuel wouldn't, and maybe not even the *Deutschland*. I could roll an opened drum of the fuel toward the riverboat and light the flammable trail, then flee back to Rork and the launch. It shouldn't take long. I stuffed the letter and envelope into my pocket and stood up from the desk.

Then a flash of lightning changed everything.

23
Old Age and Treachery

Approximately thirty miles up the Wanks River

Tuesday, 23 June 1914

I'd known the wind was picking up. The rattling windows and flaming embers from the burning barn flying horizontally across the compound had registered peripherally, but my attention was focused on solving the code. So I didn't realize that this wasn't a normal evening squall, over in fifteen or twenty minutes.

The lightning bolt that struck right at the edge of the compound and the concurrent explosion of thunder finally got my full attention. The next bolt lit up the northern portion of the sky and revealed the sight all sailors dread. A solid black wall of roiling clouds, incandescent with internal lightning, was racing toward me.

As my ears still rang from the thunder, a fifty-knot gale hit the warehouse like a solid wall. Flaming fragments of walls and wagons and debris filled the air. Seconds later, a tsunami cascaded from the sky, rain so heavy and dense it instantly extinguished the fires. In seconds, the wagon path became a raging creek running into the river. The entire compound, now a frothing lake, went dark, the lanterns blown somewhere far across the river. The roof above me lifted with a moan as the window beside me cracked. Then the window shattered, and rain gushed in like a firehose.

I had to get back to Rork and the launch! I made my way into the storage area, where the palm-thatched walls were already disintegrating, feeling my way in the blackness toward where the doors had been.

And collided with Grausame.

A lightning flash revealed his face, a mask of malevolent rage, inches from mine. When he reached for his revolver I was slow to react—old age perhaps, or simply overloaded senses. Grausame growled something, and the gun fired. The muzzle's flame erupted over my head rather than into it, and the big German fell into me, taking us both down to the muddy ground. Partially blinded and deafened by the gunfire, I lay there completely stupefied, Grausame's limp body a dead weight atop me. I struggled to push him off, slipping in the mud.

"'Tis no time to be dawdlin' about in the mud, sir," said a deep voice reprovingly above me. A hand reached down and gripped my arm. "Time for French leave, in fact, and right the hell now!"

I was yanked on my feet and would have hugged Rork for his timely intervention, but he was already out the doorway and around the corner, heading past the sawmill toward the jungle. My sight adjusted to the darkness as I hurried to catch up. As I raced by the bungalow I saw a figure leaving the verandah in the direction of the warehouse. Then I was past the sawmill and back in the jungle, right behind Rork, clawing my way through the clinging maze, trusting his instincts to lead us back to the launch. There was no worry about making noise now, and with the strength given by abject fear we took the lashing of the thorny vines and bushes literally in stride.

I have never launched a boat more quickly. And even so, we were barely in time. The river was about to overwhelm the shore and crush the launch. The bilge already held more than a foot of rainwater. I knew we would have to start bailing soon, but we had no strength left for that now. Rork collapsed on the thwart aft of the boiler as I took the tiller and steered us out into the mainstream. The waterlogged launch was sluggish to respond to the tiller, and I had to use both hands. Finally, I just let the damned thing go and sprawled across the stern sheets, knowing the current would rush us down toward the coast.

Rork tried to grin at me, but his face looked more cadaverous than mirthful. "Hell 'uva thrillin' time, sir," he gasped. "But me ancient bones're sayin' they don't wanna play this friggin' game anymore. Got no bloody stamina for a long-winded fight."

"Nor I," I gasped back. "María's right. We're just too damned old for this." Propping up on my elbows, I confessed, "That monster had me, Rork—I was a dead man. What happened?"

Another lightning flash revealed Rork's grin as he held up his left forearm, sans the rubber hand, which lay on the thwart beside him. That wicked spike gleamed for a second in the storm light.

"Old age an' treachery is what happened, me ol' friend. Aye, that Teutonic bastard lorded it over the poor native buggers, but the likes o' him never ran into an angry ol' Celt with nothin' to lose an' a proper marlinspike for a hand! Dropped like the sack of friggin' crap he was."

I reached out and clasped his good hand. "Thank you, Sean. And thank God and the Frenchmen who made that thing all those years ago. Go ahead and get some sleep. I've got the helm."

A gust of wind swept over us, heeling the launch and trying to turn it into the riverbank. I put the tiller over and kept us in the middle of the stream, more by intuition than by sight. Rork wrapped himself in soaked canvas and was snoring within minutes.

By noon the next day we'd passed the village of Chief Henry the Eighth. No one was on the bank to see us go by, because the storm was still raging. We ended up hiding the launch in the mangroves at the mouth of the river. And there we waited, eating half rations, slapping bugs, and expecting the worst—that the steamer wouldn't come.

But to our amazement—and profound relief—*Tocororo* arrived on time that Friday. By then the storm had abated, but since we had no dry fuel and a cracked steam line, Rork and I had to row the heavy launch the mile out to the steamer against the wind and tide—an excruciating ordeal for two old men.

Once the launch was hauled up to the main deck, Captain Stadlin came down to meet us as we wheezed and caught our breath. He stilled reeked of rum and stank of sweat, but now he was showing some respect. "Just who the hell are you two really? Surely not banana land-assessors. I got a cable at Bluefields from the fruit company ordering me to make sure you're taken care of in every way and get back to Tampa safe and *happy*. Never got one of those before. Hell, nobody's happy down here."

I simply trudged away, calling back, "Please have dinner delivered to our cabin at six."

Rork laughed for the first time in days and slapped me on the shoulder. "Happy seventy-fifth birthday, me ancient friend. Seems things're lookin' up on this bucket o' rust."

I'd completely forgotten the date. Seventy-five years? Three quarters of a century. Damn, that sounded old. It felt old. I was too tired to think more about it. We awoke from an exhausted sleep just before dinner (which actually tasted good) arrived. First, we sincerely thanked God for our deliverance, and then we broached the bottle of Matusalem I'd brought in my sea chest.

Thence followed a monumental celebration like old times!

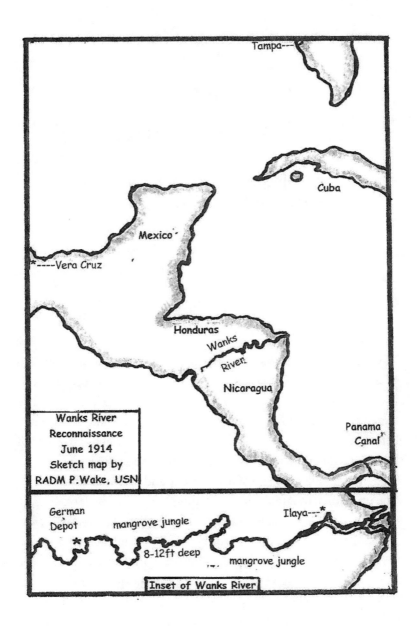

Tampa---

Cuba

Mexico

*----Vera Cruz

Honduras

Wanks

River

Nicaragua

Panama
Canal

Wanks River
Reconnaissance
June 1914
Sketch map by
RADM P.Wake, USN

German
Depot

mangrove jungle

Ilaya---*

*

8-12ft deep

mangrove jungle

Inset of Wanks River

24

The End of Innocence

Office of Naval Intelligence
1734 New York Avenue, Washington, D.C.

Thursday, 9 July 1914

Franklin Roosevelt wasn't in Washington; he was busy campaigning in New York to be the state's next U.S. senator. So I sent Rork home to Clotilda and walked two blocks to the new ONI offices, where I presented my ten-page report (typed on Stadlin's machine on *Tocororo* en route to Tampa) to the director of naval intelligence, Capt. James H. Oliver, a friend from Theodore Roosevelt's presidential days.

Though it was after the end of his workday and I was not expected, Oliver saw me immediately. After intently reading the report, he looked up at me with concern. His slow Georgia drawl made what he had to say even more dramatic. "Peter, this changes everything. Your report matches vague rumors we've heard from other sources, but it's the first with any details. And coincidentally, ten minutes ago we got a cable that Huerta's government in Mexico is falling apart; the rebels defeated him badly this morning. Von Hintze must be feeling angry and humiliated. Huerta was Germany's protégé, and the Germans spent a lot of time and money on him."

I nodded. The Germans had invested a huge amount of money in their endeavor to alienate Mexico—and the rest of Latin America—from the United States. "I read various newspapers on the train up from Tampa. Is Archduke Franz Ferdinand's murder really going to trigger the war?"

"It appears so, Peter. He was the heir to the eighty-four-year-old fellow on Austria-Hungary's imperial throne. His assassination by the Serbian Black Hand is the perfect excuse for the empire to invade Serbia, which they've been wanting to do anyway. Kaiser Wilhelm is pushing Austria-Hungary to attack Serbia as well—telling them he'll back them completely—so we expect them to declare war on Serbia any day now. That'll bring in Russia to defend their brother Slavs in Serbia, which will bring Germany in to defend Austria-Hungary from Russia. France will rise to defend her ally Russia. Then Germany will attack France, probably through neutral Belgium, and that will bring in the British. There are rumors the Ottoman Turks will side with the Germans. As for Italy," he shrugged, "time will tell. Italy's a nominal ally of Germany and Austria-Hungary, but the Italians are not enthusiastic to go to war."

"Pompous bastards're like spoiled little boys playing tabletop war with tin soldiers," I said in disgust. "It's easy for them to start a war, but damned hard on the poor peasants who will be the cannon fodder. I sure as hell hope everyone here in Washington understands that when war erupts in Europe, the European colonies in the Caribbean will be a theater of that war. And I can predict what will happen."

He nodded for me to continue. "Half a dozen of those German Type-16 and -17 submarines could be towed by freighter-motherships across the Atlantic and hidden on the Central American jungle coast. The Caribbean would be target-rich for them, especially near our new canal in Panama. And if *we* get pulled into the war, the canal will be a prime target. A torpedo or aerial bomb hit on the Gatun lock gate would knock it out for a long time."

Oliver said, "I see that you made a recommendation in your report to employ operatives to watch the coast from Nicaragua to Mexico, but you didn't say who those agents should be. Frankly, we don't have enough men for that. The few we have available don't have the language or cultural skills to do the job, or know the area."

"Use trustworthy Americans who are already there," I suggested. "Archae-ologists exploring the Mayan ruins, cartographers, and plantation managers would be perfect. Most are young and in good condition; they speak the language, know the area very well, and have the perfect cover work. They could use United Fruit Company's wireless stations to communicate in naval code."

Oliver leaned back and thought about it, then shook his head. "Intriguing idea, but no. They aren't naval officers. Can't do that."

"You could give them a special commission as ensigns. I've heard the general board is considering a reserve officer force. Make them part of that, just a little ahead of time."

He chuckled at my bureaucratically creative solution. "They would have to be recruited and run by someone there on the ground—any idea who?"

"In fact, I do. I've heard good things about a young fellow named Sylvanus Griswold Morley—a Harvard-trained archaeologist with the Carnegie Institu-tion here in Washington and an expert on Mayan ruins in that entire region. Knows the land and people in Central America well, including the Germans there. In addition to being a Harvard man, he's also a member of the Cosmos Club here in Washington, so he's connected politically."

"Very interesting indeed. I'll keep all this in mind, but I can't make prom-ises." He shook his head ruefully. "A lot of politicians here are clinging to their innocence about the world. In any event, thank you for the excellent intelligence work, Peter. Exciting stuff—just like the old days, eh?"

I laughed ruefully. "No, old friend. I'm too slow and tired nowadays to be thrilled by danger. It was just scary."

My report concluded, I headed for home. I'd cable María from the railroad station. If I could catch the six-thirty evening train to Alexandria, I'd soon have my arms around her. I did, and I did. My homecoming was all I'd hoped for. Thankfully, she never asked for the details of our Central American adventure.

On 28 July 1914, nineteen days after my meeting at ONI, Kaiser Willy finally got his war. Within ten more days all of Europe was involved in one way or another. Action soon spread to the Middle East, the South Pacific, Asia, and Africa. Much of Latin American was pro-German. Within six weeks of the war's start, the modern style of warfare had shocked the world: a German submarine destroyed a British cruiser in four minutes with a single torpedo, British aeroplanes were dropping bombs on German Zeppelin bases, massive German armies were within fifteen miles of Paris, and the Battle of the Marne had killed or wounded *half a million men* in the space of only six days.

By then, the world's last shred of innocence had disappeared.

25

The Coming Storm

Captiva Island
Southwest coast of Florida

Tuesday, 27 March 1917

*L*ibertad motored smoothly along the lower Gulf coast of Florida under her new-fangled Adolphus Busch diesel engines. Diesel was much easier to use than the old coal steam power and safer than gasoline. Rork had come down from Washington to join María and me on our houseboat and escape the frigid northern winter.

At Fort Myers we received a cable from Theodore announcing that he would be visiting Captiva Island (finally coming after I'd been suggesting it for twenty years) for a few days in late March. The next day we made our way down the Caloosahatchee River, across San Carlos Bay, and up Pine Island Sound to find Theodore's barge anchored at the settlement on the bayside shore of Captiva. As soon as we were rafted alongside, he jumped on board *Libertad*, his old grin shining from ear to ear.

We hadn't seen Theodore since we visited him and Edith at Sagamore Hill in March 1915, when he was just beginning to recover from his near-fatal Amazon trek. Thinner but hearty, he was currently embarked on a far less perilous adventure: stalking the legendary giant devilfish of the Florida coast, a beautiful creature both harmless and grossly misnamed.

"Peter! I am delighted to see you all. And I am amazed by the beauty of these islands—why didn't I come earlier! I've even gotten to see Hemp Key and the other islands I declared as sanctuaries for the birds. Bully good time!"

The four of us sat on *Libertad*'s afterdeck sipping rum and watching the sky and clouds change colors as the day faded. Despite the tranquility of the scene, it didn't take Roosevelt long to turn the conversation to politics and war.

He was angry. "This discovery of Herr Zimmermann's telegram to Mexico is an outrage and a clear declaration of Germany's intent to bring war down upon us. The Germans have invited Mexico and Japan to invade our western states! What more must we tolerate from those barbarians. They pillaged Belgium, spread clouds of poison gas across France, and have shown no human decency to civilians at sea. We must act!"

His fist pounded the chair arm to emphasize his words. "Now is the time! Democracy in Europe and here at home must be defended. The New World must rescue the Old World from tyranny! My sons and I are ready to volunteer tomorrow, raise a division of stalwart volunteers, and show Kaiser Wilhelm and the world how *American* men defeat unmitigated evil!"

He paused for a much-needed breath, then added with a sly smile, "And you two could join us. Back in action again!"

I shook my head. "Sean and I will cheer you on, Theodore, but we have no intention of volunteering for anything. We are far too old and tired for that."

"An' too damned smart," added Rork after a generous sip of Matusalem. "More rum, Theodore?"

Overlooking Rork's sarcasm, Roosevelt declined the rum and announced, "Very well, don't come along. That's understandable for you two. But *I'm* not too old! Only fifty-eight, fit as a fiddle, and rarin' to go."

I looked askance at that him. "Theodore, you are *not* fit as a fiddle. You were damn near dead after the Amazon trip, and you still have residual effects from fevers and infections, not to mention that damn bullet in your chest from only five years ago. You'd be more useless in the trenches than Shafter was at Santiago. And by the way, I know very well that both the president and the secretary of war have refused your offer—repeatedly. Let it go, my friend."

He glared at me for a second, then reined in his temper and waved a dismissive hand. "Yes, those naïve fools did refuse me, but the offer still stands. And Congress *did* want me to volunteer and lead soldiers. They'll be voting on the war next week, and I intend to get back up to Washington to support a declaration of hostilities. Peter, you know full well that the Hun must be defeated! You've warned everyone against the Kaiser's intentions for years."

"It may already be too late," I opined sadly. "It'll be much worse once Russia disintegrates internally—and it will soon—and frees the German divisions on the eastern front to head west and overwhelm the French. I'm not sure we have enough soldiers to send over there soon enough to stem *that* tide."

"Yes, Russia has always been a mess," Roosevelt admitted in disgust. "The Tsar treating his own people like slaves—no wonder they hate him. We'll have to fight on without Russia, but fight we will."

"Dinner is ready," offered María hopefully, gesturing to the table our crewman had set up on the deck nearby. She cast me a stern look. "Let us have a *pleasant* dinner on this beautiful tropical evening, gentlemen. Can we do that?"

I took the hint. "Of course, my love. You are quite right." As we seated ourselves at the table, I brought up a new topic. "Theodore, how are your children? What are they doing?"

Rork sighed and looked up at the stars. María frowned and put down her fork. For some inexplicable reason, perhaps it was the peaceful evening, I'd forgotten that all five of the Roosevelt children except Alice were already involved in one way or another with the war that was destroying the world.

Theodore beamed with pride. "They've all grown up, Peter! Ethel and her doctor husband have been working at a soldiers' hospital in Paris for two years, but they will be coming back home for the birth of their baby—my grandchild! Kermit joined the British army and thinks he'll be sent to Mesopotamia. Ted and Archie have their reserve commissions from Leonard Wood's training camp, so they'll probably head for France with the First Infantry Division once war is declared. Young Quentin is fascinated by aeroplanes. He wants to fly them for the Army."

I tried to get us off the topic of war. "I'm delighted to hear that they're all healthy and happy, and congratulations on becoming a grandfather again!" I turned to María. "And you are quite right, my dear. Let's turn our attention to this wonderful dinner. Theodore, I'm sure you'll enjoy the triple-tail fish."

He sampled a bite and exclaimed, "Delightful, María! Absolutely scrumptious!" Turning to me, he asked, "And how is young Sean Peter Wake doing these days? Is he a captain yet?"

María stared out over the water as I answered. "Yes, just promoted in December, after twenty-six years in the Navy. If war comes, he'll go to Britain to help Admiral Sims, who will be commanding U.S. forces there. Sean's specialty is destroyers, you know. Since the German submarines are stopping supplies from getting through to the British, he'll be busy."

I didn't want to go into more detail about that. María was very worried about Sean Peter. So instead I said, "Filipa and their sons Robert and Ted will remain in Alexandria, I expect."

He didn't ask, but Theodore was a grandfather, too, and I was sure he would want to hear about the rest of our family. "The other children are well, too. Useppa and Mario still live in Tampa, and their son, Peter Carlos Cano, will graduate from the Naval Academy in two years, keeping up the family tradition. Their daughter Linda is thirteen and looks just like Useppa did at that age. And my daughter Patricia and her husband, Charles, are still down in Key West; their daughter Agnes just turned six. Think of it, Theodore. María and I are blessed with five grandchildren."

That did the trick. The war wasn't brought up for the rest of the evening. Theodore never consumed much alcohol, and he didn't that night. After María went to bed, Rork and I did have a few drinks, relaxing with our remarkable friend who had overcome so much, and accomplished so much, in his crowded life. We spoke of grandchildren, the seas we'd sailed, different cultures we'd encountered, his enchantment with our Florida islands, how he had saved coastal bird rookeries around Florida, and our mutual plans to meet back in the islands two years hence, in March 1919.

The next morning, *Libertad* got under way northbound for the twenty miles to Gasparilla Island, and Colonel Roosevelt and his entourage headed back out into the Gulf of Mexico one last time to try to harpoon that world-record devilfish. He was anxious to get away, for he only had one day left at Captiva before heading to Washington to politically harpoon the "naïve fools" there.

As it turned out, the devilfish wasn't a world record, but it was very close; and Congress declared war before he had the chance to get back and urge them. This time, though, the war wouldn't be as quick and as simple as Theodore's fight against Spain twenty years earlier. And as with all wars, the bombast and glory faded once hometown newspapers published the casualty lists.

The next time I saw Theodore Roosevelt was the summer of 1918, when María and I stopped by Sagamore Hill en route to Maine. By then, everything in the country had changed.

So had Theodore's family.

26

The Real Cost of War

Sagamore Hill
Oyster Bay, Long Island, New York

Wednesday, 17 July 1918

We stayed at the Octagon Hotel on the night of July sixteenth and took a taxi over to Sagamore Hill at 10 a.m. on Wednesday to say a quick hello to Theodore and Edith before boarding our train to New York City for the next leg to Maine. We planned on a longer visit of several days when we headed back south in early September.

We were met in front of the house by Bill, the head gardener, a favorite of Theodore and his children. Normally jovial, today he was stone-faced. Something was wrong. I immediately surveyed the surroundings. On the porch, a man stood motionless, blankly staring at the copper beech tree in the front yard. The usually tumultuous house was quiet. The air was still; not a leaf moved on the trees. Even the usually loquacious summertime birds in the surrounding trees were silent.

I suddenly realized I hadn't read the newspaper that morning—we'd had a leisurely breakfast in our room and then headed for Sagamore Hill. I'd planned on reading the papers later on the train.

Bill's voice emerged as whispered agony. "Oh, Admiral. . . ."

Then I knew. My heart sank. "Which one?"

He could barely say it. "Quentin. Shot down three days ago." María gasped and reached for my hand. Bill nodded toward the man on the porch. "That AP reporter told us yesterday. It got confirmed this morning, Admiral. The Colonel just made a press statement. This copy is for the farm staff here."

He handed me a sheet of Theodore's stationery containing a one-line statement:

> Quentin's mother and I are very glad that he got to the Front and had a chance to render some service to his country, and to show the stuff there was in him before his fate befell him.

Tears streamed down María's face as she struggled to read it. I fought for composure as I asked Bill, "The other boys?"

"Kermit's somewhere en route to the front. Ted's still in the hospital from being gassed. Archie's still in the hospital—his leg was so mangled they almost amputated it."

"And Edith and Theodore?"

"Mrs. Roosevelt is resting upstairs. The Colonel was with her but is in the library now."

Bill shook his head in disbelief as he said, "He's still planning on leaving in just a few minutes to attend a political meeting in the city. Then tomorrow, he's meeting with Mr. Taft up at Saratoga Springs. Says it's his duty to keep working. In all this chaos they've forgotten you were stopping by, but I know the Colonel would surely want to see you. I'll let him know you're here. Please follow me."

María, still crying, said she just couldn't go in right then. She waited with the newsman out on the porch.

Theodore Roosevelt had had a year full of emotion: worry over his sons in battle, grief when they were severely wounded, and almost dying himself from an abdominal abscess in February. And now this unspeakable tragedy—his baby boy who loved aeroplanes, machine-gunned and blown from the sky. Like so many other American dead, he was young: only twenty.

I found my friend of thirty-two years alone at his desk. The famous thick-lensed spectacles were in a pocket. Red-rimmed eyes leaked tears that ran down an anguished face. He moved to speak, but I shook my head and pulled a chair over close to his, leaned forward, and took his hands in mine.

"Theodore, you and Edith and all your family have always been in our hearts. Now you are all in our prayers. Beyond you knowing that, words aren't needed right now. Old friends—especially ones who've been through all that *we've* been through together—don't have to talk to communicate, do we?"

He nodded slowly, his eyes locked on mine, our hands never letting go as we both allowed our tears to fall. We stayed like that for several minutes, until his secretary entered and softly said that Theodore's automobile was ready.

Out on the porch, Theodore stopped and asked me, "Peter, is it wrong to go to a work meeting right now? Many might think me a callous father."

"No, it is not wrong, and you are not callous, Theodore. I understand exactly why you have to keep working right now. Edith understands, too." I paused a moment and reflected aloud, "I think I would go to work, too, and I'm certain María would understand. You and Edith will know when and how to grieve, each in your own ways. But for now, go to your meeting in Manhattan."

I watched them drive away, then turned and saw Edith in the doorway. She nodded to the reporter and came over to María and me. María embraced her—the heartbreaking vision of two mothers who knew the terror and agony of losing a son by violence. Enduring the true cost of war.

Edith gave us a sad smile. "Thank you so much for coming. We very much needed to see you both. I'm going to go lie down for a while, I think."

Then, gazing woefully at the automobile driving her husband away, she murmured, "We must do everything we can to help him." And with that, she made her way back inside.

27

The Old Lion Is Dead

Oyster Bay
Long Island, New York

Wednesday, 8 January 1919

R ork and I stood shivering in the frigid air. We'd arrived that morning
on the overnight train from Washington and checked into the last
available room at the Octagon Hotel before leaving for Sagamore
Hill. We both gripped our canes tightly, for though the snow had stopped
falling, the icy walkways were treacherous. Seeing me shaking, Rork shared
a nip from his flask, which warmed me for a fleeting moment. I snuggled my
old greatcoat closer around me.

We'd come alone. María and Rork's fiancée, Clotilda, had decided not
to make the journey. María pleaded she would find the entire day just too
emotional. Clotilda said it was a duty Rork and I needed to accomplish alone,
without distractions.

The line of people waiting to enter the North Room of Sagamore Hill was
relatively short. The family had insisted on a small funeral for family, old
friends, and a few government leaders. They specifically did not want the
gaudy ostentatiousness of a presidential farewell or the carnival atmosphere
of thousands of mourners.

Theodore's son Archie, still recovering from his war wounds and wearing his dress uniform with the Croix de Guerre, had taken care to make sure his father's and mother's wishes were carried out. He was the only son there.

Ted and Kermit were still in Europe, at U.S. Army headquarters in Coblenz. Quentin's body was never shipped home. He was buried in France with the other fallen Americans. His sisters Alice and Ethel were somberly standing near Edith, who smiled wanly with genuine appreciation when she saw us enter the room. It took everything I had to keep my sobs inside.

I felt Rork's false left hand on my shoulder. "Steady on, Peter. . . ."

Nodding my acknowledgment, I led the way between the giant elephant tusks that framed the entryway, given to Theodore by our friend the emperor of Ethiopia, past the rocking chair draped with a leopard skin, and headed for Edith and the children at the far end of the room. First, however, we had to go by the Colonel.

In death as always during his life, Theodore Roosevelt dominated the oak-paneled, bookshelf-lined room. His flag-draped oak casket, set in front of the massive fireplace and reposing on an African lion skin, was the focal point. Two giant bison heads on the wall over the mantle flanked the casket. In front of the casket were two crossed flags from the 1st U.S. Volunteer Cavalry Regiment, his loyal Rough Riders, with a beautiful wreath of vivid yellow mimosa flowers, the traditional color of the cavalry. Presented by his old comrades-in-arms, it was the only floral display in the house.

Edith reached out to take our hands. "Oh, Peter and Sean, thank you for coming in such dreadful weather. He would *love* that you made it here. He thought of you as his older brothers, you know." She squeezed my hand. "You were a great help to him in July, Peter, but Theodore never really healed from Quentin's death." She took a deep breath. "None of us have. And now he has left us—peacefully in his sleep, thank the Lord."

I paused to collect myself before speaking. "Sean and I are still stunned by this loss, Edith. We were going to meet Theodore at Captiva Island in just two months." I swallowed the lump in my throat. "I have so many wonderful memories of him. I first met young Theodore at Delmonico's in New York just before he made the best decision of his life—to marry you. He loved you so much. You always made him very happy, my dear."

That truth prompted a gentle nod from Edith. "And so did you two gentle-men. The mere mention of either of you was sure to bring forth some story about your adventures. He was a bit envious, you know."

Archie disengaged from another conversation and shook our hands. "Admiral, Chief, I'm glad you're here. We'll be leaving in a moment for the church. Please ride in one of our family's automobiles. It's much too far to walk in this weather, especially with the three of us needing canes."

Edith added, "I'm staying home, Peter. An old tradition in my family which I now understand. So I'll say goodbye to you both now. You and your dear ladies must visit when spring comes. Our home is always open to you."

Edith embraced me, then Rork, something that shy lady had never done before. Half an hour later, Rork and I disembarked the automobile and fol-lowed Archie and his sisters into Christ Church. Every pew was filled, and many people stood around the sides. Vice President Marshall, seated on the front row, represented the U.S. government, because President Wilson, Theodore's despised political foe, was at the peace conference in France. Rork and I moved to stand in the back, but Archie insisted we sit with the family in the front. We passed former president Taft sitting in the back pew, quietly sobbing over the loss of his friend, a friendship recently renewed after years of political acrimony. Archie brought him forward to sit with the family too.

Unlike Theodore's speeches, the pastor's service was brief. A welcome, a prayer, a recitation of "How Firm a Foundation, Ye Saints of the Lord," another prayer, and the benediction, when the pastor named the deceased for the first and only time: "Theodore, the Lord bless and keep thee. The Lord make his face to shine upon thee, and be gracious to thee."

A solitary peal of the church bell signaled the end of the service. We filed out the front door and reentered the car for the mile-long trip to the cemetery, escorted by a mounted troop of Theodore's devoted New York City policemen. Once we got there, though, the entire crowd had to trudge up the hill to the grave, slipping on the ice and mud.

"Our ol' boyo Theodore surely loved climbin'—an' the rougher the better," Rork panted. "Bet the ol' sod's laughin' now."

At the summit, a brisk wind and splendid view awaited us. A mile to the north, across the farm fields and white-capped bay, was Sagamore Hill.

"Theodore knew exactly what he was doing when he picked this spot," I told Rork.

The theme of a simple goodbye was carried on here as well. The pallbearers, black-clad undertakers instead of a full military honor guard, placed the casket above the laurel-and-flower-lined grave. The flag was removed and folded. The pastor, the hem of his long surplice muddied by the climb, intoned the service for the committal of the dead. A police bugler sounded Taps. Near me, a misty-eyed police lieutenant murmured the Hebrew burial prayer.

As the casket was lowered, a flock of snow geese flew over our heads and sailed out across the bay. I said a silent prayer of thanks that I had been allowed to have Theodore Roosevelt in my life. Beside me, Rork crossed himself after offering his own prayer. Afterward, we held each other upright as we slowly followed the throng down the hill to the automobiles parked along the road.

When I reached the bottom, something made me turn and look up at the gravesite. Taft was still there, and even at that distance I could tell he was crying. As were all the people around Rork and me. The stark scene at the graveside made the cold reality set in. The impossible had happened.

The old lion was dead.

28

The Sun in Winter

Grunt Bone Lane
Key West, Florida

Saturday, 8 February 1919

The frigid ordeal of Theodore Roosevelt's funeral was the final straw. My coastal Massachusetts upbringing had been enough winter for a lifetime, and both my blood and my soul preferred the tropics. Even Washington was too far north. María instantly agreed when we spoke about it over dinner. We decided to move south to Key West, to be closer to Patricia and never again to feel Arctic pain. Patricia got a cable the next day asking her to look for a place for us.

Roosevelt's funeral was also a catalyst for Rork. His own mortality became real to him at last, and two weeks later he and Clotilda were married at St. Patrick's, the oldest Catholic church in Washington. I was best man and María the bridesmaid. A small group of Clotilda's friends and a loud contingent of Sean's pals, including no fewer than three admirals and Assistant Secretary of the Navy Franklin Roosevelt, completed the wedding party.

María and I suggested the Rorks move south with us, and I could tell he was ready. But petite Clotilda, twenty years his junior, held gentle sway over the old boy, the first woman I'd ever seen him so completely surrender to. She replied that they wanted to stay close to their church and their pub friends and the cultural attractions of the city. Sean nodded his agreement to that. He even looked like he meant it.

I was about to argue, but a nudge from my better half stopped me. "They want to live their own life," María explained later. "They should. And Sean will receive better medical care in Washington." Rork promised they would visit every winter. I made him swear to it.

We arrived in Key West on Henry Flagler's amazing overseas train a month after Theodore's funeral and settled into a two-story frame cottage on quiet Grunt Bone Lane. Our home was right across a sandy lane from the house where Patricia, her staid lawyer husband Charles Whitehead, and their delightful nine-year-old daughter Agnes lived. The circumstances of Patricia's birth had prejudiced Charles' attitude toward me when they were first married, but over the years his animosity faded and a bond developed between us. He was glad we came, and Patricia and Agnes were overjoyed.

The cottage was perfect for us. *Libertad* was moored at the fishing docks two streets away, the Methodist church where María and I had been married was around the corner, and the naval station that held so many memories was a ten-minute walk away.

We named our cottage Casita Porfina (*porfin* means "at last" in Spanish). It was slightly larger than our house up north and much more comfortable and modern. María had an *inside* kitchen, and because we were connected to the city's new electrical generator system, we had one of the new Frigidaire refrigerators, a rarity on the island. Along with a guest room there was a library for my books and charts and ship models. Out back we had a shaded patio and a garden bursting with flowers, fruit trees, and vegetables. A tool shed was converted into a simple workshop for me. We had a well for water and two good-sized cisterns to catch rain as a backup.

A month after we moved in, Rork and Clotilda left behind the cold gray skies of Washington and made the three-day train trip to our sunny island. Rork and I spent afternoons walking the town, visiting our old haunts, and reminiscing about times together stretching all the way back to 1863. The ladies conjured up wonderful meals, picked up seashells on the south beach, and attended musical performances. Useppa's family visited from Tampa and combined with Patricia's to fill the house with the sounds of youth—pure joy to my ears. The elders' nostalgia and young people's dreams and aspirations made lively conversations on the patio as we enjoyed the cool evening breezes.

It was an idyllic week of relaxation, the kind that people dream of during their working years. Then, on the eighth morning, a breathless messenger boy arrived on our front verandah with a cable from the Navy Department.

I steeled myself for grievous news about my son, Capt. Sean Peter Wake, who was currently in the Mediterranean. Or was it about Useppa's son Peter Cano, due to graduate from the Naval Academy in June? Opening it, I saw that though the telegram was from the Navy Department, the message hadn't originated there—the department was only passing it along. My heart rate eased.

When I saw the original location and sender, I was overwhelmed by memories.

29

Honor Bound

Grunt Bone Lane
Key West, Florida

Monday, 17 March 1919

Rork wandered out onto the verandah to ask if I wanted to go to O'Hara's for a St. Patrick's Day nip, then saw I was reading an official Navy telegram. His face tightened. "Oh, hell. Somethin's gone bad. Not one 'uv our boys, is it?"

I handed the cable to him without answering.

16 MARCH 1919—2013hrs REROUTE—PRIORITY ONE ONI NAVDPT—WASH DC TO: RADM P. WAKE—KEY WEST FLA ADDENDUM MSG TO RADM P. WAKE—RET FROM RADM A. NIBLACK ONI XXX—ORGL MSG BELOW—X—SENDR UNK—X—GOOD LUCK—X—NIBLACK—XXX

15 MARCH 1919—0545hrs RCVD AT NAVDPT—WASH—DC TO: RADM P. WAKE—USNAVY DEPT-WASH DC-USA FROM: SHTUR-MAN—SEVASTOPOL RUSSIA XXX—RETURN FAVOR FOR TREK NEEDED ASAP FOR WIDOWS SON—X—3 CREW HERE—X—WILL ADV WHERE-HOW WHEN RESPONSE RCVD—XXX

Rork stared at me in surprise. "Shturman. . . ." His brow wrinkled. "If I'm rememberin' rightly that's the Rooskie word for *navigator*. So that's got to be Sergei Dyvoryanin, our navigator when we was with the Tsar's fleet escapin' Russia! We've heard naught from the lad since early in the war—January of '15, maybe? He was commandin' a ship in the Baltic then. An' now he needs to get out o' there on the double-quick? Those damn Bolshies won't let even a distant cousin to Tsar Nicki live, will they?"

I'd just been reading a *New York Times* article about the chaos in the Crimea. "So it seems, Sean. Russia's so torn apart by civil war it'll never be the same again. The pro-Tsar Whites in Crimea are in retreat everywhere, the Reds are winning everywhere, and the Crimean Greens are fighting everybody else to get their independence. It's far worse even than what we saw back in '05." And that, I remembered, had been terrible.

"Young Sergei must've escaped from St. Petersburg down to Sevastopol," Rork mused. "But what's the 'widow's son'? Sergei's a Mason now?"

"Evidently. He knows about my connection, remember? In any event, he's invoking the ancient cry for help, and we have no choice but to answer. He saved our lives fourteen years ago. We're honor bound to help get him out of there."

Rork straightened. "After we'd saved *his* life, I'd like to point out, but aye, we're surely honor bound even without the Masonic bit. But what can too old relics such as the likes 'uv us actually do? Hell, you'll turn *eighty* in a couple o' months. An' I'm a wee bit older than you." He gestured inside the cottage. "An' you know the ladies won't let us go. Take us too long to get there, anyway."

He was right on all points. "All true, but I just thought of something. Franklin Roosevelt is back in Washington after overseeing the dismantling of German naval assets in Europe. As assistant secretary of the Navy he can make things happen. And he's been a Mason since 1911—Theodore told me that a while back. Franklin will understand what needs to be done and why."

"Aye, an' he owes us a big favor anyway after puttin' us through that bloody damn mess down in Honduras. But if not us, who *can* get Sergei out o' there? This has got to be done by a trustworthy man. An' he's got to be already near the Crimea 'cause there's no time for travelin' there."

Rork saw the answer in my eyes and spoke it aloud. "Aye, it's got to be Sean Peter. Isn't he someplace in the eastern Med?"

"For the last month he's been the U.S. liaison at the Royal Navy's station at Alexandria in Egypt. Prior to that, none other than our old friend Albert Niblack was the commanding officer at Gibraltar when Sean Peter had that destroyer division; so he might be able to help too. Sean Peter's supposed to leave Alexandria for London pretty soon and get his flag promotion to command Patrol Force Atlantic under Vice Admiral Sims. But to do this for us, he'll need some leave time to head north to Constantinople and get a ship there for Sevastopol."

"Didn't we just stand up a flotilla at Constantinople? They could help."

"Yes, and no. Rear Admiral Bristol's Black Sea destroyer flotilla just arrived in Constantinople. But they're responsible for dealing with the Greek-Turk mess in the Aegean, the Turkish civil war boiling all over Turkey, the Armenian massacres, the civil war in Black Sea Russia, and American missionaries everywhere. And all while trying to maintain good relations with the Brits, French, and Italians, who also have troops and ships there and want to grab land and commerce in the region. Bristol's flotilla won't have time for us."

Rork held up his hands. "Limeys, Frogs, an' Wops fightin' o'er the pickin's. Now there's a bloody perfect recipe for disaster if Uncle Sam takes sides."

"And Bristol's no fan of mine, if you recall. So he won't help Sean Peter even unofficially, and may even hinder him. No, this has to be done privately. I'm sure Franklin can quietly get him the leave time, so let's get a cable off to Franklin right now. Once we get a reply, we'll send one to Sean Peter explaining the situation. Come on."

"Right you are, sir," said Rork, adding quietly, "an' no need to tell the girls just yet."

By the time we arrived at the telegraph office on Greene Street I'd mentally formulated the message, so it took only a minute to write it out for the clerk. It was in plain language, because the codes I knew before the Great War were no longer in use. That meant this wasn't going to be completely confidential, but time was of the essence. The apathetic clerk, who was paid by the word, was more interested in the length than the content and perked up when he saw this was going to be a relatively long cable. At my personal expense, of course.

For the rest of the day, cables ran back and forth from Key West to Washington to Sean Peter at Alexandria. The messenger boy got a small fortune from me in tips, but I was assured of rapid delivery.

30

The Die Is Cast

Grunt Bone Lane
Key West, Florida

Monday, 17 March 1919

I briefed my assembled family late that afternoon on the details of the situation and the plan to rescue our Russian friend. I didn't sugarcoat it. Political and naval constraints would prevent Sean Peter from using his rank or any naval or American diplomatic assets. He must be incognito in Russia—providing plausible deniability for the Navy and our country if things went wrong.

I went through the outline of the scheme Rork and I had devised, which admittedly created more questions than answers. "Sean Peter goes by steamer up to Constantinople, Turkey. There, he'll find a steamer to take him into the war zone at Sevastopol. Sergei and his companions will find and board that ship, seek official asylum from whatever nationality's flag flies over it, and stay on board when the ship leaves Sevastopol for a foreign port. Once in another country, Sergei flees by train to a safe place and Sean Peter heads for London. He has to be there on the morning of April seventeenth to report to Vice Admiral Sims."

My son-in-law Charles frowned and offered his legal opinion. "That asylum ploy is a very thin legal veneer, Peter. European courts take forever to decide on such matters, and regardless of the country, may very well disallow it in the end and award custody of your friend to the Russian government."

"What government, Charles? Russia is pure anarchy right now. I realize this plan is fraught with difficulties. But it might work."

María, a veteran of clandestine missions, was more practical. "Bribes for the captain? And the port thugs?"

"I wired Sean Peter $950 this afternoon," I looked sideways at María, "from our savings account to the Bank of England office in Alexandria. He'll draw it out in British pounds sterling. That should be sufficient for his passage to Russia, bribes, and travel to London. Since Russian money is worthless now, solid British currency will be acceptable to everyone there."

To my relief, María didn't flinch about the money. Instead, she asked, "And the cover story?"

"Rork came up with something most thugs in war zones would understand and appreciate—and would never dream an *American* naval officer would employ."

All eyes turned to Rork, who said with a perfectly straight face, "Purveyor of opium and women."

31

Burn after Reading

Grunt Bone Lane
Key West, Florida

Friday, 1 May 1919

María laughed. "I like that, Sean. And it might even work. His alias?" I gave that answer. "John Stone, the English translation of the alias I used in Havana back in '88."

"When does all this start?" asked María.

"Tomorrow, the nineteenth, on a British P&O steamer to Constantinople, which will take about three days to do the 864 miles. Fortunately, the winds are light in the eastern Med and the Black Sea this time of year. At Constantinople, Sean Peter—or John Stone—will, we hope, find a ship for Sevastopol within two days. He'll send a cable alerting Sergei about his arrival, on the off chance he'll still be able to get it. He'll also send us a cable with a last-minute update on his next moves. It's two or three days up to Sevastopol. So if all goes well, he should reach Sevastopol around the twenty-seventh or twenty-eighth."

Then I added the hardest part for our listeners to hear. "We won't hear anything more from them until they reach a safe port in another country, one with cable connections. That means Romania or Bulgaria."

"And we just sit here and wait?" asked Patricia, her eyes darting from María to me. Charles took her hand and patted it. "It looks as if we do, my love; and we pray for your big brother and Sergei and his family to get through this to safety."

María's sad eyes reflected the truth. She knew these things never unfolded according to plan, for she'd been there when they fell apart. She knew that Sergei Dyvoryanin had risked his life to save Rork, Edwin Law, and me against overwhelming odds—and that this was a very personal debt of honor. She also knew how difficult it was for me to ask my son to do this task and not be able to do anything more to assist. María held my arm tightly.

Clotilda embraced Rork, who said, "Aye, Charles, the die is cast, an' a prayer would be a good thing right now." He looked heavenward and intoned, "Dear Lord, help our lad Sean Peter Wake in his noble cause to save three lives. We know he'll be safe with You standin' watch o'er him. An' don't let those godless Bolshie bastards hurt any 'uv 'em. Amen!"

A chorus of muted amens approved the sentiments, if not the wording.

As we rose to go our separate ways, Rork rumbled in my ear, "I'm feelin' a bit nervous, Admiral. How 'bout a bit 'uv a nip—to steady the nerves, as it were."

That sounded like a damned good idea.

The situation soon grew worse. Sergei sounded desperate in his final cable, received at Key West on the nineteenth of March.

XXX—LAST CABLE OUT—X—NOT MUCH TIME LEFT—X—WILL FIND SONS SHIP WHEN ARVS—XXX

My son's last cable was sent from Constantinople on the twenty-eighth. Four weeks is an eternity when you have sent someone you love into danger, especially for a man like me accustomed to taking action. The next four weeks of no news from Sean Peter defeated my ability to keep up my family's morale, and my own. I'd decided that Filipa and fourteen-year-old Robert in Washington shouldn't know of his private mission in the Black Sea. Outside of us in Key West, only Roosevelt and Niblack knew. I cabled Niblack three times and received the same reply each time: no information yet.

Sean and Clotilda returned to Washington at the end of March, promising to look in on Filipa and Robert without alarming them, and also to give "friendly reminders" to Roosevelt.

"'Twas the right decision, Peter," Rork said as he prepared to board the train. "Sean Peter's a wily an' resourceful naval officer, just like his ol' man. Me own heart's easy that he'll be all right."

But nothing arrived by letter or cable. On Easter Sunday, April twentieth, Patricia, Charles, Agnes, María, and I attended the service at our Methodist church, the same church where María and I were married in a double ceremony with Useppa and Mario. I sat there during the joyous service, subdued by profound worry and guilt.

At our cottage afterward, the ladies plunged into final preparations for the annual feast as Charles and I sat in the shade on the patio. Usually a reserved man, my son-in-law was even more so that day—not the companion to take your mind off your concerns. We both sat there silently brooding. I very much missed having Rork around.

Almost two weeks later, on the first day of May, as I was sitting outside deep in gloom, María called me into the house in a trembling voice, saying there was a naval officer on the verandah to see me.

I recognized him at once, though it had been many years. Ross Barnett was a full commander now, but twenty-one years earlier he'd been a young ensign and my signal officer on *Dixon* in the war against Spain. Thinking signals work too boring, he'd become a gunnery expert instead, had garnered commendations for it, and had commanded a destroyer during the Great War.

"Very good to see you again, Admiral," he said, shaking my hand heartily. "I'm sorry for the intrusion, sir, but I was sent here by express train per Assistant Secretary Roosevelt's orders to give this document to you." He unlocked an official Navy Department courier case and pulled out a plain, unlabeled dossier, which he handed to me. "I'll wait while you read it, sir. It's for your eyes only, then I'm ordered to burn it in front of you. And yes sir, I know what's in it."

María, sniffling and fearing the worst, retreated to the kitchen to wait. Barnett and I sat on the verandah while I examined the dossier. The first page was a handwritten note on plain paper from Franklin Roosevelt.

PW . . . First off, all are well. The attached report arrived here two hours ago. Knowing your bond with him from '98, I had RB (senior and trusted officer in ONI) rush a copy down to you. This is the only copy. The original report is in the ONI vault, where your reports still reside on that shadowed shelf in the back. Once you have read this you'll understand why RB will burn it in your presence, for none of it must ever become public. FDR

My heart rate slowed when I read Roosevelt's first line. The last line meant the report contained politically embarrassing information. I started reading the report and had to stop for a moment, feeling my heart race again.

This wasn't a standard naval report from an average deck or staff officer. It was a clandestine ONI report sent directly to the assistant secretary of the Navy via the highly prioritized, secret, and exclusive worldwide wireless transmission system the U.S. Navy had set up only a year earlier. And even more salient, I could tell it was written by a man who had considerable experience in espionage.

Clearly, there were darker aspects to my son's naval career that had been completely unknown to me.

32

Report of Capt. S. P. Wake, USN—Part One

SECRET—IMMEDIATE—28 APRIL 1919 TO: ASSISTANT SECRETARY OF THE NAVY F. D. ROOSEVELT FROM: CAPT. S. P. WAKE—NAVSTALOND CLANDESTINE INTELLIGENCE REPORT—BLACK SEA AREA—MARCH–APRIL 1919

1. While USN liaison officer at Royal Navy Station Alexandria, Egypt, I received confidential-urgent cable orders at 10:05 p.m. (local time) 17 March 1919 from AstSecNav F. D. Roosevelt. My orders were to:
   A. Proceed clandestinely in mufti from Alexandria to Constantinople, Turkey.
   B. There, to observe the general situation and to secure immediate false identity passage to Sevastopol, Russia.
   C. There, to observe general situation with special attention to the civil war opponents, establish contacts for future communication, information, and action, and leave for USN Station London no later than 12 April 1919.
   D. Upon arrival at London, no later than 17 April 1919, to immediately provide AstSecNav Roosevelt a secret report of said observations/ actions via priority status on the USN secure wireless network.

2a. Arrived Constantinople 20 March 19 on board 4,200-ton freighter SS *Dartmouth* (British). Stayed at low-class Hotel Toulon as "international services broker" John Stone. I avoided U.S. naval flotilla and consular officials but heard that USN Lt. Dunn, intelligence officer for RADM Bristol (USN Flotilla—Constantinople), was alerted to my presence in the city by informants and inquiring about me. Unknown if they knew my real identity. Also, the local man I hired for protection and counter-surveillance reported me to a Bolshevik group (unknown which one) in the city that surveilled me the entire time.

2b. Apparently random attempt by four bandits to rob me at docks on second night; two of them WIA. Police not involved.

2c. Contacted at breakfast in my hotel 3rd morning by member of under-ground Armenian Masonic lodge sent by cabled American Masonic request (sender unknown) to check on my well-being. He warned me Bolsheviks considered me a pro-Tsar spy for British intelligence, knew my real last name, erroneously thought me the same man who fought Bolshevik mutineers at *Potemkin* mutiny 1905 near Odessa, and warned Turk nationalists I was pro-British and anti–Turk nationalist. He believed bandits who attacked me were Turk nationalists.

The Turk nationalists are getting stronger every day under the dynamic leadership of General Kemal Atatürk, ostensibly assigned to the Ottoman Sultanate army's general staff but actually organizing a professional army to overthrow the Sultan's government, expel foreigners, and create a "modern self-reliant" Turkey. Atatürk is a very competent soldier, a charismatic leader, and not to be underestimated. Many in the city are awaiting the signal for a general uprising. They view him as a modern equivalent of Mehmet II, the brilliant multilingual Ottoman sultan who at the age of twenty-one in April 1453 roused the Turkish people, conquered Constantinople, and ended the Christian Byzantine Empire.

2d. Assessment of current situation in Constantinople:

Anarchism in the city (pop. 800,000) is worsening. Allied military occupation forces (ca. 4,000 British, French, and Italian troops) tenuously control some residential areas for foreigners (ca. 200,000 people). British are in political/military command of the Allied occupation forces. The British have another force in the Caucasus fighting Red Russian forces, without much success.

By all accounts, Ottoman government officials are decadent, duplicitous, and incompetent. Turkish nationalist rebels are strongly focused, innovative, and ruthless, using the foreign occupation very effectively to promote the overthrow of Ottoman rule, oppose foreign occupation, and persecute foreign communities in outlying areas as the causes of their nation's downfall. I have heard stories of horrible massacres going unchecked.

Discussions with Turks and foreigners indicate violence against foreigners is increasing in the city and across the country. The British have jailed several nationalist leaders and are seen as strongly opposed to Turk nationalists. Americans are viewed as slightly better and more pro-democracy, except for missionaries. Germans are seen as opportunistic friends of the Sultanate, not of the Turkish people. Turks view the White Russian refugees flooding the city as worthless whores of a moribund culture, and the Red Russian forces on the eastern frontier as Godless heathens.

The future: I predict a well-armed and -led general national uprising by Atatürk between April and July this year. Many veteran army commanders will follow him. The Ottoman army's senior leadership will fold quickly. The Allied occupation forces don't have 1 percent of the manpower they need to quell a revolution, maintain order in Constantinople, or demonstrate Allied strength and resolve.

Recommendations:

A. NO U.S. troops be made part of the Allied occupation.

B. NO USN vessels be stationed here except those needed for security of U.S. diplomats.

C. USN sailors' shore liberty should be limited and tightly controlled when ashore.

D. Continue with RADM Bristol's leadership. Give him diplomatic status as well.

E. Promote an enlightened policy; Europeans' current policy is unrealistic.

2e. Departed for Sevastopol at 3 a.m. 21 March 1919 as only passenger on 1,550-ton SS *Philos* (very old Greek freighter with multiple names, under Captain Adamos), same alias and profession, paying triple the normal passage. Halfway to Sevastopol, Adamos announced the ship was going to Balaklava, saying Sevastopol was too dangerous because of street gangsters. I believe Balaklava was always his destination.

3a. Arrived Balaklava Bay at 2 a.m. 24 March 1919. *Philos* immediately offloaded several tons of grain from the holds and then approximately 250 crates of Enfield rifles and ammunition and 50 crates of canned foods that were hidden beneath the grain.

   Adamos admitted all the cargo was destined as prepositioned supplies for the Bolshevik forces of General Dybenko, which are about to invade the Crimea from the Ukraine. Dybenko is said to work for Dmitry Ulyanov, brother of Vladimir Lenin.

3b. I disembarked later that evening and found the town of Balaklava (at the head of a narrow, winding bay) in a state of tense paranoia. Local government is a gang of thugs in uniform who accept bribes. I was instantly marked as a foreigner and targeted for robbery. This came to a head late that night while I was seeking lodging. Three armed men drove up in a truck and attempted to drag me onto the cargo bed. I broke free and used my Colt pistol, resulting in three KIAs and the acquisition of a truck with a full tank of gasoline.

   The shots woke the neighborhood, and an angry mob filled the street as I tried to crank the truck engine. The truck started just in time, enabling me to outpace the mob, find the main road (a muddy rural lane) heading northerly toward Sevastopol, and flee Balaklava.

4a. The distance to Sevastopol was much farther than the eight miles Adamos told me, and the route much rougher. The truck's left front wheel tie-rod broke on the outskirts of Sevastopol at dawn on 25 March 1919, just as a police patrol saw me and stopped.

   They didn't seem to know about the episode in Balaklava, but I was searched. The Colt pistol was found and I was taken to the local police post. I demanded to see the senior officer, who turned out to be an aged lieutenant named Grigori Gornyak. I insisted—through pantomime and pidgin English-Russian—that Gornyak accept my generous donation to his family's welfare as a token of heartfelt Christian brotherhood. We became instant friends when I told my cover story about dealing in opium and prostitution. Several vodkas later I got the Colt and the truck back, but he warned me against going into Sevastopol because there were many dangerous scoundrels there.

I thanked him and suggested he might furnish me or my friends further information in the future—for money, naturally. He agreed without hesitation, having already done such a service for a middle-aged Englishman named Sidney a month earlier. He thought Sidney had Russian roots and was pro-Tsarist. He hadn't seen Sidney since.

Gornyak pushed me to go east along the coast, where I would find many "nice places" (his exact meaning was unclear). I headed east in the truck and drove on the coast road for an hour, then turned and headed northwest over the hill country toward Sevastopol.

33

Report of Capt. S. P. Wake, USN—Part Two

4b. I arrived at the Sevastopol docks at 7:30 p.m. on 26 March 1919 on foot, having abandoned the truck hours earlier when it ran out of fuel. The streets were filled with people of all descriptions and accents, many of them coughing from influenza but very few wearing masks or taking any of the precautions normal in the West. Practically no police or military were in sight, which I thought ominous. The anchorage was mostly empty, with only a French destroyer and light cruiser and three freighters at anchor. One Russian and a few Romanian- and Bulgarian-flagged merchant ships were at the docks, their gangways guarded by armed crewmen. I spoke with the ships' captains, but each informed me he was taking no passengers. I got directions to the telegraph office and discovered the cable lines out of the Crimea were down. For a few kopeks the clerk allowed me to spend the night on a bench inside.

4c. For the next two days I walked the city gathering information. Most people seemed to believe the Red Army will soon invade the Crimea after victories in mainland Ukraine. Three days later, the Third Red Ukrainian Army under General Khudyakov arrived in northern Crimea, pushed south rapidly, and overwhelmed the Crimean defense forces under the overall command of pro-democracy Prime Minister Solomon Krym. The White Russian forces didn't offer support because their commander, General Denikin, has a personal dispute with Krym. Simferopol in central Crimea fell to the Reds on 2 April. Sevastopol was paralyzed by total panic; Krym's government fled into the mountains ahead of thousands of Red Army soldiers who arrived in Sevastopol the next day. They linked up with local Bolsheviks who were waiting for them. The British battleship HMS *Marlborough*, a superdreadnought of the *Iron Duke* class, anchored in the harbor with her escorts, but the British ships remained far out and allowed no one to come on board. Her reason for being in the harbor was unclear.

Hope of finding a ship in Sevastopol having evaporated, I decided to leave the only way possible—on foot.

4d. HMS *Marlborough* departed at noon on 6 April 1919, destination unknown. Barely evading detection by Red Army street patrols, I joined the tail end of a column of Tartar Muslim refugees walking out of Sevastopol the evening of 6 April 1919. We followed the general route the Krym government had taken to the northeast.

Eleven hours after we started in central Sevastopol, the column stopped at the Palace of the Khan, who ruled the Crimea under the Ottoman Empire until the Russians arrived in the late 1700s. The refugees seemed to think Ottomans from Constantinople would help them, out of a sense of cultural and religious duty.

After resting for half a day, in the afternoon of 8 April I left the very kind Tartars, who truly lived by the Q'uran's teachings—feeding and lodging this foreigner in their midst—and walked southeast, ironically toward the same coast where Lieutenant Gornyak had directed me a week earlier. My intention was to get to White Russian—or at least neutral—territory somewhere on the coast and find passage on a departing ship. The Tartars remained at the Khan's Palace, but an ethnic Russian family who had been a part of our group took the same road, although remaining some way behind me.

4e. A mile into my solitary trek, and out of sight of anyone else, they hurried their pace and approached me. The man cautiously called out to me, in English, "May we walk with you?" He explained he was a former Russian naval officer and introduced me to his wife and seven-year-old daughter. The little girl had a constant dry cough, a potential sign she was infected with the influenza.

After a bit more cautious chitchat, we revealed our true identities. The Russian knew my father and proved to be a pleasant companion and valuable guide as we trudged along.

4f. We crested the mountains and descended toward the coast, stopping to rest at Chufut-Kale. Although the ancient cave village appeared to be deserted, it wasn't. My Russian friend discerned another party of escapees hiding in the ruins and went over to talk with them. He used a gesture known to Freemasons, and one of the others did so in reply. Soon their chief appeared, and he too gave the sign and countersign. An animated dialogue ensued, and I was summoned. Through my father's connections with the Masonic world, I was vouchsafed a "son of a friend" of Masonry. That trust went two ways, of course, so I revealed my real name, profession, and nationality to the stranger. This led to the most candid conversation I had in Russia.

The headman of the group was none other than the deposed Crimean prime minister, Solomon Krym, en route to his dacha on the Black Sea at Feodosia, seventy miles away in eastern Crimea. The three of us spoke in English. Krym said to me right away, "Captain Wake, obviously your mission is to quietly see what is happening in this part of Russia. Good, I hope you do. America needs to know, for you have chosen to become part of it with your invasions of Russia at Murmansk and Vladivostok."

He had a kind and tired face, but his reference to America's "invasions" in the northern and eastern coasts was pointed. His eyes bored into me as he continued. "*Nothing* hopeful is happening here. People are continuing to die from the influenza because of ignorance and lack of medical help. The various factions in Russia—the Green armies wanting local independence, the White armies wanting a new Tsar to take over and restart the Russian Empire, the Red armies wanting to abolish anything remotely resembling imperial Russia, and the anarchists who want no governments at all—will continue killing each other, and anyone caught in between them, for years.

The Reds will eventually control all of Russia, plunging the country into darkness. Too much blood has already been shed for forgiveness and reconciliation. Now there is only paranoia and ruthlessness. The time for talking and listening is over. Intelligent people are getting out."

My Russian naval friend sadly nodded his agreement. Krym grasped my hand firmly and said, "American, you are in great danger. Because your country has invaded Russia, you Americans are considered enemies by the Reds. Your Russian friend and his family are also in danger. His resemblance to the royal family is unmistakable, and the Reds will surely kill him for that. You must get south to the imperial summer palace at Livadia in Yalta—quickly. Go now. There are members of the royal family there who may have the means to get you out. The Reds are just behind us."

I glanced at my friend, thinking he would be pleased and relieved that his blueblood family was so close. But he just stared impassively at Krym.

"But listen to me well, Captain Wake," Krym continued. "Even at Livadia you must trust *no one*. This information is all I can do for all of you. May you have good luck. Maybe I will see you in Paris someday. *Bonne chance*."

His depressing monologue done, Krym walked back to his group and led them off on a crude path toward Feodosia. We returned to trudging south on the main road, toward Yalta and the Tsar's surviving family. My naval friend finally admitted to me that he was uncertain how his relatives would receive him, for there had been disagreements in the past. Clearly, however, we had no other choice.

34

Report of Capt. S. P. Wake, USN—Part Three

5a. We arrived in Yalta in midafternoon on 9 April. As in Sevastopol, refugees thronged the streets, but these people seemed of a higher class; many wore elegant clothing and looked condescendingly at the poorly dressed locals. We saw dozens of expensive automobiles that had been abandoned when they ran out of gasoline.

The docks and harbor were no less crowded, although strong winds and a sizable surge made the water too rough for small boats. And here we discovered HMS *Marlborough*'s destination. She sat smugly at anchor under the lee of the breakwater, surrounded by a swarm of small boats on the verge of capsizing from the weight of the people and baggage packed into them. Royal Navy sailors were fending most of them off with pikes, although a very few were allowed to tie up and unload their passengers. People jammed the pier gazing in desperation at the British warship, their possible rescuer, so close and yet too far.

My friend and I conferred on how to get to the ship and be allowed to board. It was every man for himself ashore. No Russian police or military were keeping order. I saw no routine landing station set up from *Marlborough*, which made sense because one would quickly be overwhelmed. The few Russian bumboats remaining at the pier were crowded with people who were shoving others aside or overboard. We would have to find a boat elsewhere, and I knew that the price demanded would be more than we carried. That left armed coercion.

5b. At a small dock a hundred yards away, we found a small skiff that had just come back empty from *Marlborough*. The crowd saw it as well, however, and rushed toward us. I jumped down into the boat and held my Colt on the crew as my friend helped his wife in and then lowered their daughter into her arms. He jumped in himself, dodging a kick from a man wearing formal attire. The angry crowd pelted us with rocks and bricks. My friend fired a shot above the crowd that stopped them for a moment. The crew, terrified by my large revolver, pulled frantically at the oars.

At *Marlborough*'s gangway, my friend called his rank, royal title, and name in English. I called out my rank and name also, for I considered the order to remain clandestine no longer valid. The officer of the deck didn't hear us over the shrieks of people begging to board, but a grizzled boatswain's mate did and growled permission to come on board. Once we were on the main deck he examined our disheveled appearance closely, shook his head, and appeared ready to send us back when a voice on the starboard bridge called out my friend's name in perfect Oxford-accented English.

It was a very timely intervention by Prince Felix Youssoupoff, a cousin of my friend, who was also a prince, though further down the line of succession. Felix bounded down the ladders and ran up to embrace his cousin. Hugely relieved, our bedraggled group was led to a junior officer's stateroom.

That night, bathed and wearing borrowed clothing, we dined with the other minor royals in the junior officers' mess. The conversations in Russian were beyond me, but the relief and joy of the speakers were clear.

5c. *Marlborough* got under way for Constantinople on 11 April. During the voyage I met Empress Marie, mother of Tsar Nicholas. She was the senior royal on the ship and a very strong-willed lady. She appeared genuinely concerned about evacuating all the wounded White Russian soldiers and the civilians from Sevastopol. Grand Duke Nicholas, a six-foot-six giant with a voice as deep as death itself, was the most impressive. He turned out to be genial, kind, and generous, and profoundly grateful for my assistance to my new friend. N.B.: Both he and Prince Youssoupoff would be excellent ONI contacts.

We spent several days at Halki Island just south of Constantinople in the Sea of Marmara. The situation in Turkey had further deteriorated, and we did not go ashore. The number of royals seeking refuge had risen from the dozen or so the British had planned to take to more than a hundred. The battleship HMS *Lord Nelson* took some of them on board and headed for Genoa. *Marlborough* departed on 18 April for Malta, and arrived on 20 April.

5d. Assessment of situation in Crimea:

The Crimea, and all of southern Russia, is now in total anarchy, with the Red Bolsheviks (who themselves have many competing internal factions and leadership personalities) in the ascendency. Solomon Krym's concise summation is the best for the present and the near future. The Reds are willing to use brute force to attain their ends, unmitigated by any moral or religious restraint. The war has destroyed the main grain-producing and cattle areas of southern and central Russia, and famine has already started in parts of the south.

The monarchy will never return, in either autocratic or modern constitutional form. The excesses of the past have led most Russians to distrust all royals.

There is no chance for democracy. That takes an educated public, and the peasants and city workers are largely illiterate. Only academics, shopkeepers, and bureaucrats have any sort of education. The majority of the population is easy prey for demagogues.

The average peasant and worker distrusts or outright hates Americans for invading their nation.

The average educated Russian appreciates the charity food supplies beginning to arrive but is also angry about the presence of American armed forces in their country.

My recommendation for American policy in Russia:

A. Evacuate all American ground forces from northern and eastern Russia immediately.

B. Keep a minimum of naval assets in the Black Sea for humanitarian evacuations, but avoid confrontations and stop all shore liberty for crews.

C. Do not be seen as supporting a return of the monarchy.

D. Continue and expand the charity food distribution to civilians and somehow prevent armed factions from diverting the supplies for themselves, a difficult proposition. This will generate more goodwill than anything else we can do.

E. Do not officially recognize or support the Bolsheviks (or their various subgroups), but deal practically with them on matters of mutual need.

F. Stay out of this political/military quagmire. Wait to see what happens. Stay neutral toward Russia's civil war. America cannot dictate or even influence the outcome. Neither can the western European powers. Only the Russians can decide their long-term future. It appears it will be a dark period for a long time.

6a. At Malta, my Russian friend and his family and I disembarked HMS *Marlborough* and immediately got passage on the P&O passenger steamer *Chanda* leaving that evening for Southampton, England, along with several of the minor royals. Arrived there on 28 April 1919 after a stormy passage, unavoidably after my ordered reporting date. My Russian friend embarked with his family the next day for America on a Cunard ship. I immediately reported on board U.S. Naval Station London and am sending this report by secure wireless to Assistant Secretary of the Navy F. D. Roosevelt.

Respectfully submitted on 28 April 1919,
Captain S. P. Wake, USN, London Naval Station

35

Like Father, Like Son

Grunt Bone Lane
Key West, Florida

Friday, 1 May 1919

Appended to the last page of my son's report was a handwritten postscript note, also from Franklin Roosevelt:

PW,

You now know that I provided some bureaucratic cover to SPW's endeavor, making it a clandestine assessment of the situation at Constantinople and the Crimea, but without usual USN support. You also will have discerned that the unnamed Russian is your old friend who guided your 1905 escape. SPW omitted details that would have identified several non-naval personnel involved in their meeting and subsequent escape.

While SPW was late in reporting at his new assignment, the admiral in command (whom you once knew as a rising subordinate) was still glad to have him on board. The promotion to RADM had already been approved by Congress and was thus not affected. It became official yesterday, 30 April 1919. For the next year, SPW will serve as Commander, Patrol Force Europe. He will be the last officer in that billet, as we are reducing our postwar naval establishment in Europe. Then he will get a long-deserved shoreside tour on the General Board in WDC.

Congratulations, my friend, on raising a son with the same character, innovation, and strength as his father. The USN and the USA are the better for both of you. I know TR would have loved hearing about this adventure.

FDR

P.S. Don't forget to burn all of this after reading!

A wave of pride surged through me on reading Franklin's praise of my son. But I knew Sean Peter hadn't put everything that happened in that report—that kind of information would shock the comfortably naïve Washington leadership. Did my son have to resort to sordid methods to perpetuate his façade? Did he have to use violence to save his life, or those of Sergei and his family? I certainly had in my missions. Someday, he and I would talk, as only those who share those experiences can without being appalled.

I looked over to Commander Barnett, still sipping his iced tea as he watched a mockingbird singing in the jacaranda tree across the street. "Where is the original report, Ross?"

"On the Wake Shelf in the back of the secret section inside the ONI vault, sir. Only a few officers and senior clerks have access to that area. I'm one of them."

"The Wake *Shelf*? I know my reports are kept in the vault, but what's this about a shelf?"

Barnett smiled. "Admiral, your reports over the decades have been kept on their own filing shelf since your retirement in 1909. Your son's many reports to ONI, mostly about fighting guerillas in the Philippines and warlords in China, are kept there also. The Wake Shelf is about fifteen linear feet of intelligence reports from around the world dating back to your first report from South America to Admiral Walker in 1881. It's the first place ONI looks when we need information on some far corner of the world."

He said that with a touch of awe, and I must admit I felt grateful my work was still useful to someone. "How many of these files have you read?"

The big grin I remembered from twenty years ago on *Dixon* spread across Barnett's face. "All of them, Admiral. So has Secretary Roosevelt. In fact,

I'm told every director of the Office of Naval Intelligence and most assistant secretaries of the Navy read the entire Wake Shelf as soon as they're sworn in."

That was a surprise. "Well, how about that? I never knew. . . ."

Barnett pulled out a box of matches. "Time to burn all this, sir."

"Go ahead. I need to tell María the good news, and then we'll meet you at the firepit out back."

María was alone in our bedroom, rigid with fear. I embraced her. "Darling, it's the best news possible. Sean Peter is in London, safe and well, and has received his promotion to rear admiral. Sergei and his wife and daughter are on their way to America from Britain. I hope we'll get to see them. But right now, Ross Barnett and I need to burn the report in the firepit, so come join us."

We went into the backyard and sat around the firepit while Barnett burned every paper in the file, then the folder itself. I couldn't keep the emotion from my voice as I looked at the charred papers and said to María, "The details will always be secret, my dear, but our son did very well."

Through her tears, María murmured, "Of course he did, Peter! I never doubted that he would. Thank God he is safe."

As María sobbed on my shoulder, an embarrassed Barnett walked into the house. "And now you can tell the family and I can cable Rork the good news—everyone's safe and our lad is promoted to rear admiral!"

She kissed me gently. "Like father, like son. . . ."

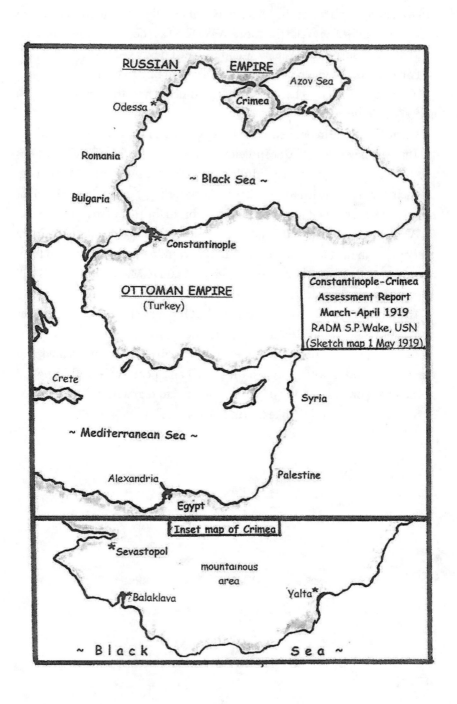

RUSSIAN EMPIRE

Azov Sea

Odessa *

Crimea

Romania

~ Black Sea ~

Bulgaria

* Constantinople

OTTOMAN EMPIRE
(Turkey)

Constantinople–Crimea
Assessment Report
March–April 1919
RADM S.P.Wake, USN
(Sketch map 1 May 1919)

Crete

Syria

~ Mediterranean Sea ~

Alexandria

Palestine

Egypt

Inset map of Crimea

*Sevastopol

mountainous
area

*Balaklava

Yalta*

~ Black   Sea ~

36

The Better Part of Duty

Grunt Bone Lane
Key West, Florida

Friday, 1 May 1919

"Telegram!" Less than an hour had passed when we heard Miguelito on our verandah. The messenger boy from the telegraph office was a great favorite of María's, who gave him a cookie and a big hug whenever he delivered a telegram; I always added a nice tip for his prompt and cheerful service.

María and I sat on the love seat and tore open the envelope. The cable was from Sean Peter in London, sent the day before. Typical of personal cables, which were notoriously expensive, it was terse and abbreviated.

XXX—AT LNDON ALL WELL—X—FRND & FAMLY SAFE IN TRANSITUSA—X—MY PROMO TO RADM TODAY—XXX

We had cabled the good news to Rork as soon as Barnett finished burning the report.

XXX—SEAN PETER IS WELL IN LONDON & PROMOTED TO RADM—X—SERGEI & FAMILY WELL & HEADING TO

USA—X—INCREDIBLE STORY—X—LETS MEET SERGEI AFTER
ARRIVAL—X—A GRAND LIBERTY ASHORE IS CALLED FOR—X—
THE RUM LAMP IS LIT—XXX

His duty done, Barnett said, "Admiral, I'm afraid I have to catch the afternoon train, so I'll take my leave now, if I may. It was wonderful to see you
again, and to be able to give you good news."

As I stood up to bid him farewell, twenty years melted away. I was back in
command. Barnett was one of *my men*. There were so many over the years,
thousands of them, on warships large and small around the world. Shipmates
with that tight bond formed between those who have gone to sea and seen
the majesty and the terrors of nature and men. Moments of joy and fear and
sorrow and victory, shared by all ranks. Remembered forever. This was one
of those moments of victory.

"Commander Barnett, the afternoon train doesn't get under way until two
p.m., and it's now only eleven," I said. "So, for the next three hours, the three
of us are going to celebrate with the best seafood and rum you've ever tasted,
over at Paula Streeter's place near the San Carlos Institute on Duval Street.
Consider that a direct order, son. And don't worry, that train won't move an
inch without you. The station master is a friend of mine."

It took Ross Barnett all of five seconds to decide discretion was the better
part of duty, so we did exactly that. The three hours of hilarious sea stories
(some of which even María hadn't heard) and delicious lobster, shrimp, and
crab, went too quickly. At precisely two o'clock, a grinning Ross Barnett
boarded the train's first-class car (courtesy of the station master), straightened
up to render me a perfect salute of farewell, and chugged off to the internecine
wars of Washington.

37
The Telegram

Grunt Bone Lane
Key West, Florida

Thursday, 15 May 1919

Sergei and his family headed south for Key West right after disembarking *Caronia* at New York City. Our tropical island was a place of wonder to them, especially after their nightmarish ordeals in war-torn Russia. Sergei's wife Natalya and daughter Katya begged him to make the island their permanent home.

The money they had used to escape Russia and get to America was rapidly running out, however, and Sergei needed income. Fortunately, Key West is a seaport and Sergei an experienced seaman fluent in several languages, including English. So I secured a job for him as a mate on a schooner carrying fruit and tobacco between Key West, Havana, and Tampa. His family lived in a small bungalow on Sawyer Lane, by the shipyard.

Both to fit into American culture and to make it easier for their new friends, they changed their last name, Dyvoryanin, to its English equivalent: Noble. I thought it a very good play on words. Although his appearance and manner marked him as an aristocrat, nobody in town suspected his close relationship to Russian royalty, which was just as well, for not even a tiny island at the end of a road to nowhere was completely safe from the Bolsheviks' revenge.

Rork, who'd made a new life in America almost sixty years earlier, and Clotilda were coming in late June to celebrate the Noble family's arrival and my eightieth birthday. Useppa and Mario were coming from Tampa, and Filipa (now Mrs. *Rear Admiral* Sean Peter Wake!) and Robert would come down with the Rorks. Things were looking up from those dark days of March and April. For the first time in a long time, I was looking forward to my birthday.

Then, on the ides of May, our young friend Miguelito arrived on the verandah with a telegram from Clotilda. Its simplicity was ominous.

XXX—SEAN SICK—X—COME NOW—XXX

I didn't need to think about what to reply: "We're coming." Miguelito, who had delivered bad news before, nodded sadly and hurried back to the telegraph office to send the message.

Suddenly I was twenty-four again and Sean was in his early thirties, both of us in Navy blue. We were at the Navy pier right here on this island, meeting for the first time in the middle of the Civil War—two young men who instantly recognized one another as friends. That vision of a young, strong, smart Rork brought many other memories. And they brought tears that wouldn't stop.

María came out onto the verandah, sat down next to me, and read the cable. After giving me a hard hug, she went inside to pack our bags.

38

Weighing Anchor

Washington, D.C.

Monday, 18 May 1919

C lotilda flung open the door when we got to their apartment. "He's in bed. You made it just in time. I'm sorry," she said apologetically, "but Sean absolutely forbade me to let you know sooner. Said there was nary a thing you could do anyway. You know how he gets, Peter." She paused to compose herself, then said, "When he said, 'It's time, my sweet girl,' I sent the cable."

We told her we understood and hugged her. I went in alone to the bedroom where he lay in the late afternoon shadows, a single track of sunlight crossing the bed. The man before me was an emaciated shadow of the Rork I had seen just two months ago in March. His India-rubber hand with the concealed spike was on the side table, too big now for his thin forearm stump. His cheeks were hollow, his eyes sunken.

But the voice was the same, the strong Rork of vicious battles and perilous storms and grand liberties ashore. And for a moment the old devilish grin emerged. "Well, me heart's happy ye made it in time, old friend, for I'm makin' ready to slip me moorin' an' get under way for Fiddler's Green. Hopin' it'll be a broad reach with a fair tide. Sorry I'll miss your birthday, but I'll hoist one for you when I reach topside."

I took his right hand in mine. "How do you know it's time, Sean?"

"'Cause me sawbones an' me priest both agreed for the first time since I've known 'em. An' truth be told, me ancient heart an' bones're ready for the voyage. I'm tired o' bein' sick, Peter. I'll miss Clotilda mightily, but I'll be waitin' when she arrives. Aye, an' won't that be a grand reunion."

To counter the sad mood, I tried our repartee of sixty long years. "Just make sure you're there when *I* arrive, you old goat, and not in some bar somewhere in the seedy side of Heaven. And don't do anything to get thrown out. I've heard Saint Peter has no sense of humor."

His voice was losing its strength now, the grin beginning to fade, but the old humor was still there. "Well, me boyo, rest assured I'll be on me very best behavior, seein' as how I'll be representin' Uncle Sam's blessed Navy an' all."

He took in a ragged breath and went on. "An' besides, 'tis well known God loves dogs an' Irishmen. But what makes you think a heathen such as yourself can get into Heaven I don't know. The Lord is a Catholic, and he mayn't think highly o' *that* intrusion."

That made me laugh. "Because God loves even us lowly Methodists too, Sean. He must, because he brought the two of us together sixty years ago. He needed somebody He could trust to get you out of trouble."

Sean squeezed my hand and sighed, his voice now almost a whisper. "Aye, that He did. We made a good partnership, didn't we, Peter? Did good work for ol' Uncle Sam."

My own voice faltered. "Yes, we did, Sean."

"An' Useppa an' Sean Peter turned out just fine. Linda would be so proud 'uv 'em. Thank ye for lettin' me into your family. 'Twas a great joy for me."

"And for me and them, Sean. And now you're blessed to have Clotilda."

María and Clotilda came into the room. María stood beside my chair, her hand on my shoulder. Clotilda sat on the other side of the bed and held Sean's left forearm. Her eyes misted and shining, she leaned forward to kiss him on his lips, and murmured, "I love you, Sean."

"An' I . . . love . . . you . . . me . . . darlin' girl." Then, after another shallow inhale, "Time . . . to . . . weigh anchor. . . ."

I didn't think I had any more tears left, but I did. I whispered in his ear, "Bon voyage, my dearest friend. . . ."

My friend's eyes lost what little light was left in them and closed. There was another sigh, and his hand went limp in mine. There was nothing else to say or do. It was over.

Sean Aloysius Rork had departed on his final and greatest voyage.

39

On Behalf of a Grateful Nation

Arlington National Cemetery

Wednesday, 21 May 1919

T he funeral was the first one of the day at the cemetery—there were so many those days with the dead still being returned from the Great War in Europe—and commenced just as the sun was rising over the misty Potomac. The Washington Monument stood tall and proud in the amber light. *Rork would appreciate that. It was his favorite sight in the city.*

The procession, in dress whites, formed near the Civil War Unknowns section and moved at the slow march for the five hundred yards to the burial site. Useppa and Mario, Filipa and Robert, Clotilda and her friends, and María, Patricia, and I walked behind the limber and caisson carrying Rork's casket draped with the national ensign. A Navy honor detail led by Cdr. Ross Barnett guarded the casket, and a naval chaplain-priest walked with us chanting softly in Latin.

Behind us was a somber gray-haired contingent of the senior petty officers of the U.S. Navy—Rork's old friends. Astern of them was a gold-sleeved array of senior and flag officers and many retired officers, led by Assistant

Secretary of the Navy Franklin Roosevelt. So many old familiar faces. So many memories.

A small Navy band was waiting at a discreet distance from the grave as the procession arrived. The ceremony was concise. A prayer by the chaplain, then the liturgy for the dead, and verses 23 to 31 of Psalm 107. The band played the Navy Hymn, "Eternal Father, Strong to Save," as the senior chief petty officers and many of the old officers sang along. "Amazing Grace," not a Roman Catholic hymn but one of Rork's favorites, was played and sung next. Then came three volleys from the seven rifles of the firing party, followed by the lone trumpeter sounding Taps.

And finally, the honor guard folded and presented the national ensign to Rear Adm. Victor Blue, Chief of the Bureau of Navigation, who in turn presented it to Clotilda with the time-honored words: "On behalf of the president of the United States of America, and a grateful nation, please accept this flag as a symbol of our appreciation for your loved one's honorable and faithful naval service in forty-eight years of peace and war."

The casket was lowered into the grave. The ceremony ended. All hands were dismissed. My friend had been sent off as he had told me several times he wanted to be, in "proper friggin' naval fashion," at the place he held dear, by the nation that had welcomed him so many years before. The attendees began drifting away. But Mrs. Clotilda Rork remained where she was, clutching the ensign to her chest, her eyes on the casket.

I started to go to her, but María, who'd been widowed herself decades earlier, told me to give her a moment. After a while, María nodded and I went to Clotilda, gently saying, "It's time to leave, my dear." We turned and walked away from her husband and my best friend.

It was the hardest thing I've ever done.

40
Anno Horribilis

Grunt Bone Lane
Key West, Florida

Monday, 1 December 1919

I write this on the first day of the last month of a horrible year. After the loss of my friend Theodore, then my dearest friend Sean, I sank into profound melancholia. María, who had endured the depths of grief for her dead first husband and then her murdered son, understood how I felt and allowed me to grieve. After a couple of black weeks, she gently tried to refocus my mind on more positive things and change my mood. But the ensuing events of 1919 only reinforced my depression.

In May, my son's prediction for Constantinople and Turkey proved true. Atatürk declared a new nation—secular, patriotic, modern, and free of the choking bonds of the Ottomans. His zeal rallied the people to him and against foreigners, including minorities who had been there for centuries and foreign powers who were there now. The American Navy flotilla stationed there was increased, and the officers did their best to help refugees without starting a new conflict with one or the other of the sides in the raging civil war.

My son's predictions for Russia also proved true. But sadly, his recommendations were not heeded; 11,000 American troops stayed in north Russia and east Russia. Hundreds were killed, wounded, or sickened as they fought the Bolsheviks while wondering why they were there.

On 6 June, our darling nine-year-old granddaughter Agnes came down with the Spanish influenza. Patricia and Charles were terrified because so many children had died of it. We were granted a miracle, though. After being dreadfully sick for two weeks—wheezing and gasping for breath—she got better, although the doctor warned us that her lungs would never completely recover.

The day he gave that prognosis, the peace treaty was signed at Versailles, ending the war President Wilson told us would end all wars. María and I knew better, of course. The treaty imposed draconian penalties on the losers, divided the world between the British and French, and came up with an idea first espoused by Theodore Roosevelt years earlier: an international forum to resolve disputes without bloodshed. Wilson, over in Europe negotiating with hard-eyed and stone-hearted men, called it the League of Nations and got the Europeans to go for it. But he couldn't convince our own Congress to agree.

As a reward for fighting as one of the Allies, Japan was given many of the captured German colonial island groups in the Central Pacific—the Marshalls, Marianas, and Carolines—as well as the German enclave at Tsingtao, China. I had no doubt the Japanese would fortify them, to our eventual peril, but by then no one in Washington listened to my opinions.

June did have one bright note: Congress finally passed an amendment to allow women to vote, and I am proud to say all of the men in our family were happy about it. The right to vote was especially meaningful for María, who cherished her American citizenship and now beheld our daily hoist of the national ensign with even more pride.

My eightieth birthday on 26 June was a subdued affair. Telegrams arrived from old friends around the world and former subordinates (all my former superiors were gone), and island friends stopped by for brief visits. My family arrived from Tampa and Washington, including dear Clotilda, and a long table was set up on the verandah for the dinner. The sound of children playing and women laughing echoed through the place in the afternoon, but all hands quieted as we sat down.

One place setting had a photograph portrait of Sean Rork and half a glass of Matusalem rum. This was María's idea as a tribute to the man she knew I—all of us—missed so much. Clotilda and I shed some tears and then launched into Rork stories. Naturally, I shared only the ones suitable for polite company. The evening of memories ended early at ten o'clock—for Sean wasn't there to keep it going any later.

The summer was long and hot, a portentous prelude to a giant hurricane that struck Key West on the tenth of September after ravaging the Bahamas. We had two days' warning from the Weather Service, and Charles and I got both homes shuttered and battened down while our wives stocked provisions and water. The houses survived the storm, but not without damage beyond our abilities to repair, especially since I'd strained my back during our preparations. So we used an old seamanship jury-rig remedy and fothered the roofs with greased tarpaulins while waiting for a carpenter to properly repair them. That took two weeks.

Worst of all, our beloved *Libertad* was crushed and sunk at her dock by a 237-foot steam yacht (one of several owned by a notorious Wall Street mogul) that had dragged her anchor for a quarter mile. We had no insurance. The mogul's insurance company declared it an act of God and refused to pay for our loss. A lawyer friend advised me the mogul's attorneys would drag out the case, force me to pay high legal costs, and probably win in court anyway. I was already exhausted by our storm recovery efforts, so *Libertad*'s remains ended up the property of salvors.

In early October, President Wilson was incapacitated by a stroke. The news was kept from the public by his wife Edith, his Navy doctor, and his cabinet. Vice President Marshall, whom Wilson despised (and I liked), was thwarted from assuming any authority. I heard about all this through ONI sources in Washington. It didn't take long for the word to get out, however, and the cover-up made the situation even worse. I was no fan of Wilson, but as a Christian I wished him no harm. The monetary inflation, financial uncertainty, political rancor, international tensions, and rise of racist violence toward black people across the country demanded public national leadership. There was none, however, and the Wilson administration's façade became a sad and ever-worsening joke.

Later in October things declined even further, for the fools in Congress passed the Eighteenth Amendment to the Constitution, prohibiting alcohol sales in America. Rork and I had known it was coming sooner or later and heartily lamented the prospect, usually over several glasses of rum. "Damned uncivilized," Rork grumbled. "Foolish," I said. "It'll make people criminals."

The draconian law would take effect the following January, so the interim was filled with even more drunken disorderliness than Key West usually saw. Many of Key West's Abaconians—immigrants from Abaco in the Bahamas— were teetotalers anyway and applauded the new regulation. Our Methodist church was quietly divided on the subject. The Cubans on the island thought it a ridiculous gringo rule, but a wonderful opportunity for enterprise. With a wink and a nod, they assured locals they would take care of any need. And they did.

The depressing litany of events was relieved by a spectacular event: at 8:23 a.m. on Saturday, 22 November, the moon crossed the face of the sun, creating an annular solar eclipse that lasted for almost ten minutes. The family gathered with other islanders—drinkers and otherwise—at the railroad dock on the harbor front and watched the show.

Agnes was absolutely mesmerized by it, asked me all sorts of questions, and afterward declared she would be an astronomer when she grew up. The rest of the family chuckled, but I had no doubt she would do exactly that and beamed with delight at my granddaughter. Clearly, she would chart her own course through life.

Part 2

Honor's Legacy

The previous chapter was Rear Adm. Peter Wake's last entry in his memoir. But the story of Wake and his family doesn't end there, for his legacy of honorable service to country lived on.

Part Two: "Honor's Legacy," tells of the final days of Wake's life and the future naval service of his family, as compiled from family letters, others' correspondence, and official reports. In a return to the literary viewpoint of the first six novels of the Honor Series, it is narrated in the third person by the author.

41

The Smile

Key West, Florida

Sunday, 4 July 1920

W ake spent the winter and spring months of the new year peacefully with his darling María. She had slowed down a bit, as was to be expected of a lady of seventy-five, but the admiral had declined noticeably. The many wounds and ailments suffered over the decades and the emotional turmoil of 1918 and 1919 had taken their toll on him. His limp grew more pronounced, his shoulders and arms less limber, and his attitude more subdued.

"I hate being in this condition," he told María. "Long past time to correct it."

His solution was predictable: address it head-on with more exercise. Accordingly, he began each morning at sunrise by walking with María, first to the Navy pier to survey the warships at Man-o-War Anchorage, then along busy Duval Street to the San Carlos Institute to take a *cafécito* with his Cuban friends. The strong, flavorful Cuban coffee served in a small cup with a tiny stick of sugarcane came with many *abrazos*, the Cuban version of a bear hug, for some of these men were comrades-in-arms who had served alongside Peter in desperate battle or shadowy espionage against the Spanish twenty-two years before. All honored him for his part in the long struggle for Cuba's freedom. The return route went along the shaded back streets to the market on Eaton Street for María to select fresh produce. Passing friends said hello all along the way, for the admiral and his lady were well known.

Once they walked all the way to the African cemetery on the south shore beach where he had married Linda in 1864, close by the West Martello Tower fort. María knew the story of Peter's love affair with a local girl who was supposed to be a Confederate spy and ended up being his wife and the mother of Useppa and Sean Peter. María never tired of hearing it, just as Peter enjoyed hearing her talk about her first husband. Both knew they were blessed to have found each other later in life.

Afternoons were for tending their gardens. The Wakes' orchids were famous among Key West's many gardeners, as was the fruit they gave to friends, especially black sapote, the famed Caribbean "chocolate fruit." Evenings were spent stargazing or reading with a glass of wine, the gramophone playing softly in the background.

On Independence Day they hosted the traditional Wake family celebration of the event. Sean Peter, home from Europe, brought Filipa, Robert (now fifteen and setting his sights on the Naval Academy), and ten-year-old Ted. Useppa and Mario brought their sixteen-year-old daughter, Linda. A delightful surprise was the arrival of Linda's older brother, Ens. Peter Carlos Cano, commissioned only two weeks before. He was due to report for sea duty on USS *Florida* (BB 30), currently anchored right there at Key West, in three days. Patricia, Charles, and Agnes came from across the street, and Clotilda took the train south from Washington to join them. Sergei Noble and his family came over from their home three streets away.

Unlike the family's gathering for Peter's eightieth birthday the year before, this time there was no recent grief and the tone was far more upbeat. The admiral was in a good mood as he sat at his desk in the library writing to friends around the world. He did something different at ten o'clock that morning, though; he closed the door to his library after telling María that he was going to write the most important letter of his life. When she asked to whom, he grinned slyly and said, "I don't know. Never met them and never will. But it's important to me they read the letter."

An hour later, the letter—along with a shiny new silver dollar—was sealed in an envelope. María fully understood the importance of the letter when she saw what was written across the envelope in Peter's neat block lettering:

TO THE FIRST WAKE TO GRADUATE FROM
THE U.S. NAVAL ACADEMY AFTER 4 JULY 2020

"We'll show this to Sean Peter today," he told María, "so he knows when I'm gone to pass it along to his son, and then on to the next generations until that day comes. I think, or at least I hope, that if a Wake becomes a naval officer in the twenty-first century, he"—his eyes twinkled—"or she, you never know, might be interested in what this old seadog learned in the nineteenth century about the importance of honor."

Overcome with love for this man, María kissed his tanned, wrinkled cheek, murmuring, "I *know* it will be read with awe and gratitude, my darling."

At high noon, the entire clan gathered and the celebration began. From posing for the family Kodak photo to the afternoon's naval and civic parade down Duval Street, to the grilled lobster and shrimp and rice and beans at their home table, to the fireworks over the harbor and the late-night sea stories around the firepit in the patio garden, everyone had a wonderful time. Sitting hand in hand with María, Peter looked around the family circle with tired satisfaction.

He'd had to raise Useppa and Sean Peter without their mother after Linda died back in 1881 when they were teenagers. Peter had always felt he hadn't been as good a father as he should have been, remembering his feelings back then of inadequacy and despair. But looking at them smiling and laughing now in the firelight he felt vindicated—and profoundly appreciative—that they turned out just fine in spite of it all.

Another Fourth of July came to mind: the 1898 Battle of Santiago, when he and Rork were prisoners in a Spanish cruiser under fire from the American battleship where Sean Peter was serving. Against the odds, they'd all survived that perilous day. There had been so many perilous days in his career, yet here he was. He looked up at the stars beyond the mango tree and whispered, "Thank you."

"It has been more wonderful than you know to see you all," Peter said to them after he checked his watch and found it was already two in the morning.

"Somewhere, your Uncle Sean is proud that we're still partying so late, but my eighty-one-year-old bones are suddenly a bit tuckered out, so we're heading up for bed."

Sean Peter and Useppa heard a bit of a quaver in their father's voice as he stood up and added, "Please know I love every one of you so very much." And then the admiral in him had the last say. "And douse that fire properly before you leave the patio tonight."

He was not allowed to retire without a long session of hugs and kisses from his family, from the oldest to the very youngest, and also from the Noble family. Useppa and Sean Peter looked at each other and then hugged him with tears in their eyes. Both knew how much their beloved patriarch had enjoyed the gathering. And they sensed what he couldn't, or wouldn't, say: that it might be his last.

As they did every night in their bed, Peter and María kissed and said, "I love you," before switching off the lamp. The sounds of laughter in the patio continued for a while. Peter yawned, and his eyes closed. María smiled in the darkness. *He loved every minute of it*, she congratulated herself, for it was she who had orchestrated it all.

Peter startled her when he reached out to gently caress her face. "It's been such a great day, dear. Thank you, María, for everything you've done all these many years. You've filled my life with love. I just wish I had been a better husband."

She snuggled up to him. "Nonsense, Peter. You've been the very best husband and father and grandfather in all the world, and I love you with all my heart."

They said no more but stayed entwined for a long time. The moonlight filtering through the open window illuminated the ghost of a smile on his face. She heard the rhythm of his barely audible breathing like waves on a beach and felt the wrinkled old hand holding hers relax. *Thank you, God, for so many years with him,* she silently prayed, and then allowed sleep to quiet her thoughts.

A warm ray of light crossed the bed at dawn and woke María. By then Peter was usually awake and reading the morning paper on the verandah, ready to begin their walk. But this morning he was still lying next to her, with that same peaceful smile taking years off his face.

And she knew her husband was gone.

42

Full Naval Honors

Key West, Florida

Wednesday, 7 July 1920

The morning was soothingly cool for July in Key West, courtesy of a strong easterly wind, but the Methodist Episcopal church was warm from those crowded inside—men in Navy blue, civilians in black, and ladies and children in their Sunday best. The lovely church with its fragrant wood paneling wasn't large enough to hold them all, and the overflow extended down the steps and out into the street. Most were there because they knew the admiral; a few onlookers had come to witness the spectacle.

María Wake, surrounded by the family who had adopted her as their mother twenty-seven years earlier, sat in the first pew staring at the flag-draped casket before her with a slight smile on her face. She was lost in remembrances—of good times and bad—grieving, of course, but still wrapped in the love that had sustained her all those years. Beside María was her remaining son, Juanito, whose life Peter had saved in battle even though Juanito was the enemy. He was now forty-five and an esteemed Spanish diplomat with a family of his own, but he never forgot that day and had been devoted to his stepfather ever since.

Useppa and Sean Peter sat on her other side. Right behind them were their spouses and all the grandchildren. Sergei Noble and his family were there also, along with Miguelito the messenger boy and many other Key Westers of all ages and backgrounds who had become close to the family. Filling the opposite side of the aisle were the naval officers and petty officers, graying now and about to retire, who had served with Peter Wake over the years in peace and war. María was surprised and grateful when an elderly man with long gray hair and a van Dyke beard, still tall and dignified, entered the church. Col. Michael Woodgerd, Peter Wake's friend and comrade-in-arms for more than forty years, had made the long train trip from Alexandria to bid farewell to Peter. María insisted that he sit with the family.

Representatives of two groups who had tremendously influenced Wake's career and life sat together in the same pew, a remarkable demonstration of respect for the admiral: ten Freemasons and three Jesuit priests. Cuba was represented by its ambassador from Washington and the family of the late Major General Calixto García, Wake's dear friend and comrade from the days of combat against the Spanish at Santiago de Cuba.

As at Rork's, the funeral included the Navy Hymn, joined in resoundingly by the officers and sailors. The pastoral prayer that followed was centered on Psalm 107, verses 23 to 31—the same vivid poem recited at Rork's funeral. Presented by *Florida*'s chaplain, the words echoed through the hushed sanctuary. The lips of many seamen moved along with the chaplain's, for they knew it well and had lived it themselves.

They that go down to the sea in ships, that do business in great waters,

These see the works of the Lord, and His wonders in the deep.

For He commandeth and raiseth the stormy wind, which lifteth up the waves thereof.

They mount up to the heavens, they go down again to the depths; their soul is melted because of trouble.

They reel to and fro, and stagger like a drunken man, and are at their wits' end.

Then they cry unto the Lord in their trouble, and He bringeth them out of their distresses.

He maketh the storm a calm, so that the waves thereof are still.

Then they are glad because they be quiet; so he bringeth them unto their desired haven.

Oh that men would praise the Lord for His goodness, and for His wonderful works to the children of men!

The chaplain ended with a few simple words: "We Christians know that the worst thing is never the last thing when your faith is strong, for that personal will and God's grace ensure life eternal, just as it has for Admiral Wake. There is always a morning after every storm."

Sean Peter rose to give the eulogy. With voice resolutely firm he spoke of his father's early life, his globe-spanning naval career of forty-six years, his loving marriage to Linda and lifelong brotherhood with Sean Rork, the tragedies—personal and professional, the triumphs and accolades earned, his father's many friends of high and low station around the world, his friendship with Freemasonry and with the Jesuits, the lifesaving marriage to María, and his father's great affection for Key West and that church. Sean Peter ended with a message his father had asked to be read at his funeral.

Dear loved ones,

Do not grieve for me, for my mortal life was full. It was never boring, sometimes painful in flesh and spirit, and frequently full of joy. I have wonderful children and grandchildren. I have known the love of two beautiful, wise, strong, and devoted women. I have seen and rejoiced in the wonders of God on earth, the sea, and the sky. Now I am on my final voyage, following my friend Sean Rork, where new wonders and joys will be found. And I will await your arrival with smiles and laughter and song.

Do not grieve for me, for I am voyaging on a glorious broad reach with a steady wind, a fair current, and all sail set, onward and upward toward those distant horizons which we sailors know so well.

Do not grieve for me. Be happy that I am free and absolutely know that we will meet and laugh and love again. . . .

In love and peace,

Peter

Preceded by *Florida*'s band playing a dirge, two long lines of men in dress whites pulled the caisson holding the casket, Marines marching alongside, down Eaton Street and then up Duval to the Navy Pier. Hundreds watched from the sidewalks, doffing hats and placing hands over hearts as the long column passed by at the slow march.

At the pier, Freemason pipers of Dade Lodge 14 played "Amazing Grace" as the casket was lowered into a launch and taken out to *Florida*. The men and boys of the family, Sergei among them, followed in other boats. Decks of trading schooners and fishing sloops, and every warship in the harbor, were lined by bare-headed sailors solemnly facing the launch being rowed across the harbor. At the halfway point, the battleship slow-fired an admiral's salute of thirteen guns.

At María's request, she and the ladies and girls of the family watched the launch shove off from the pier and then walked back to the house. It was not a mournful walk, for María wanted bright and hopeful company, and stories of "Daddy" and "Grandpa" brightened sad faces.

Once the funeral party was on board *Florida*, she got under way out of the harbor, through the ship channel, and out into the Straits of Florida. She steamed at twenty knots to the point midway between Florida and Cuba, then reversed course and pointed her bow north toward America and stopped engines. Eight hundred officers and crew gathered on the after decks, trousers rippling in the stiff late afternoon wind.

On the port beam, the sun touched the horizon, lighting the summertime clouds pink and yellow and red as the powder blue sky darkened in the east. Rear Adm. Sean Peter Wake thought about his father's final message and pictured that indestructible spirit voyaging onward and upward toward those distant horizons. He glanced at the other men of the family. They were all gazing at the magnificent sunset, their faces glowing pink in the reflection.

The executive officer called all hands to attention as the honor platoon, body bearers, and firing party marched at the slow step into position on the afterdeck, below the barrels of the massive 12-inch gun turret. The casket, still shrouded with the national ensign, was laid atop a broad plank perpendicular to the railing. At just that moment the wind piped down to a small breeze and a shaft of sunlight reached through the clouds above the western horizon. Everyone noticed it, some gasped, but all remained silent.

Florida's commanding officer, an old classmate of Sean Peter's, stepped forward. "We are here to bury a true *sailor*," he said, "Rear Admiral Peter Wake, United States Navy, who served our Navy and country for almost half a century. He tried always to do the right thing, the honorable thing, the patriotic thing, no matter how daunting the odds. He faced war and storms and overwhelming adversaries many times. He knew frustration and exhaustion only too well. But Admiral Wake is widely known and respected for *never* giving up. *Never* giving in. *Never* lowering his standard of honor. May we all follow his stalwart example. And now, we venerate him as fellow sailors should, with full naval honors."

The captain read from John 11:25–26: "Jesus said, 'I am the resurrection and the life. Whoever believes in me, though he die, yet shall he live, and everyone who lives and believes in me shall never die.' And Corinthians 15:54–56 says, 'When the perishable puts on the imperishable, and the mortal puts on immortality, then shall come to pass the saying that is written: Death is swallowed up in victory. O death, where is your victory? O death, where is your sting?'"

The captain's prayer was simple: "Lord please bless and watch over the family and friends and shipmates of Peter Wake who are left behind."

The executive officer called all hands to attention, then ordered the salute. The chief master-at-arms directed the body bearers to tilt the board, and the casket slid from beneath the flag into the sea. After the benediction, the firing party fired three shots and the ship's bugler sounded Taps.

As the last note of Taps faded away, *Florida* got under way at standard speed, the crew was dismissed, the ship resumed her routine, and Sean Peter was given the ensign from his father's casket. Drained of emotion, he and the family men watched the sunset until the last glow disappeared and the sky was carpeted with stars.

It was over. Their Dad and Grandpa was gone. With a long, sad sigh, Sean Peter led them below to the wardroom. Each of them had a life to be lived.

43

Life Goes On

Key West, Florida

1920–1941

They did move forward with their lives, of course, with all that entailed. Patricia's husband, Charles, died in 1922. She never remarried. Sean Peter Wake retired from the Navy in 1922 after thirty-two years of service, and he and Filipa moved in with María at Key West to care for her. In 1925 Useppa's son, Peter Carlos Cano, now a lieutenant (j.g.), married Anne Papillon of Martinique while serving in the Caribbean Squadron. Robert Wake, son of Sean Peter and Filipa and grandson of Peter Wake, was commissioned at the Naval Academy in 1926 and shipped out to a gunboat in the Philippines, as his father had a quarter century before.

The last of the original generation was leaving. In 1926, Col. Michael Woodgerd, old comrade-in-arms, friend, and confidant of Peter Wake, died at Alexandria at age eighty-one. His wife died a year later. The Wake family in the Washington area attended both funerals.

And in 1927, María Abad Maura Wake, beloved for her kindness and gentle advice, died at the age of eighty-three. Her last words were to her seventeen-year-old granddaughter Agnes: "Spread genuine love and kindness around—it will come back to you ten-fold." Useppa (now sixty-three) and Mario Cano came from Tampa, Clotilda Rork from Washington, and Juanito from the Spanish embassy in Havana. Hundreds of Key Westers; the Russian-American Noble family, which had grown to five; and several naval officers attended her funeral. She was laid to rest near a gumbo limbo tree in the "Wake Family Corner" between Passover Lane and the Navy's graves for the sailors killed in 1898 on *Maine*.

The 1930s saw more sadness. Sean Peter, comfortably retired at Key West, died suddenly of a heart attack in 1931. Following the funeral at the Methodist church he was buried with a naval ceremony near his stepmother.

Those were difficult times for Key West. The worsening depression, the destruction of the railroad and loss of hundreds of lives in the 1935 hurricane, and the closing of much of the Navy base meant economic decline for the island and deprivation for the people.

Useppa and Mario Cano were elderly now and didn't come down from Tampa often. By 1935, with sixteen years in the service, their son Peter Carlos was a lieutenant commander and finally due for promotion; advancement was painfully slow in the budget-slashed peacetime Navy. In 1929 their daughter Linda had married Arsenio García, a descendant of the famous Cuban general whom Peter Wake had served alongside in 1898. They moved to Key West, where Arsenio managed a tobacco factory. In 1932 they had a daughter named Useppa, carrying on that lovely name.

In 1933, Lt. (j.g.) Robert James Wake married Delores Munda, a young lady from Manila, in the Philippines where he was stationed. Their first child, María Filipa, arrived three years later at Pensacola Naval Station, where Robert's father was born in 1867.

Precocious little Agnes grew up to be an amateur astronomer and a social free spirit who divided her time between Miami, Washington, and Key West. In 1939 she began a decades-long affair with Conrad Steg, a former Florida U.S. senator and a back-room political power broker. Her diverse social circle also included Alice Roosevelt Longworth, Theodore Roosevelt's eldest daughter and the undisputed social diva of Washington. But no matter the various irregularities in her life, Agnes returned to the bungalow on Grunt Bone Lane every Easter and attended services with the Wake family. She also made sure to spend time with her bon vivant friend Ernest Hemingway at his home on Whitehead Street and the impromptu drinking sessions at Sloppy Joe's Bar, the big new one on the corner of Duval and Greene Streets.

By this time, the ominous clouds of world war once again covered the earth. The Japanese were marching across China and the Pacific and turning their eyes toward America's Pacific islands. At the decade's end, the war everyone had foreseen in Europe finally erupted. Pacifist, isolationist, and anti-Roosevelt Americans demanded that America stay out of it. The 1940 bill to reinstate the draft for national defense passed Congress by only one vote. America First Committee isolationists and the Friends of Nazi Germany put enormous political pressure on the government to do nothing to help the western European democracies stop Nazi Germany and fascist Italy.

By 1941 the Japanese had conquered much of Southeast Asia, including collaborationist Vichy French Indochina, and the Nazis had subjugated the European continent and invaded the Soviet Union. Despite the slogans Nazi and isolationist supporters shouted at rallies, the U.S. Navy quietly prepared for war. The naval station at Key West was expanded in both its antisubmarine and aviation capacities, bringing a welcome inflow of money. The island was abuzz with activity that summer, but the Wake family was worried.

Lt. Cdr. Peter Carlos Cano was commanding an ancient flush-decked destroyer escorting Lend-Lease convoys across the North Atlantic. Several American destroyers had been attacked by Nazi U-boats, and one, *Reuben James*, had been sunk with few survivors. Cano's younger cousin Lt. Cdr. Robert James Wake had just taken command of an equally old wooden minesweeper in Samoa. The family feared both would be right in the thick of it when war came.

They were right.

44

The Last Supper

Government House
Pago Pago, American Samoa

Friday, 5 December 1941

Lt. Cdr. Robert James Wake knew this was not going to be a pleasant, relaxed dinner. Too much was known, and more important, *unknown*, about what the Japanese were doing in the Pacific for anyone at the dinner to be relaxed. He tried to get Delores to stay home because he thought the inevitable discussions of war would heighten his wife's worries.

Delores was six and a half months pregnant and nervous. They'd lost their first child, heartbreakingly lovely little three-year-old María, to leukemia just four years earlier at San Diego. Delores was terrified the second child stirring in her womb might have the disease as well. Robert was terrified too but tried not to show it.

Delores shook her dark curls and reached into the closet for a dress that would fit her expanding waist. "Robert, I know you and the governor will be talking about the Japanese and the war everyone knows is coming, but I have to get out of this bungalow and see other people. I am getting more and more *balisa* staying home alone."

Delores was proud of her fluent English, learned in a Catholic girls' school in Manila, but the more emotional she got, the thicker her Filipina accent became, and eventually her native language slipped into the conversation. *Balisa*, Robert knew, meant anxious—borderline crazy. Robert looked at his beautiful wife with her sad eyes and gave in.

"Of course, dear, I just wanted to spare you the doomsday talk. Wives are invited, and next to the governor's wife you'll be the senior wife there! We've come a long way from Pearl, eh?"

He meant that both figuratively and literally. Robert hadn't been senior enough to merit a dinner invitation from the governor of Hawaii while he was assigned to staff duty at Pearl Harbor. Samoa was a backwater in comparison—in the middle of nowhere with nothing but jungle-clad mountains and a Navy captain for its governor. The naval "establishment" was a decaying fifty-year-old supply depot run by a bewildered young supply lieutenant, junior grade, and a radio relay station run by a disgruntled old CPO mustanged up to lieutenant. The area's station ship, USS *Roseate Spoonbill*, was an obsolete bird-class minesweeper-gunboat. Since Robert was the commanding officer of "old *Rosie*"—since July, when he was finally promoted to lieutenant commander—that made him the second most senior officer present on station. A moderate-sized fish in a tiny pond.

"I like it here, Robert," Delores insisted. She hadn't minded the move at all. Hadn't minded leaving behind the discrimination at Pearl, the disapproving stares at her olive skin and almond-shaped eyes when they walked into the O-Club for lunch, the parties to which they were never invited, the occasional "request" from a senior officer's wife on the patio for Delores to "be a good girl and fetch me another gin and tonic." In her darker moments she wondered whether she was the reason why her husband was assigned to an old wreck in a place inhabited by dark-skinned people nobody in the United States cared about.

Robert understood her feelings all too well. His own mother was Filipina and had endured the same trials as a Navy wife.

"And yes, it is different here," she said. "Not as many arrogant lily-white people."

Robert laughed and silently agreed. "Wear the yellow dress, sweetheart. It makes your skin glow."

Perched up on the hilltop at Observatory Point, Government House had once been impressive, but those days were long past. Lack of maintenance, termites, wood rot, and typhoons had all taken their toll. But the view was still magnificent—from the vast Pacific Ocean on the right to tall Rainmaker Mountain across Pago Pago harbor in the middle, to *Rosie* down at the Navy dock at Fagatogo village on the left. December was the rainy season, though, and a cascade of rain soon masked the view.

Capt. Laurence Wild, governor of American Samoa, had been an All-America basketball star in the Naval Academy's class of 1913. He was a gracious Midwesterner with an easy smile. Louise Wild, a former Washington debutante, was the perfect hostess, going out of her way to make her husband's visitors comfortable. In addition to the Wakes, the guests consisted of 1st Lt. Maxwell Markle, an artilleryman of Marines surveying potential gun positions to guard the harbor; Lt. Ted Nott of the radio relay station and his quiet wife, Mona; and shy young Lt. (j.g.) Johnny Gorston of the depot. The men wore the hated choker-collar dress whites, the only attire suitable for dinner with a governor in the mansion's formal dining room.

Louise kept the dinner talk lighthearted—about families back home, Delores' coming baby, Polynesian culture, sports, and literature—anything but war. Delores held her own with Louise, and both drew a reluctant Mona into the conversation. Robert was glad Delores seemed to be enjoying herself. When the last spoonful of vanilla ice cream with canned peaches was finished, Louise rose and led the ladies to the verandah, leaving the gentlemen alone in the dining room.

Wild got right to the point. "Anything about the Japs on the wireless circuits, Mr. Nott?"

"No, sir; routine admin traffic only," said Nott.

Wild sifted his gaze to Wake. "Status of *Rosie*?"

"We need to top off with fuel and provisions, sir," said Wake, then added the part he knew they wouldn't like. "And I'd like to take any extra 3-inch and .50-caliber ammunition you have. *Rosie* needs to be completely combat ready. Or as ready as the old girl *can* be. And once ready, we'll get under way. I have a bad feeling we'll be needed somewhere very soon."

Properly armed, *Rosie* would be a close-range threat to any Japanese plane or small boat she might encounter. The Samoa station might be a backwater posting, but Wake insisted on regular gunnery practice, and his gunners were among the best at the annual fleet gunnery qualifications.

Wild turned to the depot officer. "Fuel oil status at the depot, Mr. Gorston?"

Gorston spoke for the first time since sitting down to dinner. "Ah, well, we do have enough fuel in the tanks, sir. About three quarters full. But there isn't much ammo, sir. Sorry."

Markle raised a hand. "I expect to need the 3-inch and .50-cal here, sir. I'm recommending several 3-inch AA batteries be installed to defend the harbor. And my report goes off to Honolulu on Monday."

Wild was in charge of Gorston and Nott, and had some authority over Markle, but Wake's minesweeper was technically outside of his operational control. Still, it was his responsibility to allocate supplies as he saw fit. He looked around the table, gauging the men before him, remembering when he had commanded a destroyer and considering what he knew of the Japanese strategy in the Pacific.

"Gentlemen," he said at last, "Commander Wake is right. War is coming, maybe in the next few days, and the only warship here is his. So, Mr. Gorston, your priority is refueling, provisioning, and arming *Rosie* starting tomorrow at dawn. I want it done by one o'clock so she can have steam up by two. Understood?"

Gorston blinked, obviously surprised by the orders to abandon his usual leisurely pace. "Ah, well . . . yeah, sir."

Wake tried not to groan aloud. Nott almost laughed.

Wild frowned at the lieutenant. "What was that, Mr. Gorston?"

Gorston looked puzzled for a second, then said, "Oh, I mean aye, aye, sir."

Wild paused for a long moment as if he would pursue the matter but instead looked back at Wake. "*Mariposa*, the Matson liner, is stopping here on Tuesday, bound for Honolulu, then San Francisco. I'm sending all naval dependents away on it, including my wife. No exceptions. Louise can look after Delores on the trip."

When they got home to the bungalow and climbed into bed, Robert rolled over and held Delores tightly. "This might be our last night together for a bit. *Rosie* is getting topped off and ready for sea tomorrow. Don't know exactly when we'll get under way, but it may be suddenly."

She digested that and everything left unsaid. "All right, Robert. I understand," she said softly.

He kissed her. "There's more. All naval dependents are leaving for Honolulu on Tuesday, the ninth. You'll be sailing on *Mariposa*, that fancy Matson liner. From Hawaii, she's heading for San Francisco." He smoothed back her hair. "I think Key West would be a good place for you to go. My mother adores you and will be thrilled to have you there. She can help when the baby comes. Sound all right?"

Through her tears, Delores nodded. She loved her mother-in-law as well. They had much in common. "This is it, then?"

"Yes, my love, this is it. Let me hold you and our baby. I need to memorize you."

After an hour of daydreaming aloud of their future, they finally fell asleep holding each other. When Robert awoke the next morning at five o'clock, he dressed and packed his gear quietly in the dark so as not to wake her. He slipped out the front door and walked the half-mile in the rain to the Navy dock, never knowing Delores had been awake and watching him the whole time. She knew his survival depended on total concentration. She said a prayer imploring God to give him the wisdom and skills to survive and come to Key West for her and their baby.

And then she stood on their porch and cried.

45
The Signal

USS *Roseate Spoonbill* (AMG 57)
Pago Pago, American Samoa

Sunday, 7 December 1941

It was, as usual, raining. The rising sun was a faint and diffused light in the watery sky. Normally, half the crew would be released to attend Sunday services ashore. But this Sunday wasn't normal.

Everything took longer than Robert had anticipated: last-minute repairs, finding spares, provisioning, refueling, loading ammunition, obtaining medicines and medical equipment, getting charts for the areas they might be ordered, rechecking the gyro-compass, gun maintenance, and myriad other things. Starting at 0500 on Saturday and for twenty-four hours straight, every enlisted man and officer in every department and section was busy.

Fresh beef, pork, fruit, and ice cream filled the refrigerator/freezers. Each of the two 3-inch guns now had 150 rounds in the magazine; each of the two .50-caliber machine guns had 5,000 rounds; and the ship's twenty ancient M1903 Springfield rifles had 80 rounds each. The ship's four fuel bunkers were filled to the top.

After loading the supplies, all hands turned in the other direction and began lugging nonessential or flammable items off the ship, adding them to the growing pile on the pier. Finally, at ten o'clock on Sunday morning, every item on the checklist was crossed off.

Wake had just ordered his men to resume routine watches when Lieutenant Gorston pulled up in the supply depot truck. Looking quite pleased with himself, he called up to Wake on *Rosie*'s bridge, "Sir! I found four depth charges! They're old but they might still work."

Before Wake had time to respond, the governor's car careened down the road from Government House with Governor-Captain Wild at the helm. He skidded to a stop in front of the ship, leapt out, hurried up the gangway, saluted the colors, and climbed the ladder to the bridge. The entire crew stopped where they stood and watched.

A grim Governor Wild informed Wake, "A Pacific-wide war notification in regular code just came into the relay station. The Japs made a surprise attack on Pearl Harbor two hours ago. There are no details yet, but damage is expected to be major. I've already mobilized our Fita Fita Home Guard and placed them under Lieutenant Markle."

The news stunned Wake. *Hawaii? Not the Philippines? How did they get so far without being detected?* "I was going to do a sea trial today, but this changes everything. Any orders come in for *Rosie*, sir?"

"None came through. But I'd suggest you get to sea as soon as possible. You're a sitting duck here if—" He sighed. "No, *when* the Japs come."

As the Samoan area station ship, *Rosie* was officially part of the Pacific Fleet, headquartered in Hawaii. "They'll probably need us at fleet headquarters, so we'll head north for Pearl, sir."

"Good idea," said Wild, quickly doing the math in his head. "That's 2,600 miles. If you can keep *Rosie* at eight to ten knots, you should be there around the eighteenth to twentieth. I'll send a signal to expect you then. You'll be in their wireless range by the twelfth or so. Don't worry about Delores, Robert. My Louise will take good care of her."

The governor put out his hand. "I wish I had a ship of war myself right now, but what I've got is an island and a lot of people to defend, and that'll keep me plenty busy. Good luck, Commander."

Wake said, "And to you, sir," but Wild was already dashing off the bridge.

An hour later, *Rosie* sounded her horn, the battle ensign was broken out from the mast, the Fita Fita Home Guard six-piece band struck up "Anchors Aweigh," and USS *Roseate Spoonbill* pulled away from Naval Station Samoa.

As they cleared the headlands of the harbor, *Rosie's* radioman raced into the bridge.

"Sir, a signal just arrived, passed on from the relay station ashore. Standard Navy code." He handed Wake the signal report form.

TO: LCDR R. WAKE, USS ROSEATE SPOONBILL (AMG-57)
FROM: OPS-COMINCH PACFLT
COMM TYPE/ROUTE/DATE/TIME: SECRET/VIA SAMOA RELAY
STA/7DEC41—1127

XXX—ROSEATE SPOONBILL TRANSFERRED ASIATIC FLT—X—
PROCEED MANILA IMMEDIATELY VIA REFUEL AT ZAMBO-
ANGA-MINDANAO-PI—X—REPORT TO INSHORE PATROL AT
MANILA—X—PROVIDE ETA ZAMBOANGA & MANILA—X—
BEWARE ENEMY SEA & AIR PATROLS IN SOUTHERN PI—X—
ENEMY AIR ATTACKS IN MANILA CAVITE—X—MAINTAIN
RADIO SILENCE UNTIL ZAMBOANGA—X—GOOD LUCK—XXX

Wake shook his head. *Damn. They must be desperate if they're sending the likes of* Rosie *to reinforce Admiral Hart's fleet at Manila.*

Wake switched on the 1MC speakers and spoke to his crew: "All hands, now hear this. This is the captain. You know the Japanese attacked Pearl Harbor and we're now at war. I just got word we're no longer part of the Pacific Fleet. We're now in the Asiatic Fleet, and our orders are to head for Manila by way of Zamboanga. That's about five thousand miles. Because we'll need to stretch out our fuel to make it, we will not be zigzagging. All lookouts need to be especially vigilant night and day for air, surface, and submarine threats. Jap patrols have been seen in the southern Philippines and may be heading this way. Officers' call in the wardroom in five minutes. That is all."

Wake took a deep breath and contemplated what he'd just told the crew. None of them had seen combat before. *I hope they're ready. I hope I'm ready,* he thought as *Rosie* steamed west, right into the center of the Japanese Empire's Pacific-wide attack on America, Great Britain, and Holland.

46

The Ship

USS *Roseate Spoonbill*
Steaming west-northwest at ten knots

Monday, 8 December 1941

Wake's ship was unusual, to say the least. Like her sister mine-sweepers she had a wooden hull and superstructure, a passive defense against magnetic mines. But unlike her sisters she was a prototype. Most "bird-class" minesweepers only had one or two 3-inch low-angle guns and one or two light .30-caliber machine guns, relics from the Great War that were virtually useless against a modern foe attacking from the air or water.

But when twenty-three-year-old *Rosie* had been taken out of mothballs and recommissioned in 1937, she was given new guns. Her two 3-inch guns were modern Mark VII-1931s designed for combat against both surface and aerial enemies. They could elevate to 85 degrees and fire 15 rounds a minute. Her .50-caliber machine guns were air cooled and could fire 700 rounds a minute. These improvements entitled *Rosie* to the grandiose new designation of AMG: minesweeper-gunboat, a gross misnomer in Wake's eyes. The crew had thought the gunboat part a joke. Until now.

The bad news was that *Rosie* had spent the last four years, since October 1937, on boring patrol duty in Samoa and the other American islands in the south-central Pacific. Johnston, Howland, Jarvis, Kingman, Canton, Palmyra, Baker, and the other islands she watched over were mere humps of sand in the vast Pacific. The purpose was to impress the natives by showing *Rosie's* American flag and guns—and to make sure the Japanese weren't showing theirs.

But *Rosie's* main enemies turned out to be not the Japanese, but tiny teredo worms, the scourge of ships in tropical waters. During those four years her hull had not had a proper bottom job to root the little monsters out, only an annual sanding and painting to cover the problem. Unchecked, the worms spread throughout the old wooden hull, creating a constant daily challenge for the carpenter, "Chips," to keep *Rosie* afloat. The previous captain had even recommended decommissioning *Rosie* and selling her for scrap—if anyone would buy her. Wake, who privately agreed with him, worried that a broadside salvo from the main guns might shake the hull so hard it would spring the seams of the planking and sink the ship.

The main reason for *Rosie's* existence, her minesweeping gear, was still there, and somewhat better maintained, but she hadn't actually swept a mine, practice or real, since 1929. The minesweeping boom and tackle was used to load and offload provisions and equipment. None of the officers, including Wake, had ever served on a minesweeper. An old manual in the wardroom was the only authoritative source on what to do if they encountered a mine. That and the chief gunner's mate, a crochety old salt named Maloney who had learned a bit about minesweeping as part of his ordnance training. Wake ordered Maloney and Lt. George Formanski, his gunnery officer, to study the manual and devise some training drills.

Rosie's engine was another worry. Her single propeller was still powered by the original reciprocating engine. The engine was fed steam by two boilers fired by fuel oil burners. When she was commissioned back in 1917, her top speed was fourteen knots; by 1941 that had declined to eleven or twelve, and ten for any extended length of time. Her bunkers carried enough fuel to take her about five thousand miles at ten knots—if there were no storms, battles, fast currents, or minesweeping tows to eat fuel and slow her down.

Fuel was a matter of no little import. The ship's estimated range was accurate only if the fuel at the bottom of the bunkers was still usable and hadn't turned into sludge in the tropical heat. Nobody knew whether it had or not, because to Wake's knowledge, the damned things hadn't been properly cleaned out since *Rosie*'s last refit in 1937.

Thus, the wooden warship with the decidedly unwarlike name went off to fight the vaunted Imperial Japanese Navy. Wake was depressingly aware that the only way *Rosie* could help Admiral Hart's Asiatic Fleet hold the line in the Philippines was if every man on board did his job well and he came up with an innovative way to carry out their mission.

As the old minesweeper plodded west, Wake went out onto the starboard bridge wing and gazed at the setting sun, a giant coppery-pink ball just touching the horizon. But he couldn't appreciate the sight. His mind was swirling with problems his men expected him to solve.

The biggest problem was that he had no idea how.

47

A Beautiful Evening

USS *Roseate Spoonbill*
Steaming west-northwest at eleven knots

Friday, 12 December 1941

Lt. Bill Waters, *Rosie*'s executive officer, knocked twice on Wake's stateroom door, entered, and wearily sat in the tiny stateroom's lone guest chair. He was the only man in the ship who had permission to do that. The captain was just finishing his dinner, which had been delayed by sunset general quarters that had gone well past sunset due to a false ship sighting and recurring problems with the number two boiler.

Wake liked his XO, a gunnery specialist who after eight months in *Rosie* seemed to know the men and the ship well enough to anticipate and deter problems. And though Waters' past was a bit murky, he trusted him as well. A Midwesterner from rural southeast Ohio, Bill Waters had graduated from the Naval Academy in '32 and served on the operations staff of the Atlantic Fleet under the legendary Adm. Ernest King, the billet every lieutenant in the Navy wanted. Why he was then assigned—or banished—to an old bucket like *Rosie* in April 1941 was a mystery. Waters' personnel file simply noted the transfer without further comment. Waters never said, and Wake decided not to press it—King was notoriously hard to work for.

Waters handed over a signal report. "Mr. Van Dorn just decoded this signal relayed from Samoa, Captain. General message to all ships from Asiatic Fleet ops staff."

Wake turned up the brightness on the desk's red night lantern and scanned the signal, a fleetwide warning of enemy dispositions. It started with the northern Philippines. Japanese army forces had invaded northern Luzon and were advancing south toward Manila. They'd landed that day at Legaspi in southern Luzon. Enemy naval forces had been seen all around Luzon, and more landings were expected. Japanese aircraft had attacked U.S. and Filipino forces in the northern and central Philippines, destroying Cavite naval base near Manila.

It seemed to Wake the Japanese were unopposed everywhere, which made no sense. MacArthur had 100,000 men and all kinds of aircraft. *What are they doing?*

Wake quickly got down to the part that pertained to *Rosie*'s destination, the southern Philippines and northern Dutch East Indies:

XXX—ENEMY WARSHIPS & TRANSPORTS SEEN BETWEEN JAP PALAU & CENTRAL PHILIPPINES—X—ENEMY AIR PATROLS NOW REACHING MINDANAO BORNEO & NEW GUINEA—X— ENEMY SUBMARINES SEEN IN CELEBES SEA—X—EXPECTING INVASION IN MINDANAO-LEYTE AREA FROM PALAU—XXX

The message didn't provide American naval dispositions, of course, but it was increasingly clear that there was no fleet action stopping the Japanese.

Waters spread out a general chart of the region on Wake's desk and looked at his captain. "I don't get this at all. What about our subs, sir? There's at least twenty modern fleet boats based out of Manila Bay—they should be having a field day, especially at the chokepoints between the islands. And no air force to counter the Japs? What the hell is going on?"

Wake shook his head in dismay. "There's more to this than we're being told. What really happened at Pearl Harbor and Manila? My guess is that they were probably caught off guard and destroyed in the first bombing raids."

"Are we on our own, then, sir? We're still a couple of weeks out of Zamboanga."

"Unless we get word otherwise, yes, we'll operate as if we're on our own. Glad we've got the equatorial current and these storm swells pushing us at an extra knot and a half."

The duty petty officer in the wheelhouse struck the bell four times—10 p.m. Wake stood up. "It's hot in here; let's get some air."

Wake's stateroom was just abaft the bridge, so it was only a matter of opening the door to step into the wheelhouse, and another few steps out to the small starboard wing. The night was clear, and a slight breeze offered some relief. Stars dusted the inky black sky from horizon to horizon, and below them the bow wave curled away, luminescent green fringed in white.

Wake breathed in the sultry air. "What a beautiful evening." He pointed low over the port bow. "Venus is still up, bigger than ever at that low angle. Hmm, what else can I see?" Wake's hand waved an arc across the sky. "Look higher over the bow, Bill. There's Mars, bright orange tonight. And Saturn due north on the starboard bow, and Jupiter to the northeast. By God, this is a planetary conjunction! See the elliptic line connecting them all?"

In the dim red glow of the wheelhouse lantern Waters could see that Wake was smiling wistfully. "My grandfather Peter showed me my first one down in Key West when I was just a boy," Wake said. "We spent many an evening there stargazing. He said to always look up at night and pay attention to the stars for hidden clues."

Wake's hand swung east toward the rising constellation of Gemini. "Since it's mid-December we might even have some Geminid meteors transiting tonight." He let out a long sigh. "What a magnificent celestial show. Makes it impossible to believe a war is raging up ahead of us."

"Well, Venus just disappeared, sir," Waters said pragmatically. "No, there it is. Now it just blinked out again. That's strange. There's not a cloud in the sky."

Wake snapped out of his reverie, spun around to port, and focused his binoculars on Venus, which disappeared and then reappeared. There was something flying up there, blanking out the stars. When he heard the big radial engine, he knew what it was. It was coming at them fast.

"*General quarters!*" he bellowed. "Air action, low on the port bow!"

48
War

USS *Roseate Spoonbill*
Steaming west-northwest at eleven knots

Friday, 12 December 1941

*R*osie didn't have the new klaxons, and she didn't rate a bugler. The petty officer of the watch sounded general quarters by clanging the ship's bell and yelling out the order, which was relayed along the weather decks and down belowdecks. In seconds, men were racing up the starboard ladders and down the portside ladders fumbling with clothing, helmets, and life jackets, and grabbing needed gear as they passed. Four minutes and twenty-two seconds later the last station reported in, and the minesweeper was at manned battle stations.

Standing near his captain, Chief Quartermaster Seymour "Dusty" Davis cocked an ear toward the plane, then muttered, "That's an Aichi E13A scout seaplane, sir."

"You sure, Chief?" Waters asked. "Could it be one of our Kingfisher scouts?"

Davis shook his head. "Negative, sir—I know the sound of *these* particular Nip bastards. Heard 'em on the Shanghai coast as they pounded the poor Chinese to death. Damn near pounded us, too, even though we were neutrals on routine station patrol. Twice the horsepower of a Kingfisher; twice the

179

sound. Carries 525 pounds of bombs. Must be a seaplane tender or cruiser within 480 miles. That's the plane's operating range. He's on a bombing run for us. Must've spotted our wake—lit up like a runway, damn it all."

The plane was only half a mile away now, a black form getting bigger by the second, the floats under the wings discernible now. It had descended to maybe two hundred feet above the waves, the thrumming of its engine the sound of doom.

"Right full rudder to course zero-zero-zero," Wake ordered, turning the ship to bring the after guns to bear on the attacker. "Ahead flank speed. Guns will open fire when the target bears."

Engine laboring, *Rosie* pushed her speed up to twelve and a half knots. The forward 3-inch gun opened fire. Every five seconds the gun crew rhythmically ejected, loaded, and fired more shells—*Kahwump! Kahwump! Kahwump!* The gun mount was right in front of the bridge, and every man in the wheelhouse knew to open his mouth to equalize pressure in his ears from concussions and to shield his eyes to prevent being blinded by the flashes.

Wake heard the after 3-inch begin firing, then the clattering staccato of the portside machine gun as the plane closed to a quarter mile. Three-inch proximity-fused rounds burst in flaming balls all around the plane. The port machine gun sent a bright red tracer stream of fire streaking across the sky at it. But still the damned thing came at them. At four hundred yards it began to rise, and Wake knew the pilot was about to drop his bombs on them and pull up and away. In seconds the monster was over them, the thunder of its engine blotting out the sound of *Rosie*'s guns. It was too close now for the 3-inchers, but the machine-gunners held their ground, firing a steady stream right into its black belly.

The explosion took away all vision and sound and breath.

The massive concussion knocked Wake and everyone else in the wheelhouse to the deck. The windows cracked, cables fell from the overhead, and charts were flung through the air. Flaming embers and fuel rained down on the ship as big chunks of hot metal fell into the water fifty feet away to starboard.

Wake pulled himself to his feet and staggered out onto the bridge wing. A dozen fires burned on the ship's upper and main decks. Three men lay motion-less amidship as others groped their way toward them. A sailor manned the upper-deck fire hose and began spraying the decks. The foremast swayed to port and then to starboard, then collapsed over the starboard side in a mass of halyards and shrouds and antenna wiring just a few feet aft of where Wake was standing. The taller main mast rising from the aft end of the upper deck still stood, but with the top five feet broken off and hanging down.

Wake went back inside to receive damage reports. Miraculously, *Rosie* was still under way. Chief Davis was now steering, the helmsman having been sent below to Doc Stanford. The lee helmsman was standing by as a messenger. The phone talker was mumbling something into his microphone, and Wake realized the phone circuit wasn't working. Ensign Van Dorn, bloodied but calm, was picking up the charts and gear strewn about the deck.

"Left standard rudder to course two-nine-zero. Reduce revolutions to make ten knots."

Davis repeated the helm and course orders in a monotone, turned the wheel counterclockwise, then reported *Rosie* was steady on the new course. Van Dorn repeated the speed order and shifted the engine room telegraph to standard speed. Seconds later, the ship slowed.

Wake suddenly remembered what he'd just seen on the weather decks. "Mr. Van Dorn, our antenna came down with the foremast. See if it can be salvaged and jury-rigged aloft to the main mast. And if that blood is yours, go see Doc Stanford after that."

Van Dorn acknowledged the order and dashed outside. Minutes later, Waters appeared and rattled off his damage report. "Fires were caught early and are out, sir. It looks like the plane's bombs either never dropped or exploded in the air. Most of the damage was caused by the plane's high-octane fuel tank exploding and showering the decks with metal debris and flaming fuel. If that big friggin' bomb had gone off, we'd all be swimming to hell right now."

Wake nodded, and Waters went on. "Hull shows no leakage beyond the usual. All pumps are operable. All guns are operable. Ammunition magazine is safe, and ready ammo lockers topside are being replenished. Main guns expended forty-three rounds in total; portside fifty-cal fired eleven hundred. Damage appears confined to the weather decks, your stateroom, and the radio room. I think Chips can repair most of the damage, but the radio-wireless apparatus looks to be in bad shape."

"Very well. Maybe Van Dorn can figure out how to fix the wireless. Casualties?"

"One dead, sir—Seaman Castwell. Three burned, with Seaman Warnell the worst of them. Other two are Storekeeper Whitley and Radioman Boutner. Three men from deck division—Larney, Nosteros, and Clyburn—have lacerations from shrapnel. Seaman Geraci was on the helm and got a bad cut across the forehead when he was thrown on deck. All the wounded are in sick bay now, but Doc expects them to recover."

He hesitated, then said, "And Castwell's body needs to be buried soon, sir."

We were lucky, Wake thought. *If the bombs had released and fallen on the ship, we'd all have been gone in a flash.* He shivered at the thought.

"Very well. Darken ship as much as possible and get Cookie to rustle up some food for everybody. After sunrise battle stations, all hands off watch will assemble on the afterdeck to bury Castwell. We've resumed course to Zamboanga. That plane probably got a sighting message off, so the enemy will be looking for us. Take the conn, Bill. In half an hour secure from general quarters, set the regular watches, and keep the doubled lookouts."

"Aye, aye, sir."

Every muscle and bone aching, Wake knew he needed to lie down for fifteen minutes. That was the logical thing to do. Fifteen minutes of rest. But his heart told him he was the captain, and his men needed to see him right now. "I'm going to have a look around now. I need you to get at least an hour of shuteye once we secure from general quarters. Understood?"

Waters nodded. "Aye, aye, on that, sir."

49

Lame Propaganda

USS *Roseate Spoonbill*
Steaming west-northwest at eleven knots

13–24 December 1941

Twenty-three-year-old Seaman 2nd Class Jefford Roland Castwell Jr. of Pittsburg, Kansas, was buried at sea an hour after sunrise on Saturday, 13 December 1941. The ceremony was brief and tense, with every man there, including Wake as he presided, keeping one eye on the horizons. As the remains slid from beneath the ensign into the sea, Wake recalled what he had learned about Castwell in their few short conversations. He was a typical young seaman: he enlisted in the Navy as a teenager because opportunities for employment were scarce at home and he wanted to see the world and meet exotic girls. But Wake spared a moment to mourn the unique spark that had made him Jefford Castwell.

When the service was over and Castwell's body was plunging down to the bottom a thousand fathoms below, Wake walked away feeling that he'd made a poor job of it. This had been a chore, something to get over with. Castwell deserved better—a service like his grandfather Peter received off Key West. He wondered if Peter Wake would have done better. *Probably*, he decided, because his grandfather had always known what to do and had done it well.

Ensign Van Dorn and a recuperating Radioman Boutner got the antenna insulators and wires re-rigged. Because Boutner couldn't yet go aloft, he instructed the deck crew in cutting the topmast from the main mast and using it as a jury-rigged foremast, then rigging the dual antennas between them. The new setup had the advantage of lowering *Rosie*'s profile, useful in evading enemy ships. The next day, the receiver took in a fleetwide wireless message advising enemy movements. Simply put, the Japanese were reported to be everywhere. *Rosie* was surrounded.

Although they were almost certain the attacking plane had radioed back the ship's location, the lookouts saw no more enemy planes until the eighteenth, when scout seaplanes were spotted high in the overcast sky to the north coming from the direction of Palau. When a smoke smudge was spotted on the northern horizon, Wake altered course to due west to put more distance between his ship and whoever that was.

Rosie was a thousand miles from Zamboanga when Boutner pulled off another miracle and rebuilt the damaged 1932 Zenith radio to the point where it received, with a lot of static, the BBC Overseas Service broadcast relayed out of Fiji, the station closest to them. News at last! Word spread quickly through the ship, and the deck outside the rebuilt radio room was packed with officers and CPOs who gathered to hear the three o'clock news broadcast. As the announcer continued in his flat British monotone, they grew quiet and grim.

The broadcast began with the bad news. French Indochina had fallen to the Japanese, as had Hong Kong. British and Indian troops were resisting the Japanese in Malaya and British Borneo. Singapore was holding on, but its fate was certain. The Americans and Filipinos on Luzon were resisting but surrounded. The Americans were admitting that the Pacific Fleet at Pearl Harbor had sustained heavy damage. Japanese were in the Indian Ocean and roaming the Central Pacific.

The good news sounded dubious. British naval reinforcements were en route from India, and American warships were heading west from California. Australia and the British and French South Pacific islands were safe for the time being. Wake thought it was lame propaganda. Nobody on *Rosie* believed any of it.

When the BBC broadcast ended, Boutner turned the dial to find any other news from commercial or private sources. A scratchy report came out of Zamboanga from an American copra plantation manager who reported the Japanese had invaded Davao, east of him, at dawn the day before. Filipino soldiers were resisting the invaders but were outnumbered. Enemy ships and aircraft were being seen all around Mindanao. He expected the Japanese to show up any day and was begging for help. Wake wanted to question the man about the fuel situation at Zamboanga, but the Zenith was a receiver, not a transmitter, and the ship's wireless wouldn't transmit that far.

Afterward, Wake sat in his stateroom staring at the ship's only chart covering the Philippines, which offered little of value. It was a regional chart of the entire island group with no details of Zamboanga at all. One question dominated his thoughts: *What if there's no fuel left at Zamboanga? What the hell do we do then? No—what do I do then? They never covered this at the academy.*

His father, Sean Peter, had served three tours of duty in the Philippines fighting rebels in some of these same waters. His grandfather Peter fought pirates in the South China Sea in the 1880s. Wake remembered stories of life-and-death decisions they'd made. *Now it's my turn.*

As he pondered the possibilities, he remembered his grandfather's advice on decision-making in extreme situations: Do what both your enemies and your superiors never expect. Your enemies will be stunned and your superiors baffled, but you will have made at least some minor headway.

The idea came to him out of the blue a minute later.

50

Haggling

USS *Roseate Spoonbill*
Zamboanga, Mindanao, the Philippines

Thursday, 25 December 1941

Wake got his answer about Zamboanga's fuel in a fleet-wide message long before dawn on Christmas morning. Waters handed it to him without comment.

XXX—HEAVY ENEMY ACTIVITY MINDANAO-SULU AREA—X—
ALL SHIPS IN FLEET ORDERED RENDEZVOUS SURABAYA IN
DUTCH JAVA—X—NO FUEL PHILIPPINE PORTS—X—TARAKAN
& BALIKPAPAN DUTCH BORNEO HAVE SOME—X—ON ARRIVAL
AT SURABAYA REPORT ASFLTCOM HQ FOR ORDERS—XXX

Wake had already made his decision, and the message didn't impact it. And *Rosie* had run out of options anyway. Lookouts had seen Japanese aircraft many times the day before, flying high from the east to the west and southwest. The previous two nights crossing the Moro Gulf they'd seen distant gun flashes to the southwest in the Sulu Islands. No matter what the message said, Wake knew where to find fuel at Zamboanga. The big problem was getting there. Their chart was sketchy, reefs were everywhere, nights were too cloudy for accurate celestial navigation, all lighthouses were dark, and they had to discover the tidal currents the hard way.

Having dodged Sibago, Langil, and Tictabon islands to starboard; and Basilan, Tambulian, Grande Santa Cruz, and Little Santa Cruz islands to port—plus several unnamed exposed coral reefs on both sides—they arrived at Zamboanga well before dawn. Every man was at his battle station, every eye on deck watching for signs that the Japanese were already there. Zamboanga's main wharf along the waterfront was empty except for an ancient-looking passenger ferry.

Wake heaved a sigh of relief when he saw her, then looked up at the sky and said, "Thanks, Dad."

The *Sulu* was right where he'd expected her to be. Sean Peter Wake had searched the ferry for contraband and hostile Moro insurgents several times when he was commanding a patrol gunboat during his second tour in the Philippines in 1906, when the Moro Rebellion was at its bloody peak and piracy was rife. Those tales of glory were among young Robert's favorites. When Sean Peter had returned to Zamboanga on an inspection tour in 1916, the ferry's engine had been converted from a coal-burning steam engine to a diesel, one of the first local vessels to make that change. Coal was hard to find in the region, but refined fuel was readily available in the oil-rich Dutch East Indies nearby.

Sulu ran between Zamboanga and Jolo, a hundred miles to the south in the Sulu Islands. In his father's time, at least, the ferry had been the crucial transport hub of the area, and her schedule was rigidly maintained. She was in Zamboanga every Sunday, Tuesday, and Thursday without fail. Wake hoped all that remained unchanged—and that her fuel tanks were full.

As *Rosie* approached the dock, Wake ordered her main guns trained at Fort Pilar, the old Spanish fort behind the wharf, in case the Japanese had put guns in it. Fendering mats already in place on her starboard side, the minesweeper slowed to drift alongside *Sulu*. No one was out on ferry's decks, or even moving along the waterfront. In fact, Zamboanga was alarmingly deserted.

Rosie's men went about their work quietly, following whispered commands. Chief Boatswain Patrick Maloney's crew leaped over to the ferry to secure the lines, and Lieutenant Formanski's boarding party followed him to secure the ferry's bridge and upper decks. *Rosie's* usually dull engineer, Lt. Guido Portello, piratically brandished a pipe wrench and a pistol as he led his party down into *Sulu's* engine room. Wake followed and went topside to *Sulu's* wheelhouse.

A few minutes later Portello came up and reported to Wake, "Their fuel isn't a perfect match, but it will work, sir. There's enough to fill our bunkers halfway. Get us two thousand miles at ten knots, I'd say."

As Portello was finishing his report, Chief Maloney dragged an old man into the wheelhouse. "Captain, this fellow says he's Ahmad Husin, the skipper, and he's none too happy with our visit. He talks English."

Husin was not an appealing sight. His clothing, which might have once been a uniform, appeared in need of disinfecting or burning. Thin and bent over with age, he looked to be at least eighty years old and was probably older, his furrowed skin turned to teak by years at sea. Nor was he the kindly grandfather type. He cursed all present in a guttural tongue while his yellowed eyes took in everything and trusted nothing.

Wake said matter-of-factly, "I am Lieutenant Commander Robert Wake, captain of the U.S. warship *Roseate Spoonbill.*"

Husin said nothing, but his eyes turned feral at hearing Wake's name. *He remembers my father. And not fondly, apparently.*

Wake tried again, reaching out and taking Husin's hand to shake it. The man's grip was like a vise. During one of their long-ago evenings on the verandah in Key West, Wake's grandfather Peter had taught him a greeting of peace in Arabic, saying that Muslims around the world would recognize and appreciate it.

"Ah salaam alaykum, Captain Husin."

Husin made the expected reply, wishing peace also, although his tone said just the opposite. "Wah alaykum ah salaam."

He said nothing further, so Wake pressed ahead. "The war has come to us, Captain Husin, and the infidel Japanese will be here any day. They will steal your ship and fuel, and use them against your people. But if you sell your fuel to me right now, we will use it to defend your people, and all the people of the Philippines, against the infidels."

Husin shook his head. "No selling."

"Then I will have to commandeer it—without paying."

"That is stealing."

Wake, tired of negotiating, looked at his wristwatch and said, "I don't have time to waste, Captain Husin. Either we buy it or we take it. You have twenty seconds to decide."

Husin glared at him. Wake said, "Now it's ten seconds."

"Three U.S. dollars each gallon," muttered Husin. "No Filipino pesos—U.S. dollars."

"Time's up. Fifty U.S. cents a gallon or we take it. Fifty cents is double what you paid for it." He turned to the engineering officer. "Mr. Portello, rig the hoses and start pumping. Shoot anyone who interferes."

"Fifty U.S. cents each gallon," Husin growled, "but you are robbing me."

Wake responded pleasantly, "Very well, Captain. We have a deal. You will be paid immediately."

Formanski arrived and reported the entire ferry crew was over on the dock under guard. Wake gestured to Husin. "Good work, Mr. Formanski. Now, take Captain Husin to his crew on the dock. I'll have Mr. Waters give you five thousand dollars from the ship's safe, and you will give Husin the money on the dock, *in front of his crew*. Hold them under guard until we're ready to get under way, then let them go."

Husin muttered something as he was led away. Wake didn't bother to make out what it was. Hearing the fuel transfer pumps starting up, he left the bridge to check the main decks of both ships. Both fuel hoses were full and squirming with each pulse of the pumps.

"Two Jap planes, high astern!" yelled *Rosie's* bridge lookout.

Wake peered aft and finally saw a speck to the east, then another, glinting in the sunrise. He could make out no details with his naked eyes, but Waters, who was surveying them with binoculars, announced, "Scout planes, Captain. Too high for our guns."

Wake returned to his own ship's wheelhouse and rapped out orders to Waters. "Cast off all lines except forward, midship, and stern lines, and single those up for a quick getaway. Have one of the engineers ready the ferry's Kingston valves for opening—Japs might use her to transport troops. We'll scuttle her as we depart, which should be in no more than thirty minutes. Any signs of activity on shore?"

"None, sir. Not a person in sight. Eerie. Maybe they're running for the hills."

Wake glanced up at the scout planes, which were now circling high above. "I don't blame them, Bill—that's exactly what we're going to do. We'll get to Tarakan on Borneo, top off the fuel, and get down to Surabaya to join the fleet."

Waters was about to say something when the lookout shouted, "Formation of bombers! High astern—heading this way!"

51

Evasion

USS *Roseate Spoonbill*
Zamboanga, Mindanao, the Philippines

Thursday, 25 December 1941

*R*osie's guns began tracking the planes, but they were far too high to shoot at. Wake called over to the ferry, "How much longer, Mr. Portello?"

"Twenty minutes, Captain," was the harried answer.

"We may not have that, sir." Waters gave his binoculars to Chief Davis, who reported, "I count six Mitsubishi G3M medium bombers, Captain—code name: Nells. Bomb load of 1,800 pounds, range 1,000 miles. But the Nells never were all that accurate in China, especially from high up. These must be at least 10,000 feet, I think. Wait a minute, they're turning." Davis' unflappable monotone gave way to a disgusted, "Ah hell, looks like the Nip bastards're coming down, sir."

Wake heard shouts and saw the native ferry crew running from the dock, their irascible skipper hobbling after them. Clutching an armful of charts, Formanski was leading the boarding party back to *Rosie*. Every sailor topside was watching the bombers, which became fully visible as they turned, then head-on silhouettes once more as they straightened out and lined up to attack the minesweeper.

"Bridge! Warship in the haze ten miles off the port quarter and heading for us—looks like a fast small gunboat type, sir!"

Wake called to the fuel detail on the ferry's main deck, "Mr. Portello, disconnect the hoses, open the ferry's Kingston valves, and get our men back here, fast!"

Chief Davis studied the fast-approaching warship and pulled more information from his seemingly inexhaustible store. "Damn, I know that ship type, Captain. Saw that class up close at Shanghai in '37 when the Japs attacked. *Chidori* class, three 4.7-inch guns, plus AA machine guns and torpedoes, twenty-eight-knot speed. Rated as a torpedo boat to get around the naval limitations treaty, but she's armed like a destroyer with the hull of a corvette."

"Thank you, Chief. Take the helm. I have the conn."

Formanski and Van Dorn crowded onto the bridge for orders. They came fast. "Mr. Formanski, assume your midship battle station and open fire at the bombers when sure of hits. Have Chief Maloney set those four old depth charges on the afterdeck for fifty-foot depth and get them ready to roll off the stern.

"Mr. Waters, as soon as all our men are back on board, cast off. We'll head southwest at full speed with rapid course changes to dodge the bombs. Check those new charts to find a channel through the Sulu Islands to Tarakan at Borneo.

"Mr. Van Dorn, send a general signal to any ship or station in the Asiatic Fleet to relay to fleet headquarters that we are under attack and departing Zamboanga. From here on, we are following the fleetwide ship orders of this morning."

Kahwump . . . kahwump . . . kahwump—the after 3-inch gun began firing at a deliberate rate just as Portello shouted from the starboard main deck, "All men back on board, Captain, hoses're disconnected, and the ferry's scuttling!"

The deck crew threw off the lines as *Rosie's* engine rumbled into ahead gear and got her under way, with the lookouts shouting updates on the enemy bombers and warship.

The bombers were two miles away now and descending fast in perfectly straight single file behind the lead plane, as if on a routine training run. Black puffs appeared in the air around them, getting closer and closer but scoring no hits. The crew urged them on, trying to guide the shots with their body language.

The deck erupted in profane cheers when the lead plane blew apart in a fireball. The planes in line behind swerved to avoid the debris. One plane overcorrected, and the line scattered. Wake called for order and quiet. The planes were farther apart now but still coming. Only the after 3-inch gun and the .50-calibers could bear on them. Two more planes were hit, losing parts but remaining airborne and still coming at the minesweeper.

Rosie was a hundred yards from the wharf when the first plane released its eight bombs from an altitude of a thousand feet. The water between the wharf and the ship exploded in a ragged line of fountains. One of the bombs hit the sinking *Sulu* dead center. The forward 3-inch gun nailed the departing bomber as it flew overhead. Smoke poured out of its port engine, but it kept flying.

The next three bombers released simultaneously, fifteen explosions straddling *Rosie*, the white-hot shrapnel ripping into her wooden hull and superstructure. Men topside and below screamed as the deadly shards flayed their skin. Smoke drifted up from the starboard side amidships, quickly becoming thick and black. Wake knew it was probably lubricating oil in the engine room.

"Right full rudder!" Wake ordered, and Davis spun the wheel. The final bomber in the group matched their turn.

"Now left full rudder!" Davis had anticipated it and was ready, throwing his weight on the wheel with a grunt. The plane was slower to react this time. A hit from the after 3-incher jarred it as the bombs fell. One hit close aboard the starboard bow; the others straggled off to the right from there. Then the plane was past them and the attackers were diminishing specks in the southwestern distance. Wake took in a deep breath. *Rosie* was still floating, moving, and able to shoot.

But the warship was still behind them. Now only three and a half miles astern and closing fast, big white bow waves creaming away on both sides. The enemy's bow gun fired.

That very first shot hit *Rosie* dead center.

52

Innovation

USS *Roseate Spoonbill*
Near Zamboanga, Mindanao, the Philippines

Thursday, 25 December 1941

After Wake saw the gray puff of smoke from the Japanese ship's bow gun, the 45-pound, 120-millimeter high-explosive round took 6.6 seconds to reach *Rosie*. It impacted the upper deck aft of the stack, right next to the cradled motor launch, and showered the deck with splinters as it plunged below into *Rosie*'s heart. And then nothing. Every man on the upper deck and the bridge stopped breathing. No one moved. No one spoke. They waited. The Japanese warship fired a few more shots, which missed, and then stopped shooting, the captain apparently having decided to close the range before firing again.

Several minutes later—or was it just seconds?—Lieutenant Portello and Water Tender 2nd Class Schultz emerged from the starboard main deck hatch, struggling to carry an oblong, smoking object wrapped in an asbestos damage control blanket. They dropped the malevolent thing overboard, then Schultz took the blanket back below. All over the weather decks people started breathing again.

"Bill," Wake said to his exec, "assess damages and see if there are casualties. That gunboat is still coming, and things are about to get a lot worse." Portello arrived to give a brief report, clearly annoyed at having to leave his beloved mechanical beasts.

"As you'll have figured, it was a dud, sir. After hitting the upper deck, it descended forward at about a 30-degree angle through the stack trunk in the forward boiler room—which is now one more damned thing for us to have to repair—then through the ship's main watertight bulkhead and into the lower crew's quarters, punched through another bulkhead, and finally stopped in number two storeroom next to the shelf with that God-awful canned spaghetti sauce." Having said all he had to say, Portello started to turn away. "By your leave, I'll be getting back to work now, sir."

"Very well, Lieutenant. Off you go." Wake gave a silent prayer of thanks. The overhead of the ship's magazine was just twelve inches below where the round ended up.

In addition to being a dud, that accurate first round was evidently a fluke, because the warship's next half-dozen shots fell far short. Still, it was bound to get worse, for the Japanese were gaining rapidly and the range was now only two miles. Formanski's after 3-inch gun was still dueling it out with the Japanese bow gun, with neither scoring a decisive hit.

Waters' report wasn't optimistic. "Hull has dozens of shrapnel holes on both sides, including below the waterline, from stern to bow. Several seams on both sides have opened. Bilges are full. All our pumps are on line and holding the water level but not gaining on it. Engine crew reports boilers and engine are undamaged except for the boiler stack trunk, which lost part of its draw but is being patched. That black smoke was at the lube pump—quickly put out, and they reassembled the pump. We never got to top off fuel, so the tank's at one-third full. Fuel and water tanks look intact."

He paused to catch his breath, then went on. "All guns are operable, ready ammo is distributed, magazine is undamaged and functioning. We are down to about half the ammunition in ready deck lockers. Formanski is doing slow potshots at the Jap to conserve ammo and has reminded the fifty-cal gunners to hold their fire until the enemy's within half a mile.

"Five wounded and out of action from shrapnel wounds. Chief Maloney got a flesh wound tending to those depth charges on the afterdeck, but he just laughed it off. Said he'd gotten worse from the girls at Olongapo. We've got one dead, sir. Seaman Tervis, loader on the port fifty-cal, took a shrapnel hit in the head and died in sick bay."

Wake gave the automatic reply, "Very well," then realized how stupid that sounded given the nature of Waters' report. Wake pointed astern. "The enemy will be at point-blank range in less than four minutes. We won't last long once he gets close, so we're going to have to execute that crazy idea I came up with last night. Formanski's got his hands full with the guns, so I want you aft with Maloney to make sure everything's ready for when I give the word."

"Aye, aye, sir!" Waters headed aft on the upper deck.

Wake knew the timing was going to be tricky, but it was all they had. Their 3-inch guns were effective against an airplane or small ship, but against a modern warship they would be no more than a nuisance.

A round from the enemy hit the port side just forward of the after 3-inch gun mount. That one wasn't a dud. Four men went down at the port .50-caliber, and seven feet of main deck was obliterated into flying splinters. The engine room reported flooding.

All eyes in the bridge were on Wake, whose gaze remained focused on the ship behind them, calculating time and course and distance and speed and the estimated sink rate of an oil drum–sized depth charge. The enemy was a mile away now. Point-blank range. Almost time. Another round hit *Rosie*—this one in the stack top. The airburst above the upper deck blew into the radio room and the wheelhouse. The phone talker, a young kid, was led away bleeding from the face.

Half a mile now. Men's hands were clenching and unclenching. They muttered curses and prayers as they stared at their captain. Only their well-practiced discipline kept them from screaming at him. Though he never looked at them, Wake felt their intensity in the very air as he stood on the bridge wing.

Suddenly, Wake bellowed aft, "Now Maloney—*Now!* Mr. Formanski—*rapid fire!*"

The after 3-inch gun fired instantly. Below and aft of it, Chief Maloney and Lieutenant Waters felt the heat of the muzzle blast but ignored it, pushing with all their might to roll the first of the depth charges—which were even older than *Rosie*—over the stern. Waters and Maloney counted aloud to ten seconds before they rolled the second depth charge, then another ten seconds before the third, and finally the last one went into the sea.

Formanski's gun fired again and again to distract the enemy, several shells hitting and raising small bursts of debris. Wake had calculated his scheme would take about forty to fifty seconds. His heart pounded out a silent prayer. *Please God, let it work.*

The first depth charge exploded ten feet above the sixty-foot-deep sea bottom. The three hundred pounds of high-explosive Dunnite inside created a massive eruption of brown water and coral just ahead of the warship. The second depth charge lifted her hull and broke her spine. The third exploded under her stern, and the fourth on the port side. Though her engine no longer worked, the crippled ship's momentum kept her moving forward as she slid below the water. It was all over in less than a minute.

Formanski ceased firing. Except for the rumbling from the minesweeper's engine, the ship was silent. No one cheered. The men simply stood or sat where they were, stunned that they were alive. But naval discipline and duty overcame exhaustion and fear, and they began helping the wounded, cleaning up debris, and reloading guns.

Two hours later, *Rosie* slowed back down and steamed into the Sulu Sea, a maze of uncharted reefs and islands dreaded by navigators since Magellan. The sun was disappearing off the starboard bow when Bill Waters came out to stand beside Wake on the bridge wing five hours later. In the east, Mars, the Roman god of war, gave off a steady orange light.

"I can't believe that crazy idea of yours worked, sir. It damn well saved us. By the way, Merry Christmas, Captain."

"Hell, Bill, I'd forgotten what day it is," Wake said wearily. "I suppose I should make some sort of Christmas announcement to the crew."

"I think you've already made this Christmas one they'll never forget. Now, sir, may I suggest that you hit the rack and get some sleep? We'll need you rested and alert at sunrise."

53

Wooden Ships and Iron Men

USS *Roseate Spoonbill*
Tagau Island, Sulu Archipelago, the Philippines

---

26 December 1941 to 2 January 1942

When dawn finally ended the nerve-wracking night of threading through the maze of reefs and islands by starlight, *Rosie* had covered the ninety miles to deserted Tagau Island—or at least Wake hoped it was deserted. Here, on the west side of the current-scoured Sugbai Passage between the Sulu Archipelago of the American Philippines and the Celebes Sea of the Dutch East Indies, the crew could make necessary repairs and even relax a bit.

Anchored fore and aft in forty feet of water fifty yards from the island, *Rosie* was shaded from the rising sun (*literally and figuratively*, thought Wake) by a hundred-foot-high hill covered with dense greenery. Wake ordered a shore party to get palm fronds, broad leaves, and vines and bring them on board. Other men spread the deck awnings, leaving the guns exposed. By ten o'clock *Rosie* looked from a distance like just another of the hundreds of little rocky, jungle-clad islands in the area.

Repairs initially estimated to require only two or three days became a week of nonstop work. Portello took charge of repair work below the main deck, plugging the hundreds of shrapnel holes in the hull; rebuilding bulkheads and the boiler trunk; and finally getting to the long overdue maintenance of the engine, lube pumps, and boiler tubes and flues. Topside, Chips rebuilt the portside main deck and the upper deck superstructure one more time, using up all his remaining spare wood. Formanski cleaned, oiled, and serviced the guns and counted the ammunition left for them. It wasn't much, only a third of what they'd started out with at Samoa. Enough for two more engagements—maybe.

On 30 December, "Sparks" Boutner managed to pick up the Zamboanga plantation manager's last short-wave broadcast. The man gave dismal news in a dispirited voice. Jolo had been captured on Christmas Eve, which explained the distant gun flashes *Rosie*'s men had seen that night. To spare civilian lives, MacArthur declared Manila an open and undefended city on Christmas, but the Japanese bombed it anyway.

The U.S. Navy had apparently pulled out of the Philippines, and the U.S. and Philippine armies were battling the Japanese at Bataan on the west side of Manila Bay. There was still some fighting in southern Luzon and Mindanao, but the Japanese were winning. The broadcast ended with his personal goodbye. The Japanese were only two miles away from his home and would soon enter Zamboanga City. This would be his final message. The ship was quiet that night.

Ensign Van Dorn estimated that the remaining food would last three weeks on half rations. To supplement the food stores, he led a shore party to a banana and coconut grove on the other side of the tiny island, which was evidently tended by people from one of the neighboring islands.

As the week of repairs went on, Japanese planes were heard frequently, but the overcast and camouflage hid *Rosie* from prying eyes high above. Wake knew it was only a matter of time, though, before an enemy patrol came by air or sea to check out Japan's newly conquered territory. He resolved to get under way for Tarakan no later than 2 January. The 275-mile trip would take 2 days at 8 knots *if* the winds and currents were fair. They had to beat the Japanese to Tarakan. If *Rosie* could not refuel there, she wouldn't have much reserve fuel.

Accordingly, at the distressingly clear dawn of Friday, 2 January, in the new and cheerless year of 1942, *Rosie* weighed both anchors and slowly chugged away from her tropical hideaway. Her crew was at general quarters, all guns manned and ready and all eyes scanning the sky. The first fifteen miles of the voyage would involve snaking around the reefs at the southern mouth of the Sugbai Passage—of necessity a slow process—until they got to open waters. The current was against them from the first, slowing the ship's speed over the bottom to a mere six knots.

An unexpected encounter brought nerves to the breaking point. Around the eastern side of Tagau Island came a large wooden schooner, full sail up and using an auxiliary engine to make headway. Just another trading schooner, everyone in the bridge thought—until they saw the schooner's unusual deck accoutrements: a .50-caliber machine gun on a steel tripod atop the aft cabin top and two .30-caliber machine guns forward.

Formanski, officer of the watch, spotted the schooner first. "Unidentified armed vessel on the port beam—range one mile." After another second, he added, "Well, I'll be damned. It's a friggin' Jap Q-ship! Break out the battle flag!"

Wake had never heard of the Japanese using schooners as warships, but he appreciated the lieutenant's alertness and caution, if not his breach of naval etiquette. *Rosie*'s shrapnel-torn battle flag, the biggest national ensign on board, soon streamed aft from the stump of a foremast as the guns swung toward the mystery ship only a mile away.

"Lookouts—watch for torpedoes!" ordered Formanski. "If they're that well armed, they may have torpedoes too. They're tricky bastards, the Japs."

Wake lifted his binoculars for a long look. The schooner's crew were scurrying around, but he saw no one near the guns. And while some of them looked darker skinned, the tall men on the afterdeck waving at them were decidedly not Japanese. An American flag raced to the top of the foremast.

"Could be a trick, sir," warned Formanski.

"You've done very well, Mr. Formanski, and you're right; it could be a trick. But I'll handle the situation from here," Wake replied. "Those men on her afterdeck look like American naval officers to me. Signal her to come closer for inspection."

When the schooner was within fifty yards, the nationality of the schooner's officers and men was clear: Americans and Filipinos. *Good Lord. The U.S. Navy in the Philippines has come down to sailboats?*

"Lieutenant Kemp Tolley, commanding officer of USS *Lanikai*," shouted one of the officers into his speaking trumpet. "We are bound from Manila to Surabaya, as per fleet orders."

Van Dorn, reference book in hand, shook his head. "No *Lanikai* in the naval register, sir."

Wake shouted into his trumpet back at Tolley, "This is USS *Roseate Spoonbill*, minesweeper gunboat AMG 57, and I am Lieutenant Commander Robert Wake. We do not show you in the Asiatic Fleet list. When and for what reason was your ship commissioned?"

"Commissioned by Asiatic Fleet at end of November 1941 for reconnaissance of Jap movements from their base at Cam Ranh Bay on the coast of French Indochina. From 6 December we were part of inshore patrol at Manila Bay. Now we are running for our lives, like everybody else." Tolley paused and consulted with another American officer on the deck. "We have no ship of your name in *our* Asiatic Fleet recognition list, sir. Where are you bound from?"

Wake couldn't resist chuckling at his gunnery officer. "Seems you were right, Mr. Formanski. She is indeed a Q-ship—but one of ours!"

Then to Tolley he said, "Station ship at Samoa, Pacific Fleet. Transferred over to Asiatic on 7 December and ordered to Zamboanga to refuel, then on to Manila. We had just arrived at Zamboanga for fuel when Japs attacked, and never got to fill the bunkers—had to pull out fast. Now very low on fuel and bound for Tarakan for enough fuel to get down to Surabaya. You may get there ahead of us—can you carry our mail?"

We're an obvious target for the Japs. The schooner isn't, and just might get through. Please God, help them make it.

"Sure. Any sign of Japs? Any word from fleet headquarters?" asked Tolley.

Wake's answer was short. "Japs are all over. Nothing from HQ. We're all on our own."

Lanikai came closer, and one of *Rosie*'s crewmen tossed over a mailbag, which included a letter from Wake to Delores. There followed a tradition as old as the Navy. Both crews came to attention to the trilling of boatswain's pipes, both flags were dipped, both captains saluted, then the crews were dismissed. The moment of camaraderie between the American sailors ended.

The old schooner rounded the island, and the equally old minesweeper steamed south, bound for Tarakan.

"Wooden ships and iron men—that's what's left of us," muttered Waters absentmindedly to himself, echoing exactly what Wake was thinking.

Wake didn't trust himself to comment.

54

No Time to Waste

USS *Roseate Spoonbill*
Tarakan Island, northeast Borneo, Dutch East Indies

Thursday, 8 January 1942

In peacetime the voyage would have taken two days. But this wasn't peacetime, and Wake increasingly understood that they were no longer on the front lines of the Japanese invasion; they were behind them. Planes and aircraft were everywhere, and none of them were American or British. After hiding in her jungle camouflage for three days at Sibitu Island to evade Japanese patrol boats, at long last *Rosie* arrived off the southwest shore of Tarakan Island late on the night of the eighth. She was immediately challenged by a nervous Dutch minelayer, whose name he later discovered to be *Prins van Oranje*.

Because he hadn't yet officially reported to the Asiatic Fleet, Wake did not have the fleet's codebook, and thus had no idea what the proper recognition signal was for that date. And since the Pacific Fleet had changed its codes when the war started, he had no idea of a recognition signal for that fleet either. He surmised that since the Dutch warship was a minelayer, there was probably a minefield. The only way in to the fuel dock was with permission and guidance from that warship.

Aware that the Dutch warship's guns were aimed at *Rosie*, Wake decided to be candid. He ordered the after searchlight shone upward on *Rosie*'s battle ensign for twenty seconds. Most international merchant and naval ships had an American flag on board for rendering courtesies upon entering a U.S. harbor, but only U.S. warships flew a huge American battle flag. At the same time, Wake ordered a plain-language message sent to the Dutchman in international Morse code light signal: "USS *Roseate Spoonbill*, minesweeper AMG 57, recent arrival to Asiatic Fleet. Have no idea of the proper signal. We need fuel urgently."

There was no reply. Wake and Waters exchanged worried glances, each trying to figure what their Plan B might be. Then, at last, the Dutchman's light flashed back at them. Van Dorn reported, "Follow us through channel in minefield."

"Plot this channel carefully, Mr. Waters. We may well have to get through it again without an escort."

An hour later they anchored off the fuel docks and all hands breathed easier. They were a long way from safety, but at least now they had a fighting chance to reach it. The town and the oil refinery docks were black forms against the murky sky. The sound of fuel pumps drifted across the harbor. A light rain commenced, a blessed development that would help keep enemy aviators grounded. Wake kept half the crew at their battle stations and insisted the other half rest. The 90-degree heat and 100 percent humidity should have made sleep impossible, but the exhausted men flopped on bunks and decks and slept instantly, forgetting their discomfort, short rations, and uncertain future.

Sunrise revealed a dozen merchant ships anchored near the fuel docks, all waiting for fuel. The two docks still functioning were occupied by four ships that had been fueling all night. An hour later, Wake was ashore at the harbormaster's office. An hour after that, the harbormaster, a well-fed Dutchman driving a remarkably fancy car, finally arrived at his office. He wasn't pleased to see Wake, much less hear his demand for fuel and food—now.

"You Americans will have to await your turn for fuel," he huffed, "and we have no food or any other supplies to spare. The army has commandeered all of it." The harbormaster didn't look like he'd missed any meals lately, but Wake could do nothing but accept his decision.

And so *Rosie* and her men waited another two days, watching the level go down in their fuel gauges and Japanese aircraft crisscross the overcast sky. Wake spent some time ashore and learned that the Dutch army had a couple of understrength battalions, a few antiaircraft guns, four Brewster Buffalo fighters, and three B-10 bombers with which to repulse the impending Japanese onslaught. The main strategy seemed to be scorched-earth defeatism: wait until the enemy appeared, then blow up the 703 oil wells, 4 refining facilities, and 2 functioning fuel wharfs; and then surrender. He could think of nothing else for them to do. They had no chance.

At 4 p.m. on 10 January 1942, *Rosie* was finally allowed to come alongside the wharf, and two high-capacity hoses began pumping fuel oil into her bunkers. The crew did not waste time, for there was none to waste.

At 5:34, as an exasperated Portello was complaining to the Dutch supervisor about the slowness of the fuel pumps, Van Dorn was trying to use his Dutch heritage to connive fresh fruit from a grocery store, and Doc Stanford was begging for medical supplies at the local hospital, the air raid sirens wailed.

55

The Minefield

USS *Roseate Spoonbill*
Borneo, Dutch East Indies

Saturday, 10 January 1942

Half the crew were already at their battle stations when the siren sounded, and the ship's guns were ready within seconds. Guns made no difference, however, for the enemy aircraft bombed from very high in the overcast sky. The bomb explosions covered a wide area, mostly near the airfield north of town. None came close to the fuel wharf. Obviously, the Japanese wanted that for themselves.

To the east, a Japanese naval bombardment and the Dutch army's machine-gun return fire indicated a landing in progress on that shoreline, only four miles away. More important for *Rosie* was the Dutch fuel supervisor shutting down the pumps, preparing to disconnect the hoses, and cursing at the Americans to leave. He was going to follow orders and blow up the fuel tanks.

As the Dutchman stormed away to set off the charges, Wake ordered lines singled up and then cast off. Explosions sounded from all directions. Dozens of columns of dense black smoke rose into the sky and merged into an evil-looking cloud that overspread the island. The Dutch were indeed scorching the earth.

"Free of the wharf, sir," Waters said tightly.

Wake willed his own voice to remain calm. "Very well. Ahead slow. Left standard rudder."

The deck rumbled as the shaft went into gear and *Rosie* began to move forward. No one on the bridge brought it up, but everyone there knew that Ensign Van Dorn and Doc Stanford were still ashore.

"Stern is free and clear, sir," said Waters.

"Very well. Left full rudder. Come around to course one-seven-zero. Make revolutions for ten knots. Mr. Formanski, prepare for surface action somewhere to port. The enemy may appear at any time. Mr. Waters, I want a fuel gauge report immediately."

Waters checked via the voice tube. "Mr. Portello reports bunkers are 40 percent full, sir."

The stern lookout's shout startled everyone. "There they are!" Wake swiveled his gaze out to sea on the port side, looking for a Japanese destroyer.

"No, sir! On the wharf. Mr. Van Dorn and Doc are on the wharf!"

Waters muttered something to the boatswain's mate, who headed aft to reprimand the lookout to make a proper report next time. *Rosie* was picking up speed now and a quarter mile from the wharf. If she went back and was alongside when the fuel docks exploded, the ship and crew would be obliterated. Wake peered at the two men through his binoculars, feeling the eyes of everyone around him watching him, waiting for his decision. The wharf was deserted except for the two Americans waving their arms frantically.

The port lookout reported, "Two enemy patrol craft on port beam past Point Peningki, range five to six miles. They're in line ahead, course is southerly, speed is fifteen knots, sir."

Wake could barely see them against the darkening horizon. Night was coming. "Hold steady on this course. Wait to fire until well within range, Mr. Formanski. Then execute slow fire. Conserve ammunition."

A small freighter ahead of them in the harbor had weighed anchor and was drifting across their course. Another was following close astern. Like the Americans, the merchant ships were trying to flee.

"Left standard rudder to pass astern of that freighter ahead, then settle back on previous course."

The stern lookout reported, "Mr. Van Dorn and Doc Stanford are in a motorboat, sir."

Wake kept his binoculars focused on the two enemy patrol craft. Each was about a hundred feet long. They probably mounted only a couple of 20-millimeter guns, maybe a forty. Their main danger to *Rosie* was from their radios. They would certainly report *Rosie*'s course to their fleet. Then he realized it didn't matter. There was only one way to go, south toward Surabaya, and the Japanese knew it. But Wake also knew his ship couldn't make the more than a thousand miles there with fuel bunkers only one-third full. His next destination had to be Balikpapan, the last refueling port on the east coast of Borneo—almost five hundred miles to the south.

The Dutch minelayer was nowhere in sight, and they were closing on the minefield. The fuel wharf supervisor had said a hundred mines were scattered over a large area out there. Wake went to the chart table and studied the course headings Waters had drawn to show the channel through the minefield when they arrived. *Rosie* would take the opposite headings to get out.

Waters stepped close to his captain and whispered, "Mr. Van Dorn and Doc are closing on us, sir. If we maintain course and slow to five knots, we can recover them and tow their boat. We might need it later." After a moment he added, "I suggest we also tow the motor launch."

Wake appreciated him not finishing his thought: *as lifeboats when the Japs sink us.*

"Good idea, Mr. Waters," he said. "Maintain course and slow to five knots to take Mr. Van Dorn and Doc along the starboard side. Once they're on board, I want that motorboat and the ship's launch towed astern. Then we'll resume ten knots."

He added quietly, "Fill that motorboat, *Rosie*'s motor launch, and the Carley rafts with water and provisions."

"Single aircraft approaching rapidly from starboard quarter," the starboard lookout announced. "Range one mile. Elevation five hundred feet."

"Good God, it's one of the Dutch Brewster Buffalos. He must've taken off from the airfield," said Formanski before yelling, "Friendly plane! Friendly plane!" to his gunners.

The Buffalo zoomed over them, *Rosie*'s crew cheering on the Dutch pilot on as the plane curved around to the east and turned north toward the Japanese fleet. The plane disappeared into the haze, but they heard its machine guns firing, then the heavier concussions of Japanese antiaircraft fire. After thirty seconds, the gunfire ended.

A few minutes later, the oil tanks along the wharf exploded. The portside lookout reported the two enemy patrol craft had slowed and altered course away to the east. Wake soon knew the reason. Two Japanese planes appeared five miles away to the northeast, tiny specks in the fading light, heading right for them.

Chief Maloney called up from the main deck that Van Dorn and Doc Stanford were on board and their boat was being provisioned before being streamed aft; the launch was being loaded and would follow in thirty seconds. Van Dorn showed up on the bridge and silently assumed his battle station position.

Wake allowed a brief smile. "Welcome back, Mr. Van Dorn." Then, "Right standard rudder to course one-nine-zero. Resume ten knots."

"Mr. Portello says he can't, sir," said Waters a minute later. "He thought the circulating pump was fixed and we could do ten, but looks like it isn't. Seals are leaking. Best right now is eight knots."

"Very well, eight knots."

"Steady on course one-nine-zero, sir," intoned the helmsman.

The last faint light of the sunset was fading away on the mountaintops to the west. The roiling oil field smoke cloud was spreading toward it, Wake thought, *like a malevolent monster.* Then the light was gone and darkness enveloped them. The freighter following astern had slowed down for some reason. *Either they're not sure we know where we're going, or they don't want to get hit by a stray bomb from the Jap plane. If I was that captain, I wouldn't get too close to* Rosie *either.*

"Enemy aircraft still approaching from northeast on port quarter. Range about three miles. Can barely see them, sir. They're in that cloud."

Waters tapped the chart. Wake looked down at it and saw the new heading coming up, then looked astern. Darkness would be no help. *Rosie*'s bioluminescent wake would lead the enemy pilots straight to them.

"Mr. Waters, have someone pour some spare lube oil astern to dissipate that luminescence. Mr. Formanski, hold fire until I give the order. When we open fire, blind them with the after searchlight also."

Those orders acknowledged, he gave another. "Mr. Waters, have the engine room stand by for an abrupt full astern order."

Waters was alarmed. That could very well wreck the shaft gear of *Rosie*'s old engine. The ship would lose way and drift into the minefield. But Waters acknowledged the order and passed it to Portello in a deliberate voice.

The planes were dark shapes now, one in front of the other, the sparking exhausts of their radial engines flickering. One mile. Half a mile. Wake stood on the port bridge wing, his hands gripping the rail, Waters on one side of him and Formanski on the other. "We're passing the outer edge of the minefield, sir," Waters said.

Wake's eyes never left the planes. "Now, gentlemen! Open fire! Searchlight on! Full astern on the engine!"

56
Old Tricks

USS *Roseate Spoonbill*
East coast of Borneo, Dutch East Indies

Saturday, 10 January 1942

The garish white searchlight instantly transformed the night, illuminating the underside of the black clouds, the yellow-orange blasts from the after 3-inch gun's muzzle, and two glowing red streams of tracer rounds from the port and starboard .50-calibers. The Japanese planes two hundred yards astern were easy to spot now, one mechanical bird of death thundering behind the other.

Now that he had a good look at them, Chief Davis identified the planes as the new Mitsubishi A6M fighters—Zeros. He'd never seen one in person, he said, but it was rumored around the fleet that they were "a damn sight more lethal" than anything the Allies had. The light, fast long-range fighter couldn't carry big bombs, but it didn't need them against *Rosie*.

The machine-gun tracers flew straight into both planes as the point-blank antiaircraft shells, fuses set at one second, exploded around them. The planes' guns, meanwhile, were shredding *Rosie*'s decks and superstructure into lethal splinters.

Rosie's engine was much slower to engage in its part of the plan than the guns had been, going out of ahead gear just as the first plane disintegrated into a ball of flaming debris that rained down over the minesweeper. The second plane, flames streaming from its left wing-tank, banked violently to the right to avoid the debris just as the astern gear began to slow the ship. Wake watched the black 100-pound bomb arc down from the plane's belly before the fighter zoomed away into the night.

And in that sickening moment, Wake knew his plan to dodge the bombing attack by suddenly going astern and making the enemy overfly the ship had failed—by three seconds.

The blast from the fragmentation bomb knocked Wake to his knees and sucked the air from his lungs. He caught his breath and pulled himself upright to survey the scene. The bomb had hit twelve inches inboard of the starboard gunwale, right amidship, and exploded down into the after boiler room below. Both .50-caliber gun crews lay sprawled on the upper deck, dead or wounded. Half the after 3-inch gun crew looked wounded. The radio room was a shambles. Boutner staggered out, wounded again but alive. Wake felt *Rosie* begin to list to starboard.

"Douse the searchlight and cease fire," Wake ordered. "Steer course one-seven-zero. Engine ahead slow. Mr. Waters, damage report."

"Phone lines and voice tubes aren't working, sir. I'll get down to the boiler room and report back on the conditions belowdecks."

"Very well." Wake turned to his gunnery officer. "Mr. Formanski, check the upper decks and report back."

Formanski made it back first. "Fires on deck weren't bad, and almost all are extinguished, sir. After 3-inch gun still works, but Chief Maloney and two others are wounded. Portside fifty is operable but needs a new gun crew. Starboard fifty is wrecked. Radio room is wrecked and the antenna is mangled. Stack is riddled and probably losing draft. Secondary refrigeration unit is wrecked. Starboard main deck has a big friggin' hole, but it can be patched—if Chips has anything left to patch it with. Ammo is being brought topside to the ready lockers. I don't have a total ammo count yet or casualty count from topside decks, but it looks like we have quite a few wounded." He rubbed both hands across his face. "We got clobbered, sir, but *Rosie* can still fight those Nip bastards."

Waters' report was longer but equally depressing. "The bomb exploded just below the overhead on the starboard side of the after boiler room, about three feet inboard of frame forty-five. All the men there were either killed instantly or critically wounded by the blast or by scalding. Most of the damage is in there, but the after boiler room bulkhead to the engine room got weakened, and there's some damage in there too. The main fire pump is wrecked, secondary one forward works and is being used topside. It'll be reversed for pumping bilges once the fires are all out, which'll be soon. Fortunately, there was no major fire in the engineering spaces. The oil heater, secondary feed water pump, and circulating pump are damaged but can be fixed. The after boiler is riddled and heavily dented—out of operation, but it can be fixed in a yard.

"Bilge pumps still work, which is good because we're taking on water from several shrapnel gashes in the hull at frame forty-five. Bilges appear full. Don't know yet if the pumps are holding the line on flooding. Forward and after bulkheads in the after boiler room are skewed and the hatches are bent, but have been pried open. Forward boiler is undamaged and functioning. Fuel bunkers fore and aft appear unbreached. We can do six knots, maybe."

He paused, swallowed, then said, "We have nine dead and eighteen wounded, sir, six of them pretty bad, including Chief Maloney. The wounded are down in the chiefs' quarters and the after and forward crew's quarters. Doc's operating in the wardroom with Cookie and Gaspar assisting. He may be only a corpsman second class, sir, but I swear you'd never know he isn't a real surgeon. We'd be lost without him."

Another pause, then, "Mr. Portello is one of the dead, sir, and Chief McCrea is badly wounded. Motor Machinist Second Class Murphy is senior engineer now. I'll be doing up a new watch bill. We'll be short everywhere. Formanski'll need new men for the guns." In a tired but determined voice, Waters ended with, "Orders, sir?"

Wake put a hand on Waters' shoulder. "I think we both know we won't make it through another attack, Bill. Our best bet is to make them think we're already destroyed. And I know just how to do it. We're going to use the ruse de guerre that fooled my grandfather Peter when he was chasing a Spanish raider through the Caribbean in '98."

Outlandish tales of Peter Wake's exploits were part of Navy legend, and Waters had heard quite a few of them. Many officers who knew him figured Lt. Cdr. Robert James Wake would make admiral someday too—especially with the fast promotions the new war would bring. Yet, Robert Wake had never mentioned his antecedents. Until now.

"Don't think I know that one, sir."

"He was chasing the raider in a rainstorm at night. He knew his ship's guns had scored a hit, so he followed the flames—only to discover that the raider had left a flaming decoy behind and slipped away." Wake laughed. "He chased the Spanish raider another two thousand miles around the Caribbean before he finally captured her."

Waters recalled hearing something about that episode in the O-Club at Pearl, but he'd discounted it at the time as just another tall tale. "So, we'll make a decoy?"

"Exactly. A makeshift raft of flaming debris surrounded by bloody clothing and personal items, some fuel, empty ammunition boxes, and anything else that looks personal and will float. We'll put it right here, then we get out of here as fast as old *Rosie* can go. The Japs know our location, and when they come to search, they'll see what they *expect* to see—the wreckage from our sunken ship. Yet another victory for the emperor. Another round of sake for the pilots."

Waters laughed. "Captain, that's so simple it just might work."

"We'll have to hurry. We're already twenty-two miles from Tarakan. At only six knots we won't leave much of a luminescent trail astern, and we can be another fifty or sixty miles down the coast when daylight comes. We'll go up a river or alongside an island and do the camouflage bit again. Understood?"

"Yes, sir. I'll get Van Dorn and some men working on it right now. We should be ready to get under way in twenty minutes or less."

57

Silent and Dark

USS *Roseate Spoonbill*
Southbound off the east coast of Borneo, Dutch East Indies

10–12 January 1942

The decoy was still burning when Wake peered astern from the fantail, a faint sputtering light five miles back. No planes or ships had been seen or heard since the attack, so he allowed the crew to lie down and rest at their battle stations.

For the fully one-third of *Rosie*'s men wounded in the attack there was no rest. Although he had managed to find some medical supplies back at Tarakan to add to the ship's pharmacy, Doc Stanford had to ration morphine, sulfa powder, and bandages. The wounded moaned in pain as they lay in the dark berthing spaces enduring the stifling heat and humidity. Wake had spoken with each one of them, explaining what the situation was and describing the decoy and the escape plan. No one complained. All begged to be allowed back to their duty stations.

He reassured them that their crew mates could manage without them, then left them, fighting back his tears until he stood alone on the fantail looking back at the flickering decoy. No longer able to block the emotions that had been building up inside him for a month, he let the tears run freely down his cheeks. After several minutes he took a deep breath and quietly admonished himself, *There, that's done. Now carry on. They need to trust your judgment. Don't show doubt.*

Composing himself, Wake returned to the bridge and called for the burial party to assemble aft on the undamaged portside main deck. This time he didn't follow naval regulations, for the survival of the living was more important than showing proper respect to the dead. The enemy was everywhere, and possibly quite close. The dead were consigned to the sea at night, under way, with no lights showing, no Navy Hymn, no final rifle volleys, and only a handful of men attending. Wake conjured up a prayer which he whispered to the men around him. There weren't enough national ensigns to shroud all the dead prior to committing them to the deep. Wake assigned the ship's last undamaged ensign to cover Lieutenant Portello's body; the others got signal flags that barely covered their canvas shrouds. Four minutes later it was over. The men went back to work.

Dawn on the eleventh found *Rosie* at Samama Island in the Derawan group, twenty-eight miles off the east coast of Borneo. They anchored on short scope along the island's west side, and Van Dorn led a party ashore to bring back foliage for camouflage. An hour later the launch came around the point with four outrigger canoes in tow.

Looking pleased with himself when he arrived on the bridge, Van Dorn announced, "Nobody lives here, but there were eight fishing boats from a nearby island on the beach. Turns out those native guys love American cigarettes. One of them speaks a little English and told me Yankee smokes are like opium to the locals. When he asked for some, we bargained a bit. The men chipped in, and we bought four boats for two packs each."

Wake asked, "And what'll we do with them?"

"Well, sir, since we're only doing six knots, I figured we can tow them astern. You can put five or six men in each one—just in case."

Wake glanced inquiringly at Waters, who gestured at the green jungle cover quickly being spread over the ship's remaining awnings. "Sounds good to me, Captain. Helps our camouflage, too. To someone flying high overhead, it will look like native fishing boats at a little jungle island. We sure won't look like a U.S. warship. We could keep the camo on the ship until we get to Surabaya. I hear Formanski has already taken photos to show the guys at the O-Club when we get back. Figures he can make money on bar bets about whether a U.S. Navy captain allowed his ship to look like a filthy native village."

Wake laughed out loud for the first time since—he couldn't remember. "Very well. I hope Mr. Formanski makes a ton of money. And thank you, Mr. Van Dorn. That was good thinking. And once we get to Surabaya we can celebrate with an outrigger regatta."

Sheltered beneath the vegetation, the men worked to repair the damaged hull and machinery while Doc worked on his patients. All hands not otherwise occupied painted the ship and the awnings camouflage black and green. When the sun began its descent, *Rosie* weighed anchor and steered south again.

They had steamed for three hours when lookouts saw a shape dead ahead on the southern horizon. Wake was dozing in his bunk when the messenger woke him. Seconds later he was on the bridge wing conferring with Waters, who was peering through binoculars. The overcast and rain of the previous few days was mostly gone, and the half moon would be rising soon.

"It looks big enough to be a light cruiser coming north from the Makassar Strait, sir," Waters said. "If we stay on course, it will pass by less than a mile off our port side in twenty or thirty minutes."

"We'll head west, then, toward the Borneo coast," said Wake, "so as not to be silhouetted against Celebes Island by the moonrise." He walked inside to the chart table, traced the coast with a finger, then ordered, "Right standard rudder to course two-six-five."

The lookout called down softly, "There's a smaller vessel on each side of the big one, sir. All three're still heading due north toward us. Range about five miles. Estimated speed ten to fifteen knots."

"Very well," replied Wake. He pointed at the coastline on the chart and told Waters, "We'll head toward this river mouth just north of this place called Amasangkar. We should arrive around dawn. We'll hide there for the day and hope to hell the locals are friendly."

Waters nodded, and Wake continued, "Now, I need you to go around one more time and tell the men what's going on. Make sure there are no embers from the stack, no lights anywhere on the ship. Smoking lamp is out. No yelling of orders or reprimands. Stay silent and dark, or we die."

"Aye, aye, sir."

58

The River of Sullen Faces

USS *Roseate Spoonbill*
Near Amasangkar, Borneo, Dutch East Indies

Monday, 12 January 1942

The rising moon showed the Japanese cruiser and her two destroyer escorts to be continuing north, toward Tarakan. *Rosie* continued on toward the coast because there wasn't time to get anywhere else to hide for the day.

The ship entered the mangrove-lined river just as the eastern horizon was lightening, towing her brood of two motor boats and four outriggers behind her. The winding river was unnamed and undetailed on the chart, but Wake was pleased to see that it had a strong current. That meant it might be deep enough for his ship. As they cautiously crept forward against the current, a seaman with a lead line called out the depth, mostly three or four fathoms. *Rosie* needed two and a half. It would be very close.

On the starboard side of the river mouth a tiny village with huts on bamboo stilts straggled along the bank. It wasn't clear how many people lived there, because most of them seemed to be hiding from the strange warship. The few who let themselves be seen had sullen, unwelcoming faces. Waters and

Wake discussed the odds that the villagers might inform the Japanese, or even attack *Rosie* themselves. The idea wasn't that farfetched.

Wake had heard at Tarakan that some Borneo natives hated the Dutch, the deserved result of abuse they had suffered over the past three hundred years. He doubted these natives knew or cared that *Rosie* wasn't Dutch, or even European. They just knew the crew was white. Therefore, he ordered no flag to be flown. *Let them wonder,* he decided. *It might delay any attempt at violence.*

The minesweeper spent the rest of the night at the fourth bend in the river, guns manned and lookouts doubled against attack from air or ground. The following morning, they enhanced the camouflage and settled down to wait. The air was stifling and the mosquitoes a constant and vicious plague, for no sea breeze penetrated that far up into the jungle.

Only one tiny native boat went past them. The unsmiling paddler refused to even look at the warship in his river. That second night *Rosie* stayed put again, Wake hoping the enemy might forget about her or be diverted to more important operations to the north where, hopefully, the Allies were making a stand.

On the third night Wake decided it was safe enough to leave. They got under way on a flood tide an hour after sunset, running aground twice on the way downstream but backing off and moving onward. All hands breathed a sigh of relief when they passed the village and headed out to sea. Wake ordered a southeasterly course that would take them around Manghalikat Point, then south into the Makassar Strait between Borneo and the Celebes islands, and southwest toward the fueling depot at Balikpapan.

Rosie had steamed 5,271 miles since departing Samoa. Only 321 miles remained to Balikpapan. There they would find fuel, provisions, hospitals for the wounded, a repair yard for the ship, communications with fleet head-quarters in Surabaya, and information about what was going on in the war and when reinforcements from the Pacific Fleet were going to arrive. Just 321 miles—two and a half more days, Wake calculated—and they would be as safe as it was possible to be in the middle of war in the Pacific. But he knew that depended on the infamous currents in the Makassar Strait, *Rosie*'s old engine and sole remaining boiler holding up, the hull seams holding together, and the Japanese not finding and attacking.

They made it fourteen miles.

59

The Plan

USS *Roseate Spoonbill*
Off the Coast of Borneo, Dutch East Indies

Wednesday, 14 January 1942

Three hours past sunset and an hour before moonrise, lookouts sent word to the bridge that two dark forms had been spotted four miles away, broad on the port quarter, steaming south side by side at an estimated ten knots. Wake sat tensely as the reports came in. Minutes later they were identified as warships, possibly *Chidori*-class torpedo gunboats. He took a deep breath after the next report. There were eleven ships in all, steaming south into the Makassar Strait.

Fifteen minutes later, two of the distant ships altered course to the southwest. So did the nearest *Chidori* warships. All four were heading for *Rosie*.

We may not make it through this one. "Full right rudder, come to course two-two-five degrees," Wake rapped out. "Mr. Waters, I want Mr. Formanski, Mr. Van Dorn, Chief Davis, Chief Smith, Petty Officer Murphy, and Doc Stanford up here right away."

"Aye, aye, sir."

"Two destroyers, type unknown," the lookouts reported. All four enemy ships appeared to have increased their speed. A faint pink smudge of light in the east heralded moonrise as the officers and petty officers crowded around the chart table, their serious faces eerie in the dim red glow of the battle lanterns.

Wake pointed at the chart as he quickly summarized the situation. "We are here, steaming west-southwest for Perkebunan Plantation, here, about six miles away. Four enemy ships are astern of us and heading this way. Two *Chidori*-class torpedo boats are now about four miles away, and two larger destroyers are about seven miles away. We'll be in point-blank range of the 4.7-inch guns of the closest two in less than thirty minutes.

"This is what each of you will do, quickly and efficiently. Doc, your walking wounded, plus Cookie and Gaspar, will move the invalid wounded into the launch and motorboat when I give the signal. Get your medical chest ready to go too. We'll pull the boats alongside, but we won't slow down. You'll get the men in *fast*. There'll be no time to be gentle."

Wake turned to his gunnery officer. "Mr. Formanski, rig up some big scuttling charges against the lowest part of the hull in the forepeak, main magazine, forward boiler room, engine room, and shaft alley. Also, one here in the bridge. Set the fuses for fifteen minutes, but do not switch them on. Understood?"

"Aye, aye sir."

"Mr. Van Dorn, dump the codebooks and all radio and wireless parts overboard immediately. Get all the canned and boxed food you can into the motorboats when they are brought alongside. There's already some food and water in them, but I want even more."

"Three miles away now, Captain," the lookout called out.

Wake didn't wait for Van Dorn's acknowledgment. "Petty Officer Murphy, we're going to strain the boilers and engine to their limit. I want as much thick smoke as you can make while we're loading men in the boats. *After* we cast them off, I want maximum speed to go with that thick smoke. Pull out the boiler safety stops. Then open all the Kingston valves.

"Chief Rogers, you are in charge of getting those motorboats safely alongside so we can get the wounded on board. Once they're filled and cast off, get the four outriggers alongside and put men in them. Then load the Carley rafts, except for one.

"Mr. Waters, take the sextant and charts with you. Take every rifle and pistol we have, along with their ammo, with you on the motorboat. Bring every carton of cigarettes and anything around the bridge you think might be useful for barter with the natives. All right, everyone understand so far?"

After a chorus of yesses, Wake went on. "Very well, then, here's the plan. We continue on course until we come under accurate fire, then get the wounded into the motorboats and cast them off. I want Mr. Waters in the ship's motor launch and Mr. Van Dorn in the other motorboat. Chief Davis, Chief Rogers, Chief Smith, and Gunner's Mate Dorst will each be in charge of an outrigger.

"That whole flotilla will steer west for the coast. Once there, you'll head for the plantation. You may find friendly folks there, but be careful until you're sure. Get out of this area of Borneo as fast as possible and head south, overland to Balikpapan.

"After the main part of the crew is off the ship and heading west toward the shore, I will stay on board with Mr. Formanski and eight volunteers: two for the after 3-inch gun, two down in the engine room to open the Kingston valves, two to activate the scuttling charges, and two on the bridge with me. I want the guns to fire their last rounds, then the gunners will get in the Carley float. Likewise, I want the engineers to increase the shaft revolutions and activate the scuttling charges, then get in the raft. The bridge crew will turn and steer *Rosie* to the east, to draw the Japs away in that direction, then we'll get in the Carley raft and paddle for the beach. Mr. Waters, do not wait for us on the beach more than one hour. We will catch up with you on the way to Balikpapan. Any questions or suggestions?"

There were none. Wake paused and looked around at their tense faces and knew this was the moment. "I love this old ship and this great crew. You have all done magnificently, in the finest tradition of the United States Navy, and I know you will continue to do that. And when we all get to Balikpapan, it will be the greatest honor of my life to buy a decent drink for every *Rosie* man in the finest damn bar the Dutch have got there!"

That got them smiling. "Very well, let's start getting this done. Mr. Waters, send up *Rosie*'s battle flag!"

"Aye, aye, sir!" yelled Waters, looking at the signalman, who ran for the flag locker.

Then Wake quietly added to his executive officer, "Meet me in my stateroom."

A few minutes later, Waters came into the stateroom and collapsed in the chair. "Good plan, sir. We can pull it off. The men are willing and capable, and a bunch of fellas have volunteered for the scuttling crew."

Wake handed him a small metal box. "Good. In this box are some documents I want you to carry. They're in a waterproof oilskin pouch. They include *Rosie*'s logbook pages since December fifth, my commendations for the officers and men, and some letters to my wife. I'd like you to give them to her in person, Bill."

Waters hesitated, then, his eyes never leaving Wake's, slowly nodded. "I will, Captain."

Returning his friend's gaze steadily, Wake held out his hand and quietly said, "Thank you for the great work you've done, and are about to do, Bill. One of those letters is a recommendation for your promotion and command of a destroyer. I hope you get one of the new ones. God be with you and our men." He pulled his hand away and said, "Well, enough of that. Go get the men ready for their jungle trek."

From the doorway, Waters promised, "We'll all get through, sir. And make my drink a rum."

60

The Last Trick

USS *Roseate Spoonbill*
Off the coast of Borneo, Dutch East Indies

Wednesday, 14 January 1942

The chase went on for another fifty-two minutes as the closest Japanese ships—the *Chidori*-class gunboats—slowed down and warily closed the range to two miles without opening fire. The two destroyers behind them, modern *Asashio*-class monsters according to Chief Davis, were only four miles away.

The time was not wasted on board *Rosie*. Seeing the enemy's cautious approach, Wake conjured up yet another surprise for them involving the minesweeping paravane gear. The engine room, main guns, scuttling charges, Kingston valves, and bridge team were ready. *Rosie* was as prepared as she could be. Now it was up to the Japanese.

At 1 a.m., with *Rosie* now only a mile off the coast, the waiting ended. Both enemy warships picked up speed and opened fire with their forward 4.7-inch guns simultaneously, the rounds going slightly over the minesweeper. The two destroyers farther away opened fire with their 5-inch guns, closely missing on the port side but riddling *Rosie* with shrapnel.

Wake nodded to his executive officer. "Mr. Waters, get the men in the boats." Then to the gunnery officer he said, "Mr. Formanski, you may open fire."

Rosie's boats had already been brought alongside and loaded with provisions, water, and weapons, and the wounded who would board them were waiting on deck. Since the ship's bilges were full of water, her freeboard was only five feet amidship, an easy drop for them.

On Wake's orders, the crew sprang into action. The after 3-inch gun banged out a round, narrowly missing the nearest enemy ship. The wounded began entering the boats, either jumping or being lowered down. Acrid smoke belched from the stack, forming a smokescreen. The engine crew came up from below and jumped into the boats. The bridge crew followed. A lone volunteer remained to steer as Wake stood on the bridge wing watching the enemy. The deck crew sent the paravane floats over each side of the stern, the winches screeching as the four thousand feet of cable went out for each one, then they too got in the boats. Two more enemy 4.7-inch gun shells straddled the minesweeper, missing by only fifty feet this time. Wake heard men in the boats scream and curse in pain from the shrapnel lacerations.

Rosie's after 3-inch gun belched flame again, this time scoring a hit on the foredeck of the Japanese ship. Wake heard Waters shout something and looked down. The boats were away. Only the volunteers were still on board. The remaining Carley raft was ready, dragging alongside as the ship increased speed. Two more Japanese rounds exploded close alongside.

It was time.

Wake calmly said to the helmsman, "Hard left rudder. Steady her on course zero-eight-five. When she's steady on that course, lash the wheel."

Rosie heeled heavily to starboard as she began the turn, not toward the enemy but out to sea, away from the coast and the men in the boats. The Japanese swerved to avoid the paravane floats and buoyed cables that suddenly appeared in front of them, temporarily throwing their own guns off, and took several minutes turning onto the new course. The distance opened in that time. It wasn't much, Wake knew, but it was something. Enough that now both *Rosie*'s main guns could bear on the pursuers.

Wake shouted to the gun crews fore and aft. "Fire three rounds when your gun bears! Then get in the Carley raft!"

Over the repaired phone line to the engine room, Wake told the volunteers there to set revolutions for as many knots as they could and check to make sure the Kingston valves were open, then switch on the scuttling charges, run topside, and get into the Carley raft.

"Steady on course zero-eight-five, sir," intoned Quartermaster Third Class Evan Jones in a steady voice, as calmly as if they were coming into San Francisco Bay.

"Lash the helm, Jones, and get down into the Carley raft."

Two fountains erupted where *Rosie* would have been had she not just turned. Wake knew the Japanese could adjust their aim to compensate for his turn easily. But the important thing was they were turning too, following their victim and not the boats making for shore under the smokescreen. The 3-inchers banged out their last three rounds in rapid fire, then their crews ran for the raft and shoved off. Wake set the explosive charge in the bridge.

Just as Jones finished lashing the helm, the Japanese figured out the American ship's new range and bearing. The point-blank salvo from all four ships simultaneously hit *Rosie* dead center on the upper deck.

The minesweeper was obliterated in a blast of light and noise.

As Waters staggered ashore, the cloud of smoke was fading away and he could look out over the moonlit sea to his ship. The last he saw of *Rosie* was the tottering after mast and ripped battle flag as it disappeared down into the flaming fuel oil spreading across the water.

Waters didn't turn away, knowing that Wake's final trick was yet to come. The two closest Japanese ships slowed and steered for the debris, intent on capturing any survivors and interrogating them about the whereabouts of the rest of Admiral Hart's fleet. Waters looked at his watch and waited. After thirteen minutes of fruitless searching, the ships turned to leave, for this was a dangerous, reef-strewn coast.

And right then, *Rosie*'s scuttling charges went off right below them.

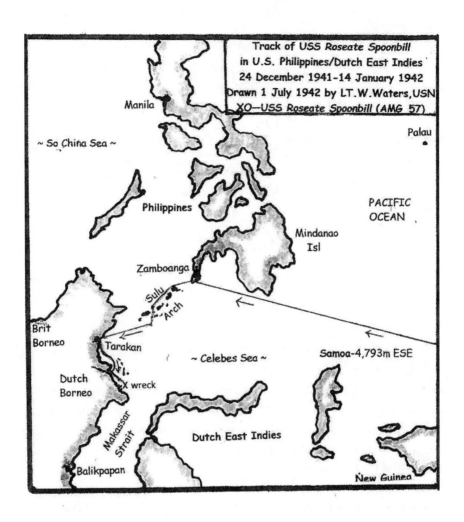

Track of USS *Roseate Spoonbill*
in U.S. Philippines/Dutch East Indies
24 December 1941-14 January 1942
Drawn 1 July 1942 by LT.W.Waters,USN
XO—USS *Roseate Spoonbill* (AMG 57)

Manila

~ So China Sea ~

Palau

Philippines

PACIFIC
OCEAN

Mindanao
Isl

Zamboanga

Sulu
Arch

Brit
Borneo

Tarakan

~ Celebes Sea ~

Samoa-4,793m ESE

Dutch
Borneo

X wreck

Makassar
Strait

Dutch East Indies

Balikpapan

New Guinea

61
The Letter

Grunt Bone Lane
Key West, Florida

Winter, spring, and summer 1942

Amid the litany of disastrous war news from the Pacific, the North Atlantic, and North Africa that dominated the airwaves and newspapers, eight-pound, six-ounce Sean Robert Wake was born at sunrise on Saturday, 14 February, in Key West's naval hospital. The nurses took one look at his sweet smile and dubbed him "Valentine." Sean Robert appeared healthy and strong, and after months of stress and despair, Delores once again had reason for hope and joy.

The journey from Samoa to Key West had been long, lonely, and tense. Delores and the other dependents had landed in Honolulu to find the air still full of smoke and the stench of burned ships, buildings, and men. The gaiety she remembered from Robert's posting at Pearl Harbor had been replaced by fear of an imminent Japanese landing. News from the Philippines was all bad. She was sick with worry for her husband, the baby she carried inside her, and her family back in Manila and Cebu.

After two days in port, *Mariposa* left Hawaii bound for San Francisco, where Delores would head for the one place in the United States she had family: Key

West. From San Francisco, she journeyed by train down to Los Angeles, across to New Orleans, then down to Miami. There, she embarked on a slow bus that clunked along the new roadway that joined the string of tiny islands to Key West.

When she finally arrived on the first of February, Filipa gathered her into a warm embrace. The house on Grunt Bone Lane became her home, and she was surrounded by family. Robert's aunt Patricia Wake Whitehead and her daughter Agnes lived across the street, and her sister-in-law Shelley—married to Robert James' little brother Ted, a Navy instructor pilot at Key West Naval Air Station—lived a block away.

The joy that accompanied Sean Robert's birth disappeared four days later. The messenger boy knew the telegram he was delivering to Mrs. Robert J. Wake from the Navy Department was bad news. With mumbled excuses, he fled the verandah after handing it to her. Delores' hands were trembling so badly that she could barely rip the envelope open.

XXX—THE NAVY DEPARTMENT DEEPLY REGRETS TO INFORM YOU THAT YOUR HUSBAND LCDR ROBERT JAMES WAKE, USN, IS MISSING IN ACTION WHILE IN PERFORMANCE OF HIS DUTIES IN THE SERVICE OF HIS COUNTRY—X—IF FURTHER INFORMATION IS OBTAINED YOU WILL BE INFORMED—X—TO PREVENT POSSIBLE AID TO OUR ENEMIES PLEASE DO NOT DIVULGE THE NAME OF HIS SHIP OR STATION—X—REAR ADMIRAL JACOBS, CHIEF OF NAVAL PERSONNEL—XXX

Delores focused on one word—*missing*. Robert was only missing, not dead. He would be found somehow, somewhere. The family gathered to comfort her, each woman echoing Delores' hope, trying to stay positive. But Ted was less sanguine and softly said, "He may be alive, but we must prepare for the worst."

Delores refused to do that. She prayed fervently for his safe return several times a day and insisted that everyone she knew pray for him as well. He would come back. He *would*. Everyone complied, unwilling to dash her hopes.

On the eighteenth of April the boy delivered another telegram. It was coldly identical to the first, except that the word *missing* was replaced by *was killed*.

The family gathered on the verandah again as the telegram was passed from hand to hand. The next day Ted made inquiries about his brother's fate with friends in Washington. They had no details except that *Roseate Spoonbill* was gone, one of many American ships lost in the Philippines and Dutch East Indies. Everyone had questions, but there were no answers. Nobody knew what had happened.

The dreaded gold star was put in the front window, one of many gold or blue stars in that Navy town. People spoke in hushed voices when they walked past the house. Some crossed themselves and said a prayer. Others left flowers. Delores retreated within herself and focused on her baby. The family's weekly dinner gatherings became monthly, then ended altogether. The Fourth of July, normally a festive occasion at the Wake home, wasn't even recognized.

On the morning of July tenth, a young man with old eyes limped up the steps to the verandah where Filipa was drinking her morning cup of watery wartime coffee. When the man introduced himself, she put down her cup and went inside to rouse her daughter-in-law, telling her a friend had arrived to see her.

When Delores came through the screen door, the man smiled shyly and said, "Mrs. Wake, you might remember me from Samoa. I'm Lieutenant Commander Bill Waters, old *Rosie*'s executive officer. I'm on convalescent leave in Miami—I got a bit banged up in the Philippines—but wanted to come down and visit."

Her voice was subdued but genuinely welcoming. "I remember you as a lieutenant, Bill. I'm glad you got promoted."

"Thank you, ma'am. It just came through and was because of your husband's recommendation. Mrs. Wake, I'm afraid I don't have good news, but I *can* tell you what happened to Captain Wake and our ship. Please don't tell *anyone* I violated security regulations by sharing this, but I think your family should know that your husband died a hero."

She reached out to embrace him. Neither bothered to hide their tears. When the sobs slowed, they sat side by side. Filipa summoned the family, who quietly assembled on the verandah. Ted came from the air station.

After first warning them about the need for secrecy, Waters spent hours telling them everything that happened on *Rosie* after they left Samoa, although he omitted the bloodier details. When Ted asked specific questions about tactics, logistics, and navigation, Waters provided the answers. He reassured them that his captain and the other man who had stayed with him at the helm died instantaneously in that final Japanese salvo. And he described how the scuttling charges severely damaged both enemy destroyers directly above *Rosie*.

He told them of trekking with *Rosie*'s men through the jungle for weeks, losing several shipmates to disease or infected wounds along the way, until they found a Dutch plantation manager in southeast Borneo who had a wireless. The Dutchman contacted the Dutch resistance in southern Sumatra, who contacted the Australians in Fremantle in Western Australia. On a moonless night a month later, an American submarine rose out of the Java Sea and rescued *Rosie*'s survivors from the Japanese-occupied shore.

After Waters had told them the whole story and they had eaten a quiet dinner, he was invited to spend the night on the couch in the parlor. The last bus for Miami had long since left, so he would have to return to Miami on the morning bus. Much later that evening, he and Delores found themselves alone on the verandah.

Waters reached into his canvas bag and brought out a battered, stained envelope. "I didn't want to give you this in front of the others. I figured you'd want to read it when you're alone. The captain put it in a waterproof box along with the ship's official documents before he sent me off the ship. I handed over the documents at Pearl Harbor, but I promised your husband I would deliver this in person." He handed her the envelope, which bore her name.

Delores clutched it to her heart and whispered, "Thank you," then went inside and up to her room. She sat in the old rocker with her baby son and softly read his father's letter to him.

10 January 1942

Tarakan, Borneo, Dutch East Indie

Darling Delores,

I love you so much. I am so profoundly grateful we met in Manila and married. Your wisdom and strength and love have always sustained me, especially during the heartbreaking days of little María's illness and passing. I think of her every day, wondering what she would be doing now at age six, what new thing she would have learned today, what she would look like, sound like. We will be with her again someday. We have to cling to that, darling, and absolutely count on it.

And no matter what happens to me, know that you and I will meet again where there is no pain, no tears, no fear, no doubt, no sickness, no loneliness. Of course, I will do my duty as long as I can, as best as I can. The Navy gave me the skills to do that, but it's the iron blood of my father and grandfather in my veins that instilled the tradition that honor is my guide and my shield, which gives me the strength to get the mission done.

Know that my life's joys come from you. I see your beautiful smile in my mind. Cherish the warmth of your gentle compassion in my heart. Feel your soft touch on my face. Hear your delicious laughter. Your spirit is in my soul.

But you have duties too—far more important than mine. Raise our new baby boy or girl to be wise and strong, and to love life and family. To love God and the natural wonders he gave us. To be kind and honorable. To be a giver, not a taker. A doer, not a whiner.

And when you feel it's time, I want you to be open to loving someone and letting them love you. It won't be a betrayal of me—not at all. Your happiness is what I want above all else, what I desperately need to know will happen someday. It's what our child should see and feel as he grows up. Promise me you will do that.

We are under way now. Bound for the unknown, surrounded by enemies, saddened by our losses but pushing on. I am so blessed to have these men—every one of them smart and strong in the face of adversity far worse than we ever imagined. But I have no doubt at all that our country will completely prevail.

If anyone can get this letter to you, Bill Waters can. He's one of the very best men I've ever known. Keep him as a friend.

Know that I will see you again in that far better time and place.

With my deepest love and respect and hopes for your future,

Your loving,
Robert

Waters buried his head in his hands as he heard the sobs coming from upstairs. But after spending the day with the family he understood that the letter he'd delivered was also a godsend, a message from beyond his friend's watery grave on the other side of the world to the love of his life and his baby son. He left the house quietly before sunrise, limped to the bus station, and caught the first bus back to the war.

In August 1942 Ted Wake received transfer orders to a new PBY squadron. He ended up fighting the Japanese in the Aleutian Islands off Alaska.

In early March 1943, Ted's older cousin reported into his new duty station amid the grand resort hotels of Miami Beach.

62

The Teacher

U.S. Navy Submarine Chaser Training School
Pier 2, Port of Miami, Florida

———

Wednesday, 20 January 1943

Cdr. Peter Carlos Cano stood in the dappled sunshine under a coconut palm and stretched. He'd just finished a breakfast of pineapple, papaya, ham, and fresh eggs accompanied by a demitasse cup of the Cuban coffee he loved. He still couldn't believe his luck. Three months of temporary duty assignment in Miami in winter, within driving distance of his hometown, Tampa.

This sure as hell beats the Iceland convoy run on an obsolete destroyer, he thought happily as he breathed in the warm salt air. His sleek black hair, beginning to show some gray after the hard years in the far north, was inherited from his father's Cuban side of the family, along with his tall, trim build. But his green eyes were pure Wake.

Dodging a company of Coast Guardsmen marching down Biscayne Boulevard, he looked back at the very nice corner room on the second floor of the Alcazar Hotel that had been assigned as his quarters. He smiled again at his good fortune, but also wondered why it had befallen him. As a U.S. Navy officer with a Hispanic name, Cano wasn't used to good fortune. And he knew very little about his new outfit, the Submarine Chaser Training Center.

When he walked past the saluting sailors on guard duty at the front door of the Spanish-style administration building, the former P&O Shipping office, Cano heard an unusual sound from the other side of the wall—drill commands in Spanish, with a decidedly Mexican lilt. *That's odd. Since when does the U.S. Navy use Spanish?*

The harried ensign in the commanding officer's chaotic outer office looked useless, so Cano went right to a bespectacled chief yeoman sitting at a corner desk and handed over his personnel file. "Commander Peter C. Cano reporting for TDY, Chief. Is the CO available?"

Chief Richard Rolfe had a hangover that morning, but only he knew it, because the gravel-voiced curmudgeon would sooner cut off his right hand than show doubt, fear, or pain. He was a *real* chief, not one of the Navy's new jumped-up, six-month-wonder senior petty officers. Rolfe had served on ships and stations around the world for twenty-nine very long years. He'd seen all kinds of officers and could tell a fake or a fool inside of ten seconds.

The one in front of him wasn't a fake *or* a fool. A brief look-see in the personnel file's previous duty station page showed quite a history. So did the "Awards and Decorations" section, along with the fruit salad of ribbons on his chest. The top-center one, he noted with respect, was the red, white, and blue Silver Star ribbon. The "Promotions" section showed the officer had been promoted to his present rank only two weeks ago, making him junior to the boss.

Rolfe nodded approvingly at the file, then looked up. "Congratulations on your recent promotion, sir, and welcome on board." The chief gestured to the next room, where a dozen officers and petty officers and several well-dressed civilians sat with faces reflecting various levels of worry or anticipation. "Commander McDaniel has a very busy schedule today—but I am sure he'll want to see *you* straightaway, so please follow me, sir."

Though Cano didn't know much about his assignment, he did know that Cdr. Eugene Field McDaniel was another veteran of the frigid Iceland run and had been in charge of the training center in Miami since mid-1942. As he waited in the doorway, Cano was pleased to see that McDaniel's corner office lacked the usual "I love me" wall of accolades and mementoes many officers, especially those with Naval Academy rings, felt the need to display.

This is a place where things get done, Cano thought. Instead of photos of the CO with various dignitaries the walls had large area charts of the Straits of Florida, the Bahamas, and the Caribbean—each with many notations. The open windows overlooked the piers just behind the building, where dozens of patrol boats and several destroyer escorts were moored and a petty officer could be heard lecturing a group of sailors about depth charges.

Rolfe laid Cano's file down in front of McDaniel, opened to "Awards and Decorations." After quietly saying something to his boss, he beckoned for Cano to enter, then departed and closed the door.

Cano stood at attention the regulation three feet in front of the desk, his eyes on the wall above McDaniel's head, and stated the obligatory, "Commander Peter Carlos Cano, reporting for TDY at the station, sir."

In his peripheral vision Cano saw that McDaniel's side table and the one behind him were piled with papers, but the desk itself was orderly, with one stack halfway perused. A cigarette smoldered in an ashtray that was made from the base plate of a 4-inch gun shell casing. The day agenda book beside it was full of notes. McDaniel's round, black-rimmed glasses and receding hairline gave him an academic look, but the strong frame, square jaw, wrinkled tan, and serious eyes negated that. *This guy is a seaman.*

McDaniel stood, showed a polite smile, and reached across the desk to shake Cano's hand. In a slight drawl—Cano guessed Virginia—he said, "Welcome on board Submarine Chaser Training Center, Commander Cano. Please sit down and give me a brief summary of your service history."

Cano knew McDaniel had it all in the file but obliged with a quick recitation of his career. "USNA 1921, sir. Assistant ordnance officer, Brooklyn Navy Yard, 1921 to 1923. Staff assistant to the chief of the Bureau of Personnel at the Navy Department, 1923 to 1925. Promotion to lieutenant, junior grade, 1925. Assistant comms officer, battleship *West Virginia*, 1925 to 1927. Assistant torpedo officer, cruiser *Marblehead*, 1927 to 1930. Promotion to lieutenant, 1930. Torpedo and antisubmarine officer, destroyer *Stewart*, 1930 to 1932. Instructor of basic antisubmarine operations, USNA, 1932 to 1934. Promotion to lieutenant commander, 1935. Executive officer, destroyer *Chandler*, 1935 to 1936. U.S. naval attaché at Buenos Aires, Argentina, 1936 to 1937. U.S. naval attaché to Cuba, 1937 to 1938. Office of Naval Intelligence, 1938 to 1941. Commanding officer, destroyer *Nygaard*, November 1941 to 10 January 1943. Promotion to commander, 5 January 1943, and now TDY here, sir."

Cano could tell McDaniel noticed he was leaving out some things—like what he did at ONI and why he was awarded that Silver Star—but he didn't ask. That intrigued Cano.

"Do you know what we do here?" McDaniel asked.

"Antisubmarine warfare training for Navy and Coast Guard men, sir."

"Correct. Do you know why *you* are here for the next couple of months?"

"No, sir," admitted Cano.

"Your operational experience and language ability are why. For the next two months you are in charge of teaching ASW to the officers and men of the Latin American navies training here. You'll have three officers and several petty officers assisting you. All speak at least some Spanish."

"Me, a *teacher*, sir?" Cano tried to hide his dismay. "For the last two years—"

McDaniel held up a hand. "You were hip deep in the freezing North Atlantic hunting U-boats. You think this is a humiliating demotion and a waste of an experienced officer's time. You were expecting to do what you do best and go after the U-boats infesting our area of operations down here. Am I correct, Commander?"

"Ah, well, yes sir, that's pretty much it. I figured I would take trainees out on real hunter-killer missions in a destroyer—hopefully one of the new ones—and show them how it's done. But I don't see any destroyers here, sir."

McDaniel's lips twitched slightly. "I thought the exact same thing when I came here from *Livermore* up on the same Iceland run you've come from. And no, there aren't any destroyers here. We teach these sailors the basics, and most of them won't ever be on full-sized sub chasers. They'll be on small patrol boats, especially the foreigners from the small navies. You will have sixty days to teach these fellows how to stay alive in their tiny 83-foot hand-me-down ex–Coast Guard patrol boats, and to coordinate operations in English with our surface and air assets, in order to find and kill the modern 250-foot type-IXC U-boats Hitler sent over here."

Having made his point, McDaniel lightened up. "The good news is this area's got pretty decent air coverage, the students are very motivated and speak a bit of English, we've got a very good training cadre, and the water's warm if you end up in it. Chief Rolfe will get you squared away. Your class starts tomorrow—135 Cubans for you to make into modern, reliable partners in the fight against Nazi subs. Can I rely on you and your staff to accomplish this mission, Commander?"

Cano straightened to attention. "Aye, aye, sir. We'll get it done."

63

"La Bayamesa"

USN Submarine Chaser Training School
Pier 2, Biscayne Boulevard, Port of Miami, Florida

Wednesday, 24 March 1943

C ano was very proud of his Cuban students. Unlike his many of his fellow American officers, he did not treat them with paternalistic condescension with racist overtones. They were naval officers and sailors, extremely focused in their studies and practice work at sea, and determined to be successful against the Nazis destroying ships along their coasts.

Near the end of the sixty-day course, the Cubans discovered two things about their no-nonsense senior instructor. First, Cdr. Peter Carlos Cano was the grandson of Rear Adm. Peter Wake, who was the legendary friend of Cuba's vaunted hero José Martí and who had long advocated independence for Cuba. Second, Cano was half Cuban himself. His mother, Useppa Wake, had married Mario Cano, a Cuban hero from the island's War for Independence in the 1890s. From that moment on, admiration for the man became total devotion.

A young ensign named Mario Ramirez Delgado got Cano's attention from the beginning with his intense desire to learn, athletic physique, and quick mind. When Cano watched him command his crew in the practical exercises at sea, he saw a natural leader. Ramirez also grasped the essence of what Cano was teaching: hunting U-boats by using teamwork between two or three surface ships and ASW aircraft while applying the new technologies of sonar and radar. The two men took to chatting informally at the end of a day's work, the Cuban learning about the American's family and career, and the American learning of the Cuban's. Cano was certain the young man would go far in his career and decided to stay in touch.

The course ended with a graduation ceremony on 24 March 1943. The Cuban graduates stood ramrod straight in their tropical dress whites on the afterdecks of the wooden patrol boats assigned to them, all nested together alongside the pier. Commander McDaniel, the chief of staff of the Gulf Sea Frontier Command, and the training center's officers and petty officers stood in formation on the pier, facing the boats and crews. The chief of staff made a brief speech thanking Cuba for helping in the global fight and praising the Cuban sailors about to face the Nazis. The senior Cuban officer spoke next, expressing gratitude to the instructors, especially Commander Cano.

After diplomas were handed out, another ceremony was held. All hands came to attention again and the small U.S. Navy band on the pier played "The Star-Spangled Banner." At the end, as bellowed commands echoed around the pier, all ten of the patrol boats lowered the American ensign on their stern staff and the Union Jack on the bow staff, respectfully folded them, and presented them to Commander McDaniel and the American instructors.

The senior Cuban naval officer then read out orders in Spanish, repeating them in English, as the flag of the Republic of Cuba was hoisted on each boat's stern staff and the band played the stirring Cuban national anthem, "La Bayamesa." The patrol boats were no longer U.S. Coast Guard cutters; they were commissioned warships in the Cuban navy.

Cano felt his throat tighten. His grandfather Peter and his father, Mario, had heard that anthem played many times while fighting for a free Cuba so long ago. When the anthem ended, the entire Cuban contingent—and Cano—shouted, "Viva Cuba Libre!" followed by "Viva los Estados Unidos!"

Cano fervently wished his eighty-two-year-old widowed father, an invalid in Tampa, could have been present. He looked up at the sky and softly said, "This is for you, Papa."

As the boats got under way for Havana, every American officer, petty officer, and sailor on that pier and the surrounding piers stood at attention and saluted them. Cano said a heartfelt prayer for God to watch over them. He'd accomplished his mission: the Cubans had earned high marks, Latin Americans were proven to be valuable allies in the war effort, and foreigners would continue to train at Miami.

Two days later, Cdr. Peter Carlos Cano left sunny Miami for the frigid North Atlantic to take command of USS *Caynne* (DD 649), a recently commissioned *Gleaves*-class destroyer, for the dreaded Murmansk convoys.

64
Validation

Havana, Cuba

Tuesday, 8 October 1946

"**L**ook there!" Peter Carlos Cano directed Anne and their sixteen-year-old son, Mario Teodoro (named for his father and for family friend Theodore Roosevelt), as the ship entered Havana harbor. The ancient city of Havana glistened across the bay. With his good right arm, Cano pointed out the location in the bay where his grandfather had almost been killed when the *Maine* exploded, the docks at Regla where Grandpa Peter and Uncle Sean Rork had escaped ashore, and the ridge behind the Cano family home where María Wake's son had been executed in the infamous laurel ditch by Colonel Marrón's Spanish henchmen in February 1898. Young Mario was spellbound. Here at last were the places he had heard about all his life.

As Mario and Peter Carlos were eagerly examining the scenery, Anne was watching her husband of twenty-one years closely from behind her sunglasses. The shrapnel wounds he had incurred a year ago in a Stuka attack off the North Cape of Norway had healed. Peter Carlos saved *Caynne* but would have lost his left arm had the ship's hospital corpsman not acted quickly to save it.

The arm would always be painful and weaker. Her husband could never go back to sea duty, and his days in the Navy would end in two months.

"Seeing this makes the old Admiral's stories come alive," Anne said. "And it's so fitting that the Navy asked you here to speak. It was *your* training that helped the Cuban navy to fight the U-boats off the coast and save so many merchant ships and seamen." She squeezed his hand and blinked back tears. "Have I told you lately how proud you have made me? Today and every day."

After they had disembarked and checked into the comfortable Hotel Inglaterra, Carlos took his family out for a night on the town. Although he avoided the more risqué nightspots, Old Havana lived up to its reputation as the Paris of the Caribbean.

On 10 October, the ceremony was held at the Casa Blanca Naval Arsenal across the harbor from the Old City. A Cuban lieutenant with golden staff aiguillettes showed them to their seats behind the podium overlooking the plaza. Arrayed in front of them were the commander of patrol boat CS 13 and his crew, standing at parade rest in immaculate dress whites. The Canos were in august company. Beside Peter Carlos Cano sat the president of the Republic of Cuba, Ramón Grau, and the U.S. ambassador, Raymond Henry Norweb. The senior staff of the Cuban navy and the U.S. naval attaché were seated behind them. On the other side of the plaza, near the seawall along the bay, the sailors' families, decked out in their best, beamed with pride.

Grau spoke briefly but emotionally, first thanking God that World War II was over and peace had come to the Americas, then praising the bravery and skill of the men of CS 13 and of the Cuban navy in the war. He thanked the U.S. Navy for the outstanding training given to the Cubans in Miami—he made a half-bow toward Cano—and the continuing camaraderie between the two navies. The wave of applause that followed those words echoed off the buildings and across the bay.

He continued, "It is my great honor and privilege to introduce to you Captain Peter Carlos Cano, a naval warrior with the blood of both the United States and Cuba in his veins, who shed that blood while facing the Nazis." He gestured at the men lined up in formation. "I am proud to ask this great warrior to tell the story of these men standing in front of me."

Cano rose to speak, as a senior officer and representative of the U.S. Navy and as the man who trained the men of CS 13. He gave his speech in Spanish while his bilingual son translated for Anne.

"I am honored to be here and to speak about Cuban patriots on this, the seventy-eighth anniversary of Cuba's declaration of independence in 1868. Now, as then, Cuba's patriots have become famous for their heroism. And I am very grateful for my small connection with some of them. Here is the story of what happened and why we are all here.

"In January 1943, I was conducting antisubmarine combat operations in the North Atlantic when I was ordered to Miami to train U.S. Navy, Coast Guard, and foreign sailors in the science of searching for, locating, and sinking Nazi U-boats. I was given charge of training 132 Cubans. I was reluctant to leave my ship and crew in the North Atlantic, but I will admit that I was thrilled to be back in the sunny tropics to savor the Cuban food of Florida, my home!"

He paused for the laughter, then became solemn. "But I was very worried. U-boats were a growing threat in the Caribbean and on the Atlantic coast. Destroyers such as the one I had been commanding in the North Atlantic were very effective against them, but there weren't enough destroyers in our fleet to be everywhere they were needed. I was worried because I knew the men I would train in Miami were going to have to use small old sub chasers and even smaller patrol boats against the best Germany had to offer.

"I knew that would be a David-against-Goliath fight: 12 men on an 83-foot wooden patrol boat with a small bow gun and a few depth charges against 50 men in a 250-foot-long steel submarine armed with torpedoes and large deck guns. How could the Cubans possibly survive such a fight, much less win?"

As Cano let them think about that, there was absolute silence.

"The answer was simple: they would have to possess national pride, professional skill and creativity, and individual courage. I immediately recognized those qualities in the Cubans I was there to train. It was obvious they understood *why* they would have to fight, and that they were determined to learn *how* to fight effectively against the unspeakable evil of Nazism.

"One captain and crew stood out from the others, that of patrol boat CS 13—the same men who stand before you today. On 24 March 1943, I was proud to watch Ensign Mario Ramirez Delgado and his crew graduate after sixty days of intense training, commission their patrol boat as a warship in the Navy of the Republic of Cuba, and go to sea.

"Several days later, I was sent back to combat operations in the North Atlantic and then farther north in the Arctic. As I endured the cold and the darkness there, I dreamed of our glorious tropical days and nights in Florida and Cuba—and I worried about the good men I'd trained in Miami. My men. The free world's men.

"In July 1943, while I was in Iceland preparing to lead a convoy to Murmansk in Russia, I received a confidential report that two months earlier a Cuban patrol boat had fought and survived a battle with a U-boat that had been the scourge of the coast. But I did not learn the details of that action until after the war.

"And it was not until I arrived in Havana that now-Lieutenant Mario Ramirez Delgado told me about the actual combat against the Nazi U-boat. For two years this was kept secret to protect our antisubmarine operations from the enemy. But that secrecy is no longer required. And today, I have been given the great honor of reporting to you, and the entire world, what happened on that fateful day in May of 1943. . . ."

Cano paused for a moment, but not for dramatic effect. He was simply thinking about Lieutenant Ramirez and the decisions Ramirez had made two years earlier that had led everyone to the ceremony. By all logic it should have gone quite differently.

65

David versus Goliath

Casa Blanca Naval Arsenal
Havana, Cuba

Thursday, 10 October 1946

The night before the ceremony, Ramirez had candidly shared the details of the battle over dinner at the Hotel Inglaterra, little changed since Peter Carlos Cano's grandfather Wake had stayed there during the Spanish colonial occupation. Over an excellent dinner of *lechon asado* followed by *flan* and *cafecitos* Cano listened closely as Ramirez explained his decisions and actions, and his fears, on that day two years earlier. Cano understood it all only too well, for he'd made similar decisions in a far different place on a much larger warship.

Now, in front of the sailors, their families, and Cuba's president, Cano pushed aside his emotions and used his professional briefing voice to tell CS 13's story to his audience.

"The battle I am here to describe began on Thursday, 13 May 1943, when a Nazi submarine attacked the Cuban tanker *Mambí*, bound from Port Everglades, Florida, to Manzanillo, Cuba. *Mambí* quickly sank five miles off Manatí, on the northern coast of Cuba. Only ten of the twenty-nine Cubans and one of the five U.S. Navy gun crew on board survived. Shortly afterward, the same U-boat attacked and sank the American tanker *Nickeliner*. The entire crew was rescued by the Cuban navy and landed at nearby Nuevitas.

"On the afternoon of 15 May 1943, three Cuban navy patrol boats—CS 11, CS 12, and CS 13—departed Isabela de Sagua, a place my grandfather Peter Wake knew well, escorting the Honduran freighter *Wanks* and the Cuban freighter *Camagüey* to Havana. This is the same coast where the U-boat had destroyed the ships two days earlier. CS 12 and CS 11 were out ahead of the freighters; the captain of CS 11 was the senior naval officer in command of the convoy. CS 13, under the command of Ensign Ramirez, was astern of the convoy.

"At 5:15 p.m., a U.S. Navy Kingfisher float plane patrolling off Cayo Megano signaled the convoy he had spotted a possible U-boat ahead of them and dropped a smoke marker in that area. The plane was low on fuel and had to depart, leaving the convoy without air cover. The convoy commander ordered CS 11 and CS 12 to continue protecting the convoy on its way to Havana and ordered CS 13 to search for and attack the U-boat. This was a difficult decision but the correct one. Ensign Ramirez and his men on CS 13 would have to face the enemy alone, but the convoy might get through.

"Ensign Ramirez raced at full speed to the area of the smoke marker. Once there, he slowed the boat and began a methodical search pattern using lookouts, radar, and sonar, just as he and his men had been trained to do in Miami. Sonar operator Norberto Collado Abreu, doing an outstanding job, located and then tracked the enemy submarine, giving Ensign Ramirez the information he needed to predict the U-boat's course and speed. I can tell you that is *not* an easy thing to do in the stress of combat. Ensign Ramirez attacked the Nazi sub using three Mark 4 depth charges set to explode at depths of 100, 150, and 250 feet.

"This too sounds simple, but it isn't. The depth charge has to explode within twenty feet of the submarine's hull in order to inflict serious damage, and closer still to sink it. That is very rarely accomplished, especially by one vessel acting alone with a limited number of depth charges. Ensign Ramirez knew that he would only get *one* chance to do it exactly right. If his calculations were even slightly off, the U-boat would surface, use its large-caliber deck gun to destroy CS 13 and all on board, then go on to attack and destroy the convoy. Once the three depth charges went over the stern of CS 13, the Cuban sailors could only wait.

"Three explosions erupted astern of CS 13. Then there was a fourth, a huge explosion so massive that the eruption partially flooded the patrol boat's engine room. Ensign Ramirez did not hesitate. He circled CS 13 back and attacked again with two more depth charges, set at a 250-foot depth. Two more explosions erupted. CS 13 only had one more depth charge remaining.

"Fuel floated up to the surface, and Sonarman Collado heard liquid and air bubbling up from tanks. Then the noises ended. Ensign Ramirez ordered samples of the fuel taken. CS 13 searched for a while longer, then finally resumed her position in the convoy, which arrived safely at Havana the next day. Ensign Ramirez reported to his superiors that he believed the U-boat was destroyed.

"There was no official public celebration, because operational secrecy was paramount. In fact, there was no absolute confirmation of the victory until we found and analyzed the Nazi U-boat records after the war, earlier this year of 1946. The analysis confirmed that U-176—which had destroyed eleven Allied ships from Great Britain, the United States, Holland, Greece, and Cuba between August 1942 and May 1943—was destroyed by the brave and skilled captain and crew of the CS 13.

"Just last month, no less a personage than the official historian of the U.S. Navy, Capt. Samuel Eliot Morison, personally verified to me that Ensign Mario Ramirez Delgado, Sonarman Norberto Collado Abreu, and the other men on board CS 13 hold the world record for being the smallest vessel in naval history to ever sink an enemy submarine. The wooden David from Cuba defeated the steel Nazi Goliath."

Cano stopped to look around the crowd. "I am greatly honored and intensely proud to be part of this ceremony to commemorate this incredible victory by the Republic of Cuba. The free people of the world owe these brave and smart sailors of Cuba their gratitude and respect." He straightened to attention and rendered a long salute to the Cuban sailors. "Gentlemen, I salute you." Ramirez returned the salute, and Cano returned to his seat. President Grau awarded Lieutenant Ramirez the Medal of Naval Merit with Red Distinction for bravery in combat. Then each man in the crew was awarded a medal for valor. Families embraced their sailors. Many embraced Cano and his family.

Two months later, Peter Carlos Cano retired from the U.S. Navy. Anne was happy but worried—would he be bored? On 5 January 1947, Rear Adm. Sidney Souers, director of the National Intelligence Authority, phoned Cano's home in Tampa while Anne was out marketing.

"It's been three weeks, Peter—tired yet of watching grass grow? Something's come up."

Cano was sixteen when his grandfather Peter Wake got a similar call from Assistant Secretary of the Navy Franklin Roosevelt in 1914—and went back to work. Now, Cano admitted to Souers that at only age forty-eight, yes, he was bored.

"That's what I thought. I've got interesting work for you to do, and that bad arm of yours won't slow you down a bit."

And so Peter Carlos Cano began a second career—in espionage. The Cold War was heating up, and he spent the first seven months in northern Europe monitoring the Russians, who were trying to expand communism far past their boundaries. The next year, Cano's espionage outfit took on a new name that would become famous: the Central Intelligence Agency.

But Cano spent most of his second career in Latin America. He was assigned to track former Nazis in Argentina from 1947 to 1950, gather intelligence on the bloody Colombian revolutions (La Violencia) from 1951 to 1953, and help run a paramilitary operation in Guatemala from 1954 to 1956. Something of a quiet legend within the CIA by then, his final assignment was Cuba, from 1956 until he reached mandatory retirement at age sixty-three in December 1961.

From that time onward he and Anne lived a tranquil life on Melrose Avenue in the Stoney Point neighborhood in Tampa. His home was only five miles from the spot where his grandfather Peter had foiled a Spanish attempt on José Martí's life in 1892, and three miles from where Peter Wake had recuperated from combat wounds in 1898. For more than two decades, Peter Carlos and Anne Cano took joy in watching their son, Mario Teodoro Cano (USNA class of 1951, ret. 1979), progress through life; tending their flower and butterfly gardens; and dabbling in amateur astronomy. Anne died three weeks after Peter did in 1985.

None of Peter and Anne's neighbors ever knew what their quiet neighbor had done for his country. But one man who attended the funeral knew what Peter Carlos Cano had done for *his* country. In the back of the church sat a descendant of Ensign Mario Ramirez. As a youth he had escaped Castro's Cuba in 1976 and with Cano's help had settled in Key West.

As his eyes misted over, he said a silent prayer of thanks.

66

Welcome to the Brown Water Navy

An Thới Naval Base
Phú Quốc Island, southwest Vietnam

Thursday, 10 December 1968

The transport dropped swiftly to avoid potshots from the Vietcong snipers in the hills and made a hard landing. After his head smacked the fuselage during a violent jink to starboard, Lt. (j.g.) Sean Robert Wake noticed the crew chief's smartass grin. "Sorry, sir," he shouted over the engine noise. "Best hang on tight . . . *sir.* And welcome to Uncle Sam's Brown Water Navy!"

Wake stepped off the Navy transport aircraft, a World War II–era C 117 D, into a solid wall of heat. The flies found him within seconds, drawn by the blood on his forehead. Wake cursed as he spat out a gnat and slapped at another. *What the hell have I done? I volunteered for a whole year of this?*

When the "White Hat Airlines" transport was approaching the island, Wake had glimpsed the naval base through the porthole by his canvas seat. The only structures that looked remotely naval to him were the two docks jutting out from a filthy beach, dozens of patrol and utility craft rafted up alongside, and a rusty barracks ship anchored offshore.

251

The rest of the place was a dump—literally. Crates and barrels teetered in untidy piles, tents and shacks straggled in rows, and trucks and jeeps slid through muddy "streets." A few dingy white cement buildings surrounded by sandbags stood out against the olive drab, mud brown, and dark gray that dominated the landscape. Even the water was brown. The camp was surrounded by rows of concertina wire and guarded by several rickety-looking guard towers.

Nobody greeted the newcomers when they disembarked. Wake was the only officer among the dozen passengers, but nobody looked at him for leadership. Instead, the enlisted sailors quickly fell in behind a second-class gunner's mate and plodded across the steel Marston matting toward a small building sporting the grandiose sign: AN-THOI INTERNATIONAL AIRPORT.

Wake followed them. Inside the terminal he found a storekeeper first class in a back room who looked more with it than the clerical types out front—this guy probably had at least ten years' service, wore glasses and a sour expression, and was intently reading a document as he listened to somebody on the phone. He was the only man in the building with his own desk fan. The storekeeper looked up at Wake and nodded a hello as he muttered on the phone, "Yeah, get me a dozen of those cases and send 'em over to my hooch, but do it *quietly*. Gotta go now, the new j.g. just got here."

Wake belatedly noticed that the man was holding the document upside down and realized the guy was a scrounger using the old *I'm really busy* façade to fool any nearby officers while he did his conniving. Omitting the usual courtesies that are supposed to signal good naval order and discipline, Wake leaned on the desk, "So, where's Coastal Squadron One?"

The fellow sighed. "Morning, sir. I'm Herb Green, airport cargo petty officer. CosRon1 is over near the docks. You must be Lieutenant Wake. The squadron's been waiting for you for two days. I'll get you a decent ride over there. Too friggin' hot and far to walk."

When Wake walked into the squadron office near the beach an hour later, a chief yeoman in green fatigues and a black beret, alerted by Green back at the airstrip, greeted him far more professionally. "Good morning, Lieutenant Wake. Welcome aboard. I'm Chief Scott Baxter. The squadron commander is off at a honcho confab with Admiral Zumwalt in Saigon, and the exec is over at Ha Tien for the day, so the ops officer will receive you. Please follow me, sir."

Wake noticed that the black ribbon on the back of Baxter's beret was cut in half and notched. From his training at Coronado, he knew that meant the man was a combat veteran, with kills. *I need to listen to this guy—and stay on his good side.*

Lt. Cdr. John Stahl, USNA class of 1958, welcomed Wake, gestured to a wobbly chair, and got straight to the point. "I'm afraid there's no time for a break-in period, Mr. Wake. Since the Tet attacks at the beginning of the year we're up to our elbows in VC. So, you'll skipper PCF-105 right away. Last skipper got a bad case of dysentery and God knows what else. Lost twenty pounds in seven days and got flown home last week. You'll have to learn on the job."

"Aye, aye, sir," said Wake. The training at Coronado in southern California had been very good, and he was confident he could do the job, but he'd hoped to have some riding time before taking command. "Is the crew experienced, sir?"

"Some of them. Let's go down the roster. Your 'Chief of the Boat' is Chief Quartermaster Andre Jour, a Louisiana Cajun who's been on the boat eleven months. Spent most of his career on tin cans before coming to us. Very squared away. Dependable."

Wake took notes as Stahl read down the crew list by the nickname of their billets.

"Your 'Guns' is GMG2 Frank Taylor. Got a rep for being a gook hater and a nasty drunk, but he knows his guns and the boat. Been here three months. Your 'Gearhead' is EN2 Randall Lincoln, black kid from South Carolina. Quiet type. None of your 'Black Power' shit. Spends all his free time reading books. Been here six months."

Wake nodded and continued writing. So far, he wasn't impressed.

"Your 'Boats' is BM3 Gary North from L.A. Been here six months. Oh yeah, now I remember *him*. Your predecessor thought the kid was doing dope but couldn't prove it. 'Comms' is a Puerto Rican RM3, Juan Rincón. Also been here six months. That's it for the regular five-man crew, but you're going to have two extra men on board."

Wake knew there weren't enough racks on the gunboat for even the regular crew. *Where the hell are* they *supposed to sleep?*

Stahl picked up another sheet of paper. "Our dear friends in the Vietnamese navy have given us GM3 Nguyen Tuan as your local liaison-translator. He's been on the boat about a month. I hear his English isn't great but he's good at telling the bad guys from the good guys on the sampans and junks."

Stahl groaned. "And now to the one you won't like having on the boat—an AP reporter by the name of Kurt Anderson. Been in-country for fifteen months, mostly the southern end, and he's already pissed off most of the Army and Navy units he's been with. Takes his own photos. Says he's a Kentucky boy and can handle a rifle if he has to. He's in the BOQ hooch now."

"That's eight men on the boat, sir. How long is this reporter going to be with us?"

Stahl grinned. "A week. Just enough to see river and coastal ops. Try to keep him alive, Wake. If he gets killed there'll be holy hell to pay, and I'll have a shitload of paperwork."

"Aye, aye, sir." *A damn reporter. On my first run. Crap.*

"Well, that's it for now. Go draw your issue gear, your weapon, grab a rack at the BOQ, and meet your chief and boat crew. Get back here with your chief at 1600 for an ops brief. Your first run is tomorrow. It *should* be an easy one." As Wake turned to leave, Stahl added, "Hey, are you related to the famous Wake naval family?"

Ah hell. Here we go. "Yes, sir. Peter Wake was my great-grandfather."

Stahl nodded. "I was at ONI for three years. Before I left I finally got to see the legendary Wake Shelf in the back of the vault. Guess you know that old Peter started out in a gunboat fighting rebels on a jungle coast too. There's a century's worth of intel on that shelf from all over the world by the various Wakes. So, Lieutenant Commander Robert Wake was your father? I read the after-action reports his XO submitted after the attack. Quite a guy."

"Yes, sir. He was my dad. I was born a month after he was KIA in the Dutch East Indies in January '42." Wake didn't mention the posthumous Navy Cross awarded a year later. Stahl had doubtless read about it in the vault.

A sympathetic smile crossed Stahl's face. "Your name's a heavy load to bear, Mr. Wake. Don't let it get to you. Listen to Chief Jour, stay focused on the mission, your men, and that friggin' reporter. Understood?"

"Yes, sir."

67

Just a Shoot-and-Scoot Recon Decoy

An Thới Naval Base
Phú Quốc Island, southwest Vietnam

Thursday, 10 December 1968

The admin stuff took longer than he anticipated, so Wake spent only about ten minutes with Chief Jour and the crew at the boat before he and Jour went to the ops brief. The Vietnamese navy liaison and the reporter weren't at the boat, which was rafted outboard of three others at the dock.

Jour was tall, lanky, and taciturn, with sun-squinted eyes, a worry-lined face, and receding dark hair. He had the ubiquitous USN fouled-anchor tattoo on his right forearm, a quartermaster's wheel insignia tattooed on the left forearm, and a lilting Cajun accent. He looked competent. The short crew meeting was unremarkable. Wake was their third skipper in five months. They were quietly respectful but wary. Inexperienced young lieutenants like Wake had a way of getting their men killed. They knew they were going out on a mission shortly, and once the introductions were over they returned to their preparations.

Along the way to Stahl's ops brief, Chief Jour summed up the crew in a soft voice. "They're pretty steady under fire. Know their jobs. Cross-trained in the basics of the other guys' jobs. No real troublemakers or goldbrickers—when they're out on the water. Most're on their second hitch, usually from tin cans. Most're gettin' out when this hitch is up. Taylor's on his fourth sea duty. He's gonna be a lifer, 'cause he knows on civvy street he'd end up in jail."

Wake wondered about Jour's laid-back demeanor. "And what about you, Chief? You like it here?"

"Me, sir? Hell, I'm just tryin' to keep everybody alive an' get the friggin' mission done. Got another two months in this brown water snake pit, then three blessed weeks' leave in Frisco. An' *then*, my salty old ass is bound for the glorious Sixth Fleet. Was there back in '61, an' had a great time." Jour sighed at the memories. "It's the *best* duty in Uncle Sam's Navy . . . Gibraltar, France, Italy, Greece. Civilized places, decent booze, real food, pretty women, and not a damned jungle for three thousand miles."

Wake chuckled. "Chief, that's all sounding pretty good to me right about now—and I've only been here a couple of hours."

"Well, here we are, sir," Jour said as they reached the ops shack. "Let's find out what we're supposed to do."

Stahl introduced Wake to the senior officer in charge for the op, Lt. Bill Minsky of PCF 106, who'd been in-country for ten months. Minsky was a huge guy with an easy smile. During the ensuing banter Wake discovered he'd played football for Woody Hayes at Ohio State, where he got an NROTC commission. He was doing his obligated five years and then planned to teach high school history and coach football. When asked, Wake found himself unenthusiastically admitting he was a lifer. Minsky's only response was a pitying look that said, *Just wait, pal, 'till you've been here a few months.*

Fortunately for Wake, Stahl didn't mention his naval heritage during the intros. Everyone quieted down as Stahl stepped to the large chart on the wall. Minsky and his boat chief, a first-class engineman, plopped down in the plastic chairs, Wake and Jour did likewise, and everyone opened their notebooks as the commander began.

"The objective is a low-key recon up the Kénh ba Hón River, eighteen clicks south of Ha Tien up on the Cambodian border, and sixty-five clicks—thirty-nine miles—east-northeast of us here. Mr. Minsky and 106 were there on a show-the-flag visit three weeks ago. Anything important about the place everybody should know, Bill?"

Minsky shrugged. "Crappy little place with some fishing and rice sampans and a couple of small coastal junks. Most of the locals looked terrified to see us. We got some evil eyes too, but no incoming. Not even a curse word—at least according to my VNN guy."

Stahl turned toward Wake. "These ops started back in October when one of our guys, Mike Bernique, stopped at Ha Tien and heard there was a VC tax collector's post up the river there. So, Mike being Mike, he took his boats up the river, got in a firefight and shot up the bad guys, and brought his boats back to tell the story. The Saigon honchos pitched a hissy fit 'cause it was a violation of the ops orders and ROE and half a dozen other things. But then Admiral Zumwalt heard about it and said it was exactly the kind of stuff he wanted and gave Bernique the Silver Star.

"Ever since, we've been pushing up the rivers to places where the VC never expected to see us. Yesterday, we got word from the intel whizzes there's a VC tax collection and conscription post—code name Vicksburg—about ten clicks up the Kénh ba Hón. We've never poked around in there, just Minsky's look-see at the village at the mouth of the river. We've had word that mañana, the local VC boss will be there just after dawn to take in his tax money and line up the new recruits for a rah-rah speech on the splendors of commie life. So that's where 105 and 106 will be, gentlemen, to let them know we care. Not sure of the exact location of the VC post 'cause air force intel overflights can't spot it—"

Somebody in the back piped up, "Pretty hard to see anything smaller than a football stadium from ten thousand feet up. And they were probably daydreaming about the evening pool party back at Ben Hoa. I hear those pukes drink martinis."

Stahl glared at the man. "Baker, we're all tired of your bitchin' so just shut your hatch." Then he pointed to a place on the chart where the Kénh ba Hón River—which looked to Wake like a straight canal—met another waterway from the southeast. "As I was saying, the VC post'll be somewhere in this area. Questions on the background info?"

"Intel source?" asked Minsky.

"Hoi Chanh defector debrief five days ago. Says VC boss is there at dawn every Friday."

Minsky nodded. "Glad it's not a KKK bastard. I don't trust *them* one friggin' bit."

The Hoi Chanhs, Wake knew from his Coronado instructors, were VC defectors; and the KKK was the Khmer Kampuchea Krom, descendants of the Cambodians who ruled the area before the Vietnamese conquered the entire Mekong region three hundred years earlier. The KKK were anticommunist but did not like the Vietnamese either. Some were suspected VC informants, but then again so were some of the Hoi Chanhs. Wake tried to remember the various other paramilitary groups, tribes, hatreds, and politics he learned about before coming over, but right then he couldn't keep it all straight.

Stahl resumed. "Okay then, on to the ops. This is part of Operation Foul Deck. It will be a recon decoy for the main swift boat thrust up the river at Ha Tien. There'll be another recon decoy by some PBRs on a canal off the Bassac River over near Châu Đốc on the inland border. The plan is to pressure the enemy on three sides and throw him off his stride, maybe get him to make a mistake. Coordination and comms will be from here at the base. All three ops should reach their objectives no later than an hour after dawn. The time frame on that is approximate. Questions?"

When no one spoke up, Stahl got to the meat of matter for the men in the room.

"Sunrise is at 0648. Weather guessers says you'll have partly cloudy skies with eight to ten knots of wind from the east and two-foot waves. Current over on the river mouth coast will be an ebb until low tide at 0538, then a flood until a two-and-a-half-foot high tide at 1513."

"Oh yeah, 105 will have an AP reporter on board, so don't do anything you think is funny, 'cause the folks back in the world won't see it that way. They'll think it's either stupid or criminal. Got that?"

Grins and nods.

He continued. "Good. As per SOP, main comms for the op will be on the AN/VRC-46 VHF FM radio at 30.00–79.95 MHZ for the Coastal Guard Frequency, channel 1. Tactical will be on the AN/PRC-10/25 VHF FM, portable field radio at 20 MHZ, channel 3. Call signs: 106 is Red Dog and 105 is Blue Puppy. Seawolves Detachment 5—call sign Shark Fin Tub—from the LST *Hunterdon* at Rach Gia on the coast east of our target area is the assigned on-call air support. They will be monitoring both radio channels. On-scene their birds will switch to the tac channel. Shark Fin Tub is also handling medevac coordination with Army dustoff birds from the 9th Division. Response time from Shark Fin Tub will be fifteen minutes minimum, so if you have a problem, call for them right away. There is no ground force rapid backup or artillery support in your immediate area. Got that?"

This time nobody grinned. "You'll get under way from the base—code name Jackson—at 0400 and make fifteen knots on course zero-five-seven for the forty-mile run over to the village of Cầu Lông—code name Biloxi—at the mouth of the Kénh ba Hón River—code name Yazoo. Remember to look out for the fishing boats near the Son Hai islands en route. Five miles before reaching the river mouth, reduce speed to ten knots to mute the sound of your approach. At one mile, reduce to five knots to get through the village as quietly as possible. You should arrive around sunrise. Pick up speed after that and get through Làng Bến Gạo village—code name Natchez—four miles up the river.

"Intel and some of the VNN guys say depths in the river up to that village should be at least seven to eight feet. Intel also says you *probably* won't get any enemy fire until you're past the village, but be careful in the lower river anyway. As you can see on the chart, the river angles from northeasterly to more northerly at the intersection of a main canal a mile past Natchez. From that point on, you're in Indian country. Rice paddies with scattered hooches. Your objective is another three or four miles up the river, which will narrow to about one hundred feet and probably get shallower.

"Hear this loud and clear: if you do find the VC post, this is a shoot-and-scoot recon decoy op. You fire and then *di-di mau* out of there. There's a hell'uva lot more of them than there are of you. Don't get killed on a sideshow op. Got it?"

A chorus of "Aye, aye, sirs."

Wake glanced over at Jour and was surprised at how tense he looked. Jour looked back and muttered, "Well, sir, this sure as hell won't be dull. We best get to the boat an' make sure we've got plenty of ammo in the ready boxes an' Taylor's got the weapons cleaned an' oiled."

As everyone stood to leave, Wake hoped it wasn't obvious that he felt like throwing up.

68

Muddy Sunrise

Kénh ba Hón River
Southwest Vietnam

Friday, 11 December 1968

Wake surveyed his crew as they crouched over their guns in the darkness, black forms who were scanning the horizon in all directions.
He wondered if they were as nervous as he was. *Probably not.*

The reporter, Anderson, was standing by the aft gun mount, a slender, quiet
fellow in his mid-twenties with a droopy mustache and hair to his shoulders. He
didn't pester anybody, didn't take flash photos in the dark or furiously scribble
notes, or do anything else to tick off the sailors. Wake could tell he was a veteran
of combat patrols because even as he stood easily swaying with the boat, his eyes
took in everything about the location and condition of the most important equipment on board—the weapons and ammo. He wore a hunting vest covered with
pockets, each one stuffed full. A first-aid pack was sticking out of one of them.

Nguyen Tuan was a question mark for Wake. The Vietnamese petty officer
kept his comments and responses quiet and concise. Whether that was from
professional self-discipline or lack of English, Wake couldn't tell, because the
man's expression rarely changed. Tuan said he'd never been up this river and
couldn't tell the Americans anything about it. That made his main function

260

interpreting—if and when they stopped and interviewed locals. Wake wondered if he was lying about his experience.

During the open-sea transit toward Biloxi in the predawn darkness, Jour and Wake got to talking about their families. Jour's father was a born-and-raised towboat man on the Mississippi. He'd been a boatswain's mate on a *Cherokee*-class fleet tug in the Pacific during World War II towing barges of supplies, and occasionally damaged ships, between island groups for three long, boring years. After the war he returned to his old job on the river, worked his way up, and was now a senior captain.

With his dad gone on the river so much, his mother had raised the family's four boys and two girls practically on her own. All of them graduated from high school, a proud first for the Jour family. And while he'd dreamed of being an architect, young Jour had joined the Navy because college was out of his reach. After retiring, Jour said wistfully, his goal was to skipper a charter schooner in the Caribbean.

"I grew up without a father, too," Sean said. "He was killed when his mine-sweeper exploded in the Dutch East Indies a month before I was born—just as the war was starting."

"Is that why you joined the Navy?" Jour asked. "Because of your old man?"

"It's just what Wake men do," Wake said, realizing that was true. "There's always a Wake in the Navy."

Although it was a subject he rarely talked about, he explained that generations of Wake men had gone to sea and served their country in far-flung places. "I grew up in Key West in the same house where my great-grandfather lived. He was a Navy man, too. I read his memoirs and thought it was the finest thing a man could do. I never considered doing anything else. I'm in for the next twenty years at least."

The sky was beginning to lighten as he concluded, "But first let's get ourselves the hell out of this brown-water hellhole."

"Hell, yeah, man," Jour agreed, "I'm with you on that!" *This Wake guy's got it right*, he thought. *Just get the job done and move on. He might even turn out to be a good officer.*

The two swift boats reached Biloxi and entered the slow-moving river just as the sun was coming up over the flat, featureless landscape. The weather guessers got it wrong—there was low-level cloud cover coming in from the Mekong Delta to the east. Wake cursed under his breath. If the clouds got thicker, there'd be no air support.

Fishermen sitting on the village docks didn't react with overt hostility, or even surprise, at the sight of two patrol boats flying American flags. Most looked away. No one waved back at the American sailors manning their guns.

"Good morning, you little slope-headed VC bastards," Taylor said as he smiled and waved with the others. Wake saw Anderson write that down in his notebook.

The two boats increased speed after they passed the village. They arrived at Natchez village a few minutes later, slowing down to reduce their waves for the sampans along the bank. Once again, the few people in sight showed so surprise at seeing the intruders.

Jour shook his head. "This ain't good. They knew we were coming."

Wake checked his men one more time. Jour was at the helmsman's seat in the pilothouse. Taylor was at the after .50-caliber mount with the underslung 81-millimeter mortar tube, assisted by Lincoln as loader. Rincón was on the twin .50s atop the wheelhouse. North was on the M-60 .30-caliber set up at the open forepeak hatchway. Impassive Tuan stood beside Jour. Anderson was sitting on the after end of the cabin top next to Lincoln. Everyone on board, including Anderson, was scanning the banks for signs of the Vietcong.

Once past the village they saw no one. The few hooches next to the river appeared deserted except for a few lethargic, skinny mongrel dogs. The boats passed the intersection of the main canal with the river. After that the river got narrower and looked even more like a canal. Wake pulled his sweat-soaked shirt away from his chest. Even this early in the morning the heat and humidity were intense. His breathing slowed as his senses sharpened, taking in the twin diesels thrumming in tune, the swish of the bow wave. He fingered his holstered pistol and reached for the M-16 in the ready rack beside him as Jour moved the wheel slightly to steer around a gentle curve in the river.

About sixty yards ahead, Minsky's 106 led the way. Wake wondered why Minsky, a famous athlete, couldn't get a staff job someplace until he finished his time and could go back home to Ohio.

Home. Wake started to lose focus as he thought of the Keys. The Ten Thousand Islands and Shark River country looked a lot like coastal Vietnam. Northerners dismissed the mangrove jungles as useless swampland, but Wake had always loved their primordial beauty and tranquility, and the incredible diversity of wildlife they sheltered. His great-grandfather had fought the Civil War on that coast. And twenty years later that same man had fought Chinese-Malay pirates not far from where Sean Robert was right now. *There's some irony for you—*

"B-40 incoming, starboard beam!" shouted Lincoln.

69
Reload

Kénh ba Hón River
Southwest Vietnam

———

Friday, 11 December 1968

Nobody had to give an order. Taylor aft and Rincón on top simultaneously opened fire with their .50s, spewing three streams of tracer and
ball rounds along the riverbank where a wisp of rocket propellent
smoke still lingered. Bushes and trees were shredded under the onslaught,
branches and leaves flying apart. Jour rammed the throttle down and spun
the wheel to starboard.

Wake's head swiveled around in time to see the rocket-propelled grenade
explode in an orange-and-black flash on the gunwale strake just aft of the
wheelhouse. Shrapnel sliced through the light aluminum superstructure,
shattering the starboard galley window and opening tiny holes everywhere.

Jour spun the wheel and got the boat headed for the other shore, then
straightened out on a course down the middle of the river. Up ahead, 106 was
jinking back and forth too. Taylor abruptly yelled, "Cease fire!" and Wake
realized the VC had fired only the single rocket grenade. *That was it? That
was nothing like the movies.*

The radio tactical channel crackled with Minsky's voice, "Red Dog to Blue Puppy. Report damage and casualties."

Wake reached for the dangling mic. "Assessing now. Will report." Jour yelled for Lincoln to get below and check for damage in the engine room. "Anybody wounded?" he added. A chorus of *nos*. Lincoln popped out of the engine room hatch to report no engine damage and no incoming water there, then went forward into the main cabin. After a few minutes he came up into the pilothouse and said the hull-deck joint was bent inward just forward of the galley, and there were a dozen small holes in the deck and hull at the gunwale.

Wake checked the crew again. North was swiveling the bow gun on its bipod left and right, looking for targets. Taylor and Rincón were checking their weapons and getting more ammo into their ready trays, which carried five hundred rounds for each machine gun. Lincoln went aft and joined Taylor. Tuan still stood next to Jour, mutely studying the river ahead. Anderson was taking photos of the damage and the shoreline.

Wake radioed his report to Minsky, who replied with a laconic, "Roger that." Right afterward the other radio piped up and Wake heard Minsky telling Stahl on the main channel what had happened and the location. Then everyone returned to crouching over their guns as PCF 105 continued upriver behind 106. *This is surreal*, Wake thought.

"You did good, Mr. Wake," said Jour. "First time's a bitch for everybody."

Wake stretched his neck to relieve the tension. "Thanks, Chief. How come there was only one B-40 shot at us?"

Jour shrugged. "Harassment. Make us jumpy an' waste our ammo. See how we react. They'll really nail us farther up, probably at a bend or narrows. And then it's gonna be a friggin' long, hairy ride home," he muttered to himself.

Wake couldn't come up with a reply that didn't sound stupid or scared. Tuan did have something to say, though. "Bad day."

Anderson came up to the pilothouse with pen and notebook in hand. "Any thoughts on that B-40, sir?"

Hell, yeah, I have thoughts. He looked at Anderson for a second, then said, "Guess the VC don't like reporters." Anderson chuckled politely, wrote in the notebook, and returned aft. Wake instantly regretted his comment. *That was stupid. I'll catch hell when Admiral Zumwalt reads that in tomorrow's paper.*

Half a mile ahead they came to a slight bend to the left. The river had gradually, almost deceptively, narrowed to about eighty feet wide. As 106 went around the curve, Minsky's gunners cut loose on the left bank and his voice came onto the tactical channel. "Armed man in black on left bank by the tall mango tree; 105, sweep the right bank!"

Before Wake could say a word, Jour was growling out orders. "North, sweep the right bank ahead of us! Rincón sweep right bank abeam! Taylor, sweep right bank on the quarter! Lincoln, watch the left bank!"

Minsky's boat heeled slightly to starboard from the sudden eruption of heavy machine-gun fire toward the left bank. Red tracer streams swept back and forth into the jungle. And then they were past the curve and the river widened a bit. Wake checked the depth-sounder and saw the bottom go from six feet to nine feet. Minsky's boat stopped shooting.

"Cease fire!" shouted Jour. "Ammo check! Taylor, do a barrel check on all guns."

Wake did a quick mental estimate of ammunition expended during the previous B-40 attack plus the thirty seconds of full auto fire during the curve and came up with about 17,000 rounds left. *We're okay on ammo,* he realized with great relief. *But we're not even halfway there.* The relief evaporated.

Taylor reported the gun barrels were not overheated or warping, and all guns had been replenished with ammo. Five hundred feet ahead of them 106 swerved suddenly. "Log in the water," Minsky radioed back. Jour followed suit, and 105 kept moving upriver, constantly searching for shoals, rocks, logs, mines, people, sampans, fishing net stakes, and anything else that could be a problem.

Tuan glanced back and saw Wake watching him. His expression didn't change.

What the hell is he thinking? Wake had heard of Vietnamese liaisons who were really VC spies. *Whose side is this guy really on? I don't trust him.*

Anderson was sitting on the deck with his knees up, leaning back against the cabin top as he wrote in his notebook. Wake remembered Stahl's warning not to let the reporter get killed. *He's exposed out there. Should I order him into the pilothouse? Hell, he's got more combat experience than I do.*

When 106 swerved again, Wake directed his attention back to the river ahead. "Another log, we think," Minsky said on the tactical channel. Jour quickly swerved to avoid it too.

"It's a mine!" yelled Taylor, traversing his .50 to blast it as the boat roared past only fifteen feet away.

The explosion sent a hail of slimy water and hot shrapnel over the boat. "You idiot!" Jour screamed.

Wake didn't react in time to brace himself, and his shoulder hit the bulkhead hard. Jour hung on to the wheel as Tuan was flung to the right. Wake looked aft and saw Taylor just standing there at his gun, either stunned by what he had done or admiring his work. Lincoln had been knocked off his feet and into the corner of the mortar ready ammo locker, and blood was pouring from a gash on his forehead. Anderson rushed over to help him sit up. Wake went aft with the aid kit and wrapped a compression bandage around the engineman's head.

"Sorry, sir," mumbled Lincoln. "I'm okay. Just a cut, right?"

Wake tied off the end of the bandage. "It's a bad cut, but you'll live. We'll get you stitched up proper when we get back. Stay sitting down for a while."

An unrepentant Taylor walked up and slapped Lincoln on the shoulder. "Ah, hell, LT, that ain't nothin'. The brother here just wants a medal for his booboo. Hell, I've had worse cuts from the whores at Mama Lola's bar."

They were still laughing—Lincoln hardest of all—when the first VC mortar rounds fell.

70

Mississippi!

Kénh ba Hón River
Southwest Vietnam

Friday, 11 December 1968

The first shell exploded ten feet off the port beam. Shrapnel peppered the hull. Jour hit the throttle and veered toward the opposite bank. Lincoln grabbed Wake's arm as the boat heeled over, and Anderson stumbled across the deck and grabbed onto the cabin top. The others held onto anything handy.

Twenty seconds later, the second round landed exactly where the boat had just been. Jour took the boat toward the other bank. He was turning the wheel again when the third round nailed the samson post on the bow. Everything forward of the pilothouse disintegrated, leaving only North's mangled corpse and a tangle of aluminum. The pilothouse windows shattered back into Jour and Tuan, ripping their faces and upper torsos and knocking them to the deck. Up on the top twin fifties, Rincón caught several shards in the face as he swept the banks with .50-caliber fire in the hope of hitting their invisible enemies.

The boat slewed around to starboard until Jour, barely able to see, dragged himself up to the controls, throttled down, and straightened out the course up the middle of the river. Two more mortar rounds exploded in the water fifty feet ahead. Another landed on the riverbank to starboard. Then the barrage stopped.

"Chicom 31, 60-millimeter knee mortar!" shouted Taylor as he flung blood off his left hand. "Two of 'em with preset ranges. But it ain't over, LT. They're scooting to another firing position now. Get ready for more!"

Wake was on the port side heading forward to the pilothouse when the second round hit the bow. He was barely able to hang on to the handrails and made it to the helm just as Jour throttled down. Having steadied the boat, Jour collapsed against the chart table holding his face. Wake rushed to the wheel. The slower speed had lowered the battered bow and allowed water to pour into the boat. Wake popped the throttle up enough to keep the bow raised.

He suddenly realized Minsky had been calling on the radio. "Do you read me Blue Puppy? One-oh-five, report condition! Report, damn it!"

Minsky's boat was slowly turning around. Rincón called down from top-side. "Skipper, you got the helm? We're heading too far toward the right bank."

"Got it, thanks." Wake grabbed the wheel and straightened the course.

Still in shock, he struggled to give a coherent report. "Blue Puppy to Red Dog. We took two mortar hits. Engines functional. Extent of casualties and damage unknown."

Minsky sounded calmer now. "Okay, I'm coming around to you, Blue Puppy."

Minsky was a hundred feet away when the next mortar barrage began landing. The third of the six rounds hit 106 on the stern .50-caliber mortar mount, which erupted in rippling bursts of light and sound. Horrified, Wake realized the round had hit the ready mortar ammo locker.

The fourth round hit 106 on the starboard beam by the galley window. The rest of the rounds hit the water one after another in a line down the middle of the river.

Minsky was in deep trouble; 106 slewed to port then went dead in the water, a cloud of black smoke boiling up to the sky—a perfect target reference for the VC. More rounds would be coming.

Taylor called forward, "Skipper, the little bastard's gotta be on that tree line about 150 yards back in the rice paddies on the port side."

"Then put some friggin' mortar rounds over there!"

"I can't load it, Skipper. Takes two arms. . . ."

Taking his eyes off 106, Wake glanced aft. Taylor stood slumped against the gun mount, his left arm hemorrhaging blood as he tried to aim with his right. Lincoln was down on the deck next to him, clutching his belly. Anderson was crawling back toward Taylor.

Wake called up to the top mount, "Rincón, forget the fifties and help on the mortar!"

"I got it, Skipper," shouted Anderson as he fed a round into the mortar tube while Taylor triggered the gun. Rincón opened up on the tree line with his twins.

Wake felt the wheel go slack and then spin uselessly, and he knew the cables had parted. Cursing, he made his way back to the after steering station at the portside end of the cabin top. The wheel and throttles there still worked, and he steered for the burning boat dead ahead.

As they came alongside 106 he called out, "Minsky—get your guys on my boat!"

The smoke lifted for a second and he saw 106's condition. Only the burning pit of the engine room remained aft of the main cabin. Minsky lay facedown on the foredeck. Two bloodied crewmen held each other up in the remains of the pilothouse.

One of them leaned out and croaked, "Mr. Minsky's still alive, sir, but in bad shape. Got another fella in bad shape, and then there's us two. They got two of us and the VNN guy, dead. Boat's sinking fast."

"Get everyone over on this boat," ordered Wake. "We're getting out of here."

"Aye, sir," said the sailor. He and his shipmate carried a wounded man over to Wake's boat and laid him out on the cabin top, then crumpled on the after deck. Anderson went forward and Rincón climbed down from the twins to help get Minsky on board. They gently stretched him out beside his sailor. Minsky's face was pale and his breathing shallow. He seemed barely alive. Rincón and Anderson went back for the other bodies and laid them out on the stern.

Lincoln was standing now, helping Taylor with a compress bandage that didn't seem to be slowing the blood flow. His brow furrowed, the black engineman jury-rigged a tourniquet—a rag twisted around a piece of handrail—and tied it above the bandage. Taylor swayed, sat down with a curse, and fell back on the cabin top next to the other wounded men.

Wake knew there wasn't much time until the VC started up again from a new position, but he couldn't leave without a final check. He went into 106's ruined pilothouse, fore cabin, and main cabin, all knee-deep in brown river water and fuel oil. There were no more bodies.

He smashed the radios with his rifle butt and called out, "Rincón, get ready to toss some grenades into this cabin." Wake got back on the after helm, opened the throttles, and yelled to Rincón, "Now!"

Six seconds later, three frags went off in 106's pilothouse and main cabin. Lincoln put a mortar round into the boat's superstructure as she settled into the bottom ooze with just the jagged remains of the pilothouse top showing. By then, Wake and 105 were weaving their way downriver at about fifteen knots, the fastest Wake dared go with his damaged vessel.

He got Anderson to steer and went forward to the pilothouse. Jour was sitting in the helmsman's chair, squinting ahead through one eye. The other was invisible in his swollen face. Tuan, his head already bandaged, leaned against the chart table and wrapped gauze around Jour's head, murmuring something in Vietnamese. Wake recognized the rhythm of the chant—it was the Lord's Prayer. When he saw the rosary beads hanging from Tuan's breast pocket, he lost all doubt about whose side he was on.

Jour grunted out, "Still floatin'. Good work, Skipper." Another grunting breath as he tried to rise. "I'll get back to work in a second."

Wake put his hand on Jour's shoulder and pressed him down. "Thanks, Chief. Rest a bit. We got it."

He took the microphone off the hook and tried to reach the base. "Jackson, Jackson, Jackson, this is Blue Puppy. We are in Mississippi. Repeat, we are in Mississippi!—on the Yazoo halfway between Vicksburg and Natchez and heading for Biloxi. Red Dog is down. Send Shark Fin Tub ASAP. Do you read me? Over."

Nothing. Not even static. He tried adjusting the squelch, frequency, and volume, and repeated his broadcast. Still nothing. The radio must have been hit by the shrapnel from the forward hit. He tried the short-range portable radio, this time getting a squelch break and some static but no reply. He tried again, directly to *Hunterdon* at Rach Gia, pretty far for a short-range rig. Seconds went by. Wake was about to try again when the static cleared and an impossibly smooth Deep South bass voice came over the radio, "Ahhh, roger that, Blue Puppy. Shark Fin Tub reads you Lincoln Continental that you are in Mississippi. Shark Fins Charlie an' Delta are liftin' off an' about fourteen out. Maintain contact on this freq an' signal when you've got ears an' eyeballs on 'em. Over."

71

Ears and Eyeballs

Kénh ba Hón River
Southwest Vietnam

Friday, 11 December 1968

*F*inally. Wake took in a deep breath. *Hunterdon* had heard them "Lincoln Continental"—slang phonetic for "loud and clear"—and was sending help. He tried to make his voice sound as composed as the one at the other end of the radio. "Roger that, Shark Fin Tub. Shark Fins Charlie and Delta here in fourteen. Please relay our sitrep to Jackson for us—we can't reach them. Over."

"Will do, Blue Puppy. What is Double-Oh Bee of Victor Charlie an' your Kilo/Whiskey count? Over."

Oh hell, I should've already given them that. Wake gave *Hunterdon* the VC's order of battle in plain English because he couldn't recall the code words for VC weapons. "No real Double-Oh Bee—never saw them. Two knee mortars zeroed in with two separate barrages on us a mile back from the north bank. Before that, one B-40 nailed us three miles to west from the south bank, and there were a couple of floating mines in between. VC are staying out of sight—we can't get a target."

He looked over at Minsky, then continued. "Need air cover down the river and medevac ASAP for four Kilos and eight Whiskeys. Red Dog is sunk a mile back to the east, but the pilothouse top is still visible. All friendlies accounted for. Recommend air strike on Red Dog wreck. Over."

"Roger that, Blue Puppy. Four Kilos an' eight Whiskeys. We're lifting two Army dust-offs for 'em. LZ will be on your right bank one mile east—repeat *east*—after takin' a port tack at Natchez. Once they hook up with you in twelve, the Shark Fins'll lead you there. Copy on the air strike request—sendin' it up the chain. Over."

A mile east of Natchez? That meant turning down a different side canal—the big one—when they got to the village. Wake couldn't find the damned chart, but he didn't waste time on it. They should see the choppers in a couple of minutes and hear their distinctive *whoop-whoop-whoop* rotor beat even before that—the "ears and eyeballs" that would tell them help was close.

He simply answered, "Roger all that, Shark Fin Tub. Over."

He looked at Minsky again, then at the others draped across the deck. *Yeah, just a simple decoy recon. Right. What a waste, and for what? We never found the VC honchos. Never even saw the ones who hit us.* A wave of exhaustion turned his legs to rubber. *I'm in charge of this shitshow and it's my first friggin' day. Oh man, I just wanna get out of here.*

When he realized that Anderson, a noncombatant, was steering, Wake cursed and looked at Jour. "Anderson's back there steering, Chief, so I'm gonna get on the helm. I need you on the radio and Rincón back on the twins. Can you see well enough to handle the radio?"

"Right eye's gettin' better, sir. I'll be okay."

"Good. Let Shark Fins Charlie and Delta know when Rincón hears and sees them."

"Aye, aye, sir. Ears an' eyeballs on the Shark Fins."

As Wake turned to go aft, Tuan held up a bandage. "Skippa, you hit many place. Much blood. I bandash most bad."

Wake was about to wave him off, but Jour squinted at him and interrupted. "You should let him help you, Skipper. You've got a nasty wound on the back of your shoulder. You're bleedin' a lot. You can't *feel* that?"

And right then he did. He flexed his right arm, and pain shot through his shoulder. Now he could feel the liquid flowing down his back. "Okay, patch me up, Tuan."

"Ears and eyeballs!" Rincón yelled. The Navy gunships were coming in fast from the southeast a hundred feet above the rice paddies.

"Thank you, Jesus," murmured Wake to the cloudy sky as Tuan cut his shirt away from his shoulder. The prayer turned into a bellowed cursed as pain stabbed through his collarbone and down his torso.

It didn't help that the unperturbable Tuan winced at the sight of the wound. "Skippa, you hit bad. Looks big pain. Want molpheen for pain?"

Damned well do *want some molpheen—with a chaser of friggin' rum!* growled Wake inwardly. Aloud he gasped through gritted teeth, "Not *yet*. I need . . . a clear head . . . for now."

Now that the adrenaline and shock had worn off, Wake couldn't move his right arm at all, so Lincoln limped over to the after helm and steered. Anderson went forward, got patched up by Tuan, then climbed topside and perched next to Rincón.

The Shark Fins separated, one staying ahead of 105 and one dropping astern, both darting through the air like angry hornets looking to sting somebody, anybody. The locals got *that* message Lincoln Continental and stayed out of sight. There was no polite slowing down at Natchez this time. The boat threw a three-foot wave against the bamboo docks and sampans on the riverbank as she turned into the large canal and headed east.

In another few minutes they saw the Army medevac dust-offs coming toward them a mile ahead. Just past the edge of the village, the lead Shark Fin circled over a flat area on the canal's right bank and fired a burst of machine-gun fire into it, then rose to join the other Shark Fin circling the LZ.

Wake yelled to Rincón, "Do you see any VC there?"

It was Jour who answered. "No VC, sir. That's standard procedure to explode any mines." Then the chief called aft to Lincoln. "Randall, slow down now an' put the bow on the bank nice an' easy, son."

Within seconds of Lincoln putting the bow into the bank, the dust-offs landed, their rotors still turning, and the crewmen frantically waved for the sailors to get their dead and wounded on board. Waving was the only effective communication in all the noise. And even that was difficult. The rotor blast filled the air with sand, mud, and debris, forcing people to squint to try to see through the sand blasting their faces.

Wake bellowed over the noise, "Rincón, Anderson, Lincoln, and Tuan, let's get Taylor and the badly wounded over there first!"

Wake and Lincoln took Taylor. Anderson, Tuan, and Rincón took the wounded crewmen from 106. Jour and Anderson brought what was left of Gary North; and Wake, Tuan, and Rincón brought over 106's dead.

As they gave the bodies to the Army medics to load, one of them circled a finger to include Lincoln, Tuan, Wake, and Anderson, and shouted into Wake's ear. "You guys're all hit. You going too? It'll be crowded, but we got room."

Wake gestured to the others and shouted back. "They're going—I'm not. It's my boat!"

Lincoln wagged his head. "I'll stay with the boat, sir—hate flying!" Anderson yelled, "I'll stay with the boat too, Lieutenant!" Tuan shook his head. Jour said something Wake couldn't hear and started walking back to the boat. Rincón was already climbing into his gun mount. The Army medic shook his head and reached for the door. The bird lifted off the moment he was on board.

"You should've gone, Andre."

The chief shook his head and smiled through his bandages. "Nah. I'm not hurt that bad, and dust-offs're only for seriously wounded. Hell, you're worser off than me. Besides, it's your first damned day, Lieutenant. You'll need my help to get this banged-up bucket home."

Wake wanted to say more but only said, "Yeah, I will, Chief. Thanks."

Weary and hurting, they set off, Lincoln steering aft, Rincón topside swiveling for targets, Anderson on the after gun, and Jour and Wake in the pilothouse. The Shark Fins buzzed above and around them as they all headed downriver.

"We're going to make this run at best speed," Wake yelled to his crew. "And I'm buying the beer for all hands when we get back to base."

"Beer, hell!" Jour yelled back. "I'm gonna need somethin' a lot stronger than beer, Skipper!"

Wake laughed. "Yeah, me too, Chief. I'll work on that."

As 105 headed down the river, the velvety voice on *Hunterdon* came over the radio again. "Shark Fin Tub to Blue Puppy. Jackson has arranged for two PCFs from Ha Tien to meet you just offshore of Biloxi and escort you home. Shark Fins will RTB at that point. Can Shark Fin Tub be of any further assistance? Over."

The guy sounded like the ultimate in cool. "Negative, Shark Fin Tub. Thanks." *Somehow, someday, I have to get to* Hunterdon *and meet this fellow.*

But not today. The cloudy skies turned stormy. One of the swift boats that met them had to take 105 in tow when it turned out the fuel tanks had been leaking and they didn't have as much as they thought. The open-water transit was long and bumpy. Once they got to An Thoi and reentered the realm of the U.S. Navy, everyone was hustled off the boat and into a hospital bed.

None of them argued.

72

Top Brass

Naval Station Saigon Hospital
Tran Hung Dao Street, Saigon

Friday, 20 December 1968

Because of their more serious wounds, Wake and Taylor were flown the next day to the naval hospital in Saigon. Surgeons couldn't save the gunner's arm, and he was flown to Bethesda for more surgery and rehabilitation. When Wake last saw him, on their fourth day in the Saigon Navy hospital, Taylor was growling at a nurse to get him some rum. Wake quietly convinced her to find some and let him have a nip.

Jour, Lincoln, Tuan, Rincón, and Anderson remained at the An Thoi base hospital for a few days before being released. The sailors were placed on light duty for a month while they healed. Anderson flew home to Kentucky the day he got out of the hospital, although his article and photos came out while he was still in An Thoi. The article, which garnered a prestigious journalism award, did not include Anderson's actions to help fight off the enemy and bring the boat back to the base. Those things were beyond his duties as a noncombatant war correspondent, and publicizing them would have endangered other war correspondents all over the world. His reputation with the bosses at AP rose considerably, and he was assigned to cover military topics in Washington. He never did tell anyone at home or at the Associated Press all the details of his role in the battle.

Wake made sure that Stahl got all his crew, including Anderson, the beer he'd promised them—two cans of ice-cold Budweiser put in their hands the moment they walked out of the base hospital. They gathered under a nearby mahogany tree and sat on some empty ammo boxes to drink them. They chugged the first beer, glorying in the taste. With the second they toasted their skipper and Taylor and Gary North, the crews of the Navy Seawolves who came to their rescue, and the Army's medevac crews.

Tuan went back to his unit. Although they never saw him again, 105's crew wondered if he and his family escaped six years later when Saigon fell. Rincón went to another PCF, survived the rest of his tour, and at the end of his enlistment returned to Puerto Rico. Lincoln transferred to a Navy supply depot near his home and stayed in the Navy. Jour did go to the Sixth Fleet in the Med and ultimately retired as a senior chief, then moved to Islamorada in the Florida Keys and opened a small towboat service. Gary North's remains were buried in a naval ceremony at the national cemetery in San Francisco near those of other young men who died too far from home. PCF 105 was deemed a total loss and ended up as a cannibalized hulk used for spare parts for other PCFs.

"So, *you're* the latest Wake in the Navy."

Wake opened one eye and saw two concerned-looking nurses and a doctor in white, several bored-looking naval officers in khaki, and, leaning over him, a bushy-browed admiral in starched fatigues. "U.S. Navy" was embroidered over one shirt pocket, and "Zumwalt" over the other. There were three stars on the collar.

Oh hell, the top brass is here to roast my ass for the recon op disaster. On further thought he decided he didn't care. Let them get it over with so he could go back to sleep. It hurt less when he was asleep. He thought of Minsky and Gary North and Taylor and the others who carried out a stupid plan concocted by a bunch of REMFs in a comfy cubicle at MACV in Saigon before heading to the O-Club for their five o'clock martinis. *Probably these same bastards standing here. So go ahead and throw me out of the Navy. I really do not care.*

"Yeah, I'm the latest Wake in the Navy," he said sarcastically. The nurses looked shocked. The doctor, a commander, studied something on the floor. Wake added a polite, "Lieutenant, junior grade, Sean Robert Wake, sir, at your service."

Zumwalt's face broke into the biggest—actually the only—smile Wake had ever seen on an admiral. "Good! We *need* officers like you, Mr. Wake, with generations of seawater in their veins and the gumption to do what it takes to accomplish the mission and save their men and ships! I'm Elmo Zumwalt. I've been in-country for two months, got responsibility for the Navy's ops here, and I want to hear your opinions on how to do things better. Yes, I know you just reported in-country, but that's good. You're not tainted yet. Doc here says we can chat for a while. Is that okay with you, Sean Robert?"

Wake glanced dubiously at the admiral's entourage. Zumwalt ordered them out, including the medicos. For the next thirty minutes Wake shared his impressions of the stateside training for swift boats, the patrol boat base at An Thoi, the coastal and river ops concept, his admiration for Lieutenant Commander Stahl and for Chief Jour, the immense value of the Seawolves, and the unrealistic and overly complicated plans hatched by headquarters. He ended with, "The Seawolves are overextended and have to stay on call at the LST when they should have enough birds to fly cover all during an op."

Zumwalt listened intently, took a few notes, and asked questions. Then he looked at his watch and said, "Gotta go, but I want to tell you something first. A Hoi Chanh defector came in three days ago from the area you were in. He said the mortar and machine-gun fire from the second boat, your PCF, nailed both his honchos—the tax collector and the conscription chief—along with the mortar team and several others. He decided the easy times for the VC in that area are over and he wants to go home to his family and farm. Says others are thinking the same thing.

"So let me tell you, Sean Robert Wake, if you think you failed, you're wrong. You did just fine. You got the VC's attention, disrupted their plans, and showed the locals that Victor Charlie is vulnerable."

Wake smiled weakly. "Didn't feel like it at the time, sir. Thanks for letting me know that."

Zumwalt patted Wake's arm. "I'll let you tell your crew about the difference they made. That's what we're here for. And now I've got something else to tell you."

He called the entourage back in. A Vietnamese naval captain had joined them. One of the American staffers produced a camera and started taking photos as Zumwalt stood over Wake's bed, brought out a framed document, and declared, "It is with great pleasure and respect that I have the honor to award to Lieutenant (j.g.) Sean Robert Wake the Navy Cross for gallantry in the face of overwhelming enemy attack, while still accomplishing his mission in spite of that attack, and bringing his severely damaged vessel home to base. I also award him the Purple Heart for wounds sustained in action against the enemy, all of this action occurring on the morning of 11 December 1968 near Lang Ben Gao in the Republic of Vietnam."

He took two medals out of his pocket and pinned them to the pillow. The staff applauded as the camera whirred. The Vietnamese captain stepped forward and read aloud from another framed document, "On behalf of the government and people of the Republic of Vietnam, Lieutenant Sean Robert Wake, U.S. Navy, is hereby awarded the Navy Gallantry Cross of the Navy of the Republic of Vietnam for his heroic actions against the communist enemy on 11 December 1968 at Lang Ben Gao in the province of Kien Giang in the Republic of Vietnam. My country thanks you, Lieutenant."

He pinned his medal to the pillow, then the room started to empty. Zumwalt stood to go, then sat back down near the bed.

"Sean Robert, you're headed to Bethesda. The doc says you'll be good as new after another repair surgery and some rehab, about a year's worth in all. That's about the time your active service commitment to the Navy is up, and I imagine you've been thinking about getting the hell out. That'll be your decision, of course, but let me just say this: you've got a good future in the Navy. I want to see officers like you change it for the better. I hope I get to see you again the next time I'm stateside. Let me know if I can help you or your crew."

"Thank you, sir," a stunned Wake replied. "I'll keep that in mind, and I hope to see you again, too. By the way, how did you know about my family?"

Zumwalt laughed. "In December 1940, my second year as a midshipman, your father lectured at the academy on gunnery tactics. His knowledge and obvious love for the Navy impressed the hell out of me. Your dad was the real deal. I wanted to be like him. Then I heard from an upper classman about the Wake family naval tradition and thought that would be a fine thing for me to start someday."

"So, did you, sir?"

Zumwalt smiled. "Both my sons are naval officers. One is on a destroyer and the other wants to be a swift boat skipper on his next assignment, probably next year. I'm very proud of them, as your father would be of you if he were here. Good luck, Sean Robert Wake."

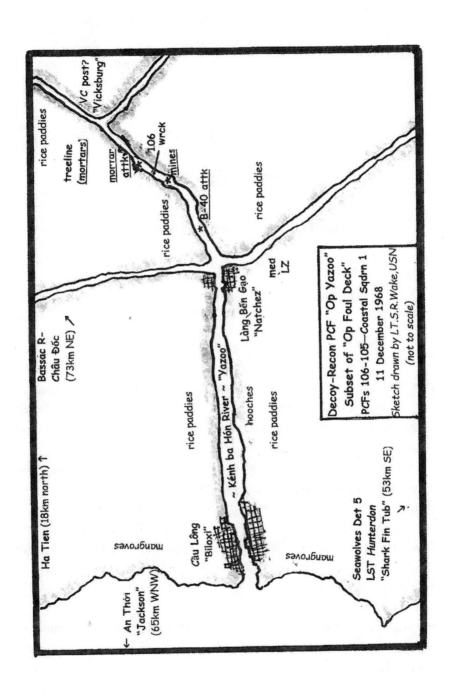

Decoy-Recon PCF "Op Yazoo"
Subset of "Op Foul Deck"
PCFs 106-105—Coastal Sqdrn 1
11 December 1968
Sketch drawn by LT.S.R.Wake,USN
(not to scale)

"VC post?"
"Vicksburg"

rice paddies

treeline
(mortars)

mortar attk
106
wrck
mines
B-40 attk

rice paddies

rice paddies

rice paddies

med LZ

Làng Bến Gạo
"Natchez"

Bassac R-
Châu Đốc
(73km NE)

~ Kénh ba Hón River ~ "Yazoo"

hooches

rice paddies

rice paddies

Ha Tien (18km north)

mangroves

Cầu Lông
"Biloxi"

mangroves

Seawolves Det 5
LST Hunterdon
"Shark Fin Tub" (53km SE)

An Thới
"Jackson"
(65km WNW)

73

The Decision

Navy Congressional Liaison Office
Pentagon

Wednesday, 15 July 1970

The surgeries and rehab at Bethesda Naval Hospital didn't take the year Zumwalt had predicted, because Sean Robert Wake pushed himself hard to rebuild his body. He was judged fit for service by the medical board in six months and released for duty.

He was shocked and angry when he was assigned to the Office of the Assistant Deputy of Staff in the Navy Congressional Liaison Office at the Pentagon. A public relations officer? Him? This was to be his final tour of duty before leaving the Navy on 1 June 1971. Whom had he ticked off? He had expected to be an assistant operations officer on a destroyer in the Med (to go after Russian subs) or, at the very least, a tactical ASW analyst at ONI—someplace near the pointed end of the spear.

Wake hated every minute of his "work," hated being a smiling flunky for the two-faced political denizens of Capitol Hill, and counted down the days until he would be free of the mind-numbing bureaucratic inertia that was the U.S. Navy.

At 6:28 on a hot Wednesday morning in the middle of July, Wake had just struck a line through the previous day on the wall calendar. Eleven months, fifteen days, and a wakeup until he could shed his uniform, grow his hair, and leave this awful place. He dreamed of sailing in the Keys again, finding adventure. *Is there such a thing as a sailor of fortune?* he wondered.

A deep voice in the hallway broke into his daydream. "This is the place, I think. I'll just be a minute, Commander. Wait for me here."

The voice didn't belong to anyone Wake worked with, but it did sound familiar. The door opened and in walked the newly promoted and appointed Chief of Naval Operations, Adm. Elmo Zumwalt. The admiral grinned at Wake's surprise, then looked around and shook his head in dismay. Wake popped up to attention and was about to introduce himself properly—after all, how could the admiral remember a banged-up junior grade from two years ago on the far side of the world?

But Zumwalt was faster. "Why, it's none other than Sean Robert Wake, PR man extraordinaire. Congrats on making full lieutenant." He returned Wake's salute and then shook his hand. "I heard you got out of the hospital early, but I didn't find out you were put in this hellhole until yesterday. Guy like you must be going crazy in a place like this. Who'd *you* piss off?"

Wake couldn't help laughing. "Been asking myself that for a while now, sir. It's my last tour of duty. I asked for ASW in the Med or at least something at ONI, but this is what I got."

"Last tour of duty, eh? Looks like you're going out with a whimper instead of a bang. Maybe I can fix that. Have a seat, son. Ever heard of the Naval Field Ops Support Group, also known as Task Force 157?"

"No, sir," Wake said. *Sounds like intel or comms.*

"Not many have. Clandestine naval intel work, just like your great-grandfather did at the turn of the century, and your grandfather did in World War I, and your older cousin is doing in the Cold War. They're all good at it—must be a family thing. I think you'd be good at it too. ONI lost its clandestine service at the end of World War II, but a couple of years ago it got started up again, *very quietly*. The unit works with CIA and DIA but specializes in maritime matters—including Soviet subs."

Wake was speechless. *The Navy has undercover spies?* Zumwalt paused, regarded Wake thoughtfully for a moment, then continued, "TF 157 has officers on assignment all over the world, and not just on Soviet or ChiCom targets. Mission is to find out what's happening, or about to happen, wherever the Navy might be involved. The Middle East is going to be one of those hotspots, but we don't have the intelligence assets there that we need. You scored high in language skills at the academy, and I think you could do good work out there, once you pick up the lingo. And you won't get bored doing it, either. I promise you that."

Learn Arabic? "It does sound interesting, Admiral, but what's the time commitment? I don't have much time left, sir." *But do I want to spend my life puttering around in the Keys? Maybe I should stay in for a while longer. Hell, the freakin' CNO himself wants me to stay in!*

"Five years," said Zumwalt. "First year is intense training, and I mean really hard work, then four years on field ops. Halfway through you'll get upped to lieutenant commander. Sometimes doing clandestine field ops, running local informants; sometimes doing attaché duty. The Middle East is where things'll be happening in the '70s and '80s, Sean Robert. Not Eastern Europe and not Southeast Asia." Zumwalt cocked an eyebrow. "Or . . . you can vegetate here until your time is up and then sail away into more boredom. Your decision." Wake didn't even have to think about it. "Okay, sir. I'm not sure how to request a transfer to a secret outfit, but I'll check today and get it in."

Zumwalt's hand was on the doorknob. "No need, Lieutenant. Your new orders will arrive this afternoon by 1600. Pack up your pencils and get ready to roll."

By the time TF-157 and the Navy's clandestine service was shut down after the congressional hearings of 1977, Wake was a commander. That year, the CIA offered him considerable incentive to join the agency as a "Language Officer" in the Linguistical Research Analysis Section of the Infrastructure Management Division in the Directorate of Support at headquarters.

Although the title made the job sound boring, that was just to deflect outsiders' inquiries into what he did for a living. It was anything but. Sean's wife, Sue, had a better idea of what he did because she also worked at the agency, although not as a field agent. She knew he had become an ops case officer and knew enough not to ask about his work and long absences. It was an unusual marriage, but both agreed it would get better after they put in their twenty-five years and retired somewhere warm and quiet.

One of the things Sue never did learn about her husband was that he had a very rare and handy skill, which was why the CIA wanted him in the first place.

74

The Pearl of the Moon

Starlight Rooftop Garden Café
Emirate Hotel, Kuwait

Sunday, 16 July 1990

Sheik Hamid Hasan Khan was nervous. A stiff whiskey would have done a lot to calm his nerves, but alcohol was forbidden to Muslims, even in a hotel catering to rich foreigners.

That was not his real name. Nor was he a sheik, or even distantly related to the ancient Kuwaiti clan—or an observant Muslim, for that matter. His identity was a ruse he had devised when setting up his first meeting with the rich Canadian gentleman who fancied himself a knowledgeable collector of Arabic cultural artifacts. That meeting had taken a month of correspondence to set up and finalize.

Hamid's nerves tingled at the very thought of the $10 million he would receive for arranging the sale of the 352-year-old Pearl of the Moon, the largest and most perfect pearl in the world. Declan O'Leery of Nova Scotia wanted it very badly. And the deal was set to close this evening. Mr. O'Leery would be arriving at the boutique hotel's rooftop garden café at any moment.

Hamid had already reserved O'Leery's favorite corner table, which overlooked the port and the ancient Mubarakiya market to the west. Beyond the port, the sun was settling into the desert through a cloud-speckled sky. Only two other tables were occupied, both on the far side of the café. Hamid had arranged that as well so he and O'Leery would have the privacy they needed to discuss such a delicate matter.

It was delicate because the Pearl of the Moon would first have to be "obtained" from its current possessor, the head of one of the ruling families of Kuwait, and unlike Hamid a very real and powerful sheik. The sheik had no hint of who Hamid was or what he was planning, of course. If he had, Hamid would have been in the Kuwaiti Security Service's dungeon by now, and "Kiss," as the service was known, would eventually dump his dismembered body far out in the desert.

He shuddered but forced his thoughts back to the upcoming meeting. Subtle hint and inducement and bargaining had led to this meeting, the third since O'Leery had arrived a week earlier. Hamid steadied his nerves with the reminder that by this time next Sunday he would be $10 million richer and flying first class to Singapore while O'Leery would be taking the Pearl of the Moon to Nova Scotia.

Or perhaps O'Leery might be the one sitting in the KSS dungeon. Hamid hadn't yet decided whether it was worth it to play both sides and notify KSS what O'Leery was carrying. Hamid had to admit it was an attractive business option. The proper owner of the Pearl of the Moon would regain it, KSS would get the credit, and Hamid would gain influence at KSS. That could be quite helpful in the future.

"Look at that sunset! And that *pearl* blue sky!"

Hamid came to his senses and spun around. O'Leery was already standing beside him. He rose as O'Leery reached out his hand.

The Canadian gestured toward the chair facing the window. "I insist that you take the seat with that magnificent view, Hamid. I've been outside enjoying this beautiful country all day."

The rich collector's boyish grin and open manner disturbed Hamid. He should be more nervous and cautious. Then he relaxed; to the few others in the café O'Leery was just another naïve foreign businessman visiting the ancient city—rich from either finance, shipping, or oil. Another dupe.

Hamid noticed that a third man, well dressed and confident looking, had entered after O'Leery and joined the table of two in the far corner. The muscular young men seated at the table next to them exchanged knowing glances. Obviously, they were bodyguards for the men at the first table, who had begun talking quietly. *Must be a big business deal,* Hamid surmised. The rooftop café was a favorite spot for deal making. At any event, they were too far away to hear Hamid and O'Leery.

"Well, Declan, how was your day snorkeling? See any pearls?"

The man laughed. "Yeah, nice day. But no pearls, Hamid—that's why I'm here with you. So, what's the word? Has the owner agreed to my price? When can I get it? Remember, I've got to be back in Halifax by the twenty-fifth for my wife's birthday party."

Hamid nodded. "Yes. It is agreed. Ten million dollars. Half to be in my escrow account by Wednesday, and the other half confirmed in my account when I deliver the item to you here at this table next Sunday at sunset. You can leave two hours later on the overnight plane to Frankfurt and be home in plenty of time for your wife's party." Hamid reached over and patted O'Leery's arm. "My dear friend, your wife will love her birthday present—the rarest and most beautiful pearl in the world, discovered by the legendary Kuwaiti pearl divers three and a half centuries ago and set in a diamond-crusted oyster shell for the emir two centuries ago. Truly, I have never seen a more superb piece, my friend."

O'Leery's face lit up at the description. "Thank you for your work on this, Hamid. It will be the *pearl* of my collection." He snickered. "Get it? By the way, I've got another project in mind for my Kuwaiti collection in the near future. A Christmas present to myself, this time."

Hamid bestowed his most sincere smile on O'Leery. "It will be my greatest pleasure to help, Declan."

The cinnamon tea arrived with dried fruit and dates, then the first course, a salad of spiced heart of palm. By the fourth course, a fragrant machboos of rice and chicken, O'Leery's cheerful demeanor had changed ever so slightly. He wasn't smiling as much. The air of lighthearted camaraderie had diminished. The Canadian seemed concerned about something.

O'Leery saw Hamid's concern and could tell that the "sheik" was wondering if his façade had failed. It was time to allay Hamid's worry—and also time to get a message out. He stood abruptly, holding a hand to his abdomen. "Sorry,

Hamid, I think that spiced-up chicken didn't agree with me. Or it could be the goats' eyes soup I had for lunch. I'm going back to my room to get some rest. I'll transfer the first half of the money to your account on Wednesday, then see you here next Sunday. Thank you, my friend. A pleasure doing business with you."

And with that and a brief handshake, O'Leery departed, leaving a perplexed Hamid to pay the considerable bill, which totaled over $1,000. It was a minor expense when $10 million was coming his way, he assured himself. Still, something wasn't quite right here.

He hadn't noticed that the third man sitting across the room had left seconds before O'Leery. He also hadn't noticed that O'Leery had been watching that man covertly the entire time. More important, Hamid didn't know his client's name wasn't O'Leery, or that he was neither Canadian nor a rich collector of Kuwaiti pearls. That was all a carefully constructed ruse de guerre.

Hamid would also never know, or even suspect, that the third man on the far side of the café was an Iraqi intelligence colonel named Kassim Zidan, who had arrived in the city a week earlier and was meeting with some of his advance team to discuss what was about to happen.

And most definitely Hamid would never know that O'Leery was actually a division supervisor at CIA headquarters at Langley, Virginia, brought back into the field to utilize his unique skill of lip-reading conversations in Arabic.

When he reached the lobby, Sean Robert Wake stepped outside to the portico and into a waiting taxi that would take him to a safe house in the Bayan section of the city, not far from the U.S. embassy. There, Wake would have the crypto-comms folks send a simple coded message to his boss at Langley: "Two a.m. on 2 August 1990." After that he would head for the airport and home.

On 2 August 1990, at 2 a.m., approximately 100,000 Iraqi soldiers invaded Kuwait. It took them only 24 hours to overwhelm the 16,000 Kuwaiti defenders. Six months after that, an American-led coalition of thirty-five nations liberated Kuwait.

On the first day of July 2001, Sean Robert Wake retired from thirty-four years of naval and federal service. In attendance at the ceremony at Langley was his son Jeff, who had chosen the Peace Corps over the Navy. After serving two tours in Rwanda he was now the assistant USAID liaison officer in the capital of Kigali. Jeff's wife, Lidia, stood next to him holding their infant daughter, Petra Ann. Jeff's younger sister Mary Ann, an assistant professor of history at UNC Chapel Hill, was also there. Cousin Raul Cano, an immigration lawyer in Miami, attended with his family. Sadly, Sue Wake could not be there; she'd died of cancer two years earlier.

The day after Sean Robert moved his belongings into the old Wake family home in Key West, just across the lane from his elderly cousin Agnes' bungalow, the United States was attacked by terrorists.

The country was at war yet again, but for the first time in 160 years, no one in the Wake/Cano family was in the Navy or the intelligence services. Sean Robert was glad of that. He knew this was going to be a long, ugly, and shadowy war. He also remembered the letter that had been passed down through the family since 1920—the letter from Peter Wake to the first Wake to graduate from the Naval Academy after 2020. It was in his safe deposit box at the bank, still unopened. *Will we still be in this war then?* he wondered.

75
Pride

Navy–Marine Corps Memorial Stadium
U.S. Naval Academy, Annapolis, Maryland

Friday, 26 May 2023

The 1,183 soon-to-be-ensigns and second lieutenants stood stiffly in formation on the field, their white choker collars and Marine dress blues already chafing their necks in the hot morning sun. For the first time since 2019 the stadium was filled with families. The pandemic had finally diminished enough to allow the age-old pageant to play out, forming indelible memories for everyone present, from admirals to little sisters.

The president of the United States gave the expected long-winded speech full of accolades for the graduates, accompanied by the expected warning to international foes, and ending with the expected homage to naval traditions that had served the nation so well for more than two centuries. The ceremony went on for several hours, but none of the graduates complained about the heat or glare. It had taken too long, and too much of themselves, to get to this point.

When the graduation and commissioning were completed and the midshipmen's head covers had been thrown into the air, never to be worn again now that they were ensigns and second lieutenants, the strict discipline gave way to elation. Families surged onto the field to embrace their loved ones and attach new shoulder boards with the shiny brass bars of their new rank to their uniforms.

Jeff and Lidia Wake beamed with pride as they attached Ens. Petra Ann Wake's shoulder boards. Her little brother Peter, a serious-looking fourteen-year-old, watched with intense interest. Petra's grandfather Sean Robert Wake, now eighty-one years old—the same age Peter Wake was when he wrote the letter just before his death—was beginning to fade in the heat. A widower for decades but still very much alert and in command, Sean Robert was now the patriarch of the family. And he knew it was time for a long-awaited event.

Clearing his throat, he announced that they had reached a moment the Wake family had anticipated for 103 years. He pulled a letter from his blazer's inside pocket and ceremoniously handed it to Petra, who nervously opened it and extracted three sheets of paper and a shiny silver dollar.

"Please read it aloud, Ensign Wake," said Sean Robert. "I think Admiral Peter would want his family to hear it together."

Petra straightened up, her light brown skin—a beautiful legacy from her Filipino great-grandmother—glowing in the sunlight. "Aye, aye, sir."

She knew whom Sean Robert meant, of course. As a little girl she had listened to her great-great-aunt Agnes' stories of her earliest years with *her* grandfather Peter Wake, who had died when she was ten: sea stories, love stories, spy stories.

Agnes died at age ninety-seven when Petra was seven, leaving an ancient Imperial Vietnamese trunk in her attic. The trunk had been there since 1942, when the widow of Robert James Wake put it there because she needed the storage space at her own house. Robert James' ceremonial naval sword, passed down in the family from Peter Wake (presented to *him* in 1907 by President Theodore Roosevelt), had been among the items kept in the trunk. It was taken out and given to Sean Robert Wake when he was commissioned in 1967. After his naval career ended in the 1970s and he went into the CIA, he returned it to the trunk because his own son had decided not to be a naval officer. And so the sword had come to Petra. Great-great-aunt Agnes had hinted to Petra that the trunk held secrets, dark secrets, of international import.

When the trunk was finally opened after Agnes' death, the naval historian brought in to catalog the contents was amazed by the trove of insightful memoirs. Most were shared with the public; a few deemed far too sensitive for public view, even after a century had passed, were transferred to the Wake Shelf in the vault at ONI.

Ensign Wake touched the gold hilt of the sword as she held the letter. *And now it's all come full circle,* she thought with satisfaction. *The sword of the naval legend whose blood is in my veins is now part of my dress uniform. I hold his letter to me in my hand. Rear Admiral Peter Wake is speaking directly to me.*

Her voice started out softly but grew stronger as she spoke.

76

Letter from
Rear Adm. Peter Wake

Navy–Marine Corps Memorial Stadium,
U.S. Naval Academy, Annapolis, Maryland

———

Friday, 26 May 2023

**To the First Wake to Graduate from the
U.S. Naval Academy after 4 July 2020**

Dear USN Ensign or USMC Second Lieutenant Wake,

First of all, I extend my heartiest congratulations to you. Four years of hard work at the Naval Academy and years of serious preparation prior to that have brought you to this moment. Enjoy it now and treasure your memories of your time here for the rest of your life.

I did not have the opportunity or desire to go to the Naval Academy before the Civil War. When I lost my merchant marine officer's exemption from conscription in the middle of the war, I chose the lesser of two evils: the Navy over the Army. I admit, though, that I was a reluctant naval officer. My commission was only for the duration of the war—one of thousands given to merchant marine officers. However, after the end of that long national horror, which took the lives of my three brothers, I decided to stay in and was one of the fortunate few whose commission was made permanent. Why did I want to stay in the Navy? What changed in me from 1863 to 1865? Why did I decide to endure the other officers' prejudice against those who did not wear the Naval Academy ring?

During the war I found a professional home among the sailors and officers of the U.S. Navy. I found a worthy and challenging mission there. And I found adventure spanning the globe. I hope you will find all those things too. But be clear-eyed about it.

The image of dashing naval officers in dress whites with medals dangling from their chests surging into glorious battle and enjoying the adulation of a grateful nation is total nonsense. The Navy was not for me, and will not be for you, an easy life. During war and peace I was often exhausted by the long hours and strain; sometimes frustrated by the few incompetents or backstabbers who also rose through the ranks; and occasionally wounded, scared, and desperate.

But I was never bored—not once—during my forty-six years of naval service. I was by turns thrilled, humbled, proud, and profoundly thankful. No other career afloat or ashore could have given me that life. I got to know the high and mighty, the quiet and productive, and the dregs and monsters of humankind. They all gave me an appreciation of my blessings: my faith, my family and friends, my Navy and country, and my past and future. Above all else, I hope you are never bored.

The Navy gave me my very best friend for fifty-six years, Sean Aloysius Rork. Our different ranks, backgrounds, and personalities created the perfect symbiotic relationship, professional and personal. Fraternization between commissioned and noncommissioned personnel is against USN regs, and for good reason. Yet our friendship was never detrimental to proper naval discipline. Rork occasionally paid a price for it on the lower decks, as I did at naval headquarters. Was it effective in dicey situations during naval battles afloat and espionage skullduggery ashore? Without a doubt, yes! Be careful about friendships in the Navy, but be open to those that make you a better officer. I hope you find your version of Rork.

I want to share with you sixteen things I've learned about being a better officer and a more effective commander:

1. Make your sense of honor your core trait. Exhibit it calmly, subtly, firmly, and compassionately, so that your subordinates, peers, and superiors know they can rely upon you. Honor should be your guide to decision making and your shield against second-guessing about those decisions.

2. Loyalty to the crew begets loyalty to their commander. Make sure your crew are treated decently and professionally by those in power above them. Never allow bullying on your ship by anyone at any time. Unless it's an emergency, never admonish a subordinate in public. On the other hand, a compliment for a job well done is far more effectively said in public.

3. Never give an order you know can't, or won't, be carried out. Understand the reason why and solve it.

4. Know at least the basics of every job your subordinates do. Let them do it without nitpicking. Give them the authority to get it done. The responsibility, however, remains with you.

5. Ask questions if you don't understand something presented to you in a verbal or written report. Do it politely. Listen carefully to the answer. If you still don't understand, ask again.

6. Solicit ideas and innovations from subordinates of all ranks. Follow through on the ones that impress you and let that person know the outcome.

7. Keep subordinates busy on truly meaningful work. Never let them get bored.

8. Keep superiors informed of your ship's readiness and progress toward the planned objective.

9. When presenting a problem to superiors, always present at least two feasible alternatives for solving it. Be candid when you make a mistake. Never mislead anyone in Navy blue.

10. Be concise and clear in communicating to superiors and subordinates.

11. Rest when you can. Insist your subordinates rest when they can.

12. Steer well clear of sycophants, malingerers, connivers, cheats, and liars. Most either cannot or do not want to change. None can be trusted—ever.

13. Simple operational plans usually work. Complicated operational plans seldom work.

14. In war, use deception against the enemy and beware of deception against you. Also beware of under- or overestimating your enemy.

15. In battle, strike first, strike fast, strike hard, and keep on striking until the enemy surrenders or is incapable of fighting further. Do not pull your punches. Go for the kill.

16. Be sure your ultimate professional loyalty is not to a person or political party—but to the Constitution of the United States of America. You may know of my friendship and admiration for Theodore Roosevelt. I gauge all the other presidents I've known by him. But we don't have a king in this country. We have a person elected by the people for a short time to fill that office. Theodore Roosevelt understood that and proclaimed it repeatedly. I hope your current president is of Roosevelt's caliber.

I hope that someday you find a special person to share this adventure called life. I found two: my dear Linda and, much later, my darling María. I hope you come to know the joy of children and grandchildren. I hope your home is a refuge where you can love and rest and play with your family.

And I hope you always keep steering Onward and Upward, toward those Distant Horizons we sailors know so well. As you read this heartfelt letter from your long-ago ancestor, know that I am out there beyond those watery horizons right now, sailing across Heaven on my greatest voyage yet, thinking of you.

Peter Wake
Rear Admiral, USN (Ret.)
Key West, 4 July 1920

Petra paused for a moment, visualizing the image of Peter Wake sailing through heavenly skies, then she read further, chuckled, and shared the addendum below his signature.

P.S. And in case you're wondering—Yes, I always hated wearing those damned choker-collar dress whites you are probably wearing right now. Good news, though—they're not expected in Heaven.

77

The Future

Navy–Marine Corps Memorial Stadium
U.S. Naval Academy, Annapolis, Maryland

Friday, 26 May 2023

Peter Wake's final words got a laugh from the assembled family. When Petra without thinking tugged at her own choker collar, the laughter got even louder.

"In the sixties and seventies I hated them too," Sean Robert chuckled. "I guess your great-great-great-grandfather knew that some things in the Navy would never change."

Petra smiled. "But he did know that at least *one* thing would change, Grandpa."

"What's that, dear?"

"His letter didn't assume I would be male."

"Well, I'll be damned. You're right. He didn't. How the hell did he know that way back then?"

"Am I interrupting a family joke? I've got something important to do."

Petra was happy to see Senior Chief Operations Specialist Glenn Lambert— a U.S. Coast Guard exchange instructor in tactical communications at the Naval Academy—approaching.

Petra liked and trusted Lambert. The Coast Guardsman had taught her about tactics, using communications for deception, and communications security. She was proud that he would be the first enlisted person to render a salute to her now that she was a commissioned officer. She knew the tradition and fished in her pocket for the silver dollar she'd put there to reward whoever was the first. *Wait.* She pulled her hand out of the pocket. Peter Wake had put a 1920 silver dollar in the envelope with the letter. *He must've somehow known this tradition would carry on too,* she marveled.

The family knew the tradition as well and hushed as Lambert arrived at the regulation three feet in front of Petra and stood at full attention, the long line of hashmarks on his sleeve gleaming in the sun.

"Good afternoon, Ensign Wake. Do I have the honor of rendering your first salute, ma'am?"

Petra came to attention and looked him in the eye. "You do, Senior Chief Lambert. And it is an honor for me as well."

The perfect parade ground salute was rendered, and the acknowledging salute given with equal precision.

"And now, Senior Chief Lambert, it is my additional honor to present to you the traditional silver dollar. But *this* one is unlike any of the others given out here today. It comes to you from Rear Adm. Peter Wake, who 103 years ago sent it to me for this purpose."

Petra opened the envelope and put the shiny silver coin in Lambert's hand along with another handshake. The year of its casting, 1920, gleamed. The chief eyed it reverently. "*The* Admiral Wake, ma'am?"

"Yes, Senior Chief. He was my great-great-great-grandfather. You've heard of him, then?"

"Yes indeed, ma'am. He was temporarily co-commissioned in our Coast Guard's predecessor, the Revenue Cutter Service, in the 1880s—one of the few Navy men to be an officer of both services. This is a treasure, to be sure. Thank you."

Lambert glanced at the family, then returned his attention to Petra and stood a bit straighter. "May I add, ma'am, that with salty blood like this family's in your veins, I know your career will be active and successful. And our Navy and nation will benefit from your work. Good luck, ma'am. . . ."

She nodded. "Thank you, Senior Chief."

"May I be dismissed, ma'am? I've other—far less valuable—silver dollars to collect."

"Thank you for all you did for me here, Senior Chief. You are dismissed. I'll never forget you. Semper Paratus."

Smiling at her use of the Coast Guard motto, Lambert nodded. "Likewise, ma'am."

As the senior chief headed off toward another new ensign, Sean Robert broke the silence. He placed a light hand on Petra's shoulder and proclaimed, "Truly a memorable day. Full naval honors aren't just for the dead. They're also for those just beginning their career. So, ladies and gentlemen, today's traditions mark the beginning of yet another Wake's adventures in the United States Navy. We all wish you good fortune, Ensign Wake."

He looked up at the sky. "And I am absolutely certain that Rear Admiral Peter Wake, Chief Sean Rork, my father Robert James, and all the Wake and Cano naval officers up there have gotten the word aloft and are damn well pleased, too." He gave her shoulder a brief shake to break the mood. "It's hot as hell out here. Let's go find something cool and tasty to drink!"

As they all turned to go, Petra looked up to see two F-35C fighters streaking across the sky from Patuxent River Naval Air Station to the south. Much had changed in the Navy since old Peter wrote that letter, but one thing hadn't: attitude and honor.

She whispered to Heaven: "Onward and Upward. Aye, sir. . . ."

Appendix: Peter Wake Family and Descendants

1638 • Wake family arrives at Plymouth, Massachusetts, from Plymouth, England
1832 • Schooner captain Jonathan Wake (1810–1879) marries Clara Clarke (1815–1885).
They have four sons: John (1833–1862, KIA Civil War), Luke (1835–1863, KIA
Civil War), Matthew (1837–1866, died of fever contracted in Civil War), and . . .

Peter Wake (26 June 1839–4 July 1920), USN career, 1 May 1863 to 4 March 1909
1864—Marries Linda Donahue (1843–1880) at Key West. They have two children:
Useppa and Sean
1893—Marries widow María Abad Maura (1850–1927). Juanito Maura, María's only
surviving son, becomes Wake's stepson.

Peter Wake's children:
Useppa Wake (1865–1941), m. Mario Cano 1893
Sean Peter Wake (1867–1931), m. Filipa Sol 1904
Patricia Wake (1889–1966, love child with Cynda Saunders), m. Charles Whitehead 1909

Peter Wake's grandchildren:
Peter Carlos Cano (1898–1985), son of Useppa Cano, m. Anne Papillon 1925
Linda Wake Cano (1904–1999), daughter of Useppa Cano, m. Arsenio García 1929
Robert James Wake (1905–1942, KIA), son of Sean Wake, m. Delores Munda 1933
Theodore (Ted) Rork Wake (1909–2001), son of Sean Wake, m. Shelley Martin 1937
Agnes Whitehead (1910–2007), daughter of Patricia Whitehead

Peter Wake's great-grandchildren:
Useppa García (1932–2009), daughter of Linda Wake Cano García, m. Dave Conn 1955
Mario Teodoro Cano (1936–2017), son of Peter Carlos Cano, m. Connie Johnson 1957
Calixto Martí Cano (1929–1994), son of Peter Carlos Cano
María Filipa Wake (1936–1938), infant daughter of Robert James Wake
Sean Robert Wake (1942–2023), son of Robert James Wake, m. Sue Smith 1974

Peter Wake's great-great-grandchildren:

José Martí Cano (1960–present), son of Mario T. Cano, m. Josee van Heflin 1987

Carla Ann Cano (1963–present), daughter of Mario T. Cano, m. Jay Jennings 1990

María Florida Cano (1965–present), daughter of Mario T. Cano, m. Eric McCrea 1989

Dave Conn Jr. (1956–present), son of Useppa García Conn, m. Paula Streeter 1979

Marilyn Conn (1959–present), daughter of Useppa García Conn, m. Joe Geraci 1986

Jeff Hollan Wake (1975–present), son of Sean Robert Wake, m. Lidia Moreno 1997

Mary Ann Wake (1977–present), daughter of Sean Robert Wake, m. Terry Brewer 1999

Peter Jour Wake (1979–present), son of Sean Robert Wake, m. Nancy Singer 1999

Peter Wake's great-great-great grandchildren, the present generation:

Mario Maceo Cano (1993–present), son of José Martí Cano, m. Ashley Mobutu 2011
    Paul McCrea (1996–present), son of María Cano McCrea, m. Maya Schwartz 2019

Dave Conn III (1988–present), son of Dave Conn Jr., m. Willow Jones 2012

Lorie Wake (2001–present), daughter of Jeff H. Wake

Carla Wake (2005–present), daughter of Jeff H. Wake

Petra Ann Wake, USNA 2023 (2001–present), daughter of Jeff Hollan Wake

Peter Hollan Wake (2009–present), son of Jeff Hollan Wake

Notes to Chapters

Chapter 1. The "Wonderful Second Honeymoon"

Wake's limp is the result of wounds sustained in the 1905 Battle of Tsushima, where he barely survived the Japanese destruction of the Russian flagship. *Code of Honor* tells the story.

Chapter 2. The Captain's Table

Nachrichten-Abteilung was Imperial Germany's efficient worldwide naval intelligence agency from 1901 to 1919. It primarily worked against the British, French, and American navies.

Telefunken, founded in 1903, worked directly with the Imperial German Navy and quickly became a leader in wireless technology. Its main competitor was the British Marconi Company. Today, Telefunken is a global communications giant.

The German South Seas Wireless Telegraphy Company, formally founded in 1912 as a partner to Telefunken, established a network of four-hundred-foot-high wireless radio towers across German (and some British) islands in the Central and South Pacific. World War I ended the project.

Japanese intelligence monitored the progress of the Great White Fleet around the world as tensions between the United States and Japan rose. Wake encountered Major Yoshida at Singapore in 1905, as depicted in *Code of Honor*. When the American fleet transited the Strait of Magellan, the Japanese freighter *Kasato Maru* followed. While the fleet was at anchor in Chile, a man called Kyoichi Aki was seen surveilling the ships.

Chapter 3. The Lady of Spain and the Gaelic Rogue

For more about Peter and María's unlikely romance in 1892, read *The Assassin's Honor*.

In 1492 the Spanish monarchy expelled Jews and Muslims from Spain. Jews were allowed to stay if they publicly converted to Christianity. Many Spanish Jews who were forced to convert continued to practice their faith in secret. A few years ago, the Spanish government apologized to the descendants of the exiled Jews (but not those of the Muslims) and offered them Spanish citizenship.

For more about the momentous (and in María's case tragic) events of 1898, read *An Honorable War, Honoring the Enemy,* and *Word of Honor.*

A sailor's queue is a short ponytail slightly stiffened by ship's rigging tar or caulking pitch. It was long out of fashion by 1908, but so was Sean Rork.

For details of their perilous mission in 1883 in French Indochina, read *The Honored Dead.*

Chapter 4. The Okhrana Man

Wake has had several encounters with the Okhrana (1881–1917), Imperial Russia's ruthless secret intelligence agency, whose techniques were passed down to the KGB (and other Soviet spy organizations). Vladimir Putin (a former KGB colonel) still uses them against democracies. Read *Honor Bound* for Wake's initial meeting of Rachkovsky in Haiti, and *Code of Honor* for their shady sparring in 1904–5. The wily Rachkovsky disappeared from public view just before World War I. I suspect he started a new life using one of his many aliases.

"Kaiser Willy" was a common pejorative term for the power-hungry Kaiser Wilhelm II (1859–1941). Wake meets him in *Code of Honor.*

Colonel Motojiro Akashi (1864–1919), sometimes called Japan's James Bond, was the head of Japanese intelligence operations in Europe (and even inside Russia) during the Russo-Japanese War. Years later he became the imperial governor-general of Taiwan.

For more about Wake's 1889 Samoan espionage mission and his friendship with Robert Louis Stevenson (1850–1894), read *Honors Rendered.*

The "United States of North America" is not the nation's official name, of course, but it reflects the way many Latin Americans, and their imperial German friends back then, viewed the country. Latin Americans still call Americans *norteamericanos.*

Chapter 6. Samoa mo Samoa

The western islands of Samoa (the eastern islands are still American Samoa) were a German colony until early World War I. The fascinating legacy of German rule can still be seen there. Governor Wilhelm Heinrich Solf (1862–1936) had an excellent reputation. His widow Johanna (1887–1954) and daughter So'oa'emalelagi (1909–1955), known as "Lagi," joined the anti-Nazi resistance in Germany in World War II, were arrested by the Gestapo in late 1943, and ended up in Ravensbrück concentration camp. They were liberated by the Soviet army in April 1945 before they could be executed. They were witnesses for the prosecution at the 1947 Nuremburg Nazi trials and are considered heroes in Germany today.

Lauaki (1848–1915) was exiled in 1909 to German Saipan. He never returned to Samoa.

Chapter 7. Venganza

For more about Wake's long conflict with the Spanish secret police in Cuba and Florida, read *The Darkest Shade of Honor, Honor Bound, Honorable Lies,* and *An Honorable War.*

Chapter 8. Connections

"Kanaka" was an ethnic slur used by white people to describe Pacific natives. It is no longer used by decent people.

Chapter 9. The War Will Come

Sir Osmond de Beauvoir Brock (1869–1947) was in charge of British naval intelligence operations. He saw combat in World War I, was knighted, and eventually rose to the pinnacle of the Royal Navy as Admiral of the Fleet.

Tsingtao in northeastern China was a German colony from 1898 until it was captured in 1914 by the Japanese, who were on the Allies' side in World War I. It is now called Qingdao.

Weihaiwei, now called Weihai, is not far from Tsingtao. From 1898 to 1930 it was a British colony and naval base.

John (Jacky) Arbuthnot Fisher (1841–1920) is one of the most famous Royal Navy officers in history. At this time he was First Sea Lord, the Royal Navy's most senior rank. Wake first met him in 1874 when Fisher rescued Wake from Barbary corsairs off the coast of Morocco. For that story, read *An Affair of Honor.* They remained friends ever after.

Chapter 10. Death for Breakfast

The Russians' (or was it Germans? Wake was never sure) attempt to kill Wake at the Maryinsky Theater in St. Petersburg was foiled when María killed the assassin with a candle sconce. Read *Code of Honor* for the chilling details.

The Black Dragon Society, the clandestine appendage of Japanese military and naval intelligence for more than half a century, was officially disbanded with Japan's defeat in 1945. But is it really gone? For more about it, read *Code of Honor.*

Chapter 14. Simple, Gentle, and Predictable

The impressive Latrobe Gate entrance to the Washington Navy Yard was designed and built by Henry Latrobe in 1806. It was one of only three buildings to survive the British destruction of the Navy Yard in 1814. It still exists and is now officially designated "Main Gate," but many use the traditional name.

Chapter 15. Kaiser Willy's Dream

The occupation of Veracruz, Mexico, by U.S. forces lasted from April to November 1914 during a civil war inside Mexico. U.S.-Mexican relations went from bad to worse over the next few years.

Wake was right. Franklin Delano Roosevelt's career did end up mirroring Theodore's in several ways. Both were former New York assemblymen who served as assistant secretary of the Navy, governor of New York, and president of the United States.

Chapter 17. The Mosquito Coast

The Wanks River—also known as the Río Coco, Wanki (in native Miskitu), Río Segovia, Cape River, and Yara River—at 523 miles is the longest river in Central America. It descends from an altitude of 2,200 feet down to the sea and has been the official Nicaragua-Honduras border since 1915.

A fathom is six feet. The term comes from the Old English word for the distance between a grown man's outstretched arms and fingertips.

The Körting Company (officially Körting Brothers AG), founded in 1871, was an innovator in engines with offices and plants across Europe and in Philadelphia. In 1906 it was making V-8 engines for early German airships and six-cylinder two-stroke paraffin/kerosene engines for German submarines. A U-boat had two such engines, each rated at 200 bhp at 500 rpm. The company still exists as Körting Hannover AG and is a leader in pump engine technology.

The overall king of the Miskito people (who occupied an area covering hundreds of miles) during this time was King Robert Frederick (1855–1928). He reigned from 1908 until his death sometime around 1928.

Chapter 20. "Heil dir im Siegerkranz"

"Heil dir im Siegerkranz" (Hail to thee in the victor's wreath) was the Imperial German anthem from 1871 to 1918. The Germans were not the only ones to use the melody of Great Britain's "God Save the Queen." In America it is still sung as "My Country 'Tis of Thee," and Hawaiian monarchs used it in their national anthem, Hawai'i Pono'ī (Hawaii's Own), which is still played in Hawaii at sports events as the state anthem, sung right after "The Star-Spangled Banner."

Chapter 21. Chaos in the Lair

Elizabeth Cochrane Seaman (1864–1922), better known by her pen name, Nellie Bly, was an investigative journalist, inventor, and businesswoman. In 1887 she wrote an undercover exposé of the horrors at the New York lunatic asylum. In 1889, in a widely publicized journey, she circumnavigated the world by land and sea in seventy-two days. In the early 1900s she ran her deceased husband's company, Iron Clad Manufacturing, and oversaw the invention and production of the fifty-five-gallon steel drums now ubiquitous in the world. In World War I she was a combat correspondent on the Eastern Front.

Germany's Type 16 U-boat was commissioned in 1911 and had the following dimensions: displacement (surfaced), 489 tons; length, 189 feet; beam, 19 feet; draft, 11 feet; speed, 15 knots surfaced, 10 knots submerged; test depth, 160 feet; crew, 4 officers and 25 crewmen; armament: four 17.7-inch torpedo tubes (2 forward/2 aft) with six torpedoes; one 2-inch deck gun. In World War I the Type 16 sank eleven ships, damaged two others, and captured another in the First Battle of the Atlantic. After Germany surrendered, the boat "accidentally" sank in 1919 as it was being taken to Britain. No others were built of this class because it was soon surpassed by the newer German designs.

Master spy Paul von Hintze (1864–1941) was a German naval officer, protégé of Admiral von Tirpitz, and diplomat. In 1898 von Hintze was in the German squadron that faced off against Admiral Dewey's Asiatic Fleet at Manila, nearly going to war. As the ambassador to Mexico in 1911, von Hintze helped to stir up anti-U.S. sentiments. In July 1914 he got war postings in China and later in Norway. In 1918 he was made foreign minister under Kaiser Wilhelm II and was instrumental in setting up the armistice negotiations with the Allies. When he left the foreign ministry in November 1918, his replacement was Wilhelm Solf, whom the reader has already met as governor of Samoa in 1908. Von Hintze lived a quiet life in retirement and died in Italy.

Karl Boy-Ed (1872–1930) was yet another of the effective German naval intelligence officers working in the Western Hemisphere, mainly as an attaché in the United States. His urbane manners made him many friends there, even among his adversaries. After he was expelled from the United States for espionage in 1915, he took over command of the global operations of the Nachrichten-Abteilung (naval intelligence). He married an American woman in 1921 and in 1926 tried to emigrate to America. The State Department denied him a visa. He died in a horse-riding accident on his fifty-eighth birthday.

Chapter 23. Old Age and Treachery

"French leave" is a sailor's slang term meaning to flee quickly. The French do *not* use it. "Stern sheets" is a thwart (seat) across the stern adjacent to the transom in a small boat.

Chapter 24. The End of Innocence

Franklin Roosevelt lost that senatorial election and returned to his position as assistant secretary of the Navy.

James H. Oliver (1857–1928) had a very unusual career. In 1904 Oliver was in command of USS *Culgoa* when she collided with a schooner in Delaware Bay. Twenty-nine of the schooner's crew died. Oliver retained his command but was placed under technical arrest (and his sword taken from him), an impossible position. After waiting *a year* for his court-martial, he was cleared "with honor" and his sword was returned. Oliver promptly broke his sword, threw it into the ocean, and resigned from the Navy. In 1906 President Theodore Roosevelt restored his commission, saying, "I would've done the same thing," and Oliver was simultaneously promoted to commander. He made captain in 1910, worked in intelligence in 1914, made rear admiral in 1916, and was the first American governor of the U.S. Virgin Islands in 1917.

Archduke Franz Ferdinand of Austria (1863–1914) was the heir to the throne of the Austro-Hungarian Empire. He and his wife, Archduchess Sophie, were assassinated at Sarajevo (capital of Bosnia and Herzegovina) on 28 June 1914, several hours after surviving a grenade attack that same day. Ignorance, arrogance, and long-standing hatreds fueled immediate saber rattling and threats of war among the neighboring countries and then all of Europe. Kaiser Wilhelm actively urged Austria-Hungary to go to war against her enemies. On 28 July 1914 the warmongers got their wish, and World War I began. Four years later, 10 million military personnel and 9 million civilians had been killed.

The Black Hand was formed in 1901 by a group of radical Serbian junior army officers who wanted to establish a pan-Serbian empire through assassination and intimidation. The organization dissipated after World War I, but similar European groups in the 1920s and 1930s adopted many of its techniques.

Sylvanus Griswold Morley did become a spy for ONI in Central America, eventually running a complicated network of his colleagues. I've read his reports and found them detailed and accurate. After World War I he concentrated on archaeology.

The Cosmos Club still exists. I've been a guest at that fascinating place.

Chapter 25. The Coming Storm

Adolphus Busch (1830–1913) not only made world-famous beer, he founded one of the first U.S. diesel engine companies (American Diesel Company) under a license from Rudolf Diesel in Germany. Busch-Selzer Inc. began building diesel engines for U.S. Navy submarines in 1916. The legendary American submariner Adm. Chester Nimitz got a lucrative offer to join the company in 1913 but refused and stayed in the U.S. Navy. The Navy might have fared much worse in World War II in the Pacific without him.

The channel at Captiva anchorage is still called Roosevelt Channel. Check the chart.

The magnificent "devilfish" should be called by its proper name: giant manta ray. They are harmless despite their enormous size.

Three of the islands Roosevelt established as sanctuaries are still important bird rookeries. Over the last century the sanctuary has expanded to include thirty-eight islands, administered by the U.S. Wildlife Service out of "Ding" Darling Sanctuary on Sanibel Island.

The Zimmermann telegram, a coded cable from German foreign secretary Arthur Zimmermann to his ambassador in Mexico City, proposed a military alliance between Germany and Mexico in the event the United States went to war against Germany. Germany agreed to support Mexico if it attacked the United States to recover lost territory in Texas, New Mexico, and Arizona. The British intercepted the coded signal, deciphered it, and (rather gleefully) gave it to the Americans. When it was made public, the telegram backfired on Germany, cementing anti-German feelings in the United States. For their part, the Mexicans wisely refused the German offer. By April, America was at war with Germany, and a year and a half later Wilhelm was no longer Kaiser and the German empire had ceased to exist.

Matusalem was the favorite Cuban rum of Peter Wake and Sean Rork—and is mine as well. Since the Castro dictatorship began in 1959 it has been made in the Dominican Republic.

The reserve commissions Theodore Roosevelt referred to were among the very first in the Reserve Officers Training Corps (ROTC), begun in 1916. This program was, and still is, enormously successful. As of 2017, ROTC commissions accounted for 58 percent of U.S. Army officers. The camp was at Plattsburgh, New York, and the idea for the program was that of U.S. Army Chief of Staff Maj. Gen. Leonard Wood.

Leonard Wood (1860–1927) was quite a man. A Harvard athlete and medical school graduate in 1884, he joined the Army in 1885 for adventure and a steady income. He was awarded the Medal of Honor for saving a combat unit in a battle in Arizona during the 1886 Geronimo campaign. In 1893, while he was stationed at Fort McPherson, Georgia, he coached and played on the Georgia Tech football team. In 1895–98 he was presidential physician to Presidents Cleveland and McKinley and became a friend of Theodore Roosevelt (assistant secretary of the Navy at the time). In the Spanish-American War, Colonel Wood commanded a cavalry regiment (the Rough Riders, with Roosevelt as his number two) and subsequently a cavalry brigade as a brigadier general—both in harrowing combat. In 1903 he was a provincial governor in the Philippines. Then, as a major general, he commanded all army forces in the entire Philippines until 1908. In 1910 he became the only medical officer to ever become the U.S. Army chief of staff, the service's highest command. After four innovative and successful years in that position he continued his service in administrative commands during World War I, and finally retired in 1921. From then until 1927, he was governor-general of the Philippines. He died in 1927 and is buried at Arlington. Fort Leonard Wood in Missouri, the World War II attack transport USS *Leonard Wood*, and a Masonic lodge are named in his honor.

William Sowden Sims (1858–1936), a brilliant naval officer, is still renowned for his innovations in gunnery and antisubmarine tactics. He had experience in naval intelligence during the Spanish-American War, and later became a protégé of President Theodore Roosevelt. In World War I he commanded all U.S. naval forces operating out of Great Britain. In 1921, while commanding the Naval War College, he was awarded the Pulitzer Prize in History for his book *The Victory at Sea*. He retired as a vice admiral in 1922, died at age seventy-seven, and is buried at Arlington.

Chapter 26. The Real Cost of War

The Octagon Hotel building, constructed in 1851, still stands in Oyster Bay.

Twenty-year-old Quentin Roosevelt of the 95th Aero Squadron was shot down on 14 July 1918 (Bastille Day) during aerial combat against the Germans over Chamery, a hamlet of Coulonges-en-Tardenois, then under German occupation. The German army rendered full military honors. When the American Military Cemetery was created in Normandy after World War II, Quentin's remains were reinterred there, next to those of his eldest brother, Ted, who died of a heart attack at age fifty-six, a month after he landed in the first wave at Normandy. They remain there to this day, the only children of an American president to die in war.

All three of Quentin's brothers survived World War I, though Archie and Ted were severely wounded. All three (by now in their forties and fifties) volunteered for and served in combat in World War II. In 1943 Archie was severely wounded again while commanding a battalion of the 143rd Infantry Regiment during brutal fighting in the New Guinea jungle. Kermit served with the British Army's Middlesex Regiment in combat operations in Norway (1940) and North Africa (1941). He returned home in 1943 and got a commission in the U.S. Army. His already severe alcoholism worsened, and in 1943 he died by suicide while stationed in Alaska. Brig. Gen. Ted Roosevelt, assistant commander of the 4th Infantry Division, was the only general officer who landed at Normandy in the first wave. His son landed with a different division farther down the beach, the only father-son pair to land at Normandy on 6 June 1944. In a desperate move and under intense enemy fire, Ted (on his cane from his World War I wound) led the way off the beach and inland for his men, an action for which he was later awarded the Medal of Honor. He and his son reunited for a dinner three weeks later. An hour after his son left to rejoin his unit, Ted died of a heart attack in his sleep, just like his father did.

Chapter 27. The Old Lion Is Dead

Sagamore Hill has reopened to the public after a long refurbishing. I urge readers to visit.

For more about Wake and Roosevelt's first meeting in 1886 at Delmonico's in New York, read *The Darkest Shade of Honor*.

Christ Church of Oyster Bay was founded in 1705. The current building was constructed in the 1870s. The Roosevelt family attended services there, and I urge readers to do so as well.

Chapter 28. The Sun in Winter

Construction of the Florida Overseas Railroad from Miami to Key West, an extension of Henry Flagler's Florida East Coast Railway, was begun in 1905 and completed in 1912. Though never as financially successful as the company hoped, it operated daily until the Labor Day Hurricane of 1935 destroyed much of it. In the 1940s, many of the surviving bridges and some newly built ones were incorporated into the Overseas Highway from the Florida mainland to Key West. The highway is a wonderful early-morning drive in the summertime, when there is less traffic.

The name Grunt Bone Lane (originally Grunt Bone Alley) refers to bones of the white grunt, considered a "poor man's fish" because of the many small bones in the meat. "Grunts and grits" was a common dish in old Florida. The street was later renamed Peacon Lane after the Peacon family of fishermen, some of whom lived and worked near my home island a hundred miles north of Key West.

Chapter 29. Honor Bound

Sergei Dyvoryanin was the young Russian naval officer (and cousin of the Tsar) whose life Wake saved at the Battle of Tsushima in 1905 (read *Code of Honor* for details). Wake is not a Freemason, but José Martí designated him a "Friend of Freemasonry" in 1886, creating a symbiotic relationship with both sides honor bound to help when it was needed.

Chapter 31. Burn after Reading

The Methodist Church still stands and has a beautiful sanctuary. I have taken readers there during my Key West Reader Rendezvous and they love it.

Chapter 32. Report of Capt. S. P. Wake, USN—Part One

In 1919, Lt. Robert Steed Dunn was a Naval Reserve intelligence officer for the flotilla based at Constantinople during that tumultuous time.

Mustafa Kemal Atatürk (1881–1938) was the founding father of the Republic of Turkey. He served as its first president from 1923 until his death in 1938 and undertook massive reforms that changed the old Ottoman Empire into a secular, industrialized, modern Turkey. I doubt that he would approve of the current regime.

Pavel Efimovich Dybenko (1889–1938) was a Russian sailor before he joined the revolutionaries and worked his way up to general. In 1938 he was one of hundreds of senior military officers Stalin suspected of disloyalty and had arrested, tortured, and executed. In 1958, five years after Stalin's death, Khrushchev "rehabilitated" Dybenko's reputation. Such is life and death in a dictatorship.

"Sidney" was probably the fascinating British-Japanese-Russian double and triple agent Sidney Riley (1873–1925). Born Georgy Rosenblum, he was a master of disguises and alibis; had many aliases (Sidney Reilly, Sigmund Georgievich Rosenblum, Karl Hahn, among others); escaped certain death in several wars, prisons, and countries around the world; had a complicated love life; and was executed by the Soviets outside Moscow on 5 November 1925 after fifty-two extremely eventful years. The BBC broadcast a twelve-episode miniseries based on his life, *Reilly, Ace of Spies*, in the 1980s with Sam Neill in the title role.

Chapter 33. Report of Capt. S. P. Wake, USN—Part Two

Solomon Krym (1864–1936) was an agronomist and a Crimean Karaite politician. He escaped the Crimea in April 1919 and lived the rest of his life in Bormes-les-Mimosas on the Côte d'Azur, a very nice place for a desperate Russian émigré to land.

Krym was referring to the Allies' invasion and occupation of Russia around Murmansk in the north and Vladivostok on the Pacific coast during the Russian Revolution. Thousands of American troops (hundreds of whom were killed or wounded) were in Russia from 1918 until late 1919 and even into 1920. All Russians are taught about this in school. Few Americans know anything about it.

The 1,500-year-old fortified cave village of Chufut-Kale was still a place of refuge for those seeking shelter.

Chapter 34. Report of Capt. S. P. Wake, USN—Part Three

Yalta was the scene of a World War II summit meeting between Winston Churchill, FDR, and Stalin on 4–11 February 1945. FDR was very ill at the time and would die at age sixty-three only two months later.

Chapter 38. Weighing Anchor

Fiddler's Green is the Irish sailor's mythical Heaven full of mirth, music, and free-flowing alcohol.

Chapter 39. On Behalf of a Grateful Nation

Written three thousand years ago, Psalm 107 (verses 23–31) depicts God's power over the sea and still deeply resonates with sailors today. "Eternal Father, Strong to Save" was a British hymn written by William Whiting in 1860 and inspired by Psalm 107.

It soon became popular in the Royal Navy and U.S. Navy. In 1879, Wake's friend Capt. Charles Train, then teaching at the U.S. Naval Academy and head of the choir, adopted it as the Navy Hymn, as it is known today.

Chapter 40. Anno Horribilis

The Spanish flu (February 1918–April 1920) didn't come from Spain, although Spain was the first country to truthfully report it. The disease swept the world in four waves, killing an estimated 25 million people.

The League of Nations (1920–46) failed to prevent war. Dictators simply ignored it.

Fothering is an old seaman's technique for plugging a crack or small hole in a hull by lashing a sail around the hull to cover it. The water pressure against the sail helps to mitigate the leak or seal it. I had to do that myself fifty years ago.

An "annular solar eclipse" occurs when the sun, Earth, and moon are aligned. When the moon is between the Earth and the sun, the sun appears as a very bright ring, or annulus, surrounding the dark disk of the Moon.

Chapter 43. Life Goes On

This was the original Sloppy Joe's Bar, started by Josie Russell in the 1930s. Peter Wake knew the building in the latter 1800s as the telegraph office. In 1938, Sloppy Joe's landlord raised the rent a dollar a month, and the bar moved a block east to its present location at Greene and Duval. Agnes drank there too. In 1968, the old original building was named Captain Tony's Bar after the new owner, Captain Tony Terracino. I knew Captain Tony, a very colorful fellow.

Chapter 44. The Last Supper

"Mustanged up" is a Navy term (originally from the Army) for an enlisted man who rises into the commissioned officer ranks.

A roseate spoonbill is a large, rose pink wading bird. Easily distinguished by the flattened, spoon-shaped bill, these beautiful birds are found in wetlands from southern Florida down through the Caribbean to South America.

SS *Mariposa*, built in 1931, was an 18,000-ton, 20-knot luxury ocean liner that carried 704 passengers. During World War II she was a troopship able to transport 4,165 passengers on each voyage. She was scrapped in 1974 after serving the Home Lines as SS *Homeric*.

The Fita Fita Guards are a very proud part of Samoan history (*fita fita* means "courageous soldier" in Samoan). Formed in 1900, the unit eventually reached one hundred strong and guarded the islands under the direction of the U.S. Navy. Each man wore a lavalava (a long wraparound kilt) and a T-shirt, no shoes. In World War II they also wore a standard fatigue uniform. The unit was disbanded in 1951, but the legend lives on.

Chapter 46. The Ship

Commonly known as the "bird class," the official name of these minesweepers was *Lapwing* class, after the first built ship. Forty-nine of the 188-foot ships were built in World War I and the 1920s, and many served for twenty or more years. The last U.S. Navy bird-class minesweeper, *Flamingo*, was decommissioned in 1953. *Auk* went to Venezuela in 1947, and her hulk is still visible near La Guaira.

Chapter 48. War

Aichi E13A scout float planes flew for the Japanese Navy from 1941 to 1945, their three-man crews enduring arduous long-range patrols (up to fourteen hours). Most were stationed on board warships. The Allies' code name for them was "Jake."

A "lee helmsman" in the days of sail was the assistant to the helmsman in rough weather. In the modern Navy, the lee helmsman is the sailor stationed at the engine telegraph or throttle control.

Chapter 50. Haggling

Kingston valves are large seacocks for allowing seawater into the interior of the ship, usually into a tank. They can also be used to scuttle a ship.

Chapter 52. Innovation

As the name implies, a water tender monitored the water in the boilers and stoked the fires that boiled the water to make steam. This naval rating no longer exists.

Chapter 53. Wooden Ships and Iron Men

Q-ships are innocent-appearing civilian ships that are actually heavily armed decoys manned by naval crews. This sort of deception has been used for centuries, but the term "Q-ship" originated during World War I when the Royal Navy converted cargo ships into decoy ships at Queenstown in Ireland, thus the name Q-ships. The Imperial Japanese Navy used Q-ships in 1944, with no success.

Lieutenant Tolley survived many harrowing ordeals in World War II and went on to make rear admiral. His memoirs (*Yangtze Patrol*, *Cruise of the* Lanikai, and *Caviar and Commissars*) of service in China, the Pacific, and Russia in the 1930s and 1940s are some of the very best ever written by a U.S. naval officer.

The 89-foot schooner USS *Lanikai* was built as the *Hermes* in California in 1914 for a German company trading in the Pacific. She was seized by the Americans in World War I and served during the war as a USN patrol vessel in Honolulu, being sold after the war. Between the wars she was a leper colony supply vessel and a fishing vessel. In 1937 she became the MGM movie studio's yacht and appeared in the John

Hall/Dorothy Lamour film *The Hurricane*. The U.S. Navy bought her in October 1941 and transferred her to the Royal Australian Navy in May 1942. She was used as a patrol boat for the rest of the war. She sank in a typhoon at Manila in 1947.

Chapter 55. The Minefield

Carley floats (or Carley rafts) were lifesaving rafts designed in 1903 and in widespread naval use by World War II. The raft had a kapok-filled floating perimeter and a rope-webbing floor, so anyone in or on them would still get wet. Most carried twenty to thirty men; the large ones could carry fifty.

The Brewster F2A Buffalo was designed in the 1930s and came into U.S. naval service in 1939 as the Navy's first monoplane fighter. The underpowered, under-gunned plane was inefficient at high altitudes and performed dismally against the superior Japanese fighters in the first months of the war. The Navy canceled the contract in January 1942.

Chapter 56. Old Tricks

The Mitsubishi A6M naval fighter, which began service with the Japanese navy in 1940, completely outclassed Allied fighters in the first six months of the war, with an astounding kill ratio of twelve to one. By June 1942 Allied designs and tactics had begun to catch up, and by 1943 U.S. Navy fighters were holding their own. In July 1942 the Navy assigned the Mitsubishi A6M the official code name "Zeke," but it was already commonly known as the Zero for the final numeral in its Japanese designation. It could carry two 130-pound bombs.

Chapter 60. The Last Trick

The fast (35 knots), heavily armed *Asashio*-class destroyers served the Japanese navy from 1937 to 1945. They were used in battle from the Aleutian Islands down to the Solomon Islands. None survived the war.

Chapter 61. The Letter

A blue star displayed in the window signified that the family had a member serving in the armed forces. A gold star meant that one of the family had been killed in action. The tradition continues to this day.

PBY Catalinas were big, long-range flying boats that flew patrols for the U.S. Navy from 1936 to 1945. The Catalina carried a crew of seven to nine and was armed with three .30-caliber and two .50-caliber machine guns along with bombs, torpedoes, and depth charges. They are beloved by aviators to this day.

Chapter 62. The Teacher

The U.S. Navy's Submarine Chaser Training School was located just south of MacArthur Causeway, a bridge connecting Miami to Miami Beach. The school operated there from 1942 until 1945. After the war the P&O Line used the building and pier for its ships steaming weekly to Havana, Cuba. The building is gone now, and the former berths at Piers 2, 3, and 4 were filled in (you can still see the ends of the piers). The area is known for its museums and the Maurice A. Ferré Oceanside Park.

Cdr. Eugene Field McDaniel (1902–1977), USNA class of 1927, was a respected naval officer who made a huge difference in the fight against Nazi U-boats in the Atlantic and Caribbean. He did much to cement U.S.–Latin American ties during the war, and later made rear admiral.

Chapter 64. Validation

Casa Blanca Naval Arsenal is still functional, but few Cuban naval vessels remain in operation. For the details of Peter Wake's 1898 experiences in that area, read *An Honorable War*.

Dr. Ramón Grau San Martín (1881–1969) was a university professor and physician who became a moderate-reform politician. He was an interim president for one hundred days in late 1933, and in 1944 was elected (a rarity in Cuban history) for a four-year term (1944–48). He is generally remembered as a good national leader.

Raymond Henry Norweb (1895–1983) was an English-born American career diplomat well known for his difficult but successful work in Portugal and Latin America during World War II. He and his wife were also numismatic experts on coins of the world.

The small Cuban navy did outstanding work in World War II. Cuban ships steamed 134,206 miles escorting convoys, 66,778 miles on offshore patrols, and 12,032 miles in rescue operations that saved the lives of 221 merchant seamen. During the war, Cuba's merchant marine lost 79 men on 6 ships sunk by U-boats.

Ensign Mario Ramirez Delgado (circa 1920–1988?) is a Cuban national hero to this day. He stayed in the navy until 1962, achieving the rank of lieutenant commander, then resigned and joined the Cuban merchant marine. He retired in the 1980s. His sonar operator, Norberto Collado Abreu (1921–2008), made history again in 1956 as the captain of the 60-foot yacht *Granma* in its voyage from Veracruz, Mexico, to eastern Cuba carrying Fidel Castro and eighty-two of his revolutionaries. *Granma* has been preserved and is displayed in downtown Havana. Collado Abreu retired from the Cuban navy in 1981 as a lieutenant commander.

Chapter 65. David versus Goliath

The Hotel Inglaterra is the oldest continuously operating hotel in Cuba. Many world leaders have stayed there, and it's my favorite place to stay in Old Havana.

The OS2U Kingfisher was a USN/USCG long-range scouting float plane that could carry two 325-pound depth charges. More than 1,500 were built, and the last one flying in service was with the Cuban navy in 1959. It is on display at the same museum as the boat *Granma.*

Samuel Eliot Morison (1887–1976) was a Pulitzer Prize–winning historian tapped by his friend FDR in 1942 to write the history of the U.S. Navy in World War II. As a Naval Reserve officer he served on ships in combat during the war, and later in Reserve assignments, until 1952, when he retired as a rear admiral. I heartily recommend his fifteen-volume *History of United States Naval Operations in World War II.*

Sidney William Souers (1892–1973) was a businessman turned Naval Reserve intelligence officer who rose in rank and responsibility from 1941 until 1946, when President Truman put him in command of the newly formed National Intelligence Authority, which soon became known as the Central Intelligence Agency. In 1947 Souers left the NIA to head the new National Security Council at the White House. He remained in that position until 1950, when he became Truman's special consultant on military intelligence matters. Little known by the general public, he was one of the most influential founders of the modern U.S. intelligence system.

Bahía de Cochinos, the Bay of Pigs, was the site of the doomed invasion of 17–20 April 1961 where CIA operatives and Cuban exiles tried to invade Cuba to liberate it from Castro. The invasion was a disaster for many reasons, most of them connected to the American leadership.

Chapter 66. Welcome to the Brown Water Navy

An Thới Naval Base was built by the South Vietnamese navy in 1960, was expanded greatly by the Americans in 1964, became a major coastal naval base for the U.S. Navy and U.S. Coast Guard, and is still used by the Vietnamese. The base included a four-thousand-foot runway.

From 1949 to 1992 the C-117D transport was the USN/USMC version of the venerable DC-3/C-47. They were extensively used in the Korean and Vietnam wars.

Navy PCFs (Patrol Craft, Fast) were commonly known as "swift boats." These heavily armed boats were 50 feet long with a 13-foot beam and 5-foot draft. Malta (in the Mediterranean) still uses two old American PCFs.

GMG2 is a gunner's mate (for guns instead of missiles or other weapons) second class, EN2 is an engineman second class, BM3 is a boatswain third class, and RM3 is a radioman third class. All are junior petty officers. BOQ is the bachelor officers' quarters. A hooch was a shack.

Chapter 67. Just a Shoot-and-Scoot Recon Decoy

Michael R. Bernique (1943–2016) is a legend among swift boat sailors. He left the Navy after Vietnam and became a very successful businessman in the technology field.

Elmo Russell "Bud" Zumwalt Jr. (1920–2000), USNA class of 1943, became a famous and widely respected naval officer. After running coastal ops in Vietnam, he was jumped over several senior officers and made the Chief of Naval Operations by President Nixon. He retired in 1974. Both of his sons served as naval officers in Vietnam, one on PCFs. That son tragically died of Agent Orange–induced cancer at age forty-two.

ROE is the acronym for rules of engagement. A PBR (River Patrol Boat) was a heavily armed 31-foot fiberglass boat able to operate in only two feet of water. Each carried a crew of four. The U.S. Navy had hundreds of them.

Seawolves were U.S. Navy helicopter gunships of HA(L)-3 (Helicopter Attack Squadron [Light] 3). The Seawolves flew the Bell UH-1 Iroquois "Hueys" and were dedicated to air support of the patrol boats. They were heroes to the men on the boats.

USS *Hunterdon* was a World War II LST that served the Navy from 1944 to 1974. She ended up with the Malaysian navy and was later scrapped.

Di-di mau was Vietnamese for "get out fast!"

A B-40 was the North Vietnamese version of the Soviet RPG-2, a 40-millimeter rocket fired from a lightweight launcher. The simple but deadly system has been, and still is, used by America's enemies since 1954.

Chapter 70. Mississippi!

A Chicom 31 knee mortar was a Chinese Communist (ChiCom) copy of the World War II American M2 light mortar. It was lightweight, small, simple, and easy to use—perfect for guerillas on the run.

RTB means "return to base."

Chapter 72. Top Brass

MACV was the American acronym for Military Assistance Command, Vietnam. REMF was an impolite acronym for rear-echelon personnel who did not see battle action.

Chapter 74. The Pearl of the Moon

For centuries Kuwait was famous for the quality of its pearls, which were extremely expensive. In the last one hundred years oil has become the country's big money-maker. There are very few pearl divers left.

"Blessed are the peace-makers, for they will be called children of God" is the ninth verse of chapter five (the Beatitudes) in the book of Matthew from the Bible. One of my favorites.

Chapter 75. Pride

The tradition of presenting a silver dollar for the first salute goes back to colonial times. Back then, the dollar amounted to an entire first month's pay for the new officer, so it was quite a sacrifice.

Semper Paratus (always ready) has been the motto of the U.S. Coast Guard and its antecedents since 1836.

Acknowledgments and a Final Word to the Reader

I conceived the Honor Series twenty-five years ago to tell the story of an average nineteenth- and early twentieth-century American naval officer's life, loves, and career; the places he saw, the battles he fought, the missions he endured, and the people he met. I wanted the books to illuminate the history of this country and the world as well, to show how we ended up where we are.

Little did I imagine what a fantastic voyage of discovery it would be for me. The Honor Series took me around the world. I met royalty, admirals, generals, sailors, soldiers, gangsters, priests, pirates, fishermen, and farmers. I have eaten in the finest restaurants in major cities and gagged on unidentifiable glop in remote and rugged places. I have been detained by authorities in three countries, eluded mortal peril in several others, and known perfect tranquility in a few.

And now, after 17 books, 7,100 pages, and 1,785,000 words in print, the story is told. Peter Wake's family—five generations onward from him—has entered the twenty-first century. They are still honorably serving our country, still facing daunting challenges at home and around the world.

My heartfelt thanks go to the hundreds of people on five continents who helped me along the way with incredible research information, kindness to this stranger, advice and encouragement (Kaydian Wherle), protection from various enemies lurking in the jungle, and some decent rum (Randy Wayne White) on the porch at sunset. The editorial, graphics, and marketing crews at Pineapple Press and at the Naval Institute Press were consummate professionals and a pleasure to work with. Special thanks go to June Cussen, David Cussen, Shé Hicks, Mindy Conner, Tom Cutler, Glenn Griffith, and Jim Stavridis. Thank you to the many booksellers around the country and around the world on the Cunard Line who were such wonderful hosts. I very much appreciate that the book profession's critics and literary award juries understood the intent and effort that went into the Honor Series, and am profoundly honored by the awards I've been given.

My beloved "Wakians" around the world get a very special thank-you. They have been nothing less than the finest readers any author, anywhere, in any century, could hope to have. Thank you for lifting my spirits, making me laugh, telling your stories, rekindling my curiosity and energy, and letting me have fun with you. You are a crucial part of every book in the Honor Series.

And a very sincere and humble thank-you to the one and only Nancy Glickman, to whom this book is lovingly dedicated. As many of you know, Nancy has been my overworked and underpaid business manager, ever-ready morale officer, extremely efficient logistics officer, brilliant astronomy and nature researcher, talented photographer, eagle-eyed editor, stalwart co-adventurer, culinary coach and co-perpetrator, and a damn good steady hand on the helm. But more than all that, she is my lover, wife, and fellow dreamer. Nancy is my life.

Finally, I truly hope all of you follow Peter Wake's sage advice: keep steering your lives onward and upward toward those distant horizons sailors know so well. I certainly will be. . . .

Robert N. Macomber
Distant Horizons Farm
Pine Island, Florida

Research Bibliography

Theodore Roosevelt's Presidency, 1901–1909

The Autobiography of Theodore Roosevelt, 1920 edition, Theodore Roosevelt (1913).

The Bully Pulpit: Theodore Roosevelt, William Howard Taft, and the Golden Age of Journalism, Doris Kearns Goodwin (2013).

Colonel Roosevelt, Edmund Morris (2010).

Grover Cleveland: The 24th President 1893–1897, American Presidents Series, Henry F. Graff (2002).

Imperial Cruise, James Bradley (2009).

New York Times, 1897 and 1898 newspaper articles, http://spiderbites.nytimes.com /free_1897/articles_1897_02_00001.html.

President McKinley: Architect of the American Century, Robert W. Merry (2017).

"The Right of the People to Rule," 1912 Roosevelt campaign speech recording (recorded by Thomas Edison), Vincent Voice Library, Michigan State University.

The Rise of Theodore Roosevelt, Edmund Morris (1979).

The Rough Riders, Theodore Roosevelt (1902).

Theodore Rex, Edmund Morris (2001).

"Theodore Roosevelt in Europe," Frank Harper, *Reader's Digest* (1910).

Theodore Roosevelt's Naval Diplomacy, Henry J. Hendrix (2009).

The True Flag: Theodore Roosevelt, Mark Twain, and the Birth of American Empire, Stephen Kinzer (2017).

William McKinley: The 25th President, 1897–1901, American Presidents Series, Kevin Phillip and Arthur M. Schlesinger (2003).

Intelligence Operations

Ace of Spies, Bruce Lockhart (1967).

"A Century of Japanese Intelligence," LCDR W. M. Swann, Royal Australian Navy, Naval Historical Society of Australia (December 1974).

A Century of U.S. Naval Intelligence, Capt. Wyman H. Packard, USN (Ret.) (1996).

Coaling, Docking, and Repair Facilities of the Ports of the World, Office of Naval Intelligence, U.S. Navy (1909).

Espionage and Covert Operations: A Global History, Vejas Gabriel Liulevicius (2011).

The Friedman Legacy: A Tribute to William and Elizabeth Friedman, Sources in Cryptologic History 3, Center for Cryptologic History, NSA, 2nd printing (1992).

The German Secret Service, Colonel Walther Nicolai (1924).

A History of the Russian Secret Service, Richard Deacon (rev. ed., 1987).

The Illustrious Career of Arkadiy Harting, "Rita T. Kronenbitter," *CIA Historical Review, Studies in Intelligence* 11, no. 1 (declassified 1993).

Masked Dispatches: Cryptograms and Cryptology in American History, 1775–1900, Series 1, Pre–World War I, vol. 1, Ralph E. Weber, Center for Cryptologic History, NSA (2nd ed., 2002).

The Ochrana: The Russian Secret Police, A. T. Vassilyev and René Fulop-Miller (1930).

The Office of Naval Intelligence: The Birth of America's First Intelligence Agency 1865–1918, Jeffry M. Dorwart (1979).

Practice to Deceive, David Mure (1977).

"Russia's Naval Intelligence in the 19th and 20th Centuries," Vitaly Belozer, *Military Thought* 17, no. 4 (October 2008).

Secret Servants: A History of Japanese Espionage, Ronald Seth (1968).

Secret and Urgent: The Story of Codes and Ciphers, Fletcher Pratt (1939).

Top Secret Directive for Establishment of the Naval Field Operations Support Group, Secretary of the Navy Paul Nitze (Clandestine Intel Ops, AKA: TF 157) (1965).

Turnabout and Deception: Crafting the Double Cross and the Theory of Outs, Barton Whaley (2016).

Twenty-Five Years in the Secret Service: The Recollections of a Spy, Henri Le Caron (1892).

The World That Never Was: A True Story of Schemers, Anarchists, and Secret Agents, Alex Butterworth (2010).

The Great White Fleet, 1907–1909

Annual Report of the Pacific Steam Ship Company (30 April 1907).

"Auxiliaries Off to Form Wireless Chain," *Pacific Commercial Advisor*, Honolulu (19 July 1908).

"Cruise of the Great White Fleet," JO2 Mike McKinley, USN, Naval History and Heritage Command (2017).

"Czar's Naval Officer Following Course of the Fleet," *Washington Evening Star* (18 January 1908).

The Great White Fleet, Robert A. Hart (1965).

"The *Kasata Maru* and Her Strange Mission," *Hawaiian Gazette* (21 February 1908).

The Last Voyage of the SMS Leipzig, vol. 1: *1906–1914*, Kapitänleutnant Walter Schiwig (1973).

"Linking up the Pacific," *The Age* magazine, Melbourne, Australia (10 August 1909).

List of Wireless-Telegraph Stations of the World, Department of the Navy (1908).

"Local Brevities," *Pacific Commercial Advisor*, Honolulu (25 July 1908).

"A Striking Thing: Leadership, Strategic Communications, and Roosevelt's Great White Fleet," James R. Holmes, *U.S. Naval War College Review* (2009).

"The Struggle for the Australian Airwaves: The Strategic Function of Radio for Germany in the Asia-Pacific Region before World War I." Presentation by Peter Overlack at the 2007 King-Hall Naval History Conference, Australian Department of Defence (printed 2012 in *Naval Networks: The Dominance of Communications in Maritime Operations*).

"Today Fleet Sails for the Southern Cross and the Colonies," *Pacific Commercial Advisor*, Honolulu (22 July 1908).

Central America, 1912–1918

The Archaeologist Was a Spy, Charles H. Harris and Louis R. Sadler (2003).

The Incredible Yanqui: The Career of Lee Christmas, Hermann B. Deutsch (1931).

In Plain Sight: Felix A. Sommerfeld: Spymaster in Mexico, 1908–1914, Heribert von Feilitzsch (2012).

Latin America and the War, Percy Alvin Martin (1925).

In Plain Sight: Felix A. Sommerfeld: Spymaster in Mexico, 1908–1914, Heribert von Feilitzsch (2012).

"Spying by American Archaeologists in World War I," David L. Bowman, *Bulletin of the History of Archaeology* (2011).

"*Ypiranga* and *Bavaria* Unloaded Cargoes at Puerto Mexico," *New York Times* (28 May 1914).

U.S. Naval Operations in the Black Sea and the Russian Civil War, 1919

America's Black Sea Fleet: The U.S. Navy Amidst War and Revolution, 1919–1923, Robert Shenk (2017).

"The French Army and Intervention in Southern Russia, 1918–1919," Kim Munholland, *Cahiers du Monde Russe et Soviétique* (January 1981).

"The Russian Masonic Movement in the Years 1906–1918," Ludwik Haas, *Acta Poloniae Historica*, Institute of History of the Polish Academy of Sciences (1983).

"Sidney Reilly's Reports from South Russia, December 1918–March 1919," John Ainsworth, *Europe-Asia Studies* (1998).

U.S. Naval Detachment in Turkish Waters, 1919–1924, Henry F. Beers, Department of the Navy (1943).

Samoa, the Philippines, Minesweepers, and Asiatic Fleet Operations, 1941–1942

Cruise of the Lanikai: *Incitement to War*, Kemp Tolley (2014).

"Fighting the Submarine Mine: How Navies Combat a Deadly Sea Weapon," Rear Adm. Yates Stirling, USN (Ret.), *Popular Science* (October 1941).

The Fleet the Gods Forgot, Capt. W. G. Winslow, USN (Ret.) (1982).

Kaigun: Strategy, Tactics, and Technology in the Imperial Japanese Navy, 1887–1941, David C. Evans and Mark R. Peattie (2012).

The Rising Sun in the Pacific, 1931–April 1942 (History of United States Naval Operations in World War II, vol. 3), Rear Adm. Samuel Eliot Morison, USNR (1948).

Samoan Historical Calendar (1941), Stan Sorensen and Joseph Theroux (2007).

Ship plans for *Lapwing*-class minesweepers, U.S. Navy, Bureau of Construction and Repair, (1941).

"Tutuila in WWII: In the Crosshairs of History, Part 1," John Enright, *Samoa News* (15 March 2011).

War in the Pacific: End of the Asiatic Fleet. The Classified Report of Admiral Thomas C. Hart, Charles Culbertson (2013).

U.S.–Cuban Navy Antisubmarine Warfare Operations, 1943

Admirals and Empire: The United States Navy and the Caribbean 1898–1945, Donald A. Yerxa (1991).

"Coast Guard Pays Tribute to WWII Veterans," staff writer, *Coast Guard News* (2015).

History of United States Naval Operations in World War II. The Battle of the Atlantic, vol. 1: *1939–May 1943*, Rear Adm. Samuel Eliot Morison, USNR (1947).

Report to the Secretary of the Navy of Pre-War and Wartime Combat Operations of United States Navy (to 1 March 1944), Atlantic Section, Adm. Ernest J. King (23 April 1944).

"Submarine Contact and Attack by Cuban Sub Chaser," declassified report of F. R. Dodge, USN, Gulf Sea Frontier (24 May 1943).

U.S. Coast Guard: Small Cutters and Patrol Boats, 1915–2012, HMC James T. Flynn Jr., USNR (Ret.) (2014).

Operation Sealords, Vietnam, 1968–1969

Brown Water, Black Berets: Coastal & Riverine Warfare in Vietnam, Lt. Cdr. Thomas J. Cutler, USN (Ret.) (1988).

Navy Medicine in Vietnam: Passage to Freedom to the Fall of Saigon, Jan K. Herman, Naval History and Heritage Command (2010).

"Operation Sealords: A Study in the Effectiveness of the Allied Naval Campaign of Interdiction," Lt. Cdr. Eugene F. Paluso, USN, Research Paper at USMC Command and Staff College, Quantico (2002).

War in the Shallows: U.S. Navy Coastal and Riverine Warfare in Vietnam, 1965–1968, John Darrell Sherwood, Naval History and Heritage Command (2015).

Maps, Charts, and Sailing Guides

The 1907–9 Great White Fleet in the German South Pacific
Map of Apia, Upolu Island, German Samoa (1897)
Map of British Ocean Telegraph Cables (1901)
Map of German Pacific Colonies (1911)
Map of Honolulu, Hawaii (1893)
Map of Upolu Island, German Samoa (1910)

Central America, 1914
Chart of Nicaragua-Honduras coast of Cape Gracias a Dios, British Admiralty 2425 (1900)
Map of Central America (1912)
Map of Honduras (1917)
Map of Mayan Empire extent in Central America (2020)
Map of United Fruit Company Central & South American Ship Routes (1908)

Black Sea, 1919
Map of Europe (1919)
Map of European Russia's Civil War 1918–1921 (2020)
Map of Istanbul (Constantinople), Turkey (Ottoman Empire), British War Office (1919)

Map of Russian Civil War military positions in March 1919 (1919)

Map of Sevastopol, Russia (1919)

The Philippines and Dutch East Indies, 1941–1942

Area chart of the Philippines with USN notations from LSM-133 (1940–45)

Chart of Pago Pago, American Samoa (1940)

Map of 1941–42 Japanese invasion of Philippines, Louis Morton (1953)

Map of 1941–42 Japanese invasion of the Dutch East Indies (2015)

Map of the Dutch East Indies (1940)

Map of Philippine Islands trade and transport (1920)

Southwest Vietnam, 1968

Map of Sealords Operational Theater (1968–70)

Map of Vietnam, Operational Navigational (ONC K-10), Defense Mapping Agency (1968, 1984)

Map of Vietnam-Cambodia Coast (Long Xuyen), Joint Ops Graphic (Air) NC 48-6, Defense Mapping Agency (1972)

About the Author

Robert N. Macomber is an award-winning author, internationally acclaimed lecturer, former Department of Defense consultant/lecturer, *New York Journal of Books* reviewer, and accomplished seaman. When not trekking the world for research, book signings, or lectures, he lives on an island in southwest Florida, where he enjoys cooking the types of foreign cuisines described in his books and sailing among the islands.

Visit his website at www.RobertMacomber.com.